# THE
# NIGHT
# THIEF

A gripping crime thriller full of stunning twists

# JOY ELLIS

*DI Jackman & DS Evans Book 8*

JOFFE
BOOKS

Joffe Books, London
www.joffebooks.com

First published in Great Britain in 2021

ISBN: 978-1-80405-030-9

# CHAPTER ONE

It was a hot, stuffy night, unnaturally warm and dry for mid-September on the Fens. The curtains were drawn back and the windows opened to capture the few night breezes there were. Annie Carson had replaced her duvet with a single cotton sheet, but even so she was restless, tossing and turning, endlessly seeking a cool spot in her uncomfortably warm bed.

She had just drifted off when something woke her. Annie slowly opened her eyes and saw a figure standing at the foot of her bed.

Her vision blurry with sleep, she thought the figure was her son. Or was this a dream? It had to be, Callum was a good foot shorter than the figure staring at her. But, now, she was fully awake. Fear gripped her, and she screamed.

Trembling, Annie fumbled for the switch on her bedside lamp, and the room was flooded with light. The figure took the shape of a man, running from her room. She shouted for her son, just then emerging from his room, tousle-haired and bleary-eyed.

'Mum? Was that you? What's wrong?'

She pushed past him down the stairs, and Callum followed a few steps behind, still asking what had happened. All she could do was repeat that it had been *a man, a man.*

1

The front door stood wide open, but there was no one in sight.

They stood there, afraid to step too far outside in case he lay in wait for them. They peered up and down the empty road, turned and hurried back inside.

Looking increasingly alarmed, Callum listened to his mother's account of what had happened. 'Mum, what if he *didn't* go out the door?'

Fresh waves of fear coursed through her and she swallowed. She told herself to be strong for Callum, a skinny lad of twelve. 'Don't worry, son, he went out. I know he did.'

Callum looked unconvinced. So was she, but she kept it from her boy. 'If it makes you feel better, we'll check the whole house, okay?' She cast around for something to use as protection and settled for a metal doorstop.

Room by room, her son at her heels, she pushed doors wide and flipped on light switches. With every light came the thrill of fear. What if Callum had been right? As the last door swung open, she heaved a sigh of relief. 'It's all clear, son. He's gone.'

'How did he get in, Mum?' the boy asked. 'I heard you lock up last night, so it wasn't through the doors.'

*Good bloody question.* 'I'm not sure, Callum.'

'I'm scared.'

She held out her arms. At twelve, Callum was still a child, but more artistic and creative than his older brother, Andrew. Andrew had been a little Action Man at the age of five, whereas Callum was sensitive and thoughtful, more likely to be found with his head in a book than slaughtering insurgents on his PlayStation. She cuddled him for a moment or two, then led him down to the kitchen, where she made them both a comforting hot chocolate.

He seemed relieved, but she knew that Callum wouldn't relax until he understood how their intruder had got in. Nor would she, for that matter.

Callum had his hands around his favourite Hogwarts mug and looked down into the swirling, frothy drink. 'What did he want?' he asked without looking up.

Another good question, and it scared the shit out of her. What *did* he want? Why just stand there and stare at her? How long had he been watching her? In her bedroom! She dreaded to think. 'I suppose he was just a burglar, and I woke up before he could steal anything.' It sounded pretty lame, even to her, but it was all she had to offer. She could hardly express her worst fears to her fragile boy. She frowned. What was it? Something she'd half noticed when she checked the rooms just now. 'I'm just going to the lounge for a moment, son, won't be a moment.'

Annie pushed open the door. The light was still on. Most of the lights were still on. She told herself it was for Callum's sake.

Her eyes roamed around the room, trying to recall what had bothered her. Something small, something that she'd pushed into the background in fear during her hasty inspection.

Then she saw it: a gap in a row of five matching framed photographs. Now there were four. The first, a picture of Ned, her late husband, grinning broadly and leaning against the bonnet of his precious MGB Roadster. Second, their wedding day. Next, Andrew, taken just before he left to start his basic training with the RAF. Then the gap, and finally her mum and dad on their ruby wedding anniversary.

Annie stared at the space and her mouth went dry. The missing picture was of Callum.

She walked slowly back to the kitchen, cursing herself for not calling the police immediately. But in the absence of any actual harm and with nothing missing, what was there to say? More than likely they wouldn't even send anyone out. This was a small Fen village, and she hadn't seen a police officer in years. She wasn't even certain where the nearest police station was anymore, they had closed so many. But that missing photograph changed everything.

'I think you should try to get some sleep, sweetheart. It's four in the morning and you've got school tomorrow.' She tried to sound casual. 'Take your drink upstairs, I'll come up with you.'

'Are you coming to bed, Mum?' He clearly hadn't been totally reassured by their hurried patrol through the house.

'In a little while. I should ring the police. He could be going around bothering other people.' She tried to keep it light.

He nodded. 'Yeah. Good.'

She followed him up the stairs. 'I'll leave your door open. I've already checked — the windows are closed and the doors all locked, so he won't come back now. Try to sleep.' He climbed into bed and took his phone and his earbuds from the bedside cabinet. 'I'll call in when I go to bed, okay?'

He was already scrolling through his playlist. The music would help.

'I'm leaving the light on,' he stated firmly.

She stuck a thumb up and winked, like his father used to do, and hurried back down the stairs.

In the kitchen, she picked up the phone and dialled. 'Police, please. Someone broke into my house, got into my bedroom and stole a picture of my son. We're on our own here, and we're scared.'

She had expected to be given an incident number, fobbed off with an excuse about shortages of personnel, so she was taken aback when she was told that a car from Saltern-le-Fen would be on its way immediately.

Thirty minutes later a marked police car pulled up outside. Even so, she waited until she saw the uniforms.

The two PCs introduced themselves as Stacey Smith and Jay Acharya. They were quick to assure her that she had done the right thing in calling them. Handing them mugs of tea, she began to describe waking up and seeing that silent figure staring down at her. At that point, the shock overwhelmed her and she burst into tears.

4

'It's okay, it's okay.' PC Smith handed her a tissue and sat down next to her on the sofa. 'It's delayed shock, Mrs Carson, don't worry. It's a good thing it's coming out.'

It took a few minutes, but after a couple of deep breaths she began to regain control. 'It's Annie, please. Oh dear. I'm so sorry.'

They were all nods and encouraging smiles.

'No need to apologise, Annie. This sort of thing is horrible,' said Stacey vehemently. 'When you're ready, please tell us the rest. In your own time.'

She sipped her tea. This time she got through the whole story, noting the swift puzzled glance the officers gave each other when she mentioned the missing photo frame.

'And you've no idea how he got in?' Jay asked.

'No. The top windows were open in some rooms because it's been so hot, but they're too small for anyone to pass through. I always make sure to lock the doors. As I said, it's just me and Callum here. My other boy is in the RAF and my husband died three years ago, so I'm very careful about security.'

'No cameras?' asked Stacey.

'I've never even thought about it. It's a small, peaceful village, and I don't know anyone else with cameras, except the people who live in the big house on the edge of the village, but that's a very expensive property.'

'An inexpensive system might give you a little more peace of mind,' offered Jay. 'My brother installed one so his wife feels safer when he's working nights.'

She had fleeting thoughts of stable doors and bolting horses, but was it such a bad idea? 'I'll look into it.'

'Would you mind if we take a look around, Annie?' asked Stacey. 'We'll try not to disturb your boy. Anyway, from what you told us, your man didn't get in through his bedroom. We'll be really quiet, I promise.'

'Please, go ahead,' Annie said.

They pulled on gloves and walked from room to room, spending a lot of time near the windows. Annie was beginning to wonder why she was getting so much careful attention. The officers seemed to be looking for something specific. This bothered her.

She grew still more bothered when the tall young policeman called Jay asked her if she could please be at home later that morning. She should avoid touching the front door any more than necessary. 'We'll get a forensic officer down, Annie. We know that he opened the door, so he might have left prints. We'll take yours and your son's for elimination purposes, and they'll be destroyed afterwards, so don't worry about that.'

'You seem to be taking this very seriously,' she said. 'Has this sort of thing happened around here before?'

Jay seemed not to know how to respond.

Stacey, the older of the two, hastened to say, 'We take all such incidents seriously, Annie. And, no, it hasn't happened around here. We just want to stop him scaring anyone else. Now, is there anyone you'd like to call to come and stay with you? You look pretty anxious.'

She forced herself to smile. 'I'll be fine, honestly. Thank you for being so understanding.'

'No problem. One last thing.' Stacey still had her notebook out. 'Could you describe the photo that was taken? You've told us the frame was the same as the others, and that it was of Callum — what did the picture actually show?'

'He was about ten, wearing navy shorts and a Hogwarts T-shirt, and holding Cocoa — that's his rabbit. I took it here in the garden. I have the image on my computer if you'd like it.'

Stacey wrote that down and pocketed the book. 'Thank you, Annie. Maybe you could print us off a copy? Someone will contact you later about that, and don't forget the forensic officer.'

Jay opened the front door with his gloved hands and they went out to the car. 'Try not to touch that door,' Jay called back. 'Have a good day, thank you for all your help — and the tea!'

Annie put the mugs in the dishwasher and went to check on Callum, who was fast asleep with his earbuds still in. It was still early, but she knew she wouldn't sleep again.

* * *

In the car, Jay and Stacey looked at each other, their faces grave.

'He's upped his game, hasn't he?' said Stacey after a while.

'And he's extending his area. He usually sticks to town.' Jay frowned. 'Same MO, but he's never got in knowing there's two people in the house before, has he?'

'No. It's usually single people living alone.'

'Maybe he didn't know about the son.' Jay looked thoughtful. 'He's a real opportunist, isn't he? Leave one window open, and he's in.'

'Usually,' said Stacey flatly. 'Let's hope he's not testing the waters, pushing the boundaries. I just don't get why he took that picture. That shifts the whole thing up into burglary. Odd that. He's never damaged or taken anything before, and we've never caught him inside a property. That's why we've never been able to nick him.' She put the car in gear. 'Better get back and tell the skipper, I suppose.'

She and Jay had been crewing together for a month, and they'd hit it off straight away. He wasn't like some of the younger guys, pumped full of testosterone and trying to prove themselves. Jay appreciated that she'd been in the job for nearly fifteen years and he could learn from her expertise. He was worth making an effort for. She would have liked to know more about him, but so far all she'd gathered was that he'd transferred up from the West Country and was one of two brothers and three sisters. Even Lisa Arnold, the civilian in charge of the evidence store, and who made it her business to know everything about everyone at the station, could tell her little more. She said she thought he was Hindu and was single, but that was all. It was unlike the forthright Stacey to hold back like this. Why not simply ask him? For some reason, she felt she'd be invading his privacy. Still, what really mattered was his quick smile, his empathy for victims of crime, and the cool and controlled way he dealt with the suspects they ran up against. All things considered, he was a top bloke to be teamed up with. Plus, of course, he was bloody good looking, with those white, even teeth, neatly clipped beard and the raven black hair.

'That single photo frame is really bugging me,' she said as she pulled on to the main road towards Saltern. 'D'you reckon CID might want to take a look at this?'

Jay pulled a face. 'Not really their thing, is it, Stace? Peeping Toms aren't high profile enough for the detectives, are they?'

Stacey laughed. 'I'll forgive you this time, Jay, but you'll soon learn that the Saltern-le-Fen detectives aren't like the ones back where you came from.'

'What? Not a bunch of toffee-nosed gits who think they're better than us plods? You're having me on.'

Stacey laughed even louder. 'If you're good, PC Acharya, tomorrow I'll introduce you to DI Jackman and DS Marie Evans. Then I'll watch you swallow your words.'

Jay made a face. 'Thanks a bunch. Really looking forward to that.'

'I think you'll be pleasantly surprised, sunshine. Now, back to our Ratty. He's been up to his tricks for years. Why? Because he can. He gets this weird kind of pleasure out of just being inside someone's house without them knowing he's there. The psychologist said it's a sort of game, a control thing, just to prove he can do it. He's never touched anyone or taken anything, and he's not a voyeur. Plus he's never actually broken in, never damaged a lock or forced a window. He looks for weak points and takes advantage of people's carelessness. Up until a few years back, even if we had caught him inside, it was a civil matter.'

'You saw him in action once, didn't you?' said Jay.

Stacey laughed again. 'Did I just! Ratty is about six stone wringing wet, skinny as a rake. He's in his fifties but he can scale a wall in seconds. I heard climbing's been classed as an Olympic sport — well, Ratty could be our hope for gold.'

Out on the main road, she changed gears. 'I was only a few minutes away when I got a call to say someone had seen this sneaky-looking little guy hanging around a house in Cedar Grove. It was an oldish property with this climber up the wall, and he'd just started up there when I arrived. He went up the side of that house like a spider. He saw me, swung into a tree near the house, jumped down and was gone in seconds.'

'Impressive!' Jay grinned.

'You can say that again.' She became serious. 'But why did he suddenly want to take something? It bothers me, that does.' She shook her head. 'I really hate it when someone acts out of character!'

'Deep breaths, Stace!' said Jay, grinning. 'Think of your blood pressure!'

'PC Acharya, you're lucky I'm driving, otherwise you'd be going home with a thick ear. Now, come on, tell me why someone who's been following the same pattern for years suddenly does something so out of the ordinary.'

They drove on in silence. Neither had an answer. For her part, Stacey was well aware that most people would consider the appropriation of a family photo to be a minor problem, low on the list of issues the police had to deal with. But things that made no sense bothered her. Ratty was no thief, and he wasn't a voyeur. As far as they knew, getting inside other people's property gave him no sexual gratification whatsoever. He simply relished the challenge of gaining access and seeing how close he could get to the occupant without being seen. So, why on earth steal a simple photograph and finally risk arrest?

# CHAPTER TWO

Rowan Jackman awoke to the sound of a blackbird singing. He yawned, looked at the clock and turned towards his partner, Laura. It was five thirty but her side of the bed was empty. He sat up and looked around. Downstairs, a door closed. Rubbing his eyes, he padded down to the kitchen, where, through the window, he caught sight of her wandering around the garden in her dressing gown and slippers.

Puzzled, he opened the door and went out barefoot. 'Laura?'

She turned, apparently surprised to see him there. She looked unusually drawn and pensive.

'You okay, sweetheart?' he asked, planting a kiss on her forehead. 'You look worried.'

'I had a bad night. Couldn't sleep, and I've got a full schedule today. I thought some fresh air might help clear my head.'

'Come back inside. You don't need to be up for another hour yet. Go back to bed and I'll make us some tea.'

Meekly, she allowed him to lead her back inside. Jackman was worried. He'd never seen her look so distracted. He hoped that she wasn't ill and covering it up. She wasn't herself at all.

Upstairs, he set down her tea and slipped back into bed beside her. 'Something's wrong. No secrets — remember?'

Laura sighed. 'I'm sorry, darling. I try not to bring work home, but every so often I get a case that I can't seem to let go of. I even dream about it.'

At least she wasn't ill. But she was visibly anxious, and that in itself was unlike her. 'Anything you can share?'

Laura sat up. 'I'd love to, but this one's complex and you know how patient privacy works.' She gave a little shrug. 'So it looks like I'm stuck with it at present.'

'Well, if you need to discuss a . . . purely hypothetical situation, I'm your man.' He took her hand and squeezed it. 'Always.'

She snuggled into him. 'If it becomes any more of a conundrum than it is already, I will, I promise.'

It wasn't easy being the partner of the force psychologist. Naturally, Laura was bound by the Hippocratic Oath, whereas he could quite properly consult her on the psychological aspect of tricky cases. So, they generally kept work chat to a minimum, unless it was about friends they had in common — friends like DS Marie Evans.

'Is she back yet?' asked Laura, sipping her tea.

'Back on shift this morning. She'll be full of stories from the Welsh mountains, no doubt.' Jackman put his mug on his bedside cabinet. 'I've really missed her. It's only been a week, but work isn't the same without Marie.'

'Did she go alone?' Laura raised an eyebrow.

'Yes, she did, Madame Matchmaker!'

Laura laughed. 'Then I bet you're not the only one who's missed her. I can think of a certain detective sergeant over in Fenchester who'll have been pining quietly in her absence.'

Laura sounded more relaxed, and Jackman felt easier. 'You're probably right, but they're not an item, you know. They've just been out to dinner a couple of times.'

'Marie looks happier than I've seen her in years since she bumped into Ralph again. You aren't going to try and tell me that's a coincidence, are you?' She rolled her eyes at him.

'Well . . .'

'Rowan Jackman! Crawl out from under that stone. Ralph Enderby has fallen for Marie in a big way, and unless I'm way off the mark and don't deserve to be called a psychologist, she's pretty smitten too. In fact, I'm inviting them to dinner here next week so you can judge for yourself — and I can grill them.' She looked at him smugly. 'And no arguments.'

He held up his hands. 'As if I'd dare!'

'Ask her which day will suit them best, would you?'

'Hey! This was your idea. You ring and ask.'

'Okay, I will. I'll cook. You're in charge of the wine.'

But as they ate breakfast, Laura looked pensive again. 'Honey?' Jackman said, 'I know you can't talk to me, but why not ring Sam? He's a colleague and a damned good psychologist. Don't try to shoulder this case alone.'

'Okay . . . maybe I will.'

'No maybes, Laura. Talk to him.'

* * *

Sylvia Wilson awoke at seven thirty and lay back for a few minutes, luxuriating in her comfy bed. She was on a late shift at the nursery today, so she could indulge in a slow start to the day. Perhaps she'd make a drink and have half an hour with her Kindle. Then a soak in a hot bath before getting ready for work.

She looked around the room. She was planning on redecorating and still couldn't decide on a colour. Maybe blues this time? Or lavenders? Or . . . Sylvia stared at the bedroom door. That was odd. She never closed her door at night, and it was pushed to. Not fastened, but certainly not as she had left it. A draught? Had to be. She had locked all the downstairs windows but left all the upstairs top openers partly open because of the heat. She had been out watering until almost ten o'clock, so her planters and pots of late-summer flowers wouldn't die. A draught. Of course it was.

She pulled herself up in the bed and leaned back on the pillows. Then she froze.

Glancing down at the floor in search of her slippers, she saw a footprint.

Her gaze travelled to the windowsill. She swallowed hard. There was another! As she slept, someone had crawled in through the fanlight window, stepped right over her, leaving a muddy footprint on the duvet, and on to the floor. She stopped breathing for a moment. Then she looked over the side of the bed. On the cream carpet, a third footprint, and another, closer to the door.

Sylvia lay wringing her hands, unable to move. Oh, my God! Was he still in the house? She listened, straining her ears, but there was no sound. Slowly, she began to regain her courage. She slipped out of bed, found her slippers and dressing gown and took a couple of steps towards the door. She stopped and went back to pick up her mobile phone.

Five minutes later, Sylvia Wilson stood in her kitchen looking at the unlocked kitchen door. She had definitely locked it the night before, so whoever it was had obviously chosen an easier route out than the one he came in by.

Nothing had been taken that she could see, and nothing was damaged, but even so, she rang the police.

After being passed around a bit, a cheery-sounding woman gave her an incident number. She told Sylvia that as the intruder had left and nothing had been taken, she couldn't promise a visit. If Sylvia could get to the station sometime this morning and make a statement, it would be attended to as soon as possible.

'Actually, no, I'm not coming to the station,' she said angrily. 'I want someone to see this. He stepped right over me, for heaven's sake! I live alone! Have you any idea how frightened I am!'

There was a pause, during which she heard the woman talking to someone else. A few moments later she was back. 'Can I have your address, please? If you stay at home, an officer will be with you as soon as someone is free.'

Sylvia realised that she was shaking.

She went back upstairs, pulled on some clothes and rang work to tell them she'd had an intruder and was waiting for the police. She wouldn't be in until tomorrow. They didn't sound too happy about it, but sod them. She was in no fit state to work.

It was an hour before an officer arrived, looking less than enthusiastic. He seemed more inclined to tell her what he couldn't do than what he could. Then Sylvia burst into tears and he softened.

'Are you up to showing me these footprints?'

She led the way upstairs.

PC Simon Laker stared at the dried mud on the duvet and the floor and let out a low whistle. 'I see what you mean. That must have given you quite a scare.'

'You have no idea,' said Sylvia shakily. 'And I never heard him, I didn't even wake up.'

'Maybe that's for the best, Mrs Wilson. I'm just going to take some photographs, if that's okay?'

'Please do, and then this bedding goes straight in the washing machine.' She was inclined to bin it, but it was her best linen, and it hadn't been cheap.

'Er, well, if you could leave washing it for a bit.' PC Laker frowned. 'I suggest you place it in a black refuse sack and tie it up. We may not need it — normally we wouldn't — but as I drove here I heard that there'd been another call about an intruder last night, and it could be the same guy. There could be some trace evidence on your bedding.'

All at once, she was drained. 'I need a cup of tea. Can I offer you one, officer?'

'White, one sugar, please, Mrs Wilson.'

Downstairs, he joined her in the kitchen and sat opposite her at the table, his tablet in his hand.

'No pocketbooks anymore?' she said rather wistfully.

'This *is* my pocketbook, Mrs Wilson. Soon we'll be taking witness statements electronically too, but for now—' he produced a pad of statement sheets from a case he'd brought with him — 'it's the old-fashioned way. I'll write this all down and then I'll get you to read it carefully and sign it top and bottom. Okay?'

It took a while to take the statement.

'Now, you're sure nothing is missing?'

'I haven't checked everything, I was too shaken, but as far as I can tell, nothing, and no damage at all.'

'Are you usually a heavy sleeper?' he asked.

She smiled. 'Yes. I slept through that summer storm a few weeks back. Next day my neighbour told me there'd been thunder and lightning and a dreadful high wind.' She shivered. 'Even so, I'm usually quite sensitive to anything out of the ordinary inside the house. A small picture fell down in the hall one night — the fixing had come apart, nothing sinister — but I woke up at once.'

The policeman nodded. 'I get what you mean. So, you think an intruder coming in would have roused you?'

'Absolutely. He must have been as silent as a ghost.'

'I think I know who it was, Mrs Wilson.' PC Laker laid down his pen and drank a mouthful of tea. 'It might help to put your mind at rest if I tell you we have a habitual intruder in the area. We've even got a name for him — Ratty. He's like a spider monkey and could be up your wall and through a big top opener like yours with no trouble at all. But he's never hurt anyone, not even touched them. It's a bit of a game to him, just getting in is enough. But here's the thing, he's been doing this for years and he's never been back to the same house twice.'

'But you've never caught him?'

'We've apprehended him in the vicinity many times, but never actually inside a property. It's a very difficult crime to deal with, Mrs Wilson, grey areas between civil and police matters, and never enough evidence to get him even near a court, so each time we've had to let him go.' PC Laker frowned. 'It's a case of *we* know he's done it, *he* knows we know, and he also knows we can't prove it. The law is an ass sometimes.'

15

'Some game! He's made me feel as if my home, my own private refuge, has been violated. I loved this little house, and now, well . . .' She sighed. 'Now I don't know if I even want to stay here.'

PC Laker gave her a look of understanding. 'You'll feel better when the shock's worn off. Do you have any family you can call? A friend who could come round? Talking always helps in these situations.'

She shook her head. 'No family hereabouts. No brothers or sisters either. My kids are all grown up and have flown the nest. Even Luke, my oldest grandson, is at uni now. He has his own room here. He often stays as he doesn't get on with his stepfather. Oh, my neighbour could come round, but . . . maybe not, she's quite elderly. It might scare her.'

'I'm sure you have other friends. Bend their ear, you'll feel better for it, I promise.' He drained his mug and thanked her for the tea. 'If you just read and sign, I'll be on my way. Now, I don't suppose I need to tell you to shut all those windows tonight, do I? It's supposed to get much cooler in the next day or so anyway.'

After he'd gone, Sylvia sat down and began to worry all over again. She wasn't stupid, and for all his reassuring words about this Ratty, it was time to consider her options.

\* \* \*

As PC Simon Laker drove away, he reported in on his mobile.

'I'm pretty sure it's not Ratty, Skipper. He left footprints in the bedroom. The occupant had watered the garden the night before and the borders were still wet. Ratty is skinny and has small feet, plus he always wears light trainers with grippy soles. These were more like large climbing shoes with distinctive smooth soles, and they had a logo like a cross in them. I reckon someone else is muscling in on our Ratty's turf. No idea what his game is. It doesn't feel right, Sarge, not at all.'

At eleven o'clock, Simon Laker took a call on his mobile.

'I'm so sorry to bother you, PC Laker. It might be nothing.'

'Yes, Mrs Wilson. How can I help you?'

'I thought nothing had been stolen, but I've had a more thorough look and I missed something. But it doesn't make sense. I mean, why would someone want a school photo of my two younger grandsons?'

# CHAPTER THREE

Jackman spent the entire morning ensconced in Superintendent Ruth Crooke's office being briefed on the latest policies on public safety. As far as he could see — and Ruth too, he suspected — the string of objectives and initiatives were a mind-numbingly boring waste of police time.

Hence, it was midday before he was free to welcome DS Marie Evans back to work. Admiring her radiant countenance, Jackman was forced to agree that Laura was most likely right. Marie looked five years younger than when she left for her holiday, and he doubted that the mountain air was entirely responsible for the glow.

She sat in his office, beaming at him from across his desk. 'I had the best time, Jackman! Mum and I went to places she's always wanted to visit. We hiked around the Bearded Lake near Aberdovey — it was magical. It's not hard to understand why our Celtic ancestors considered it a spiritual place. Another day we went to the beaches at Borth and saw the petrified forest. It was amazing. Mum was in her element — she knew all the legends, of course. I felt like a little kid again. And I've got some fantastic photos. I didn't want to come back — well, except to see you, of course.'

Jackman almost added, 'and . . .' He sat back and contemplated her rosy features. 'Well, I have to say a week away from Saltern's most wanted has done you a power of good. You look great, Marie.'

'Thank you, sir!' She inclined her head regally. 'Anyway, my walking boots are back in the cupboard, so I'm ready to hear what you've got lined up for me today.'

'You timed your trip perfectly — it's been paperwork, paperwork and more paperwork. Right now, you may not believe this, but there's very little on.' He sifted through a couple of files. 'We've been informed that a lifer's being released today from Full Sutton maximum-security prison in the East Riding.'

Marie grimaced. 'Oh, there. They've got some nasty pieces of work locked up in that place.'

'Including Dennis Nilsen and Charles Bronson. They say plans for a new "mega prison" have been approved for the site, but as you can imagine, there've been thousands of objections.' Jackman grimaced. 'I wouldn't want one of those on our doorstep either.'

'So who's the inmate, and why would he be of interest to us?' asked Marie.

Jackman looked at the report. 'Giles Bannon, thirty-four, served three years of a life sentence for a crime to which he pleaded not guilty. In light of new and compelling evidence, he was acquitted of murder.' Jackman looked up. 'He was supposed to have killed his wife and child in their home in Northumberland. I don't remember it at all. You?'

Marie shook her head. 'Aside from a headline somewhere, nothing. So has this gone out to all forces or just us?'

'Just us. Seems he's relocating here. His parents sold his home for him while he was inside, and the village he lived in doesn't want him back. They probably don't trust the new evidence.'

'So *we* get him. Great. Even if he's innocent, he'll bring a shedload of trouble with him. You never know, his old neighbours might turn up to give him a house-warming party.' She raised an eyebrow. 'Anyway, I suppose it won't hurt to read up on the case. At least we'll know what we're dealing with.'

'I was just going to suggest that very thing, Marie. Forewarned and all that.' Jackman returned to the small pile of reports. 'The only other thing is Uniform's department really, but Ruth Crooke has suggested we might take a look, since we're quiet.' He picked up a memo. 'She says here, "There have been several complaints of someone hanging around the school gates in the mornings when the children are going in. He doesn't have a child with him, and although he is smartly dressed and fairly young, some of the parents have registered their concern." Thing is, it's not just one specific school but multiple. Uniform haven't managed to catch him, but the complaints are still coming in.' He shrugged. 'We have no known paedophiles in the area or anyone on the sex offenders list that fits the bill.'

'Sounds like he's looking for someone in particular, doesn't it?' Marie said. 'There could be a simple explanation. Remember that guy who was hunting for his wife? She'd done a bunk and taken the kids. He watched all the schools for months, poor man, just trying to find his children.'

'I thought that too. We could try asking around the women's refuge centres in the area. It would help if we could get a good description from one of the parents. Then there's the CCTV from the schools. If nothing else, it would put the parents' minds at rest to know we're taking it seriously. Good for public confidence.' Jackman smiled. 'Ruth will like that.'

'Well, if we've nothing else on, I'm happy to take that one.' Marie stood up.

'Take Gary with you. He's up to date on all his work. Robbie and Max are still completing their reports on the last big case, so they'll have their heads down for a bit longer. Oh, and Marie — while you were away, Robbie and Ella split up. Amicably, as far as I know, but just so you know the score, in case he's a bit remote.'

Jackman was just about to say something else when there was a knock on his door. He was mildly surprised to see PC Stacey Smith and the good-looking Asian lad he'd been seeing around lately.

'Come in, Stacey. Everything okay?' Stacey had been around for a long while now, and Jackman liked her. She was a good solid beat bobby — if such a thing even existed these days.

'I wondered if I could run something past you, sir. I've had a word with our skipper, and he said it was okay, as long as you're not too busy?' She gestured to the young PC at her side. 'This is PC Jay Acharya, sir, my new crewmate. Transferred here last month.'

Jackman nodded to him. 'Sit down, both of you. How are we treating you, PC Acharya?'

'Oh, very well, sir. It's great here, and I'm learning a lot from Stacey.'

He had a ready smile, even if he did look a little surprised at receiving such a warm welcome — from a DI, no less.

'This is DS Marie Evans.' Jackman indicated to Marie and grinned. 'Our Welsh dragon. Okay, Stacey, spill the beans.'

As she relayed events, he began to understand her concern. Stacey knew the area and its population well, good and bad. Grassroots knowledge like that was of enormous help to CID.

'So,' Jackman said, 'looks like you have two possibilities. Ratty is escalating into something a little more dangerous, or there's another intruder at large in the area.'

'That's how we see it, sir. PC Simon Laker dealt with another one later on this morning. Same kind of thing, but he swears it wasn't Ratty because of the size of the footprints they left behind.' She pulled a face. 'I know this isn't a CID thing, sir, but I have a bad feeling about it, and I thought you should be aware, just in case it turns nasty and our intruder does more than just stare at his victims.' She looked angry. 'And they are victims, sir. He's scaring these women half to death.'

'I appreciate your concern, Stacey. Perhaps you'd keep me up to speed as things progress?'

Stacey nodded. 'I certainly will, sir.' She glanced at Jay. 'We're both quite worried about what's going on.'

'Have you considered paying a visit to Ratty?'

She nodded. 'I asked the skip and we're off to do that right now.'

'And if indeed there are two of them, Ratty might have an alibi for when our new guy was making his nocturnal calls. If he does, you'll know what you're dealing with.'

Stacey stood up. 'Thanks, sir. We'll update you as we go.'

When the constables had gone, Marie said, 'I don't like the fact that the only things taken were photos of kids.'

'Neither do I,' Jackman said. 'I wonder if it could be connected to the guy at the school gates.'

'Well, this *Welsh dragon* should do some work, I guess,' Marie said. 'I'll gather up Gary and we'll hit the road.'

* * *

By four o'clock, Marie and Gary were back in the CID room. Having written their report on the afternoon's enquiries, they were now going through the record of the Giles Bannon trial.

Half an hour or so later, Gary pushed the files aside. 'Everything pointed to the husband, didn't it?'

'It did,' Marie said, 'but there wasn't nearly as much actual evidence as I would have expected for a jury to come up with a guilty verdict. I'll need to read this more thoroughly, but I'm starting to understand why he got his acquittal.' She frowned. 'Which is not to say I believe in his innocence, of course. We all know how a good lawyer can swing a case, but even so, a lot was missed the first time around.'

Gary nodded. 'True, and as you say, it needs more than just a skim through to get a proper feel for it.' He smiled at her. 'Marie Evans, you look absolutely radiant.'

'Fresh Welsh air, my mother's cooking, copious wine, time away from the scrotes, sleeping the whole night through with no call-outs . . .' She sighed contentedly. 'What more could you ask for?'

'I think you've left something out.' Gary looked at her pointedly.

'Oh? I don't think so.'

'A certain Fenchester detective?'

'Ah, yes.'

'And?'

'And what?' A flush stole up her cheeks.

'Oh, come on, Sarge. Must I spell it out for you? Are you or aren't you seeing him?'

'Sort of.'

Gary threw up his hands. 'You want to watch me beg, don't you? All I need is a yes or no.'

She glanced around and lowered her voice. 'Well, nosey, we had dinner before I went to Mum's, and we talked pretty regularly while I was away . . . And if you must know, I'm seeing him tomorrow evening, caseloads allowing.'

'That's good, I'm glad to hear it.' Gary beamed at her.

'And if you recall, Gary Pritchard, you told me that if I took the plunge, you would too. So? Your turn.'

Gary shifted his chair closer. 'I haven't said anything because of the business with Robbie and Ella, and the last thing I want to do is rub salt in the wound.' He coughed. 'However, I did find the courage to ask a certain lady out for a drink, and we seemed to get on rather well. Early days, of course, but it's nice to step away from the job for an hour or so.'

Marie was almost bouncing in her seat. 'Oh, that's the best thing I've heard today! What's her name?'

'Gilly. Do you remember my friend John Beard who helped us in our last big murder case? Well, she's his sister-in-law. She's only been here a year, so I thought I could take her around — you know, show her the Fens.'

Only now did she notice how much better Gary looked. Their last investigation had been pretty gruelling, not to mention Alistair Ashcroft's continual harassment. Under the weight of it all, Gary had begun to look older than his years. Now he looked much brighter, more relaxed. He'd even swapped his signature ancient wax jacket for a smart navy coat. 'I think she's just what you need, Gary. I've got a good feeling about it.'

'Well, I kept up my side of the bargain. It wasn't an easy move to make, I must say. And now I've done it, I'm beginning to think I've been acting like a bit of a prat since I lost my sister. Even if it doesn't work out, at least I know I'm not a prisoner to myself anymore.' He shook his head, looking embarrassed. 'As I said, a prat.'

'These things only happen when the time is right, Gary. It was the same with me, I could only move on when I was ready for it. Now it's your turn, so stop calling yourself a prat.' She grinned. 'After all, in our job there's always plenty of others ready to do that for you.'

Just then, Jackman called from his open office door, 'How did you two get on?'

They moved themselves over to his office and Marie began. 'Well, boss, we've managed to find a couple of reliable parents with good visual memories. One guy — his twins are at one of the schools — he's a photographer, so he reckons he's good with faces.'

'And,' added Gary, 'his description ties in pretty well with one of the mothers at a different school. She's a hair-dresser, and she remembered he had medium-length hair with a fashionable cut.'

'He doesn't seem to change the type of clothes he wears either,' Marie went on. 'Jeans, a casual zippered jacket, a T-shirt and trainers. Around thirty, maybe younger, fairly tall and slim. No one saw him get in or out of a vehicle. Our civilian techni-cians are trawling through the schools' CCTV footage.' Marie looked at her notebook. 'He's certainly not your stereotypical pervert in appearance. He doesn't talk to anyone, just waits, then goes. It's making people nervous. It's nothing like that case of the distraught father hunting for his kids — he talked to everyone, begging people to look out for them, showing them photos. That was understandable, this guy's just creepy.'

'So what's the overall opinion of him among the par-ents?' asked Jackman.

'They don't have one, boss,' Gary shrugged. 'They're just baffled by his behaviour.'

'And it's not going to be long before someone challenges him,' added Marie. 'So far, one or two have tried to engage him in conversation, but he just mumbles. There are a couple of mothers who could well take him on, especially if they gang up.'

'Nothing quite so dangerous as a lioness protecting her cubs,' said Gary sagely.

'Mmm, it is odd, isn't it?' Jackman mused. 'I think we need to have a word with this guy ourselves. Maybe Uniform could scatter a few officers around the schools when the parents drop their kids off. And that's odd too — why not at home time? Why always the mornings?'

Marie shrugged.

'Could mean he's working and can't get away,' said Gary. 'Or if he's looking for a particular child, that could have a bearing too. Like, he knows the mother drops them off, and the father collects them, and he doesn't want the father spotting him. Who knows?'

'I'll have a word with the duty sergeant. We can speculate all we like, but we need to get face to face with this guy.' Jackman scratched his chin. 'So, have you had a chance to get the lowdown on Giles Bannon yet?'

'We've done a shufty through the records, but we need to really look at the whole thing — transcripts, media coverage, the lot. Bottom line, frankly I'm surprised at the verdict, but that's only after a cursory look. But if he didn't do it, someone should be looking for who did.'

Jackman began to clear his desk. 'That's something for tomorrow, then. You guys get home. It's a welcome change to clock off on time, so make the most of it.'

Which they did.

'Oh, Marie?'

She stopped at the door.

'Nice to have you back.' Jackman winked at her.

'Good to be back, sir, despite what I said.'

# CHAPTER FOUR

'Mum! Mum!'

Lizzie Coupland swore under her breath. 'How many more times, Tommy? Don't run down the stairs yelling your head off. Your dad's watching *Gogglebox*.'

'But, Mum. There's someone in Nan Cutler's back garden. I was watching out for the International Space Station and I saw something move.' Tommy, dressed in spaceship pyjamas, looked at her wide-eyed.

She looked at her son suspiciously. 'You sure it wasn't a cat? You've got a wicked imagination, our Tommy. It was aliens last week.'

'It's a man, Mum, I saw him. Honest.'

'Is there, by heck. Eric! Get that tyre iron you keep by the door. Our Nan Cutler's got an unwanted visitor in her back garden.'

'Fuckin' hell! Right, I'll have him.' Eric leaped up, showering the carpet with crisps, and raced into the hall. Moving surprisingly fast for someone of his weight, he grabbed the iron and was out of the back door in seconds. As he went, he flipped a switch and the whole back garden was flooded with light.

They kept a close eye on their elderly widowed neighbour, even having a small gate installed that connected the two properties and gave them swift access if required — like now.

Cursing, Eric floundered around in the old lady's overgrown garden, flailing the tyre iron like a sabre. 'Where are you, you bastard?' After a few minutes of this, he stopped, panting, and looked around. No one. Nothing moved among the weeds and spindly shrubs. 'Come back here, you, scaring people, and it'll be the last thing you do! Creep.'

Eric's wife and son waited apprehensively on the kitchen doorstep.

'Has this little toerag been telling porkies again?' growled Lizzie.

'No, love. There was someone there all right, but he slipped away before I could get to him. I reckon I scared the bugger though.' Eric sat down heavily on one of the wooden kitchen chairs. 'Hope I didn't wake our Nan up, I was yelling like some crazy, but she didn't put a light on.'

'She takes her hearing aids out at night and has that herbal stuff to make her sleep. I wouldn't mind going over to make sure she's okay, but I don't want to frighten her.' They kept a spare key for emergencies, but it seemed silly to scare the old biddy now it was all over. At least she wasn't too forgetful and always locked up at night. Lizzie smiled at her husband. 'Well done, our hero. You could have saved our Nan from having all her precious treasures nicked.'

'Maybe we shouldn't tell her about this, Lizzie. Like you said, we don't want to scare her. But I'll give the Old Bill a tinkle, just in case he hits someone else's house tonight. They'll most likely do sod all, but at least we'll have done our bit.'

Lizzie agreed. 'Now, bed for you, our Tommy, and no more stargazing tonight. You've seen quite enough for one evening.' She rumpled his hair. 'And good boy for spotting that prowler. Well done.'

* * *

Nan Cutler awoke groggily from a deep sleep. She'd taken her water tablets too late again and now she needed the toilet. 'You'd think I'd learn at my age,' she muttered to herself. She sighed and pushed back her duvet.

She didn't put the light on, it was far too bright for her old eyes, and she certainly knew the way by now. She left the room and padded across the landing to the bathroom, idly noticing that Eric had forgotten to turn off his outside light. Not that she minded, a little light in the darkness was no bad thing.

She used the toilet and slowly made her way back to bed. She'd never really believed in herbal sleep remedies, but these ones certainly worked. She was grateful — since her husband died all those years ago, sleep had eluded her.

About to pass the top of the stairs, she came to a sudden standstill.

Standing at the bottom, staring up at her, was a tall, dark figure.

Nan blinked, still half asleep. 'Henry? Is that you?' A trickle of light from a streetlamp seeped through the glass in the front door and lit him up. Yes, there he was. Her Henry.

'My darling! You've come back to me! Oh, my darling!'

Nan moved forward, missed the top step and pitched forward, into the waiting arms of her beloved husband.

* * *

Not another one. Every day this week. PC Simon Laker was starting to think he'd been jinxed.

He'd just started to get his head around a silent intruder climbing over a sleeping woman without waking her, when he got another shout. Another prowler, but in this case someone had died.

He arrived at the location to find two anxious neighbours, still in their nightclothes, waiting at their door. 'Hello there,' he called from the gate. 'Was it you called this in?'

'Our poor Nan. We just found her, twenty minutes ago. She's dead. Fell down the stairs.' The woman clutched at her dressing gown, distraught.

'Okay. You stay here while I take a look, then I'll come back and we can talk.'

The door was open, the key still in the lock.

He pushed it gently, and immediately saw the old lady, lying on the hall floor, still and lifeless. He knelt down and felt for a pulse, even though the cold flesh told him it was far too late for that. The old soul had been dead for hours.

Looking about, the whole thing seemed obvious. One slipper was still on her foot, the other remained at the top of the stairs. How old was she? She had to be about ninety, so what was she doing alone in a house with steep stairs and no chairlift? It was all wrong. Where were her kids? Why wasn't she in a nice, warm, sheltered flat somewhere?

He told himself he should know better than to make assumptions — he knew nothing about her. She might not have kids. She might be one of those stubborn old rural folks. 'This is my home and the only way I'm leaving it is in a box,' and all that.

He sighed. *Well, you got your way, dear.*

He called in his findings, requested a doctor to confirm life extinct and asked for a member of CID to attend, then he closed the door and locked it, taking out the key, and returned to the neighbours to get some details.

Once the basic facts had been established, he asked about the intruder they had mentioned.

'I keep wondering, blaming myself,' said Eric Coupland miserably. 'Could I have disturbed her so she got up to see what was going on and then fell? I'd never live with myself if I thought I was to blame.'

'I very much doubt that was the case, Mr Coupland,' said Simon.

Eric related how his young son had seen someone from his bedroom window.

'And then you went outside and saw them yourself?' asked Simon.

'Fleetingly. I heard running footsteps, and then nothing. There was definitely someone there, no question.'

'So, why did you go in this morning? Did something bother you?' Simon asked.

'Our Nan is an early riser,' said Mrs Coupland, 'always has been. One of us goes in every morning at around seven — by that time she's got herself up and washed and dressed — and we make sure she gets down the stairs safely.'

'So she never came down the stairs without your help?' asked Simon, feeling suddenly uncomfortable.

'No, never. Our Nan was dead organised for ninety-one. Anything she wanted brought down she put in a little pile, and either my Eric or me carried it for her. She never went back upstairs until we took her, which was at nine every evening. She had a downstairs toilet, so she didn't need to go up until bedtime.' Lizzie Coupland wiped her eyes. 'We're really going to miss the old dear. Salt of the earth, she was.'

So she never attempted the stairs, but she did last night. The night of the prowler. Without expressing his concerns to the Couplands, Simon suggested they go in and make themselves a cuppa while he waited for the doctor and the detectives. He needed to think. What if the prowler hadn't run away at all? What if he'd got in? Did he startle the old lady?

As soon as the others arrived, Simon wanted back in that house and fast — number forty-seven Connaught Road was now a crime scene.

* * *

Marie was just stepping out of the shower when the phone rang.

'Sorry to call so early, DS Evans, but they said you might like to take a look at this one. It's a prowler and a possible intruder.'

'That's got my name on it, Sergeant. Address?' She picked up a pen and scribbled it down, then dashed to the wardrobe. 'Show me attending.'

In twenty minutes she was at the victim's address, parking behind the car of a local GP she knew.

'Doc Mason! Morning!' she called out. 'Is this a patient of yours?'

He came out of the house to meet her, a stocky little man with a thatch of prematurely white hair and black-rimmed glasses. 'Was, I'm afraid, DS Evans. Nancy Eliza Cutler. Lovely old woman. Frankly, I'm shocked to find her like this. I saw her for a check-up a week or two back and I swear she was fitter than me.'

'Do you have time to go back in with me?' Marie asked.

'Of course, but it's pretty self-explanatory.'

'DS Evans, can I have a word before you go in, please?' PC Laker had been stationed outside the property.

Marie frowned. 'You look anxious, PC Laker. What's the problem?'

The young constable frowned. 'I don't think this is quite as straightforward as it appears, Sarge. I don't know how much you've been told yet, but there was a prowler in her back garden last night. The neighbour thinks he did a runner, but I'm not so sure. I think he might have got in and scared the old girl.'

Marie didn't know PC Laker well, but he'd been policing the area for several years and, according to Stacey Smith, he had a reputation for being observant and efficient. 'Okay, come back in with us, and as soon as I've spoken to the doctor here, we'll do a careful walk through.'

Laker looked relieved.

The doctor was gazing down at his elderly patient and shaking his head. 'Had to be an accidental trip — she never had dizzy turns, and her blood pressure was amazing for a woman of her age.' He pointed to her feet. 'I would guess that the missing slipper at the top of the stairs is probably the culprit.' He sighed, then a slightly puzzled look stole over his face. He knelt down and examined her feet. 'That's odd.'

He pointed at her bare foot. A clearly defined red mark ran across the top of it.

'There'll naturally be tissue damage from the fall, although she died instantly from a broken neck, but this looks, well . . .' He stared at the thin, dark-red line.

Laker had been right in his suspicions, but there was something even more sinister. 'I think I know exactly what that is, Doctor.' She'd seen it before. A girl who'd been tied around the wrists. The cord had left a thin, red weal, just like the one across Nan Cutler's foot.

Marie went up the stairs and took note of the position of the single red velour slipper. Then she knelt down a couple of stairs below and scanned the top step, as well as the wall on the other side of the lone slipper. She looked more closely at the top step, got her torch from her pocket and directed the light along the paintwork. There! One tiny hole.

She swung the beam across to the other side of the stairs and found a corresponding hole in the upright of the newel post. Two slim nails, or maybe even picture-hook pins, had been enough to secure a tripwire. Afterwards the killer had removed the wire and pins, but there was nothing to be done about the holes.

'Simon, can you ring this in, please? We have a crime scene. I want the area sealed off and a log set up immediately.'

'Murder?' Dr Mason sounded incredulous. 'Surely not?'

'Tripwire, Doc, that's what caused the welt on her foot. She steps forward, catches her foot on the wire and, leaving the slipper behind, lurches forward and down the stairs — with considerable impetus, I should think — hence the broken neck.'

'I don't understand,' Dr Mason said. 'Who would want to hurt Nan Cutler? She was just a harmless old lady.'

'That's for us detectives to figure out, Dr Mason,' said Marie angrily. This was unforgivable. There was no room in the world for someone who could commit such a despicable act.

While she waited for Forensics and a uniformed team, Marie spent the next twenty minutes going over in her head the possible reasons for wanting Nan Cutler dead. A red-eyed Lizzie Coupland had brought tea for her and Simon, and they stood with their steaming mugs hypothesising over different possible scenarios. By the time the police vehicles were pulling up outside, they were still none the wiser. At least Simon had been able to assure Eric that he was definitely not to blame for Nan's death.

Marie was surprised, given how early it was, to see the Home Office pathologist, Professor Rory Wilkinson, draw up in his battered lime green Citroen Dolly.

'Well, well, well! DS Marie Evans, recently returned from the land of my fathers — I mean land of *her* fathers. And a good *bore da* to you.'

Marie grinned somewhat mischievously. 'And *cyfarchion i chi*!'

'Now don't get smart with me, Evans. At least I managed good morning — give me some credit.'

'Oh, but you said it so beautifully, Rory, I thought you must be fluent.'

'Mmm.' He raised an eyebrow. 'I'm told we have quite a conundrum here. Would you talk me through it?'

Marie related the events of the night before and what she'd subsequently discovered.

'So you worked out what a simple red welt meant. How very astute of you. I've got Cardiff Erin on her way and a couple of SOCOs.' Rory was referring to one of his two technicians, Erin Rees, who he fondly referred to as Cardiff, from her birthplace. 'We'll need to comb that garden for traces of the prowler. As you suggest, it looks very much like our prowler was actually a killer.'

'Good luck with that, Prof,' said Marie. 'It's a bit of a jungle out there. The neighbour seems to have charged in there like a rhino.'

'Typical! Oh well, no one ever said a SOCO's job was cushy. They'll cope.'

They stood back while a constable placed a pile of bags containing coveralls and overshoes by the door.

'Suit-up time. Let's take a look at our hapless lady.' Rory pulled on the protective clothing and secured a mask in place. As he did so, another uniformed officer arrived with a clipboard and scene log forms, and two others strung yellow plastic tape around the front entrance, while yet others cordoned off the rear. Crime scene management and proper evidence preservation and recovery were vital to seeing a successful case through the court.

Marie watched them put down protective boards on the front path and into the house. It reminded her of the trial of Giles Bannon. She'd suspected that procedure had been sloppy, and the smart new lawyer had jumped on it. The actions of first responders could have a massive impact on a case. Luckily, everything here was textbook. She wanted to make things right for the old lady, to make up for her callous, violent end.

She turned to Rory. 'Regarding contamination, when we arrived at the scene, we had no idea that this was anything other than a sudden death. The doc did his bit and we also checked, as did the neighbour who found her, but all of us spent minimal time with the body. And I climbed the stairs just that one time to check for indications of foul play.'

'And you found some, dear heart. As I said, very astute.'

She shrugged. 'I'd seen those injuries before, Rory. You don't forget.'

'That you don't.' Rory looked at his watch, then back at Nan Cutler. 'This is very much off the top of my head but, considering it was a warm night, it's my guess she fell around midnight at the earliest, possibly an hour or two later. Would that fit in with the sighting of the prowler?'

'PC Laker said the neighbour was leaping around in the back garden at around eleven. So, yes, if he managed to gain entrance quickly, it wouldn't have taken him long to attach the tripwire. Apparently, she was quite deaf, so he wouldn't have disturbed her while he was setting it up.' She frowned. 'There's lots of loopholes yet, like how did he know she would wake? We've also been told that she never went down the stairs alone, so why then?'

'You'll work it out. And I'll provide you with as much evidence as I can. As soon as we're through here, I'll give you a call so you can go through the place from top to bottom.' He glanced towards the path outside. 'I see my other Welsh witch has arrived, so I'd better get down to some work.'

Passing Cardiff on her way out, Marie gave her a friendly smile. The woman had settled in well and seemed remarkably unfazed by Rory's numerous quips. His larger-than-life, camp personality could be off-putting if you didn't know him.

'Sorry about the early start, Cardiff. My fault, I'm afraid.'

Cardiff smiled back. 'To be honest, like, it's nice to get out of the underground kingdom for a while, even at this hour.'

'I'll see you later then.' Marie stripped off her coveralls, tossed them into a bin and signed out. She checked the time. Perfect. Jackman and the others would be in the office by the time she got back. Before she left, she had a word with Simon Laker. 'Nice one, Simon. Looks like your hunch was spot on. Now we can get straight on with the investigation, rather than stumbling into it days later when something shows up in the post-mortem. By that time, all trace evidence would have been obliterated. I'll make sure I mention that to your skipper.'

'Thanks, Sarge, that's kind of you.' Simon beamed. 'And thanks for believing me. I wasn't sure at first, but the more I thought about it, the more the whole thing smelled bad.'

'Yeah, I know that feeling.'

'But even I didn't consider premeditated murder. You were shit hot on that.' He stopped and blushed. 'Sorry, Sarge, that was rude.'

'Shit hot's fine by me, as long as you include the "hot" part. Thank you. I've got to get back now. Are you staying on for a bit?'

He nodded. 'Yes. It feels like my baby.'

Marie patted him on the shoulder. 'Good work, Simon. I'll see you later.'

It happened so often. Some seemingly inconsequential job turns out to be more difficult, more dangerous even, that you imagined. She'd left the nick last night thinking she was investigating some harmless intruder and was returning this morning with a murder investigation.

'I guess that's policing for you,' she murmured to herself.

CHAPTER FIVE

Laura Archer returned home from her early morning meeting at Greenborough police station at around ten thirty and let herself into her consulting room. A renovation of part of the old mill, it was an idyllic setting to work from. The building was separate from the main house and provided the perfect environment for her meetings with clients. No one came to Laura's rooms except by appointment, so she had quite a shock when the doorbell rang.

She opened the door to Professor Sam Page, her old mentor and dear friend. He was smiling broadly. 'Sam! Come in. I wasn't expecting to see you today.' For a second, she wondered if Jackman had rung him and told him she needed his help, but Sam didn't seem at all concerned.

'I hope I haven't picked a bad time. Have you got appointments this morning?' he asked.

'Not until midday, so you timed it just right. Want a cuppa? I'm just about to put the kettle on.'

It had been over a week since she had last seen Sam. She and Jackman kept in regular touch with him because Sam had a heart condition and lived alone in an isolated spot on the marsh. They had offered him a permanent home at Mill Corner, in a completely self-contained flat above her consulting room, but he had declined. They suspected that Sam was reluctant to intrude just as they were embarking on a new life together, but he said he preferred the remoteness of his little cottage. It was situated in a bird reserve, and Sam was a keen birdwatcher.

'I'm on my way to Cartoft. I like to stock up with fresh produce from the farm shop at least a couple of times a month. I'm not exactly a brilliant cook, but I do try to eat healthily. Plus, they sell this amazing ice cream. You should try their chocolate marshmallow one. Heaven.'

'Stop it, Sam. Some of us need to watch our figures, you know.'

'Rubbish! Eat what you enjoy, you're a long time dead.'

His choice of words sobered Laura somewhat. Not that long ago, a killer had roamed the streets of Saltern-le-Fen, and Sam had been so badly injured that she had feared for his life. Maybe a close call like that gave you a different perspective on life.

She handed him a mug of tea and they sat down on the couches.

Sam eyed her over his tea. 'It's all right, I'm not being maudlin. It's just my standard excuse for eating too much ice cream.' He sat back and looked around. 'There's a lovely atmosphere here, Laura. Are you okay with working "from home," so to speak?'

'I love it, Sam. And in any case, a lot of my work takes place outside, mostly in police stations or hospitals or prisons. This place is pretty under-used really, but it's perfect for my referrals and private patients.'

Sam sipped his tea. 'I did have an ulterior motive for calling in, actually.'

So Jackman did ring him. 'Really?'

'Something that's been on my mind for a while now, and might even have crossed yours . . .'

Okay, not Jackman. 'Go on.'

'As you know, I'm officially retired, but I occasionally get a call from an old colleague asking my opinion on some issue they're working on. Well, last week I heard from Trevor Blackstone, a retired prison governor I worked quite closely with when they were reassessing the psychological evaluation of dangerous prisoners.'

Laura nodded. 'I remember you telling me about that. Took ages, didn't it?'

'It certainly did. Well, although he too is retired, he's been doing a consultancy with another governor, whom I also happen to know quite well. You've heard of him, I expect. Ross Cadman at HMP Gately?'

'Oh, yes. That was where you and DCI Matt Ballard had to go, wasn't it? The repentant murderer and the copycat killer. We were both involved, weren't we?' It had been a nerve-racking investigation, Matt's final case before he became a private investigator.

'That's right. At the time, Ross Cadman was pioneering a special PIPE unit at Gately, called the "Harbour." PIPE being Psychologically Informed Planned Environment, in case you've not been in one. His was the best I'd ever seen.'

'I've read about them,' said Laura. 'Matt didn't want me directly involved, did he? So I never got to see one in action.'

'Ross's worked very well, and now he wants to make it even better.'

Laura tried to recall what she'd learned about them. 'They aren't treatment units as such, are they? More like progression programmes for Cat A prisoners with personality disorders and the like.'

'In order to get into these units the relevant prisoners need to have completed high-intensity treatments, after which they're assisted with personal development, so they don't lose the ground they've already made. The conditions are much better, but they have to work closely with their psychiatrists and psychologists, and they must be willing to participate in in-depth probing sessions that often refer to the crimes that put them inside. It's no walk in the park, that's for sure, but for those that put in the work, there are rewards, and if a parole board sees that he or she has completed the course, it counts in their favour.' Sam took a mouthful of tea. 'But I digress. Trevor knew I'd seen several of these special-ised units and studied the various programmes used, so he wondered if I might have any input as to ways to improve the system. Anyway, we chatted, and at some point, he started talking about HMP Belmarsh, so naturally I pricked up my ears.'

Laura understood immediately. The man who had insti-gated a reign of terror throughout Saltern-le-Fen and who had tried to kill Sam was incarcerated there. 'Don't tell me they're going to open a PIPE unit there?'

'No. What caught my attention was the mention that several of the Cat A prisoners are being moved.' He paused. 'Our nemesis is one of them.'

'Alistair Ashcroft,' she whispered. Laura swallowed. 'Where is he going? Do you know?'

'Trevor didn't know about my history with Ashcroft. Now he does, he's going to make sure that I'm made aware of exactly where and when he's going. At the moment it's probably HMP Frankland in County Durham, or possibly HMP Gartree in Leicestershire.'

'Do you know why they're moving him?' she asked.

'It's not unusual for prisoners to be moved around, and there's no reason for it to have any impact on us. Of course, considering his profile as a dangerous killer, the move will be a high-security operation.' He set down his empty mug on the coffee table in front of him. 'No, what bothers me is that both those prisons have special PIPE units. Ashcroft has apparently volunteered for every form of psychiatric treat-ment on offer. I'm wondering if he's playing the system with the sole intention of getting into a special programme.'

Laura narrowed her eyes. 'With what in mind?'

'Perks. All those little extras he might use to manipu-late the people around him. He's a master deceiver, a mind-bender, and to my mind should be refused all such options. He surrendered his rights to any privileges when he chose to terrorise a whole town and murder innocents.'

Laura had rarely heard Sam speak so harshly. 'He has a whole-life tariff, doesn't he? He'll never get out.'

'He won't. It's life, without any possibility of parole or conditional release.' He paused. 'But others he comes into contact with might, and there are suggestible folk that work in those places who, out of altruism and an honest desire to help, could just fall under his spell. We must never lose sight of the fact that Ashcroft can be a charismatic and very, very convincing liar. He only needs one admirer on the outside and we could all suffer the repercussions. It's something you've considered yourself, isn't it? You know exactly how dangerous he is.'

She was forced to agree. 'I never mention it to Jackman, but Ashcroft is always there, waiting in the shadows. I'll never forget what he did. The others seem to have moved on, relieved that Ashcroft got his just desserts. They're getting on with their lives, they're happy again. Maybe it's the nature of my work, unravelling the skeins of people's twisted thoughts every day. I cannot let him go.'

Sam leaned across and patted her hand gently. 'Then let's keep this between ourselves, Laura my dear. Let the others enjoy the freedom of knowing he's safely confined and cannot harm them. We can always talk to each other if we feel anxious.'

'You will tell me everything you find out, won't you, Sam?'

'Of course I will. In any case, I'm probably reading far too much into it. It doesn't help that I'm personally involved, I know.' His face darkened. 'Sometimes I wish there'd been a different outcome.'

He didn't need to explain. Laura had often wished the same. Yes, it would have been better if Ashcroft had died.

She glanced at her watch. 'Oh dear, my midday session. I'd better get ready.' She collected up the mugs. 'Before you go, Sam, I've got a tricky patient at present. Do you think we could discuss him sometime?'

'Of course! Can you give me a general idea of the problem? Maybe I can have a think about it, or swot it up for you?'

'Well, if you don't mind. It's somnambulism. Not just sleepwalking, and it's not a youngster who'll grow out of it. It's an adult man who's scared to death because not only does he go out of the house, but he drives his car while he's asleep. He's a GP referral and I suspect there's a complicated history there, but he's not ready to share it yet.' She put the mugs in the sink. 'Could you find some case histories for me?'

'Interesting. Yes, I'd be pleased to, and we'll talk soon. Now, I need my ice cream fix.' He gave her a hug.

'I'll ring you tomorrow. Take care.'

Laura watched him drive away. It was always good to see Sam, but he'd done nothing to reassure her. It seemed her fears were real after all.

* * *

'I don't get it, where has the little shite disappeared to?' Stacey flopped on to a mess-room chair and glowered at Jay. 'Day two already, and we still haven't got hold of Ratty.'

'It seems a bit out of character, I must say. According to his somewhat dubious neighbour, he never goes away,' said Jay. He opened a large plastic lunch box and stared hopefully at the contents.

'Another healthy option, Jay?' Stacey smiled, wondering who it was that took such care with her workmate's diet.

He sighed. 'Looks that way. Oh, but there's two bran muffins in here. They're delicious — made with apple sauce instead of fat. I'll save one for you if you like.'

Stacey was more of a full-fat girl but hated to offend her crewmate. 'Smashing — if you can spare it.'

'Of course.' He handed her a carefully wrapped muffin.

Surprised at how tasty it looked, Stacey thanked him. 'So what's the main course today?'

'It's a stuffed spinach chapati with masala corn.' He raised his eyes from the box, apologetically. 'Not pretty to look at, but it's really very tasty.'

'You don't cook all this yourself, do you, Jay? Only you never seem to know what you've got until you open it.' In for a penny, thought Stacey.

'I'm living with my brother and his family until I get settled. His wife Ravinder treats me like their fourth child.' He showed her the lid of his lunch box where someone had written "Jay A" in felt pen, with a sticker of a smiling spider.

'The kids have a new sticker every day. I see it's mini-beasts today.' He shrugged. 'As I said, I'm kid number four.'

'I think that's lovely!' said Stacey, eyeing her supermarket sandwich. 'I wish someone cared enough about me to make me a personalised home-cooked lunch.'

Stacey lived with her sister. If anyone was going to cook in their household, it had to be Stacey. Danielle didn't do cooking. Actually, Danielle didn't do much of anything. The place would be a dosshouse if it weren't for Stacey's frantic clean-ups after her shifts finished. She wished she could leave, but the house belonged to her. She had inherited it from their father, who had known exactly what would happen if Dannie got her hands on it. The will had stipulated that Stacey must look out for her sister, and she was determined not to let her dad down. After a rocky start, the confirmed dropout was finally in full-time work. Even better, she seemed to love it. If she could only come to love housework too . . .

'So what do we do about Ratty?' Jay was asking.

'Find the bugger. What else?' Stacey ate half of her sandwich and threw the rest in the bin. She rubbed her hands together. 'Now, time for that muffin.'

Stacey bit into it and experienced the oddest emotion. Sure, the muffin tasted nice, but it wasn't that. It was the fact that the cake was home-made. It struck her that no one had ever baked her a cake, made something just for her. How sad that was.

'You don't like it, do you?' Jay said.

She swallowed, unable to speak for the lump in her throat. It wasn't the muffin. 'It's the nicest thing I've ever tasted.'

He gave her a pleased smile. 'I'll tell Ravinder. She'll be really happy to hear that.'

'Her children are very lucky to have her,' she said rather shakily.

'We are, aren't we? Next time I'll make sure she adds another muffin to my lunch box. Now. Ratty. We've checked his home, his usual haunts, and we've spoken to the few people he hangs around with. Where next?'

Stacey licked the last of the crumbs from her fingertips. 'I think I know where his mother lives. He might be there. She's in the static caravan park at Teasel Woods, and be warned, she's mad as a box of frogs.'

Twenty minutes later they pulled up by the site manager's office. The tatty statics at Teasel Woods had all seen better days. A while back, the place had been at the centre of a drug investigation. The gang that ran it had all been apprehended, and since then the park had been virtually deserted.

'You do bring me to the nicest places,' said Jay, stepping over a wide muddy puddle. 'And considering we've had no rain, where has all this water come from?'

Stacey chuckled. 'I don't think you want to know.'

'Some holiday camp — who stays here anyway?' Jay wrinkled his nose. 'It's not going to feature in any tourist brochures, is it?'

'It's a dump, little more than a gypsy camp really. The people here are just one step up from homeless. Some are transient seasonal field workers, some can't afford a proper home. Some just finished up here and never left, like old Ma Jones.'

'Ratty's mother?'

'Yes — and a word of warning, never call him Ratty to her face, okay? I've seen her deck someone for that. His name is Reginald.'

'Got it.'

Stacey stopped outside a small, old-fashioned caravan with frilly net curtains at the windows. Thirty years ago it might have looked pretty, but the curtains were unwashed, the paintwork peeling. She knocked on the door, then stood back. Ma Jones didn't appreciate visits from strangers.

'Mrs Jones? Can you spare a minute?'

After a while, the door cracked open just wide enough for them to see an elderly woman peering through the narrow gap. She was tiny, extremely thin, and her grey hair stuck out in all directions. Her eyes were small, colourless, disconcertingly piercing and suspicious. 'What do you want?'

'Hello, Mrs Jones. We were wondering if Reginald is staying with you at the moment. We need to have a word with him.'

'Oh, it's the filth, is it? Well, sod off, he ain't 'ere!'

'We just need a few words, that's all,' Stacey said, smiling.

'I said he ain't here.'

'Then do you know where he is? It's quite important, Mrs Jones. We think someone's looking to get Reginald blamed for something he didn't do, so we just want to prove it wasn't him. A few words and we can put him in the clear.'

'Coppers don't help the likes of us, certainly not my Reginald. You lot have been hounding him all his life, so don't come to me with your "proving it isn't him" bullshit.'

'True, we've felt his collar at times, but he shouldn't be shinning up people's drainpipes and getting in their houses, should he? Look, we know he's not a thief. All we want is to know where he was on a certain day at a certain time so we can put him in the clear. Otherwise he'll be done for burglary, and you know what that means.'

The old woman pulled the door to and they heard a whispered conversation. The door opened again, and Ratty Jones stepped out. 'I ain't no tea leaf, PC Smith. You know that. You know what I do, but I never stole nothing when I got in them houses.'

'Yes, I know you didn't. But there's someone doing the same as you now, and they *are* stealing things,' said Stacey.

Like clouds across the sky, Ratty's expression passed from anger to fear. 'I know. But before you ask, I dunno who it is. I swear.'

'What do you mean, you know, Reginald?' asked Jay.

Ratty gave him a startled look. 'Night before last I went out to a nice little cottage I had lined up for a visit. I saw him when I was walking down one of the lanes along the back of the houses. He was going into this house, straight through a top-opening window. Thought I was seeing things. He went up like greased lightning.'

'Where was this house?' asked Stacey.

Ratty described the location.

'That's where PC Laker saw the footprint on the bed,' Jay muttered.

'Hmm,' Stacey said. 'Pity. That doesn't give you an alibi, all it does is put you right in the vicinity of the theft. So, how about last night? Where were you from around eleven p.m. onwards?'

'Right here, playing cards with Harry Moore — he's the caretaker of this dump — and a bloke called Keith who lives two vans up, and my mum.' He pointed his thumb backwards over his shoulder. 'Ask her. She won.'

'What did you play?' asked Stacey.

'Seven-card stud. Ma's a class act. Dunno why we let her play. She always cleans us out.'

Stacey knew when a man like Ratty was lying. It seemed he had an alibi for last night, after all.

'Why aren't you at home, Reginald?' asked Jay politely. 'How come you're here?'

'Ma's sprained her ankle. Went to hospital, she did, and it's all strapped up. I'm looking after her for a few days.' He pushed the door wider. 'Look.'

The old lady was sitting down with her leg propped up on cushions. The strapping was unmistakably a professional hospital job.

Stacey nodded. 'Now, listen to me, Ratty. This is serious. Do yourself a favour and stay out of those houses. Keep your head down and make sure you have people around you. You might need alibis for other dates and times, and not for just minor stuff either. You'll see it on the news tonight. Just make sure you don't step out of line, or your ma could be looking after herself from now on.'

They saw Ratty's Adam's apple move up and down as he swallowed. 'On the news?'

'Yep. It's bad, Ratty. So be warned, keep that head right down.'

They called at the site office on their way out, and as Stacey had expected, the card game had gone on until almost one in the morning, and yes, Ma Jones had made a killing.

Ratty might have lost at cards, but the game had been very lucky for him.

# CHAPTER SIX

By two in the afternoon, Jackman had been to the crime scene, talked to the neighbours and begun enquiries into the background of the victim, Mrs Nancy Eliza Cutler.

Marie and he had walked silently through the house, examining all the insignificant objects that constituted her life. Everyone but Marie had been made to leave, so that the two of them could absorb it all, fix it in their minds, to reflect on later. Marie had seen Rory do the same thing on many occasions. In fact, it was understood that you always waited for the prof to do his bit before you went in.

Both he and Jackman were trying to capture some remaining trace of the killer. Often this wasn't even tangible. You might say it was something in the air.

Now that they were back in his office, Jackman was still quiet and ruminative. Thoughtfully, he spun the globe on his desk and watched the continents flash past. Marie was just beginning to think he must be getting dizzy when he stopped the globe and looked up at her. 'Coat hangers.'

'Pardon?'

He laughed. 'The old lady was especially neat and tidy, wasn't she?'

'Yes,' she said. 'The place was full of souvenirs, ornaments and all that, almost cluttered, but they were all dusted and clean. The pictures hung perfectly straight, everything in its place.'

'And her wardrobe was the same,' Jackman said. 'Coats at one end, then jackets, skirts, dresses and finally blouses. Everything was spaced out along the rail, so it wouldn't get creased, and spare hangers, just four of them, lying on the bottom shelf.'

Marie frowned, wondering what was coming.

'Okay, so, in the spare room, another wardrobe. From the smell of mothballs, these must have been her late husband's clothes that she'd never been able to part with. Everything hung in the same order — coats, jackets, suits and so on, except—' he raised a finger — 'two empty coat hangers, still on the rail, with the clothes on either side pushed back. Looking at where they were taken from, I'd say an outdoor jacket and a pair of trousers had been removed. And removed hurriedly too — an adjacent jacket had practically fallen off its hanger. It looked like someone had grabbed them quickly and shut the door. I'll ask Forensics to check carefully for prints in that wardrobe.'

'He stole clothes?' She grunted. 'Weird. It's usually the family silver.'

Jackman chuckled. 'It's one of those strange little clues — so easily overlooked. It could be the crucial piece in the puzzle.'

'The bit where we go: "Of course! Why didn't I think of that at the time?" Trouble is, it's not helping us now. We still know sod all.'

'Maybe,' said Jackman, still sounding reflective. 'And before I forget, smart work finding those tiny holes. If it hadn't been for that, it would have been put down as an accident. Damned good work.'

'I'm sure Rory would have picked it up, boss. I just got there first.' She changed the subject. 'Anything about the woman herself yet? She must have had some kind of skeleton in the cupboard to get herself murdered. People don't set up elaborate traps to kill old ladies unless they have a good reason.'

Jackman stared thoughtfully at her. 'My money's on her knowing something about the killer. It must have been about to come out, so he had to stop her.'

'Possible, or this was payback for something she'd done in the past.'

'Also possible.' Jackman grinned. 'Maybe she'd criticised his prize dahlias or sung out of tune at the harvest supper . . . Sorry, Marie. I'm being flippant now.'

She smiled back. 'My money's on the dahlias.'

'Ah well, we'd better go and organise the whiteboard. We don't have much yet, but things are moving quite fast. A simple request to help out with an intruder, and now we have two thefts and a murder.'

'In a matter of days,' added Marie. 'As you say, things are hotting up.'

'Enough to warrant a team campfire, I reckon. Could you tell the others, Marie? Four p.m. in the CID room. We'll keep it in-house to start with . . .' He looked at her. 'What about bringing in Stacey Smith and her new crewmate, and PC Simon Laker?'

'Good idea. They're on the ground, and they've been a massive help so far. Shall I go have a word with their sergeant?'

'Please,' Jackman said. 'See if we can pinch them for a quick meeting today, and sound out how he feels about them joining our investigation. They're up to speed on it, and their local knowledge could be invaluable.'

A few short minutes later, Marie paced back into Jackman's office. 'Result, boss. Skip is fine on all counts, just so long as they can deal with any ongoing jobs of their own. Basically, they're ours whenever we need them.'

'Excellent.'

'Oh, and I put in a good word for Laker while I was there. He sensed right away something wasn't right in that house. He's got a good nose, that one.'

Marie followed Jackman out to the main CID room to, as he put it, "play with the whiteboards."

* * *

At four p.m. everyone was present, with the exception of Gary Pritchard.

'He'll be here in a few minutes, boss,' said Marie. 'He went back to Connaught Road, said he wanted to check something out.'

Jackman nodded. 'Then we'll start. We don't have a lot to begin with, I just wanted everyone to see the whole picture at the outset of the case.' He looked around him. 'Detectives, you'll see we have Stacey, Jay and Simon with us today from Uniform. They were the first responders, and their input could be invaluable. Well, in two days what started as a suspicion that our local infiltrator, Ratty Jones, was stepping up his game to theft has turned into a murder inquiry. So, please make use of our colleagues' street knowledge as and when you need.' He looked towards the two half-empty whiteboards. 'Right, this is what we have.' He paused as the door opened to admit Gary.

'Sorry I'm late, boss.'

'We're just starting, so nothing missed, Gary. Now, this case kicked off with an intruder, who did not break in but found an open window big enough for him to gain access. He terrified the occupant by standing at the end of her bed and then fled, taking a framed photo of a young ten-year-old boy.'

'Any description, boss?' asked DC Charlie Button.

'None at all,' Jackman replied. 'The lady in question did put on a bedside light, but by then the intruder was off down the stairs. Her son saw only a blur as someone rushed past his bedroom door.'

'Even I'd probably shit myself if I woke up to see a stranger standing over my bed,' said DC Max Cohen. 'It must be terrifying.'

'Indeed,' Jackman said. 'Next came another unauthorised entry into a private house, again using a top-opening window, and this time leaving a clear footprint on the bed of the occupier. Which to my mind would have been even more frightening.'

'The lady in question, sir,' said Simon Laker, 'was distraught. I rang her this morning, just to check on her. She said she slept in a chair in the lounge last night — too scared to go to bed.'

'Not surprising. Again, a photo was taken, of her two grandchildren, one of whom is ten years old. Having pictures of children taken is worrying, although during the last incident, the murder, no picture was removed.'

'Hold on, boss.' Gary Pritchard held up an evidence bag. 'I've just been to Connaught Road, and I found this.' Pulling on a pair of gloves, he removed a photograph album and placed it on the desk beside Jackman. Carefully opening it, he pointed. 'Look, a page has been torn out, leaving a tiny scrap at the bottom. Although the full name of the subject has gone, you can still make out the letter "Y" and the words ". . . at age eleven." The rest of the album is intact, just that single picture was taken.'

'Of someone aged eleven,' mused Jackman. 'Well done, Gary. This most likely connects the murder to the two uninvited guests. In one way that's a blessing, as it means we're only looking for one man.' He narrowed his eyes. 'And given the age of these children, we also have to consider the reports of a youngish man waiting at various school gates when children are arriving for the day. As of yet there's no clear connection, but we can't ignore it.' He looked at Stacey. 'I believe you and Jay spoke to Ratty?'

'We did, sir. He has an alibi for the night of the murder, and it checks out. The odd thing is that he saw the other intruder a couple of nights ago — he couldn't give a description, but he definitely saw him go through the window of Mrs Sylvia Wilson's house.'

'Are you sure that none of this is Ratty's doing, Stacey?' asked Jackman.

Stacey glanced at Jay. 'We're both certain, sir. He was bricking it, and not because he felt guilty. This other fella scares him — badly. Plus, Ratty always throws up his hands to what he does. It's a compulsion. He's no thief, and he has no history of ever going near children.'

'Well, that's good enough for me,' said Jackman. 'I hope you warned him to butt out of his "compulsion" for a bit. We don't want him muddying the waters.'

'Stacey has already done that, sir,' said Jay. 'Firmly too.'

Jackman smiled. 'She has a way with words, our Stacey.' He looked around. 'Now, anything else?'

There was little more to discuss, so Jackman brought the meeting to a close. Back in his office, Marie asked about Giles Bannon. 'In light of the murder, shall we drop our background checks on him, boss?'

He pulled a face. 'No, better not. As soon as the initial flurry of activity surrounding the old lady's death dies down there'll be a pause. It won't take long to conduct our house-to-house enquiries and so on, and then we'll be left waiting for Forensics to fill in the gaps. I'd rather not let our friend Giles escape our minds. I think we'd better be prepared.'

'Good. I wish I could get a sense of whether he's really guilty or not. It helps if you find yourself talking to the man himself.'

Jackman smiled at her. It was good to see Marie so on top of things, so relaxed. 'So, the next thing is to start delving into Nan Cutler's past. Apart from a few snippets from the next-door neighbours, we know precious little about that old lady.'

'Me and Gary will press on with that,' said Marie. 'We've already brought back a load of personal papers from the house, which'll help us build up a picture of her background.'

'Okay. Meanwhile, it's time I brought Ruth up to speed.' He paused. 'But get away on time tonight, Marie, and make sure the others do too. We could get busy soon, so take advantage of an early night while you can. Or maybe you have plans for this evening?'

'Might have.'

'Ah.'

She laughed. 'Better put you out of your misery, I suppose.' She rolled her eyes. 'Yes, I'm having dinner with Ralph Enderby.'

'Good for you! Have a lovely evening.'

'I'm sure I will. Oh, and tell Laura we'll be happy to join you both for dinner.'

He beamed at her. He'd waited years for this. One of his greatest aims in life had been to see Marie happy again.

But as he watched her leave the office, his warm feelings were replaced by anxiety. Suppose she got hurt? He'd made a few discreet enquiries about her new friend Ralph, and so far he'd passed the Jackman Test with flying colours. He seemed to be a brave, well-respected detective sergeant, known to be fair and reasonable, and was generally very well liked. Which led him to another problem. What if he lost her for good? He'd missed her desperately when she'd been away for a week, what if she decided to move away or even give up police work altogether?

Disgusted with himself for being so selfish, Jackman strode out of the office. *Be happy for her, for goodness' sake.*

\* \* \*

Sam Page dished up his grilled lamb chops, adding new potatoes and a selection of fresh local vegetables. A dash of homemade mint sauce and the meal would be complete. Apart from a nice glass of wine, that is. However, he only drank wine with dinner every other day and he'd had his ration yesterday. He was often torn between looking after his health and, in the words of an old friend of his, "living for today." As that friend had said, there might not be a tomorrow.

Sam had always considered this attitude to be rather irresponsible, but as he grew older, he could see the reasoning behind it. Sam had powered through his busy life with no thought of either his age or his body, until suddenly, the latter began to fail him. This was doubly irritating, because in his head he was still around thirty.

He got out the wine, filled his glass to the rim, and raised it in a toast to his old friend. Here's to tomorrow — or not.

Furthermore, he did something he never did. His father and mother would have been appalled had they seen him now, for he sat with his laptop before him and read while he ate. Laura had wanted case histories of somnambulism and he had come across very few in his long career. This was mostly because somnambulism was treated as a medical condition, not a psychological one. However, he'd remembered a former colleague having expressed an interest in it and had sent him an email.

He checked his messages and saw a reply.

*Hi Sam, glad to help. Mind you, you've picked on a pretty contentious subject. Views on sleepwalking are often based on misconceptions and, to be frank, the established diagnostic criteria are inconsistent with the research findings, especially my own! How about we meet up? I'm in Lincoln tomorrow, any chance of you getting across and we grab lunch together? I don't often get a chance to expound my theories on my pet subject! All the best, Hughie.*

How fortuitous! Hugh Mackenzie was exactly the man he needed. He sent a quick reply: *Perfect. Midday at the Birdcage? Very tasty food.*

Hughie's response came almost immediately. *See you there. And remind me to tell you about the Reece case. H.*

Sam had heard of Reece, a man who had murdered his sister and attacked his brother-in-law, claiming that he was asleep at the time. It would be good to hear the story from someone in the know, rather than rely on the media.

He googled various medical sites. Hughie had been right, there was much debate as to the cause of the condition. And, as yet, he had no information about Laura's patient, other than that he was driving in his sleep. That one fact was disturbing enough — where would he be going? And why? He would have liked to ring Laura and question her further, but she would be with Jackman now, so he would have to wait.

He cleared away the dishes and washed the grill pan. No wonder Laura was so concerned about her mystery sleepwalker. The case would require extensive research, and Sam was glad he had the free time to help her. A challenging case always excited and worried you in equal measure. Often it shed new light on the issue, which was the exciting part. She was right to start with case histories, and where better to start than with Hughie Mackenzie's murderer?

He carried the remainder of his wine through to the lounge. If he was to get any sleep, he must switch off his brain and immerse himself in a film. He checked through the channel guide and found the perfect one. The 1920 version of *The Cabinet of Dr. Caligari* was the feature film tonight. He recalled that the plot centred around a hypnotist who uses a somnambulist to commit murders for him. How appropriate.

# CHAPTER SEVEN

The night was cooler than it had been of late, the temperature far more suited to the time of year. Fleur Harper toyed
with the idea of closing the windows, but she did like fresh
air, so she left the fanlights open.

She hadn't been sleeping particularly well recently.
Insomnia came and went with her, according to her moods.
Tonight, sleep evaded her. She tried reading and watched
TV for a couple of hours, but at midnight, she was still
wide awake, and conscious that she had an early start in the
morning.

'Oh hell. Better take something, I suppose.'

She padded downstairs. A milky malt drink and a couple
of magic pills would give her a few hours' respite. Despite
having natural ingredients, they weren't available in this
country and had to be ordered online. So far, they hadn't
failed her.

Back in bed, she finished her drink and turned out the
light, already feeling drowsy. Oh, the relief of sleep!

Fleur awoke to the sound of the alarm clock and reached
out to stop its buzzing.

She was mildly fuzzy and still clinging to the vestiges of a
strange dream. She blinked and stretched, parts of the dream

still with her. It had almost been erotic. A man had entered the room and stood beside her bed. He had watched her sleeping and then bent forward, as if to kiss her. She had stirred in her sleep, welcoming his attention. Even this morning she felt his warm breath caress her skin and smelled a hint of cologne.

'Phew! Shame I woke up.' She only ever dreamed when she took her sleeping pills. Nonetheless, that was some dream, and so vivid!

Fleur roused herself. She needed to keep moving this morning. Today, she was embarking on a new, long-overdue fitness regime. She showered quickly and pulled on her swimming costume, followed by a loose sweatshirt and joggers.

She ran downstairs and into the kitchen and stopped, looking around. Something wasn't right. Hang on. Where was the picture of Jason? A photograph of her son always hung next to the Welsh dresser, and now it had gone. A slight draught caused her to turn away, and she saw that the back door was ajar. The door she had carefully locked when she went to bed. The door she had rechecked when she came down to make her drink.

Images from her dream flooding back into her mind, Fleur walked slowly back up to her bedroom. She stopped just inside the door and sniffed. It was faint but unmistakable. Cologne.

She ran from the room.

\* \* \*

'He's made another night-time sortie, Jackman, this time in your village.' Marie sounded remarkably awake for six in the morning. 'Another boy's picture taken and another woman half scared to death. Sorry to ring you so early, but I've just had a call from Control. Uniform were going to attend, but as we have an interest in this creep, they wondered if we'd want it. I suggested you might like to do a house call on your way into work. I could meet you there if you like?'

'Er, yes, sure. What time?'

'How about seven? It'll give you time to shower and grab something to eat. The address is three, Glebe Close, Cartoft. The woman's name is Fleur Harper. Do you know her?'

He thought about it. 'I knew a Bob Harper, but he moved away a few years back. Could be his ex-wife. Anyway, I know where it is. See you there.'

'You will.'

Marie had hung up before he could ask her how her evening went. Never mind, he'd get it out of her later.

'Off early again?' Laura asked.

'Sorry, sweetheart. Duty calls. But at least I've got time to grab some breakfast before I go. I'll bring you some tea.' She looked so beautiful with her tousled hair and sleepy eyes . . . He sighed.

'Nothing I can do to convince you to stay?' She gave him a slow smile.

'Plenty. But right now, another woman needs me.'

'Oh well. In that case I'll have another half-hour's sleep.' She pulled the bedclothes up and settled back down.

Jackman showered, dressed and made a pot of tea and some toast. He took a mug up to Laura. She was always so difficult to leave. He hurried back downstairs and let himself out, careful to lock the door behind him.

* * *

'Morning, boss.'

Clad in her black-and-red riding leathers, Marie stood waiting for him beside her motorcycle. She struck an impressive figure.

'Morning, Marie. You look ready for anything.'

She grinned at him. 'As always. It's one of my finest attributes. I must say, I'm surprised he was back on the prowl after the previous night. I assumed he'd back off and regroup. He's certainly a very cool customer.'

59

'He is indeed. I didn't expect to be chasing after him this soon. Shall we go in?' He directed his gaze to number three. 'Nice, neat, little house. Does she live here alone?'

'Yes. She's divorced, so she could be your Bob Harper's ex. Anyway, we'll soon find out.'

The front door was opened before they got to it. 'DI Jackman and DS Marie Evans of Saltern-le-Fen CID, Mrs Harper. Can we come in, please?'

She looked at their warrant cards and held the door wide. 'With pleasure. I must admit I've been in shock.'

They followed her through to the lounge, where she offered them seats facing an expensive sofa. Jackman noted the neatness of the room, the tasteful decor and several beautiful orchids adorning the fireplace and windowsill. No children or animals.

'Are you up to telling us what happened, Mrs Harper?' Jackman asked gently.

'There's not much to tell,' she managed in a shaky voice, 'other than that some . . . pervert got into my house last night.'

Marie rose and sat close to her on the sofa. 'There's no rush. Why not let me make you a cup of tea and we'll take it slowly.'

'Would you? I was shaking so much that I didn't trust myself to pick up the kettle.'

'Of course. You just sit there, I won't be long. Kitchen straight through?'

Fleur nodded. 'Everything's out on the work surface near the kettle. Just milk for me.'

Jackman smiled at her. 'Do you mind if I ask whether you were married to Bob Harper?'

'Yes. Bob and I divorced a couple of years ago. We're still in touch, for Jason's sake. That's our son.'

'And Jason's with your husband?' Jackman asked.

'He is, although I have him every other weekend. Bob remarried and lives in Greenborough now, with his new wife.' Jackman gathered this was an amicable arrangement.

'I knew him in passing. I live in the village too.'

She smiled faintly. 'I know. Mill Corner, yes? I know Hetty and Len Maynard.'

'Most people do,' he said cheerfully. The Maynards, an old local family, looked after him — cleaning, gardening and doing any other odd jobs that came up. Jackman couldn't have done without them, especially Hetty's wonderful home-cooked meals when he worked late. What's more, Hetty Maynard knew everyone in the village and what they got up to, and wasn't afraid to share her knowledge with him. If Fleur Harper was a bit reticent, he'd soon get the info from Hetty.

'I didn't take my husband leaving me very well, DI Jackman. I had a kind of breakdown, so we felt it best, for Jason's sake, that he went with his father for a while. I was in no fit state to care for him properly. He's eleven now, but he'd only just turned nine when Bob left me. It wouldn't have been fair on him, and I love him dearly.' She swallowed. 'Bob and I have agreed that when he's older, he can choose which one of us he would like to live with, and the other won't object. None of it was his fault, and we've tried to make the split as easy as we can on him.'

'That's good to hear, Mrs Harper. We see too many cases where the children become a kind of possession to be fought over. You really wonder how people can disregard their children's feelings.'

Marie arrived with three mugs of tea. 'Hope you don't mind, Mrs Harper, I thought we'd join you.'

'Of course not. I should have pulled myself together and made it for you. I'm not usually this feeble,' Fleur said.

'It's just the shock,' said Marie. 'But tea always helps. We live on it.' She looked around. 'What a lovely home you have. Mine never looks as tidy as this, even when I've cleaned up.'

Fleur smiled ruefully. 'To be honest, DS Evans, I needed to take a long hard look at myself after my divorce. I'll be frank, my ex-husband had good cause to be unhappy with me. I wasn't the best wife, or the best housewife really, although no one could ever say I wasn't a great mother. I adored my baby boy, to the exclusion of everything else — including my home and my husband.'

Jackman was starting to feel mildly uncomfortable. It seemed strange she should want to share all this with two complete strangers, and it bothered him that a mother who apparently doted on her son would let him go so easily.

Marie sipped her tea. 'Up to talking yet?' she asked gently.

'Yes, although there really is little to tell.' She cupped her hands around her tea. 'You see, I'd taken two herbal sleeping pills — melatonin. So, I slept soundly and, as I often do when taking the pills, I dreamed. I dreamed there was a man in my room.'

Jackman could see she was becoming tense again. 'It's okay. In your own time. So, it wasn't a dream?'

'After I woke up properly, I smelled his cologne — after-shave or whatever it was — still in the room. That's when I knew it wasn't a dream. Oh God, I felt his breath on my cheek! He must have been really close to me.' She put her mug down and wrapped her arms around herself.

'Look, I'm going to suggest we get someone to come in and talk to you, Fleur. A counsellor, someone who can help you through this.' He was thinking of Laura. 'And if you can just give us a few more basic details, we won't bother you until you're feeling stronger.'

Rocking backwards and forwards, she nodded. 'What can I tell you?'

'Did you leave any top-opener windows open last night?' he asked.

'Yes. I like fresh air. I always have windows open.' She looked startled. 'Is that how he got in?'

'We think so. And this isn't the first time he's done this. He can get through these narrow windows surprisingly easily.' He paused, considering how much to share. 'And he exited how?'

'Through the back door. I'd locked it from the inside. He unlocked it and left it ajar.'

The same as before. 'And he only took one thing, a photo of your son?'

She nodded. 'That really scares me, DI Jackman. Why did he want a picture of my Jason?' Her eyes were wide, frightened.

*I wish I knew.* 'We can't say, not yet. But I promise we'll keep you up to date on every new development, Mrs Harper. Now, I'm afraid we'll need to bring some specialist officers in here to see if we can find any trace evidence. I hate to cause a mess in your lovely home, but it's absolutely essential. I'll make sure they aren't too disruptive.'

'Do what you have to. Just catch him.'

'Thank you. Is there anyone you can ring to come and be with you while I arrange a support officer?'

'Yes, I'll phone Helen. She'll come over.' She pulled a face. 'That's Bob's wife. Sounds weird, doesn't it? But in the past year we've become friends. Initially it was for Jason's sake, so he still had some continuity, then we really did become friends.'

'Why not ring her now?' said Marie. 'And while you're doing that, perhaps we could have a look around?'

'Of course. Please, go ahead. I'll just get my phone.' She stood up.

Jackman and Marie did a walk-through of the whole house.

'Intense, isn't she?' murmured Marie. They were standing in the main bedroom.

'Very. I find her quite overwhelming,' Jackman said. 'I can still smell that fragrance, can't you?'

'I can, though I'm not very well up on men's colognes.'

'I don't think it's a cologne.' Jackman vaguely recognised it. 'More like deodorant. I kept something similar in my gym bag when I used to play badminton. I had a shower gel and deodorant in the same fragrance. I'll check it out.'

They continued their inspection.

'I bet he got in through the boy's bedroom window. It's at the back, and not particularly overlooked,' said Marie.

'Agreed. We'll get Forensics to concentrate on that area, then the back door and the main bedroom. Now, let's go see where that photo used to hang.'

'I saw the gap when I made the tea,' said Marie. 'It was a good size, and according to Mrs Harper, in a black resin frame to match the other pictures.'

'Let's ask her about it, then I'll get an FLO in to chat to her — and I'm also thinking of Laura. I'd like her to assess her mental state, just in case this situation pushes her over the edge.'

'I'm with you there, boss. I get the feeling she could do with a lot of support right now.'

Downstairs they found Fleur in the kitchen, staring at the space where the photograph had hung.

'Would you describe the picture for us, Mrs Harper?' Jackman asked.

'I can do better than that.' She picked up her handbag, removed her purse and took out a small passport-sized photo. 'It's my favourite. I've got several of them.'

Jackman took it from her and saw a studio portrait of a smiling youngster wearing a smart white shirt and a striped tie. He saw at once why she loved it so much. The boy looked happy. 'Mind if I take a picture of it?' he asked.

'Not at all.'

Jackman took out his phone and took two shots of the photo. 'Perfect, thank you.'

'Any luck with Helen?' asked Marie.

'She's on her way. I knew she'd come. She's a good woman, full of heart.'

*So much heart she took your husband away from you, mmm?*
'Good. I'll make arrangements for our support officer, and then we must get back to the station.'

'You said he'd done this before, DI Jackman.'
'Yes.'
'Did he steal photographs?'

'Yes, Mrs Harper. He did.'

'Of young boys?' Her eyes were narrow, flinty.

'Well, this is an ongoing investigation, so we'd be obliged if you kept this to yourself, but yes, it appears that way.' He returned her hard gaze. 'So I suggest that until we either apprehend this man or have some answers, you do not have Jason to stay here.'

'You don't have to tell me that! Jason's coming nowhere near here. This animal's a paedo, isn't he? He's after children.'

Marie touched her arm gently. 'Mrs Harper, it may not be that. We aren't at liberty to give you all the details, but it's a rather complicated case. We only suggested you keep Jason away as a precaution. If the suspect follows his usual pattern, you'll never see him again. Just keep an open mind if you can.'

'And above all, please do not mention paedophiles to anyone, or you could jeopardise the case. Work with us if you want him found and brought to justice.'

'I'm sorry,' she said. 'Of course I will, but will you keep me informed of what is going on?'

Jackman said, 'We will, I promise, and I'm sorry we can't say more at this stage, but you will be brought up to date very soon.'

Twenty minutes later the liaison officer arrived, along with Helen, and Jackman and Marie were able to leave.

'Oh my! I need to get back to the factory and get a bloody strong coffee inside me,' said Marie.

'You've forgotten something,' Jackman said. 'That's *two* bloody strong coffees.'

# CHAPTER EIGHT

At around eleven o'clock Marie re-joined Jackman in his office, and they went over what they had achieved that morning.

'Stacey and Jay have ascertained that Ratty didn't go wandering last night,' said Marie, pulling up a chair. 'So it wasn't him breathing all over the sleeping Mrs Harper. Ma Jones wasn't well, and several of their neighbours saw him there, looking after her. Stacey says he's scared shitless over his rival interloper.'

'Apart from the fact that he's probably never even heard of deodorant, what's been going on is way beyond Ratty's remit, isn't it?' Jackman said. 'With the exception of the way he gets into the houses. That's creepy.'

'So is having some wingnut lurking in your boudoir in the dead of night,' said Marie. 'Those poor women will be living in fear, probably sleeping with a light on for months or years. If they sleep at all.'

Jackman leaned forward. 'Any theories as to why our man is doing this? And why the pictures? Why just take them?' He produced several prints of Jason Harper's portrait and pushed one across the table.

Marie stared at the cheeky smiling face. 'So why don't I think he's a deviant? Everything points to it. Fleur Harper thought so as soon as she heard he was collecting photos of young boys. But something keeps telling me it's not so simple.'

'Then there's the death of Nan Cutler,' Jackman said. 'He took the picture from her album, but then why kill her so deliberately? I mean, she was an old lady — a *very* old lady. It doesn't make sense.'

'Any hunches yet, boss?' Marie asked.

'Nothing substantial, no.' He exhaled. 'And yet, something's telling me it's all a carefully constructed plan, like he's set himself a task and he's working through it.'

'To what end, I wonder?' Marie said.

'I've no idea, but I think we might learn something when we find out more about Nan Cutler's life. If she had to be eliminated, she either knew something or had done something unforgivable. If we can find what that was, we might gain some insight into his master plan.'

'Gary and I are working on that now, boss, and we've roped in DC Kevin Stoner as he was at a loose end.'

'Excellent. Anything of interest shown up yet?' he asked.

'Believe me, you'll be the first to know, but she seems to have been so ordinary. We're putting together a potted history of her life and we'll let you have it once we're done.' Marie glanced at the clock. 'Anything back from Forensics yet?'

'Rory told me he'll be calling in before lunch and he'll bring everything he has so far. I'll give you a shout when he gets here.'

She stood up. 'Great. Meanwhile, I'll press on with Nan Cutler.'

'Er, meant to ask . . . Good time last night, Marie?' He tried to sound casual.

'Very nice, thank you.'

'And, er, will you be seeing him again?'

'Probably — if that's all right with you?' She gave a laugh. 'Oh, Jackman! Why not just ask? Yes, I'm definitely going to see him again. He's a really nice man and I enjoy his company. I know he's another copper, and yes, that may make things more difficult, but at least we both know what the job involves. If either of us has to work late and break a date, the other will understand.'

'I'm pleased for you, Marie, I really am. It's good to see you looking happy again.'

'But?'

'No buts, honestly.'

All the same, Marie had caught the concern in his eyes. 'Don't worry about me, Jackman. I'm a big girl now. I'm not making any life-changing decisions, I'm just enjoying myself. It might last, it might not, who knows? Just don't worry.'

'I can't help worrying about you, Marie. You're very special to me. I couldn't bear to see you hurt again.'

*Oh, Jackman.* How lucky she was to have someone care so much about her. 'If it wasn't inappropriate, I'd hug you, Jackman!'

'And I'd hug you back, but since my office door's wide open, maybe you'd better bugger off and do some work.'

With a smile, Marie turned and left. What would she do if Jackman ever left? She couldn't see herself working with anyone else.

'What are you thinking about? You're miles away.' Gary was grinning at her.

'Oh, just thinking how bloody lucky I am.'

'Well, that's nice to know. Just won the lottery then?'

She beamed at him. 'As good as. I've just realised I have friends who care for me.'

'You've been at the magic mushrooms again, haven't you? I've told you before, not while you're on duty.'

Marie gave his arm a playful cuff. 'Okay, Pritchard, make my day and tell me you've got something juicy on old Nan Cutler.'

'Ah. Well, that's where your day goes tits up, I'm afraid.' Gary threw up his hands. 'Guess what! She's ordinary!'

'That's what I said to Jackman, but the fact remains someone murdered her and tried to make it look like an accident. You don't do that to an ordinary person, especially one who's over ninety.'

'And nick her dead husband's clothes. Are we dealing with a fruitcake here?' Gary said.

'I'm not sure what we're dealing with,' said Marie. 'But I'll be a lot happier when he's locked up downstairs and not creeping around Saltern in the depths of night.'

\* \* \*

Sam Page drove to Lincoln, found somewhere to park and strolled across to the Birdcage. He guessed Hughie would be late. Time meant little to his friend — he tended to become embroiled in his thoughts and lose all track of time.

Today, however, proved the exception to the rule, and both men arrived together. Sam had known Hughie Mackenzie a long time. He was a somewhat eccentric character who often wore his favourite Mackenzie kilt to lectures. He was lively and talkative, and possessed of a keen and perceptive brain.

'I hear you've been in the wars, old man,' Hughie began. 'Shot, no less.'

Sam pulled a face. 'Yes, it was touch-and-go for a while. The bullet managed to nick an artery.'

'Well, I must say you look remarkably healthy for it,' Hughie said.

'Thanks to Laura and her partner Rowan Jackman. They looked after me so well I had no choice but to make a splendid recovery.'

Sam opened the door for Hughie and they sought out a table.

'So, Sam, why the interest in sleepwalkers?' Hughie asked once they'd caught up with their news and finished their respective meals.

'It's Laura, actually. She has a GP referral that's worrying her. I don't have the full story yet. All I really know is that he drives in his sleep. Laura's asked me for case histories and I've almost none to offer.'

Hughie sat back. 'I have quite a few, in fact.' He opened the briefcase he'd been carrying and pulled out a file. 'I printed off several of the more interesting ones for you. It's a fascinating subject. I can tell you now that it would be perfectly possible for this patient of Laura's to drive while sleeping, but only if he was on home territory and knew the roads. Sleepwalkers need to be in familiar surroundings to orient themselves.' Hughie smiled, beginning to warm to his subject. 'You see, sleepwalkers are essentially awake and asleep at the same time — the part of the brain that controls motion is awake while they are in a state of deep sleep, and the part that controls awareness and cognition remains unconscious.'

'So, the part of the brain related to thinking and voluntary movement is asleep, and the movements they make are controlled by other parts of the brain and are sort of reflexive?' asked Sam.

'Exactly,' Hughie said. 'People can do amazingly complex things in their sleep, quite bizarre things sometimes, and have no memory of them afterwards. Listen, Sam, give Laura these studies to read and tell her that if she wants to discuss any aspect of the subject, I'll be happy to talk to her.' He grinned. 'I'm a bit of an expert on somnambulism.'

'Is it true that sleepwalking can run in families?' asked Sam.

'Yes, it can. You're much more likely to sleepwalk if other members of your close family suffer from sleep disorders or night terrors. We're pretty sure it has a genetic component, but we have yet to establish how the condition is passed down.'

'You told me to remind you about the Reece case,' said Sam. 'I read the basics: Reece adored his sister and her husband, yet he apparently drove twenty miles to their home, where he brutally killed his sister and savagely attacked her husband. His defence was that the whole episode occurred while he was asleep. Is that right?'

'You'll find a brilliant paper from an eminent scientist/ neurologist in the file,' Hughie said. 'It's one of the most widely discussed trials in which somnambulism was used as a legal defence. The most remarkable thing about it was that Reece was acquitted. However, I'm in agreement with my colleague, who writes that a lot was missed at the trial, factors not brought to light that really should have been considered. Read it, Sam, it's a bloody good insight into a mind on the rampage.'

Fascinated, Sam assured him he would.

'You know about the state of dissociative analgesia that can occur in sleepwalkers?' asked Hughie.

Sam nodded. 'I've heard they can injure themselves and feel no pain at the time.'

'In Reece's case, immediately after the attacks he went to the police station to give himself up, arriving with badly slashed hands. He'd done it to himself but was completely unaware of having done so. This was a major argument in the case for the defence. He also registered serious abnormalities on an ECG.' Hughie looked at Sam, eyes bright. 'I'll be very interested to hear your thoughts once you've read that paper. And you've whetted my appetite. I'm keen to learn about Laura's new case. It's perfectly possible to drive asleep, but thankfully not a common occurrence. She could have an interesting case history of her own there. I'd love to share it.'

'I think she'll be more than happy to do that. She didn't say too much, but from the little she did, I could tell she's worried about it. Very worried, in fact.'

'Then tell her I'm all ears.' Hughie passed Sam the folder of papers. 'There you go. Bedtime reading.'

'I really appreciate it, Hughie.' Sam accepted the file gladly. He wasn't often able to help his protégée these days, and he was pleased to have found a way. 'I'm glad to have been able to tap into your fount of knowledge.'

'Anytime. But now I have to press on, unfortunately. I have a lecture to deliver — on Capgras delusion of all things.'

'Ah, that's an interesting one,' said Sam. 'I had a case once where a woman believed her father had been replaced by an imposter. It was one of my most unusual cases, Hughie. I wish I could sit in on your lecture, but I need to get back.'

'You'll be missing a rare treat, Sam Page. It's a stonker. I'm using a study of a woman who believed that her son had been replaced by an alien. It's unsettling, to say the least. In her case they used electroconvulsive therapy, and the condition stabilised, but it took years to get to that point. It was finally traced to an old brain injury — great stuff for the students.'

Hughie was one of the most popular tutors Sam knew. He appreciated learned people who were not possessive about their knowledge, and Hughie was generous with his expertise, happy to share it with anyone who wanted to learn.

They rose to leave.

'Ring me!' Hughie called out as he rushed off to his next appointment.

Sam promised he would, but he was eager to get home and read those papers.

\* \* \*

Rory Wilkinson breezed into Jackman's office carrying an official-looking folder and a large white box that Marie hoped had come from the local bakery.

'Well, cherubs! You certainly are keeping my SOCOs on the hop, aren't you? They're running from one house to another after your portrait-pinching Spiderman.' He placed the folder and box on Jackman's desk and flopped on to a chair. 'My goodness. I still can't believe he got in through those tiny windows. Though there is a rare condition called voluntary anterior dislocation, where a person is able to dislocate one or both shoulders at will. Maybe that's how he managed it.' He looked around. 'Any chance of a coffee?'

'Only if you tell me what's in that white box,' said Marie hopefully.

'Get me one of your, erm, "delicious" vending machine specials and I shall reveal all. Deal?'

Marie opened the door and called to Kevin Stoner. 'Would you be an angel and get us three coffees, please?'

She held out a handful of pound coins. 'And get some for yourselves as well.'

She ducked back into the office, where Rory was ceremoniously lifting the lid. 'Chocolate or salted caramel eclairs? All the way from Café des Amis in Greenborough. Enjoy!'

Marie had every intention of doing so.

'So, what have you got for us, Rory?' asked Jackman. 'Apart from a load of calories.'

'Well, from the houses where he simply scared the daylights out of various ladies and nicked a picture, pretty well nothing. The only definite finding is the make of the shoe, which we obtained from the footprints he left on the windowsill and the duvet cover. He was wearing special, lightweight rock-climbing shoes, size eleven. Pricey, but perfect for the job.' He produced a printout from the folder and passed it across to Jackman. 'Notice, the soles are slightly textured and slip resistant. And here—' he pointed to a second picture — 'is the logo. One arm of this cross has been gouged almost off, probably on something sharp.'

Kevin brought their coffees and tiptoed out.

'So, other than that,' Rory continued, 'our careful investigations have thrown up nothing at all. He wore gloves and left no fingerprints in any of the houses he visited.'

Jackman shrugged. 'No more than we expected, I guess, but what about the crime scene in Connaught Road?'

Rory sipped his coffee and pulled a face. 'The coffee never gets any better, does it?'

'Nope,' said Marie.

'The crime scene is a little different.' Rory wiped his lips with a tissue. 'We suspect he spent some time there, even after he'd murdered Nancy Eliza Cutler. But let me get the sequence of events in order — I'll start in that jungle of a garden.' He took a breath. 'As you said, Marie, it was no easy task. The Lost Gardens of Heligan have nothing on the Lost Garden of Nan Cutler. I reckon that patch last saw a lawnmower at the time of the Great War. That should have helped us because he'd have flattened the grass and so on, except that the neighbour ran amok in it and trampled most of the tracks and evidence. Still, we were able to find another print in the soft soil of a convenient molehill, and it matches the one we already have.'

'Excellent. So that's concrete proof it's the same man.' Jackman nodded.

'Indeed. Now, he gained access through an open fanlight window in the downstairs toilet. It's situated at the side of the house, and I suspect that as soon as the neighbour's garden lights came on, he legged it around the corner of the building, wriggled his way inside and pulled the window closed behind him. That way the neighbour wouldn't have seen him enter the house.'

'So, if Eric and Lizzie Coupland had actually gone in to check on Nan, they would have run into the killer,' Marie said.

'Undoubtedly.' Rory shuddered. 'So perhaps it's all for the best they didn't. I could have had three bodies in my chiller cabinet, along with the nice little Italian bubbly that Sainsbury's has on special offer this week . . .'

Marie snorted.

'We believe he got in just after eleven p.m. and went immediately to prepare the tripwire. He used very slim pins, most likely the ones that come with picture-hanging fittings. They were driven in quite deeply and at an angle, in order to hold the wire firmly and not come loose when her foot caught it.' He took another printout from the folder. 'We examined the welt on the old lady's foot and decided it was indeed wire that he used. In fact, after finding minute particles of metal fibres embedded in the welt, we deduced that it was actually picture-hanging wire. Electro brass-plated twisted steel wire to be exact.' He sniffed. 'Unfortunately, this can be purchased anywhere online or in the major hardware stores.' He drank more coffee. 'Anyway, we think he then went into the spare bedroom and took two items of clothing from the wardrobe there, and here, I am happy to say, we had some luck.'

Marie and Jackman both leaned forward. 'What kind of luck?' Jackman said.

'Oh, the best. What do we love more than anything, my dears? We love blood!'

'Blood? Why? Whose?' asked Jackman in surprise.

'His, for sure. Because it wasn't hers — that was the first thing we checked. And it was miniscule, just a tiny smear, but it didn't escape the eagle eyes of our Cardiff. She found it on the outside of the wardrobe door. I'd say he caught his finger or thumb on something sharp and tore a tiny hole in his glove. Maybe it was on one of the strands of the tripwire as he twisted it taut. He would never have seen it in the dark or by torchlight.'

Jackman laughed. 'That's massive, Rory! When we get a suspect, we'll be able to prove whether or not he was in Nan's house. Say thank you to Cardiff for us.'

'Oh, I shan't do that. It'll give her ideas above her station. Anyway, there's more to come.' He drained his beaker of coffee. 'We now think that he managed to wake the old lady, but without startling her. We have no idea how. Now, what happens if an elderly person is roused from sleep? They inevitably want to pass water, and we know she took furosemide, a diuretic tablet. So, half asleep, she wanders off to the bathroom. Meanwhile, Spiderman goes downstairs. And here is where I stray into hypothesis . . .'

'We do a lot of that, Rory,' said Marie, 'and it's often right, so hit us with your theory.'

'All right. See if you agree. Bear in mind, the clothes disappeared from the house along with Spiderman, so it's reasonable to suggest he was wearing them, yes?'

They nodded.

'Now, your man gets through tiny spaces, so he's wiry and lithe. Nan's deceased husband, whose clothes she couldn't part with, was heavily built. So, why steal clothes that didn't fit?'

'He put them on over his own clothes for effect,' Marie said.

Rory beamed at her. 'My thoughts precisely.'

'Coat hangers,' sighed Jackman. 'They bothered me from the start. He deliberately picked a distinctive jacket and matching trousers because he wanted to look like the dead husband.'

'Exactly! There's a street light right outside her front door. He dressed up in the husband's clothes and showed himself to the old lady. Woozy from her sleeping tablets, she either took a step forward to see better or started to go down the stairs. We'll probably never know which it was. Suffice it to say, she fell to her death.'

'Lizzie Coupland told me that Nan often talked about "seeing" her Henry around the house,' Marie said. 'She talked to him all the time, apparently, as if he was still with her. So, if she was half asleep, it's perfectly reasonable for her to think she was seeing her husband.'

'Calculating bastard,' growled Jackman.

'Absolutely. Anyway, moving on,' Rory said. 'He then spent some considerable time looking for her photo album, which he found upstairs in a bedside cabinet. We know that because of what had been disturbed. She was a very tidy person, and he left the room in some disarray. And we know he took his time because he left a faint footprint in her blood in the hallway. Since it came from a small wound caused by the fall, it would have taken some time to seep into the spot where he trod in it. He tore the relevant page from the album and left the book in the lounge, where your Gary found it. And then he slipped out into the night. End of story.'

'Wow!' breathed Marie. 'I never expected actual evidence.'

'Me neither,' said Rory. 'Apart from the teeny, weeny, little smudge of blood, and the edge of his shoe catching the pool of Nan's blood on the floor, it was a perfectly executed, premeditated murder.'

'And your post-mortem results showed nothing else untoward?' Jackman asked.

'I reckon that lady would have made it to a telegram from the Queen, no trouble at all. For her years, she was as fit as a butcher's dog. Okay, she had arthritis and needed a couple of blood pressure tablets, but overall, our Nancy was in the rudest of good health.'

'So what on earth did she do to get herself so ruthlessly killed?' said Jackman.

'That's where I hand over to your department,' said Rory. 'I haven't the foggiest. Do tell, won't you, as soon as you find out? It's giving me sleepless nights, and you know how I need my beauty sleep.' He stood up. 'And now I must return to the Kingdom of the Dead. Good luck, and don't forget — the moment you know . . .'

# CHAPTER NINE

Ratty Jones sat in the caravan and stared at his mother's sleeping form. She was ageing so fast it scared him. In the space of a month, she seemed to have gone from being active and fiercely independent to feeble and helpless.

He stood up, went through to the tiny kitchen and put the kettle on. She never slept for long. Soon, she'd be waking and demanding a cuppa. He'd drunk more tea in the last week than he ever had before.

Ratty was struggling. He needed to get out. Being cooped up in this stinking old van did him no good at all. The nights were especially hard. The nights belonged to him. His greatest pleasure was walking the deserted streets in darkness, slipping from the shadows into other people's gardens and private spaces. He found the motion-activated sensor lights particularly annoying, but he knew who had them now. In any case, most people installed them and then turned them off, after finding that every passing cat, rat, bat or night bird set them off.

He made the tea, placed one mug by his mother's bed and returned to his chair with the other. It wouldn't be long before he was forced to leave her at night, if only for an hour or two. Despite knowing what he might be accused of if he were stopped, the compulsion to go out was becoming too strong to resist.

It was a craving, this impulse to get inside strangers' houses unnoticed. To invade their personal spaces unseen. Uneducated but by no means stupid, Ratty supposed it was a form of power. Control. He suspected it came from a childhood blighted by a violent father who hated him. Whatever the cause, it was too late to address it now. The bastard was long dead, leaving Ratty a legacy of shattered self-esteem that only the nights could assuage.

Ratty gave a ragged sigh. Why did this other creep have to move in on his territory and spoil everything? It was too much.

Then he sat up straight. He recalled the figure slipping through that top opener and an idea occurred to him. He could never have identified that slippery figure as it slid silently inside, but he had, subconsciously, noticed something about it.

Ratty bit his lip. He'd never voluntarily contacted the police before, but needs must. He had to do something to get this interloper off his patch.

He went outside, out of earshot of his mother, and rang the police station.

'I want to speak to PC Stacey Smith . . . No, no one else, just her.'

Finally, he heard a vaguely familiar male voice.

'This is PC Jay Acharya. PC Smith is busy right now. Can I help you, sir?'

Damn, it was her oppo, the Asian bloke. Ratty thought hard. Same difference, he supposed. 'It's Reginald Jones. Ratty. Your mate asked me about the geezer I saw getting into that house the other night. Well, tell her it might help her to know that he was wearing them poncy tights you see on cyclists. I don't know about the top 'cause he was already halfway through the window, but the tight pants caught the moonlight, and they were stretchy and shiny.'

'Thank you, sir. That's a great help. I'll pass it on as soon as she's free.'

Ratty hung up, a half-smile playing on his lips. Sir, eh? He chuckled to himself as he went back inside.

His eyes on his mother as she began to stir, he sipped his tea and had another idea.

There was a way of getting back out! Who better than him to help the police find this guy? He knew the kinds of houses and the types of windows matey boy would choose. Well, if the coppers accosted him while he was out, he could say he was helping PC Stacey Smith track the intruder.

He closed his eyes. Oh, relief! He wouldn't have to endure another night imprisoned here. And as long as he was careful and didn't stay out too long, he'd be able to resume his normal activities. He drank his tea and grinned happily at his mother. 'Hello, Ma. Back with us? There's a nice cuppa there, drink it while it's still hot.'

\* \* \*

Marie called Gary and Kevin over to the whiteboard and jabbed a finger at the picture of Nan Cutler. 'We have to find out why this woman died, lads. Have to! She's the key, the reason why our man took all those pictures of youngsters, I'm sure of it. Somewhere along the line she did or knew something that led to her murder. It's particularly frightening because children are involved. So, tell me everything we have on her.'

Gary took a breath. 'Right. She lived here all her married life but was born Nancy Eliza White in Winterborne Whitechurch, a village near Blandford Forum in Dorset. It's not clear why her parents moved, but most likely they were following work around the country. Her father is recorded as being a labourer. Last mention of them as a family was in Thorney, outside Peterborough, where the father was working on the land as a picker.'

'She married in Crowland in 1950,' Kevin added, 'and her husband, Henry Cutler, served in the RAF as ground crew. We've found photographs that put them together at

RAF Binbrook, and it looks like he was stationed there until he retired at fifty-five. He then took a civilian job working with agricultural machinery, and they moved to Connaught Road, Saltern-le-Fen.'

'Did she ever work?' Marie asked.

'Hard to tell from the records, Sarge,' said Gary. 'It looks like she did small cash-in-hand jobs around the local neighbourhood. She helped out at the library and the cottage hospital. She was a popular woman, happy to chip in and help with local charity work and church events. No regular job that we can trace.'

'Children I know about,' Marie said, 'as I was checking up on them. Nan had two girls, Babs and Christine. Babs, now dead, never married, and the other one moved with her family to South Island, New Zealand. I've passed the word to her local police force so they can break the news to her.' She paused. 'The odd thing is that the photo the killer took wasn't of any of her grandchildren. Christine had two girls, Ava and Coco, and a boy, called Dermot. The one of the lad the killer took had the letter "Y" next to the age. Dermot has no "Y" in it. So, if it was another boy's photo that he took, we have no idea who that boy is.' She shrugged. 'Of course, we're only assuming it was a boy because the others were, and of the same age. Having said that, even though I'm pretty sure it will be another lad, we need to keep an open mind.'

'You said the other daughter never married. That doesn't mean she never had a child,' said Kevin. 'It could have been hers.'

'Good point, Kev, but I checked that out. Definitely no kids, and she died in her twenties in a car crash. So, who is he?'

'A nephew, or a niece?' said Gary.

'Possibly, but it would be on her husband's side. She was an only child. That's one to check out next, followed by friends, which isn't going to be easy. So far, most of our info has come via the neighbours, but they aren't likely to know about her friends or where they live, are they?'

They all fell silent until Kevin said, 'You mentioned helping out at the church. If we found out which one, maybe that's as good a place as any to start.'

'Can I hand that over to you, Kevin?' Marie said. 'And, Gary, follow the husband's family tree. I want to know who was in the missing picture.'

They returned to their desks. Marie's phone buzzed. A text from Ralph.

She went outside to the corridor and leaned against the wall to read the message.

*Intel says the case I'm on is going to kick off tonight. Might not be able to ring. If anything changes, I'll contact you.*

She smiled to herself. So this is how things would be. Two cops whose jobs came first. Marie, of course, had been here before and knew it was possible to make it work. Ralph, on the other hand, had always had girlfriends from outside the force. So, if one of them decided it was too difficult to continue, it would be him. Time would tell.

She texted back: *Stay safe, ring when you can.*

She sat back down at her desk. This was all quite foreign to her. Her and Bill's romance had begun a long time ago now, and she had been a lot younger. She remembered the intensity of it. From their first date, she had known they would marry, and so had he. She smiled at the memory. They had driven to Skegness, then up to the nature reserve at Gibraltar Point and walked on the beach. There they had sat on the dunes and watched the sea, eating crisps and drinking tea bought in the Visitor Centre. When the sun set and they were alone, Bill had kissed her. She saw again the setting sun and felt his lips on hers. On the way back to the car park Bill had said, 'You know you're saddled with me now, right?' She remembered the thrill his words gave her, she could think of nothing better. It wasn't long before they moved in together, and looking back, she was glad that they had. At least it had given them some time together. Bill died on the last day of their honeymoon, killed riding his precious vintage motorbike.

Marie blinked. Time to move on. They had a killer to catch.

* * *

Having just finished a meeting at Greenborough, Laura drove home, readying herself for her appointment with her latest patient, the one that was causing her such concern.

Freddie Shields. His was probably the most complicated case she'd ever had. On the surface, he appeared to be an intelligent and well-balanced young man, but she felt certain that whatever triggered his sleepwalking, he wasn't sharing it with her. The purpose of today's meeting was to try to get him to open up more. She'd seen him three times now, and at least he seemed somewhat more relaxed than during their first session. They'd covered all the standard questions that helped establish a picture of the client, their problem and how they saw it. Now it was time to dig deeper.

Back in her consulting room, she adjusted the lighting. She varied its brightness and direction according to the patient and their problem. People reacted differently in different lighting, and she needed to make them feel comfortable and at ease. It was important to create a healthy, peaceful environment for her patient and herself.

For the umpteenth time, she went through his case notes. Shields was thirty-nine years old, divorced and currently in a relationship with a teacher at the Saltern Academy. He lived in Saltern-le-Fen, in a Victorian end terrace close to the park. Being at the end, his garden was bigger than the others and had room for a small annexe that he'd built for his mother. He had described this in great detail. It was designed to allow her to live independently while being close to him, giving them both peace of mind.

She stared at her notes. He seemed to care very much for his mother and spoke of her fondly. His partner, Julia, lived mainly with him, but had kept her own flat until they were sure about their relationship. Laura detected a similarity to her early days with Jackman. Afraid to take that final step, to commit to a future that would no longer be entirely yours. With her, the decision to commit had been taken pretty early on. Freddie and Julia had been debating their future together for two years. Even so, she couldn't see this being the trigger for his sleepwalking. Something much deeper lay behind that.

The doctor's referral letter lay open in front of her:

*Dear Dr Archer*

*Thank you for agreeing to see this gentleman, Mr Frederick Shields, for me. After a year of regular bouts of sleepwalking, I have finally ruled out, as far as I can ascertain, any medical condition that is either causing or exacerbating this condition. We have counted out an adverse reaction to medication or drugs, and he is not a drinker, so alcohol is not a factor. He gets adequate sleep and does not suffer from sleep apnoea or restless leg syndrome, both of which sometimes trigger an episode.*

*It is my belief that stress and anxiety may lie at the bottom of this, but he denies having any issues so serious that they might cause such severe occurrences.*

*I would be very grateful for your opinion on this gentleman, and any suggestions you might have as to future management of his condition.*

*Yours sincerely*

*Dr Peter Mason*

The doorbell rang and her stomach clenched. Tension. This wasn't like her, and it wasn't good. As a therapist she had to be calm and in control, both for her patient's sake and for her own well-being. She had been told that she had all the qualities and personal skills of an excellent therapist. So why did this man unsettle her so much? She got up to answer the door, deciding that she'd give him one more session. Then, if she still felt uncomfortable, she would suggest he see a different psychotherapist. Maybe Sam Page might be interested.

She held the door open for him and smiled. 'Mr Shields. Do come in.' On their first visit they had agreed not to use first names. She always gave her clients the option. Some people assumed that the use of first names indicated friendship. She was not making friends, she was counselling them, and it was a professional relationship.

'Dr Archer.' He nodded politely. 'I'm not late, am I?'

'No, not at all. Come on in and sit down.' She closed the door and ushered him to one of the sofas.

Today he was wearing a light grey sports jacket with a Nike logo, denim jeans and a banana-coloured polo shirt. He looked as if his hair had been recently cut. Spoiling the relaxed, sporty image was his anxious expression. As soon as they were both seated, he said, 'I've done it again, Dr Archer. I've taken the car out while I was asleep.'

'When was this?'

'The night before last. My girlfriend had a relative visiting, so she wasn't with me. When I woke up in the morning, I was lying on the bed wearing my outdoor clothes. My nightclothes — a T-shirt and pyjama bottoms — were on the floor and there was mud on my shoes.'

'And you say you took your car?'

'It was parked differently, not particularly well, and in a different spot in the drive. I spoke to my mother. So as not to scare her, I just said I hoped I didn't wake her, and she said she heard me come back at around one a.m. I told her I'd popped across to Julia's flat as she had a leaking washing machine and didn't know how to turn the water off. I think she believed me.'

His voice had risen slightly, and Laura heard the anxiety in it.

'At least this time I know where I went,' he said.

'Can you explain?'

He drew in a breath. 'I dreamed that I was at my father's grave — he's buried in St Saviour's Churchyard. In my dream, I felt compelled to take him yellow flowers. I went everywhere looking for them, but no one had any. I finally found some and took them to his grave. I remember crying and asking for his forgiveness — no, *begging* his forgiveness, although I have no idea why or what for. Anyway, when I realised yesterday that I had been sleepwalking again, I went to the churchyard, and there on his grave was a bunch of yellow flowers. I drove back via the service station on the main road, and they had a bucket of the same yellow chrysanthemums and roses, in the same yellow-and-white cellophane as the bunch on the grave. When I got home, I checked my online banking transactions. I'd been at the service station at midnight and had paid by card.'

'And you're sure you have no idea why your father should need to forgive you?'

'None at all. We had a good relationship. There were no recriminations when he passed away.'

'Tell me about him. How would you describe your relationship with him? Do you think he was a good father to you?'

He sat back. 'Oh yes, although he was often absent. He worked a lot. I would have liked to have seen more of him. Still, he always did his best to make those times we were all together happy ones.'

'And your mother? I know you're very fond of her. What kind of mum was she when you were a boy?'

He smiled. 'The best. Always there for me, always supportive — ready to talk, explain, discuss absolutely anything. She was a star.'

'I imagine she would have liked your father to be around more?'

'I suppose so, but she never complained. They had an understanding. He worked hard and put food on the table and gave us a comfortable, secure place to live, and she looked after the home, and me.' His smile widened. 'To this day, she never complains. She's a real angel, my mother.'

Laura smiled warmly at him, while hearing what he wasn't saying as much as what he was. 'Tell me about your school life. Was it a positive experience, or couldn't you wait to leave?'

He thought for a moment. 'I always knew that whatever I achieved at school would affect the rest of my life, so I was a bit of a swot. I strived to do well and hated coming up against a subject that I found hard. My grades weren't good enough for university, but I was assured of a decent job after I left. So, yes, it was a positive experience.'

And school friends? Teachers? Any other social contact? Not a mention. In an earlier session he had described his interpersonal and communication skills as average, but she doubted the veracity of that. She believed Freddie Shields was a loner, with very few friends, if any.

'Who do you turn to when your heart hurts, Mr Shields?'

There was no hesitation. 'My mother.'

'And yet you haven't told her about your sleepwalking,' she said.

He looked down, avoiding her gaze. 'No.'

'Can you tell me why?'

'I don't want to worry her. She's in her seventies, it wouldn't be fair.' But he hadn't raised his eyes.

'All your life, she has been your rock. She even moved house to be closer to you, and I'm sure that was a two-way thing, so you could care for each other. Why do you feel that on this occasion, you cannot turn to her when your heart hurts?'

He was rubbing his hands together now, as if he were cold.

'I used to sleepwalk as a child. It scared her then.' He swallowed. 'It would scare her even more now, Dr Archer.'

'What form did this childhood sleepwalking take?'

'Getting up. Walking downstairs.' He bit his lip. 'Er, going outside.' He sighed and looked at his feet. 'This is embarrassing, but I suppose you should know. I sometimes opened the wardrobe door and peed in it.'

She smiled at him. 'That's called inappropriate behaviour, and it's common in child somnambulists. I'm sure you never remembered doing it. It's simple confusion — the sleepwalker often thinks they're somewhere they're not. In your sleep, you probably believed it was the bathroom.'

He smiled back sheepishly. 'I wish someone had explained that to me years ago. I was so ashamed.'

'Any other unusual activities?'

Laura noted his hesitation before he said none that he knew of. He was lying.

'Nothing you tell me ever goes further than my supervisor. All therapists have one to ensure that we're coping well and can deliver the best possible outcome for you. If I ever deemed it necessary, I would always ask your permission before discussing your case with another professional.' She gave him what she hoped was a reassuring smile. 'I'm not here to judge you, Mr Shields, I just want to help you to help yourself. Sometimes it's hard to tell the truth about something, and sometimes we don't even admit that truth to ourselves, and that's when it comes out sideways, if you understand what I'm saying?'

'As in I'm repressing something, even from myself, and it's coming out in the form of sleepwalking?' This time he was looking directly at her.

'Exactly.' She sat back. 'So, Mr Shields, can you think of anything in your past that was not adequately addressed at the time? Even if you can't share it with me, perhaps it's time to get it out into the open and face it. If there can be a release, a catharsis, then healing will follow.'

'And the sleepwalking would stop?'

'I'm certain of it.'

There was a silence. Then Freddie Shields shrugged. 'There's nothing.'

She had expected this. Keeping her voice even, she said, 'Talk to your mother. You're an adult now. Talk to her about what scared her when you were small and walked in your sleep. If we can't address the main issue, let's start with smaller things. Think of taking down a wall, brick by brick.'

He nodded. 'I will, if you think it would help, but I don't think I can mention what is happening now.'

'One brick is good enough. But maybe she'll understand more than you give her credit for. Mothers can be remarkably tough where their offspring are concerned.'

Soon, the time was up. Before he left, she said, 'Earlier, I mentioned a professor of psychology that I work with. May I share your history with him? No names, just the background and your present somnambulistic activities.'

He agreed without hesitation. 'Please do. Anything that might put an end to it. I'm terrified I'll injure someone.'

'Thank you. I'll see you again later in the week, if that's all right?' Laura checked her diary. 'Shall we say Friday at two? That's good for me.'

'I'll be here. And thank you, Dr Archer.'

After he had gone, she made herself a strong coffee and called Sam Page.

# CHAPTER TEN

Jackman paced his office. He had just left a meeting with Superintendent Ruth Crooke. Between them, they had been trying to thrash out this man's motive. Why would he be stealing photographs of boys? They hadn't managed to come up with anything helpful, so in the end Jackman had gone back downstairs.

Sadly, speculations were all he had. He couldn't afford to sit around and wait for the next intrusion. He stopped pacing and sat at his desk, idly spinning the globe.

*How does he even know these photos exist?* he thought to himself. *Does he actually know each of these women personally? Why get into the house at night when the occupants are there? Why not wait until they're out? He appears almost to want to be seen by them. And why kill the old lady, when he hadn't harmed anyone else? What the hell was that all about?* None of it made sense.

Though he had already tried to find a common denominator among the women whose photographs had been stolen, he decided to look at them again.

He began with Annie Carson. The picture of her son, Callum, had been taken two years before, when he was ten. Annie worked from home as a part-time bookkeeper and lived in a tiny Fen village called Fenton Mere.

Number two on the list was Sylvia Wilson, an older woman who lived on the outskirts of Saltern, in an area called Leetoft, who worked in a local plant nursery. In her case, the photo showed her two grandsons, one of whom had been ten at the time the picture was taken.

Then came Nan Cutler, the murder victim. They had no idea who the subject of her picture was, other than that the boy — if it was a boy — had a name ending in "Y" and was eleven years old. Nan had lived in Saltern-le-Fen town.

The last one had been Fleur Harper, in his own village of Cartoft. The intruder had removed a framed photo of her son, Jason, aged nine or ten. He was now eleven.

Uniform had interviewed the three women, none of whom knew each other or Nan Cutler. Their lives didn't seem to overlap anywhere. They had no shared interests, neither church, clubs, libraries or gyms. They even shopped at different supermarkets.

He remembered the man who had been watching at school gates. What was going on with him? He called out to Marie.

'Anything back about our watcher?'

'Not yet, boss. Robbie and Charlie are now up to date with their work and are with us at last, so I've given them that one to chase up. Charlie's down with Uniform, and Robbie's catching up on the CCTV footage. Hopefully, we'll have a report by late afternoon.'

'Okay. Let me know if there's any progress. Oh, and Marie, how *is* our Robbie?'

She shook her head. 'I had a long chat with him earlier. He's a lot more cut up about it than he's letting on. He said it had been a joint decision, but now he's beginning to think he made a big mistake. He's well confused.'

Jackman felt for him. His relationship with Laura had almost ended in the same way, but luckily they had both realised what they were losing and had got back together. 'Tell him that if he ever wants to chat, he knows where my office is. All that paperwork probably didn't help. I'm sure he'll be better off doing something physical.'

'Absolutely,' Marie said. 'I'll make certain he's run off his little feet. Gary and Kevin are trying to build up a picture of Nan Cutler. I'll report what we have at close of play.'

'Good.' He paused. 'Off out on the town again tonight?'

'Not tonight. Ralph's received intel that a job he's working might come to a head this evening. It's the planned raid that our uniforms have been asked to support, if we are needed. It's really big.'

'Sounds it. Our Fenchester brothers and sisters will be busy tonight, that's for sure,' Jackman said.

'I just hope he stays safe,' Marie said. 'Those raids can get messy, especially when there's drugs with such a huge street value at stake — like, millions.'

He laughed. 'Ah, the joys of being attached to a police officer!'

'Tell me about it. I've been there before, remember? Still, it's a two-way thing. He'll be just as worried when I do something equally hare-brained.'

He laughed. 'Like get on that beast of a bike of yours. That's dangerous enough.'

'Excuse me, *sir*,' Marie retorted. 'Shall I quote you the figures on horse-related accidents? Head injuries, spinal cord injuries, crush injuries . . . Do you know that back in 1985, a study was published suggesting that motorcyclists suffered a serious accident once every 7,000 hours, whereas equestrians could expect one every 350 hours! Which, I do believe, makes you a much higher risk than me!'

'Ah, but consider the health benefits of riding,' Jackman said.

They both laughed. Bikes and horses weren't actually so different, if you thought about it. Both had speed, freedom, excitement and fresh air. And for the two of them, best of all was the complete escape from their work.

He winked at her. 'How about bringing a coffee in with you when you drop off those end-of-day reports? Seeing as how you aren't in a hurry, we'll go through everything after the others have gone home.'

'I'll do that.' Marie returned to her desk.

He still worried about her.

\* \* \*

It seemed like no time at all before the lads were clearing their desks ready to leave. Marie gathered every piece of info she could find and knocked on Jackman's door.

She caught a preoccupied expression on Jackman's face as she went in, although he quickly assumed a smile. She wondered whether to ask but decided against it. He'd tell her if he wanted to.

'You don't have the aspect of someone who's solved a case, Sergeant Evans,' he said.

'Too right, Inspector Jackman. I bloody haven't.' She set down their drinks, took a seat and flipped through her notes. 'Just a few snippets that might interest you.'

'Enlighten me,' he said.

'Well, Jay took a call from Ratty, of all people. He remembered something about the man he saw going through the window that time. He said he was wearing cycling tights — those skintight, shiny jobs that serious cyclists wear.'

'Sensible of him,' Jackman said. 'Wouldn't snag on anything, and they don't have the bulk of normal clothing.'

'He's treating it like a professional job, isn't he?' said Marie. 'And those clothes belonging to Nan's husband would have slipped on over them easily.'

'And they'd make him less likely to attract attention if spotted. Well done, Ratty! That's a turn-up for the books. He must really be anxious to get this other guy caught.'

'It's probably driving him stir crazy having to stay put with Ma. Just in case, we've had a couple of officers drop by the park unannounced, and his car hasn't moved for days. Stacey says he's shit scared of having a murder added to his record.' Marie turned a page. 'Our man at the school gates seems to have gone to ground. He hasn't been seen for two days. But we do have this.' She showed him a still from some

CCTV footage. 'Robbie sourced this from the primary school in Seagate Road in Saltern. One of the mothers confirmed it was the man that had been worrying her. It's not brilliant and not full face either, but it gives us an idea of what he looks like.'

Jackman took the picture from her and stared at it. It showed a man, possibly in his late thirties, wearing a hoodie, a plain T-shirt and smart denim jeans. He looked clean cut, unthreatening. 'As you say, better than nothing, and it matches the description given by the parents. He looks about as far from the usual image of a paedophile as you could get. But as we know all too well, appearances can be deceptive.'

'What I don't understand is why he's there at all,' Marie said. 'Bloke shows up, doesn't speak to anyone and just goes away again. Weird.'

'What I want to know is whether he could be connected to our night stalker.'

'Robbie's asked several of the parents to call us immediately if they spot him again, and we'll have a car there pronto,' said Marie. 'It's the best we can do. There are too many schools to post officers at every morning, and it might have nothing to do with the case. It might even be perfectly innocent — if we can only nail him and have a chat.'

'What we don't need is a panic among the parents,' Jackman said. 'It would only take one big mouth saying there's a paedo watching their kids to have a witch-hunt on our hands.'

'Maybe even a lynch mob, since kids are concerned,' added Marie. 'All I can say is that the parents we spoke to seemed sensible, just a bit disturbed at his appearing outside the school with no child in tow. Understandable really, and I reckon they were reassured to see us taking their concern seriously.'

'So, is that it?' Jackman said, taking a packet of chocolate biscuits from his desk drawer and offering it to her.

'I have one more item on my short agenda, courtesy of our Kevin. He found out where Nan Cutler went to church and had a few words with the vicar and some of his helpers.'

Jackman grinned. 'Very appropriate, considering his family.' Kevin Stoner's father was the diocesan bishop.

'Well, he came back with some interesting stories about the deceased. It seems that although her neighbours considered her a sweet old thing, not everyone felt the same way. One or two thought Nan was a busybody, always sticking her nose into other people's business. The vicar told Kevin that she'd even had to leave her last church because she'd had too much to say about one of the other women on the church committee. Got quite nasty apparently, and she was asked to go.'

'Is that a fact?' Jackman looked interested. 'She must really have upset someone to be forced to leave. If she acted like that with a comparative stranger, what was she like with people close to her? Maybe she interfered in the killer's life?'

'My thoughts exactly,' Marie said. 'So, I've asked Gary and Kevin to draw up a list of all her relatives, close and more distant. I want to know what the family thought of Nancy Eliza Cutler.'

'Good move. Maybe we'll find our man somewhere in Nan Cutler's past, along with why he's stealing pictures of ten-year-olds.'

'That's the plan.' Through a mouthful of biscuit she said, 'I was also thinking of doing a search on any incidents occurring in the last five years that involved youngsters of that age.'

'Sounds a bit "needle and haystack," Marie,' Jackman said. 'We're just making wild guesses. Don't waste your time. Stick with the old lady's relatives for now, okay?'

'You're probably right.' She closed her notebook. 'And that's that! As I said, not much.'

'But considerably more than nothing.' Jackman glanced at the clock. 'We'd better be getting off home. Laura's last appointment was in her consulting room at the mill, so hopefully she's got dinner on the go.'

He was wearing that faint look of anxiety again. Before she could ask, he said, 'Poor Laura is a bit down and distracted right now, and there's nothing I can do to help.'

'What's up, Jackman? You guys share everything.'

He sighed. 'Not everything. Patient confidentiality, you see. It's one of her cases, and it's really bugging her. I've never seen her quite so preoccupied with a client. I've told her to talk to Sam Page, and I hope she has. I've never known Laura to be unable to find the key to a problem before. That's why it's so worrying.'

It was true. Laura was streaks ahead of any other professional in her field — apart from Sam, of course. 'Sam'll help her,' Marie said. 'And if even he can't find a solution, he'll know someone who can.'

'Anyway, enough of my worries. You get on home.'

'You and your worries are important to me, Jackman. Anyway, Sam loves Laura to bits. He'll help.'

'You're right, Marie. No use fretting when she has Sam to call on.' He held the door open for her. 'See you tomorrow.'

'Let's just hope our creeper doesn't go on another midnight jolly tonight!'

# CHAPTER ELEVEN

As midnight approached, two figures slipped through the shadows, like vampires avoiding the light. Each had been driven to walk the streets by an overwhelming compulsion that was leading one of them towards a nightmare.

\* \* \*

On his way to a hospital appointment with his mother, Ratty had spotted a property with his name written all over it. Perfect. Now he just needed to find out who lived there, where they slept and whether they worked at night. In this agricultural community many places operated round the clock — notably the food processing and vegetable packing industries that employed many of the workers in the area. As the summer drew to a close, harvesters too worked all night in the fields gathering the crop before the weather worsened and rain set in. Thus, you could never tell which householders would be asleep at home.

Now, at midnight, he was back to have a closer look at the place. A sweet choice, probably inhabited by a pensioner or someone who had no need to work. The cottage looked neat and cared for, but what enticed him were the windows. The owners had obviously replaced the original wood-framed sash windows and installed double glazing but kept to the traditional design, so they were easy to get through.

He watched the cottage for a while, noting the position of the windows, the layout of the rooms.

Another lover of fresh air. The windows on the upstairs floor were partially open, as well as a smaller one on a latch downstairs. He would enter through the one above that very conveniently placed conservatory. It even had a tiled roof instead of the usual glass.

The nearest house was two hundred yards away, a blank wall turned towards the cottage. No dog barking, no toys, no drinking bowl in the garden. No warning sign on the gate. He went in, crept around the single garage and peered in through a small window. One car, and at the back of the garage a bike. He saw no crossbar, so it was probably a woman's.

Having made his decision, he had no need to roam further tonight. He'd be back with his mother before she even noticed his absence. Mind you, she wouldn't have objected even if she had. They had spoken about it once, never mentioning it again. She had spent her married life confined at home by Ratty's abusive father and understood all too well his need for escape.

* * *

Ratty drove home in his borrowed car, singing happily to himself, basking in the joy of being back out again, free and alone in his secret shadowy realm.

Across the Fens another man, who never sang, was watching a different property. He knew exactly who lived there and what he wanted. His decision was already made.

He took a breath, opened the bedroom window and slipped inside.

* * *

Natalie Miles put her book down, uneasy. It happened some-times, especially if she'd sat up late with a glass or two of wine and a scary film. This time the book was to blame. She'd been off work for a while — a back injury caused by a machine left unguarded at the factory where she worked. Nowadays she was bored and unable to concentrate.

Now she stood on the patio, a torch in her hand, staring into the dark, having let the cat out into the garden for a last pee before bed. Where was that bloody cat? An owl hooted, causing Natalie to jump. 'Arthur! Get a move on!' she hissed. The long back garden was full of close-growing trees and shrubs, and mostly in shadow. She had never got around to installing that garden lighting.

Finally, she saw him, sauntering in her direction as if he hadn't a care in the world. She shooed him inside, locked the door and checked it. She began to relax. With Arthur weaving around her legs, she made herself a hot drink and took some strong painkillers. Time to call it a day.

Still a little nervous, Natalie shut all the windows and settled into bed with Arthur and her drink. She tuned her bedside radio to an easy-listening station and turned the volume down. Leaving the bedside lamp on, Natalie finally drifted into sleep.

\* \* \*

He stood in the doorway, watching her, his eyes as narrow as those of the cat staring back at him. He froze. A cat! He hadn't reckoned with one of those. And it was growling at him. He backed away.

He turned and ran back down the stairs. It had been going so well until he'd spotted that animal. He'd been fortunate, getting in before she locked up and concealing himself in the integral garage.

He went into the lounge and cast around. Where was it? Photographs lined the shelves and windowsills, hung in clusters on the walls, framed memories instead of artwork.

There it was, grouped with two others on the top of a bookcase in a solid silver frame. He picked it up in a gloved hand and slipped it into his bag.

He should go back upstairs and finish his work. He wanted to look closely at the woman and then make his decision about what should happen, but he couldn't face the cat. At least he had what he'd come for. He let himself out of the back door, leaving it open and blowing in the draught. Only the cat knew he'd been there.

* * *

Startled from sleep, Natalie looked at the clock — 3.14 a.m. Hadn't she left the light on last night? She leaned across and pressed the button. Nothing wrong with it. She must have switched it off in her sleep.

Arthur blinked at her accusingly. Maybe he was the culprit. He had been restless last night. Even in her sleep she had felt him move, grumble to himself and even hiss at one point. She wondered if cats had bad dreams.

Then she heard it. A rhythmic banging, coming from downstairs.

It was no good, she had to go and see what it was. There was no one to send anymore. She put on her dressing gown and crept downstairs. The noise was coming from the kitchen. She wondered if she had put the washing machine on and frowned. She seemed to be getting very forgetful these days.

As she opened the kitchen door to see, the cold air hit her. Not the washing machine but the back door, wide open and banging against the outside wall.

Natalie stood in the doorway and stared. How could that be? She had definitely made sure the door was locked before she went up to bed. She even pictured herself turning the key, and then checking the handle. So, why . . . ?

She edged into the kitchen and found it empty. She flung open the pantry door and jumped back, but it was empty too. Where was the person who had opened the door? Out? Fled into the night? Or still inside?

Natalie swallowed hard. Her mobile phone was still there on the counter, charging up. She grabbed it, ran outside into the garden and dialled 999.

* * *

Marie and Gary got to the village of Old Fleet within twenty minutes of receiving the call. They soon found Crosswinds, the bungalow they'd been called to, and parked outside.

'That'll teach us, won't it?' Marie said. 'Remind me *not* to tell Uniform to alert us to these calls in future.'

'Well, think of it this way, at least we are in at the beginning.' Gary released his seat belt. 'And that must be Mrs Miles.'

They both looked at the woman waiting at the gate, a dressing gown held close around her.

They introduced themselves. She looked slightly surprised when they said they were with CID but she didn't question it. She told them she was waiting outside because she'd been too frightened to stay inside the house.

Gently, Gary took her arm. 'Don't you worry, Mrs Miles, we'll check the house right through. Come and sit in the kitchen, you look frozen.'

'I can't stop shivering. I don't understand how he got in. I shut all the windows before I went to bed and locked the doors.'

Gary drew out a kitchen chair for her. 'You sit there. We'll take a look around and then tell you what we think, okay?'

They removed themselves to the hall. 'He'll be long gone,' Marie whispered.

'Oh yes,' said Gary, 'and most likely with a child's photograph clutched in his sticky little mitt.'

They walked slowly through the whole house, Marie stopping to pet the gorgeous long-haired tabby cat that had sidled up to her, purring contentedly.

They finished up in the lounge, where they stopped and stared at the vast array of photos, hunting for a telltale space. 'Ah, got it,' Marie said. 'Look, Gary.' She pointed to two small, framed photographs on top of a bookshelf. Between them was a slim, clean line in the dust. They asked Mrs Miles if she remembered what had stood there.

'It was a picture of my nephew, Davy, and it was in a silver frame. Where's it gone?' Natalie looked utterly confused.

'Mrs Miles,' said Marie softly, 'you are the fifth person this week to have had a photograph stolen. We still don't know why this man is doing it.'

'But you can rest assured that he isn't here, Mrs Miles. I just have to check the garage, then we'll be done. He's a long way from here by now, I promise you.' Gary went back into the kitchen and opened the door to the integral garage. The place clearly wasn't used for a car, housing instead a chest freezer, garden tools, a mower, several stepladders and a pile of boxes all marked 'Xmas Decs'.

The main garage door was locked fast, and there was no personnel door. You accessed it either from the main door or the kitchen. It was chock full of stuff, but there was nowhere to hide a man. Gary went back into the kitchen.

'Is the door from the kitchen normally locked, Mrs Miles?' he asked.

'No, the garage is a handy dumping ground — as you probably noticed,' she said. 'I'm always in and out to the freezer. No one could get through the outer door without a key and it sticks dreadfully, you'd hear anyone who tried.'

They sat around the kitchen table. Marie asked Natalie if she would talk them through her evening. 'And Gary will make you a cup of tea.'

Gary smiled. 'Of course.'

Natalie stood up. 'No, I'll do it. You've been very kind, and I feel much better now. It's good to know I'm not the only one this man's targeted. I don't feel quite so much a victim.' She made them all tea, then described her evening.

At first, Marie couldn't help wondering if Natalie's nervousness had been down to the book she was reading or just her enforced idleness. By the time Natalie had finished recounting her movements, she was certain their killer had slipped inside before she closed the windows, hiding somewhere until she had gone to sleep. She kept this to herself.

'Tell us about that picture of Davy, your nephew,' Gary said.

'It was taken here in the garden,' Natalie said. 'He used to stay here sometimes. He's a lovely child, rather bookish and fascinated by nature. He prefers being outside in the garden, enjoying the birds and insects, rather than playing games on the computer. The garden is so overgrown now that it's become a haven for hedgehogs, frogs and all sorts of other creatures that interest a youngster. The picture was taken by the wildlife pond. It was just . . . just *Davy*, in his wellies and shorts. I love it.'

'How old was he when it was taken?' Marie asked.

'Oh, nineish, I suppose. Maybe nearer ten.'

'And now?'

'He's twelve. His birthday was last week as a matter of fact.'

Marie wrote this all down.

'He isn't in danger from this man, is he?' Natalie asked anxiously.

'We don't think so,' Marie said. 'He's made no attempt to go near any of the other children, nor has he gone back to any of the places he's entered. It's a bit of a mystery, to say the least.' Marie glanced at Gary. 'We'd better go and get this all logged.'

'There'll be a uniformed officer out to take your statement, Mrs Miles,' said Gary. 'And I'm afraid there'll be a scene-of-crime officer too, to check for prints and so on, but that will be a little later. Is there anyone who could come and keep you company?'

'My friend Patsy. I'll give her a call as soon as I think she'll be up. She was going to do some shopping for me later anyway. I've hurt my back and carrying shopping bags isn't good for it. The supermarket couldn't deliver this week.'

Marie was glad she had a friend to call on. It didn't do to be alone after a shock like that. It would be a while yet until sunrise, and Natalie Miles shouldn't be alone in the dark. 'Gary, give the station a ring and get someone out here now. I'm not leaving this lady alone.'

Natalie gave her a grateful smile. 'Thank you, Sergeant, I appreciate it. I don't mind saying this has really shaken me up.' She took their empty cups to the sink. 'Do you think these boys are connected in any way, Officers? Only my Davy doesn't have a lot of friends. He's quite a loner for a boy of his age.'

'So far,' said Gary, 'we can't find any at all. Not between the boys or the women whose houses were broken into. Though technically he's not breaking in, he gains access without damaging any locks or property. As the sarge here says, it's a mystery.'

'How did he know I'd have a photograph anyway?' she asked anxiously. 'If he'd got into Patsy's house, for instance, she doesn't have a single photo of children.'

Marie shrugged. 'It's early days yet, and so far we know very little. As soon as we know what we're dealing with, we'll tell you, I promise.'

A few minutes later, a patrol car drew up outside. Marie and Gary stood up.

'We'll be in touch,' Marie said. 'Here's my card. If you think of anything else that might help us, please ring, day or night.'

Natalie accepted the card. 'I will, and thanks for your kindness. You must think I'm just a silly, frightened woman.'

Marie smiled at her. 'I don't think you're silly at all. If it happened to me, I'd react just the same. But maybe steer clear of the scary stories for a while?'

'Don't worry, Sergeant. It's chick lit and rom coms for me from now on.'

Just as they were leaving, Natalie said, 'He was in here all the time, wasn't he? Before I locked up. He was in here with me.'

They glanced quickly at each other. Well, no point in lying. 'It looks that way, I'm afraid,' Marie said. 'But try not to think about it. He had no intention of hurting you, he just wanted that photograph, nothing else.'

'Thank you for your honesty, Sergeant.'

But Marie had seen the expression on her face. The coming night was going to be hard for this woman.

# CHAPTER TWELVE

Jackman waited for the kettle to boil, going over the previous night's conversation with Laura. She had already spoken to Sam, but she was still anxious. It seemed out of all proportion to the case and he was beginning to think there might be something else worrying her. Maybe he should have a private word with Sam. If Laura couldn't — or wouldn't — tell him what it was, maybe Sam could put his mind at ease.

He made the tea, still mulling over what to do, then heard his phone ringing.

Marie still managed to sound cheerful despite having been dragged out of bed at three in the morning. 'Just giving you an update, boss, no need to rush in. Gary and I have done all we can, now we're off for a double sausage and egg McMuffin.'

She told him about their visit to Old Fleet village and relayed the victim's questions. It was a good one. How had the intruder known she had the photo? Why choose her and not someone else? The thought had been bugging him too. He could only surmise that the man had been in her house before, on a recce. More to the point, he'd been in *all* the houses at some point. Jackman knew exactly how that could come about. It would be his first job when he got into work, asking them all whether they'd had workmen in recently. Telephone engineers, window cleaners, security or double-glazing salesmen, anyone seemingly legitimate that gained access to their home. All he needed was a common denominator.

He took Laura's tea to her and found her sitting up, still looking pensive.

'You're starting to really worry me, sweetheart,' he said softly. 'Isn't there anything I can do to help?'

Laura smiled at him. 'I'm so sorry. I never meant to worry you, darling. But now I have Sam and another expert in the field with me, I'm sure we'll sort it in no time.'

'And that's all it is? Nothing else?' he asked.

For one fleeting second there was an expression of . . . what? Surely not guilt. Or maybe just tension, and then it was gone. But he was a policeman, trained to notice such indications.

'It's just work, really it is.' She held out her arms to him.

He lay down and put his arms around her. She wasn't telling the truth. He was determined to ring Sam as soon as possible.

\* \* \*

Sam was sitting up in bed with a large mug of decaffeinated tea — for his heart — surrounded by Hughie Mackenzie's case studies. It was heavy stuff. By far the most shocking was the brutal attack on an apparently well-loved sister and her husband. But there were other cases too, ones that hadn't made the tabloids. He read about a young man who in his waking life had no real creative talent, but in his sleep he produced the most beautiful and elaborate artwork. He had even held exhibitions in famous galleries. Hughie had included copies of some of his work, which was truly amazing. Apparently, an art expert had been shown a selection of this artist's nocturnal paintings and had believed each one to have been made by a different artist, so varied were they in technique and style.

Sam sipped his tea and turned a page. He read of a chef who would get up in the night and prepare a full meal. His wife would find him eating, still fast asleep. Amusing, but think of those sharp knives being wielded by a sleeping man.

Hughie was right, parasomnia was a fascinating phenomenon. Some people suffered terrifying hypnagogic hallucinations, where a person believes they can see a mysterious stranger standing at the foot of the bed. Others acted out their dreams — people had been observed dancing barefoot in the rain. Some raided the fridge, and then when awake, wondered where yesterday's leftovers had gone. A few drove in their sleep. Others had sex. A rare disorder called sexsomnia had been used as a defence in rape cases. What they all had in common was the fact that they had sleepwalked as children.

Sam pushed the papers aside and leaned back against the pillows, his mug in both hands. He knew about some of these conditions, but because they were usually assumed to be medical or drug-induced, no cases had come to his personal attention, so he wasn't surprised that Laura hadn't met one either. He was to meet her today at the mill to discuss her observations. She had said there was something about Shields that she found disconcerting, but she could not pinpoint what it was. It was this that had sent her to him for help. She wanted Sam to meet Freddie Shields so he could observe him in person and help her understand why she felt this way.

It was some years since he'd felt so excited by a new case.

* * *

After a supreme effort, Annie Carson had returned to sleeping in her bedroom at night. If it hadn't been for her son Callum, she would have slept downstairs all night with the TV on. But she didn't want Callum to know how frightened she was. So frightened, in fact, that it was in her mind to talk to her eldest son about selling up and moving. She didn't want to uproot Callum, but her house was no longer her home, her safe place.

What troubled her most was the theft of Callum's photograph. It left her unwilling to allow Callum out of her sight. Oddly, it had affected him badly too. She had expected him to be dying to get back to school and tell all his mates about the strange man in his house and the police coming around looking all serious. But he didn't even want to go in. He said he felt ill, and asked could he stay at home for a few days?

For once, she accepted this excuse without demur, happy for them to stick together until this man was caught. Her older boy, Andrew, had offered to take compassionate leave and come home to look after them, but he was doing so well at work that she was reluctant to disrupt it. Luckily, she worked from home, so she had no need to leave Callum at all. It would get better with time, and eventually the man would be brought in, hopefully sooner rather than later. Until then she would just have to be strong and see them through it. At first, she had been surprised at the attention the police were giving the case. Then she learned that on the following nights, he had got into more homes and had even killed an old woman.

Annie stretched and yawned. The sun was up now, and a new day was dawning. She went downstairs and thought about breakfast. Callum wouldn't be up for another hour at least, so she decided to treat herself to a cooked breakfast, something usually reserved for holidays. Maybe the smell of bacon would even tempt her lad from his pit.

The police would be calling today. They were trying to find something that connected her with the other women the intruder had visited. As she dumped an egg into a sizzling frying pan, she had an idea. What if she and the other women actually met up and shared not only their experience but what they might have in common? You never knew, they might come up with whatever had led this dreadful man to seek them and their children out.

She bustled about, relishing the mouth-watering aroma of fried breakfast, feeling a bit of the old feisty Annie returning. *Come on, Annie. You managed to raise two lovely boys while mourning the death of your beloved husband, surely you can do something to help get this wretch off the streets?*

The other women would feel the same, she was sure, and if any held back, she'd make sure they came forward in the end.

The breakfast was delicious. Annie enjoyed every mouthful, and then repeated the process half an hour later for her pleasantly surprised son.

She had been given the names of the other women, to see if she recognised either of them — Sylvia Wilson and Fleur Harper. The names remained engraved in her brain. She'd seen on the news that the dead woman was called Nancy Cutler. Annie decided that as soon as she'd cleared the breakfast things, she'd track down Sylvia and Fleur and invite them for a coffee. She had no idea what kind of women they were, but if dearly loved children were involved, they had to be keen to do what they could.

She had little work to do today, so she'd get her business stuff out of the way, see the police and then set about organising her little group of avenging angels. Amid a determined clatter of dishes, she decided that the best way to combat this horrible feeling of powerlessness was to fight back.

\* \* \*

When she and Jay arrived at the house that morning, Stacey was delighted to see a remarkable change in Annie Carson. Leaning forward in her seat, she listened intently to what they said.

'So there's been another one?' she said. 'What's her name?'

'Natalie Miles. Ring a bell at all?' asked Stacey.

'I used to know a Natalie. She was a secretary — for an accountant I work with. I can't remember her surname though. Where does she live?'

'The village of Old Fleet, not far from Saltern.' Stacey noticed Annie writing this down. 'You seem to have made a remarkable recovery, Annie. You were shaken to the bone the last time we saw you.'

'I have a young and impressionable son, Stacey. I have to put on a brave face for him.' Annie gave a dry laugh. 'Sometimes, if I try really hard, I even convince myself.'

'Good for you,' Stacey said. She pointed to Annie's notes. 'Thanks for taking this so seriously. I see you're really trying to find a connection between yourselves, and we appreciate it.'

'It's the least I can do. I want him found and locked up.' She frowned. 'This Natalie I used to pass on work to, I even had a drink with her one evening, though it's ages ago now. I'm not sure if I still have her number, but if not, I'll ring the accountant and ask him what her surname is.'

'If you would let us know, that'd be great,' said Jay.

When he and Stacey were back in the car, Jay said, 'I feel easier about her and her son now. She's made a big effort for his sake. Let's hope she manages to find a connection.'

Stacey started the engine. 'So, why do I feel uneasy? Did you notice her expression when we told her about last night's victim?'

Jay looked blank. 'She was interested, but why wouldn't she be? It would make her feel less like a target. The more houses he gets into, the greater the likelihood that it was a random selection, which would mean less threat to her son.'

'Very logical, young man,' Stacey said. 'But I saw something different. Our Annie's up to something.'

'Is this a woman thing?' asked Jay. 'My sister's always saying we think differently. So, what did you see?'

Stacey grinned. 'It's not a woman thing, Jay, at least not in this case. It's instinct, something you learn in the police after years of mixing with liars and villains. You start to read what people are *not* telling you, rather than what they are. And don't worry, you'll pick it up, even if you are a man.'

Jay sighed. 'Years, eh?'

'At least ten.'

'Marvellous. And in the meantime?'

'In the meantime, we keep a bit of a watchful eye on Annie Carson.'

* * *

Annie watched the car draw away. Another woman, maybe someone she knew. She wouldn't contact Natalie yet, she'd be in shock. She went to the room she used as her office.

She googled their names, tried Facebook and Instagram, but only came up with one private account and an unidentifiable picture for a Sylvia Wilson. So, having failed to find them online, she turned to good old-fashioned footwork. She decided to start with Fleur Harper, who lived in Cartoft village. Cartoft was small, with no amenities other than a church and a village hall, as far as she could remember. Which meant that the inhabitants all knew each other.

Cartoft was around twenty minutes from Fenton Mere. Now, what to do with Callum? She really didn't want to leave him home alone, but he was watching a Harry Potter film and would object to being dragged away from it.

Annie went up to his room. Callum paused the film and blinked at her. 'You all right, Mum?'

She decided it was time to take him into her confidence. 'Son? Can we have a chat?'

'Sure.' He patted his bed.

Annie thought fast. She would make her idea into a sort of game. 'I've been thinking, Callum. We can't let that horrible man get away with scaring people, can we? He's a bad person and he has to be stopped. I think we can help the police, but we'll have to do it in secret. Then, if we find something out, we can tell them, and they'll be really pleased. What do you think?'

His eyes lit up. 'You mean like we were secret agents?'

'Exactly!' She smiled at him. 'So, I thought of going to see if we can find some people to help us. Are you up for a ride in the car?'

'Where to?'

'Cartoft village.' She stood up. 'To find another lady who this man scared. Want to come?'

'Cool!'

'But remember, Callum, not a word to the police just yet, or anyone else. I want to find everyone who's been scared by the bad man.' She winked at him. 'Why not get one of your notebooks and write down our findings? You can record times, places, people, just like we're real detectives.'

Harry Potter forgotten, Callum jumped up and went to his bookshelf. He took down a spiral-bound notebook with a picture of Dr Who's Tardis on the cover. 'Here we are, a police box — well, sort of.'

'Perfect, son.' She smiled to herself. Somehow it pleased her that in the era of smartphones and laptops, her boy was still fond of paper. Callum must have over twenty new notebooks on his shelves. 'Ready, Partner?'

'Good to go!'

They locked the house, made doubly sure it was secure, then headed out of the village in Annie's Ford Fiesta.

'Our first mission is to locate a lady called Fleur Harper. The bad man got into her house the other night, and we need to interview her.'

Callum nodded seriously. 'Does she have a son? Did his picture go missing too?'

'Yes, she does, but the police say he lives with his dad and just visits at weekends.'

'Ah, like my friend Jamie. Divorced, I guess, like Jamie's parents. He says it's not so bad. He gets two homes, two bedrooms, two lots of clothes and loads of presents.' He looked up at her. 'I can see what they're doing, Mum. It's because they feel guilty about splitting up.'

Annie glanced at him, impressed. 'You could be right there, son.'

'How are we going to find this lady, then?' he said.

'Well, we'll park in the village, and . . . suppose we see an old couple walking a dog? I'll ask them if they know where Fleur Harper lives.'

'Yes, that would work.' He nodded to himself. 'Hey, see that children's play area? And the field? Jamie's dad took us there for a friendly match with some other kids the other Sunday. If there's any kids around I could ask them if they know where Mrs Harper lives.'

Annie smiled. A kid asking directions to someone's house would give less rise to suspicion. 'Great idea. We'll see what we find when we get there, shall we?'

They pulled up in the church car park. 'Target at three o'clock!' Callum pointed to a young woman emerging from her front garden with a child in a pushchair. 'Quick! Interrogate her, Mum!'

Annie opened the car door, trying hard to look serious.

She strolled across and smiled at the young woman. 'Excuse me, I'm sorry to bother you. I suppose you don't know where I can find Mrs Fleur Harper, do you?'

The girl brushed her hair from her face. 'I'm sorry but we haven't been here long. I've heard the name, but I'm afraid I don't know where she lives.'

'No problem, thanks anyway.'

As Annie turned to walk away, the girl said, 'If I was you, I'd go over to the churchyard. You'll find old John there, pottering about. He knows everyone in the village.'

Annie thanked her, went back to the car and told Callum.

'Can I come with you, Mum?'

'Sure, hop out.'

They found old John tinkering with an elderly petrol mower. 'You're not from round 'ere, are you?'

'No. I wonder if you can help us,' Annie said.

'If I can.'

'I'm looking for a lady called Harper, I—'

'That'll be our Fleur.'

'That's right! Would you be kind enough to tell us where she lives?'

John pointed to a lane that ran along the far side of the churchyard. ''Bout halfway down Glebe Close on the left-hand side, semi-detached with a dark-red front door. Number three.'

'Thank you so much, sir. Much appreciated.'

Back in the car, Callum bent over his notebook, scribbling furiously. 'Right, Mum. Got that. Let's go.'

She drove down the lane and parked outside the house. There was no mistaking the large number three on the gate. 'I want you to sit tight, Callum. I don't know what kind of person she is, so you just keep your eyes peeled, okay?'

'Okay. I'll be backup if things turn ugly.'

A cartoon image of the boy flashed into her head, storming in, all guns blazing.

She rang the bell and waited.

'Who is it?' The voice behind the door had a slight tremor.

'Fleur Harper? You don't know me, but I wondered if I could have a word, please?'

'If you're the papers, you can just go away and leave me alone!'

'I'm not, honestly, Mrs Harper. I just want to talk. He broke into my house too. That awful man, he stole a photo of my son.' Silence.

After a while Annie heard the key turning in the lock. A woman peered anxiously through the narrow gap. 'You aren't just trying it on, are you, to get a story?'

'No, I promise. Look, my son is in the car with me. I daren't leave him alone and he's too upset to go to school. My name is Annie Carson.'

'Oh, yes! The police told me your name. You'd better come in.'

'Can I bring Callum? I haven't let him out of my sight since that night . . .'

Fleur stepped back. 'Of course, you must keep him close. Bring him in.'

Annie hurried back and told Callum to get out of the car. 'Be polite, now. This lady has had a terrible shock, just like us. Just keep quiet and remember what we say for your book. Okay, partner?'

'Got it.'

Callum followed her into the house.

'Come into the kitchen,' said Fleur. 'I'll make tea.' She looked at Callum. 'Would you like a cold drink?'

'I'm Callum, and yes, please.'

'Diet Coke or orange juice, Callum?'

'Orange, please, Mrs Harper.'

'Sit down.' Fleur indicated the kitchen table. 'You'll have to forgive the mess. I'm a total wreck at present, I'm afraid. I'm so on edge I can't concentrate on anything.'

This woman wasn't coping well at all.

When they were all seated, Annie began. 'The thing is, I was wondering if it might help if we — that's all the women who've had this intruder come into their house — got together and discussed what has happened and how we might help the police.' She looked hopefully at Fleur. 'I thought we might be able to work out what connects us and why he stole photographs from us in particular.'

'That's been on my mind every moment since it happened. Why take a picture of my Jason?' She rubbed her hands together nervously.

'That's what my mum's worried about,' said a small voice. 'And me too.'

'How were you thinking of going about it?' Fleur said.

'I'm going to try to contact the other two women — Sylvia Wilson and Natalie Miles — and then have you all over to my house for coffee. Maybe if we all get together we'll be able to solve the puzzle, rather than struggling on alone.'

Fleur nodded vigorously. 'I'm all for that. Everybody says talking helps, don't they?'

Annie smiled. 'Just to start with, I think it best that we don't tell the police about it. They might discourage us, and then we would lose out on a brilliant support group.'

'I see what you mean,' Fleur said, 'but I'm not very good at telling lies, I'm afraid.'

'No lies, we just don't mention it. And if we come up with something, we take it straight to them,' Annie said.

'Ah, I see. Okay,' Fleur said.

'Well, you're the first. I'm going to try to hunt down Sylvia Wilson next,' Annie said. 'She lives in the Leetoft area of Saltern, and she won't be so easy to find. I'm not sure who I can ask.'

'I think I heard one of the police mention that she lived near to where she worked — in a nursery? Plants that is, not children,' Fleur said.

'Great! Thanks for that. I'll check out the nurseries. That's fantastic, Fleur. We're on the way!' Annie fished in her bag. 'This is my business card, but my telephone number, mobile and email are all on it. I'll ring as soon as I find the others, and we can all meet up.'

Fleur tore a sheet from a shopping list pad and wrote her details down. 'I think this will work. I feel better just for talking to you.'

'Me too,' Annie said.

'And me,' piped up Callum. 'My mum's dead bright.'

Fleur laughed. 'You're right. I'd certainly never have thought of such a clever idea.'

Fleur offered them more drinks, biscuits, cake. It was obvious she didn't want them to go. But Annie was keen to keep moving. They left, promising to keep in touch.

Back in the car, Callum asked, 'Are we going to Leetoft now?'

'Sure are. Let's have a look for that nursery.'

'I'm on it.'

Callum got on his phone.

'There's two nurseries in Leetoft, Mum. Starr-plants and M. L. Prescott and Sons.'

'Addresses?' Her boy was turning out to be rather useful.

'Starr-plants is on Main Road. The map shows them next to a big house called Carlton Lodge.' He scrolled down. 'And the other one is in Rabbit Lane, all on its own, nothing else for miles.'

Fleur had said Sylvia lived close to her work, so it would be the first one.

'Okay then. Starr-plants, here we come.'

They found it easily. The nursery consisted of a vast area of polytunnels. The entrance was fashioned to look like a big glass greenhouse, with a cash desk, a row of trolleys and a pile of wire baskets, followed by dozens of low tables stacked with colourful plants. A big sliding door at the back led to the polytunnels. Annie could see acres of benches holding more plants. A bored-looking woman was lounging against the desk. Business was obviously far from brisk today.

Annie picked up a tray of bright red flowers that were marked up at £3.99. She had no idea what they were, but they gave her an excuse for being there. 'Afternoon,' she said brightly. 'You're quieter than usual?'

'Comes and goes,' the woman said in a dull monotone. 'We're either rushed off our feet or dead, like this.'

'Is Sylvia in today?' Annie asked.

'She's off. Boss ain't too happy either.'

Poor Sylvia, what a miserable place to work. A zombie for a co-worker and a boss who clearly had no sympathy for her plight. Fumbling in her purse for change, she wondered how to get this miserable woman to give her Sylvia's address.

'Mum? Can we go visit her? See if she's all right? She might be sick.' Callum was nudging her in the ribs. 'She said to call in any time we're passing, didn't she?'

What a son I have! Destined either to become a police officer or a successful criminal. Annie gave a little laugh. 'She did, but your stupid mother has forgotten the address.'

'Jasmine Cottage,' the woman said, accepting the money. 'Four houses down. Can't miss it — she spends most of her pay on garden plants.'

Annie smiled gratefully. It was only half past two and they had located two women. 'Thank you very much. We'll say hello for you, shall we?'

The woman shrugged and went back to lounging against the counter.

Back in the car again, she smiled at Callum. 'You're pretty good at this, aren't you?'

He grinned. 'S'all those cop shows on TV. See, they *are* useful.'

How could she argue? 'Right. Well, don't forget to charm Sylvia Wilson with those manners of yours, will you?'

# CHAPTER THIRTEEN

Marie was starving. The morning had flown by, and she hadn't had lunch yet. She was just about to dash to the canteen when her phone rang.

'Ralph. You okay?'

'More than okay, Marie. We made a blindingly good collar last night. A couple of dodgy moments, but we got a good two-thirds of them, including the ringleaders, and all of the merchandise, so we're well chuffed.'

Marie knew all about that magical buzz. She could feel it now — her phone was almost vibrating with it. 'Well done! Bet you're knackered.'

'I'll say. The minute the adrenalin starts to wear off it hits you like a steam train.' He laughed. 'It's taken until now to process them all. So, I'm off home to hit the sack. I just wanted to tell you I'm safe, and happy as a pig in shit.'

She laughed. 'You have a good wallow. Ring me later?'

'Sure. Speak soon.'

She sat smiling idiotically at the empty screen. Finally, she grabbed a sandwich and hurried back to her desk to look at her list of things to be done. She saw that she had neglected to check out their new resident Mr Giles Bannon, who might or might not be a murderer. She had promised Jackman not to let this slip, but their intruder had got in the way.

If only she could just pay him a call, but that would be frowned upon. There was nothing in the memo sent from his home area constabulary but a notification that he had basically been hounded out of his neighbourhood and had decided to move to their patch.

There was so much she didn't know about Bannon, like where he was living, what he looked like and how he was spending his time. His address had been given as Hobhole, an odd place consisting of a few scattered houses placed at seemingly random intervals along a stretch of a canal known as Hobs Drain. Arable farmland extended beyond and below it as far as the eye could see. The buildings stood like solitary little islands, edged with trees or conifers protecting them from the relentless North Sea gales.

She glanced at the clock. Almost three. Hobhole was about fifteen minutes away by bike. 'Going out for half an hour or so,' she called to Robbie. 'When Gary comes back, tell him I'm just doing a recce of Giles Bannon's new home.'

'Will do, Sarge.'

Soon, Marie was heading out of town and across the sunlit Fens. She arrived at a straggling collection of dwellings and slowed down. She was looking for a house or cottage called Moorcroft, but after almost half a mile she still hadn't spotted it. By now she was almost out of Hobhole.

Ahead of her were only two more houses, and then nothing but fields.

She passed the first, which bore the name Pemberley, a rather rambling house with several buildings attached to it.

So, Moorcroft had to be the last house on Hobs Drain.

Cold Blow. Damn it. Marie turned around. She must have missed it, though she could have sworn she'd noted every plate and plaque she passed.

'Who you lookin' for, mate?'

An old man in shabby clothes, carrying a green plastic trug full of hedge clippings, appeared from around a hedge.

'I think I'm lost,' she said.

'Sorry, lass, thought you were a bloke on that big machine.' He looked at it admiringly. 'Used to have a smasher when I was younger, a Matchless. You probably won't even have 'eard of one of them.'

Marie pulled off her helmet and grinned at him. 'What model?'

'A Silver Hawk,' he said proudly.

'Really! Wow! That was a 1930s luxury model, four-cylinder machine. It was a Bert Collier design, wasn't it?' Marie gazed at the little old man in awe.

'Well, I'll be jiggered. You know your bikes, lass. My pride and joy it was.' He beamed at her, his eyes almost brimming with nostalgia.

'How come you had a bike like that, if you don't mind me asking? They were like, well, *really* expensive back then, and rare too.' Marie had only ever seen one in the National Motorcycle Museum in Solihull.

'I had an uncle, rich as Croesus, the old bugger was. Well, he had to have every newfangled machine he could get his hands on. So, he buys this beautiful motorbike, hasn't got a clue how to ride it and crashes it. So what does he do? He throws it in the dyke! Luckily my dad saw him do it and went and got a tractor and towed it out. He brought it home and we rebuilt it. Best thing that ever happened to me, lass, and that's no lie. Time with my dad, and the best bike in the world at the end of it.' He cackled. 'I felt as rich as that old sod, my uncle.' He stood running his eyes over her Triumph Tiger. 'That one's beautiful too, in its way.'

'But not a Matchless. Don't worry, I understand.' She smiled at him. 'Nice to meet you, sir, but I'd better get a move on.'

'Well, I gather you're a courier. If you're looking for a house along this stretch, some of them have changed their names in the last year or so. Birchwood is now called Long

Eaton, and the Hawthorns is called Moorcroft. Don't think either have their proper name plates up yet. Dunno why folk have to do that, do you?'

'Confusing for us, that's for sure,' she said. 'Thanks anyway. You take care.'

She rode off. She remembered passing a long, low, chalet-style house with a big double garage called the Hawthorns. So that was Giles Bannon's new home.

She slowed and cruised past. The house wasn't luxurious, but still pretty upmarket. She counted three, maybe four bedrooms, and what looked like a granny annexe. It was surrounded by shrubs, trees and conifers, and the nearest neighbour was at least 500 yards away. Not a bad spot, if you wanted to hide.

There had been no car in the drive, and blinds at all the windows. The place looked shut down, the life of the occupant invisible to the world. His neighbours had turned on him in the past, so this didn't come as a surprise.

She opened the throttle and sped away. Now she knew where to find him, she could get on with her day — and look forward to a late-night telephone conversation with a certain detective . . .

\* \* \*

At around four p.m., Laura drove home after a gruelling day. She had been part of a crisis team dealing with a client who had suffered a serious episode and was in danger of injuring himself. Normally, she was able to deal with such issues and move on. Today, however, she had been unable to maintain her usual detachment. She longed to be home and wrapped in the comfort of Rowan's arms, but he was involved in a difficult case, so she'd probably be spending the evening alone.

As she pulled up beside the mill, her heart sank. Another car, and she knew who it belonged to. Fuming, she parked and got out, just as Freddie Shields emerged from his.

'Mr Shields. You know I can't see you without an appointment. Patients can't just turn up when they choose.'

'I know. I'm so sorry. Normally I wouldn't consider doing such a thing, but I didn't know who else to turn to. Please, can I talk to you for a few minutes?'

He did look frantic with worry, and Laura relented. 'Five minutes, Mr Shields, and then you have to go. We have an appointment for Friday, as we arranged.'

He followed her into her consulting room. As soon as she'd shut the door, he blurted, 'It's getting worse. I drove again last night. I have no idea where I went, but this morning I saw thirty more miles on the clock. Thirty miles! Where did I go? What did I do?'

'Did anything happen yesterday evening to make you especially upset or anxious before you went to bed? Was your partner with you?'

'As you suggested, I spoke to my mother. She told me she had always been terrified for my safety when I tried to open windows or wandered off outside. She said that nothing else frightened her apart from that.' He looked down at his feet. 'I think there was something else, but she wouldn't say what it was. I've told Julia not to spend the night for a while. I . . . I'm scared I could hurt her, Dr Archer. I've read about people hurting others in their sleep. My grandfather had shellshock, and he had nightmares he couldn't wake up from. Once, he tried to strangle his wife because he thought she was an enemy soldier. That really scared me, which is why I told Julia to stay away.'

'Those thoughts will have preyed on your mind and prevented you from getting proper rest. Having to send your partner away puts stress on you and your relationship. Have you considered giving either Julia or your mother your car keys, so you can't drive?'

He pulled a face. 'I still haven't told Mother about that. We only spoke of my sleepwalking as a thing of the past, one of those stories from childhood you tell each other. If I gave her the keys, she would know I was driving. I don't want that. It wouldn't be fair on her.'

'It wouldn't be fair on her either if you were injured or even killed in a car crash,' Laura said. 'You really should share this with her, Mr Shields. I urge you to do so.'

'Dr Archer, if this keeps on getting worse, is there somewhere I could go to be treated, somewhere safe? I don't have a great deal of money, but I would be willing to spend some of my savings if it meant I could be cured.'

'I can make enquiries for you, Mr Shields. The situation is clearly having a detrimental effect on your mental health, but we need to find somewhere with counsellors who have experience in this disorder. I will shortly be meeting an eminent psychologist who specialises in somnambulism. I'll put it to him and see what he suggests.'

'Thank you! I knew you'd help me.' He stood up. 'I'm sorry to have taken up your time. You've been very kind, and I apologise for just arriving like I did, Dr Archer. I was at my wits' end.'

'I'll see you on Friday then, and you can meet Professor Page. Meanwhile, I'll look around for a suitable clinic.'

Laura stood in the doorway and watched him get into his car. She couldn't quite decipher the expression on his face. Relief? Or was it something else? For a moment he had looked — what? Triumphant? No, that didn't make any sense. Laura made her way into the house, wondering what she might have said to have caused that strange look.

Inside, she went straight to the phone. She needed to talk to Sam.

\* \* \*

To Annie's delight, Callum was putting on a stellar performance. Sylvia Wilson was totally captivated. Poor Sylvia. Fancy waking up to find a muddy footprint on your duvet cover. She was full of admiration for Sylvia, who, after the initial shock, had rallied and was now furious at the intruder.

'I think it's a splendid idea, and I'll certainly join you. One of my ancestors was a staunch suffragette, you know.

She led marches, spoke at rallies and wasn't afraid of being dragged off to the cells. I keep remembering that remarkable woman and I refuse to let myself cower at home.'

'Excellent! Tomorrow, I'll see if I can find Natalie Miles, his latest victim, and then we'll all get together at my house — if that suits you, Sylvia?'

'I'll be there, never fear.'

Annie finished her tea. 'It was your grandsons in the stolen photo, wasn't it?'

'Will and Bobbie,' Sylvia said. 'They were about nine and ten, almost your lad's age. Lovely boys, but cheeky, not polite like your Callum here. He's a credit to you, Annie.'

Callum put on his angelic expression. Annie ruffled his hair. He'd definitely earned himself extra TV time or a new book. 'Thank you. He's not too bad, all things considered.'

Sylvia was somewhere in her late sixties. She admitted that the intrusion had knocked her sideways for a while. She was so frightened she was even thinking of moving — and then she remembered her doughty forebear and her fear turned into anger. Imagine what it would do to someone of a nervous disposition. Why should they put up with it? No, that sneaky bastard wasn't going to make her leave the home she loved.

Once they were back in the car, on their way home, Callum looked up from his detective's notebook where he was carefully making notes. 'Mum, what's a suffer . . . suffra . . . ? You know, what she said. Is she one of those? They sound pretty tough.'

Annie chuckled. 'Suffragette. Well, she could have been, I reckon, if she'd lived back in those days.' She glanced at her son. 'Okay, partner, what do you fancy for tea? Anything you like, you've earned it!'

\* \* \*

DC Kevin Stoner stood outside Holy Trinity Church and looked up at the somewhat plain exterior. He had a vague memory of coming here with his father once for some special service, although he remembered nothing about it.

He hadn't planned to visit this church on the outskirts of Saltern, but it felt like the right thing to do. He went inside and found that in contrast to the almost forbidding facade, the interior was actually rather beautiful. His entrance happened to coincide with the end of a meeting about the flower displays and an exhibition of amateur art at a charity fundraising event.

He looked around. So this was the church that had dismissed Nan Cutler for upsetting a member of the council. Learning what had actually happened to cause this rift might help them understand who Nan Cutler really was, other than a "sweet old lady." And where better to start than with the vicar?

Josephine turned out to be a friendly, chatty woman, passionate about her church and everything to do with it. He was surprised that she recognised him, and even more so when she recalled his name. Perhaps being the bishop's son had its advantages after all.

After a few minutes' idle conversation, he asked Josephine if she had heard about the death of Nan Cutler.

Josephine nodded sadly. 'I wouldn't have been surprised to hear that she had died — at over ninety it could have been expected. But murdered?' She shook her head. 'Now that came as a shock.'

'I'm trying to build up a picture of her past and wondered if you or anyone here could help?' He looked at her hopefully.

'I didn't have much of a chance to get to know her, Kevin. I arrived not long before she left. But the others told me that although she was quite devout and helpful, she did have very set notions of how things should be done, and she wasn't afraid to voice her opinions. Not often, but if she did find something that offended or upset her, she wouldn't let it go.' The vicar looked around, then said softly, 'The best person to talk to would be one of my churchwardens, Amy Shipley. She was on the parish council at the time.' She turned and beckoned to a woman talking to a group of others nearby. She made the introductions and left them to talk. As she hurried around organising her army of helpers, Josephine put Kevin in mind of an enthusiastic sheepdog, complete with collar, herding her flock.

Amy Shipley was in her late seventies or early eighties with sharp eyes and a straight back. He explained who he was and asked if she could tell him anything she remembered about Nan Cutler.

'Come and sit down,' she said, ushering him to a pew in the main body of the church. 'It was uncomfortable business, DC Stoner. The lady Nan upset so much has since left us. She was a lot younger than any of the women in the church group, and to be honest I found her a bit overpowering. I got the feeling that Nan knew her from before she joined the church, and that something had happened between them that caused them to dislike each other so intensely.' She shrugged. 'I could be wrong, but that was the impression I got. Andrea, the younger woman, had a lot of friends here, and she took against Nan from the first.' She lowered her voice. 'As far as I could see, Andrea's friends closed ranks against Nan and forced her to leave. Personally, I suspect that Nan was actually right in what she said.'

Kevin frowned. 'Really? You mean she was deliberately driven away from the church?'

'Deliberately driven away from Andrea is more to the point.'

'Do you know what it was all about, Mrs Shipley?'

'Not exactly. No one here will even talk about it, but what I do know was that it concerned a child, a boy. Something to do with this lad upset Nan, but I don't know what.' She spread her hands. 'And that's all I know.'

'What was this Andrea's surname?' Kevin scribbled in his notebook.

'Becker, but I have an idea that she divorced and went off with another man, possibly even married again, so it could be different now.' Mrs Shipley kept glancing around, as if she was concerned not to be overheard. 'She lived in Connaught Road back then, like Nan, but I don't know the number, and she's certainly not there now.' She looked around. 'A lot of the committee members joined us after the event and know nothing about Nan or what occurred, but her death has sent a few ripples through the aisles, I can tell you!'

Kevin smiled at her. 'You've been really helpful, Mrs Shipley. If I give you my card, would you contact me if you recall anything else, or even hear anything? I'm certain it was something from her past that caused this shocking thing to happen.'

'That wouldn't surprise me at all,' she said. 'Not everyone who steps through our hallowed portals is without sin.'

He noticed her wry smile. 'You're right there, Mrs Shipley,' he said. Hadn't the murderer Ashcroft conceived the most terrible of his acts while sitting humbly in a church pew?

As he got up to leave, she said softly, 'I liked Nan Cutler, Kevin. I hope you find the truth.'

'I'll do my best.'

# CHAPTER FOURTEEN

When Jackman arrived home, he was pleasantly surprised to find Sam Page's car there. He'd been meaning to ring him all day to talk about Laura but had never found the right moment.

Sam and Laura were in the kitchen, deep in discussion. Jackman kissed Laura and smiled at Sam. 'How are you, Sam? Can you stay for supper?'

'Actually, Laura's already invited me, so if there's enough to go around and it's not an imposition . . .'

Jackman laughed. 'As long as you like chilli con carne.'

'Love it,' said Sam.

Jackman took off his jacket and sat down. 'I was lucky to get away more or less on time tonight. Our murder case is hotting up and I can see some late nights coming.'

'Well, I'm so glad you're here now,' said Laura. 'I was thinking of opening a bottle. Any preferences?'

'As long as it's alcoholic, I don't mind,' said Jackman. 'I'll just go and freshen up and then I'll get the dinner ready.'

'It's all ready, just needs heating up, and I've made a green salad and some guacamole to go with it. All you have to do, my darling, is choose the wine.' Laura was smiling, but he noticed the worry lines around her eyes.

'Be back in ten.'

Jackman hurried upstairs to shower and change. Back in the kitchen, he opened a bottle of red wine and poured three glasses. 'The guest room is all ready, Sam. Why don't you have a couple of glasses with us and stay the night?'

'For once,' Sam replied, 'I'm going to take you up on that. I think it might be a good idea if we all have a chat.'

Jackman wondered at this. 'Sounds serious. Maybe we should get dinner going?' Sam and Laura nodded.

Twenty minutes later they were seated before steaming bowls of chilli. Jackman said, 'Okay, you two, what do you need to talk to me about?'

Laura glanced at Sam, who took a sip of wine and said, 'You start, Laura.'

'The thing is, my darling, you're worrying yourself sick over me — and I you. It's going to affect our work if we don't sort it.'

'Very true.' Jackman reached across the table and touched her hand. 'I do understand about patient confidentiality, but it's just distressing to see you so troubled.'

'I'm going to tell you what I can, without mentioning the patient's name or anything about his condition.'

Sam looked at him. 'We want to put your mind at rest, Jackman. It's a difficult case, but Laura isn't going to shoulder it alone.'

'That's a relief,' Jackman said, quietly wondering why Laura needed Sam along to tell him this.

Laura began.

'My patient is a GP referral, as I told you before, and he has a condition that's usually considered medical rather than psychological, which is why I haven't had a case like this before. Having exhausted the medical possibilities, his doctor turned to possible stress issues and felt that I could help.' She leaned forward. 'I sense a lot of problems in my patient, but even after several sessions he's not opening up. Despite this, he's showing signs of becoming reliant on me, which is not acceptable. I could simply tell him that I can't see him anymore and refer him to a trusted colleague, but I believe his problems to be very serious indeed, and I don't want to cause him further stress. So, with his permission, I've brought Sam in.'

'And in turn,' said Sam, laying down his fork for a moment, 'as this condition is beyond the scope of my expertise, I'm bringing in an expert, Professor Hugh Mackenzie.'

Jackman thought about this. 'Is this patient a danger in any way — to himself, to someone else, or more to the point, to you guys?'

'We don't know,' said Sam flatly. 'But we're doing all we can to make sure that doesn't happen. If you think about it, by their very nature, many psychological problems can be dangerous if not properly treated. We're trying to make sure the patient gets the best treatment and as swiftly as possible.' Sam broke into a smile. 'And on the plus side, it's a fascinating case — it interested Hughie Mackenzie enough for him to beetle all the way down here from Scotland at the weekend. So fear not, Jackman, your Laura has the finest working with her.'

Jackman frowned. 'I know that should reassure me, but actually I think I'm even more concerned. As a humble plod, I see the danger in everything, and your "fascinating case" sounds more like a "danger to public health" to my ears.'

Sam laughed. 'It would! Because you are a policeman! Well, rest easy. Just before you came home we decided that, if appropriate, I may take over his care completely.'

To Jackman that sounded like a bloody good idea.

Sam said, 'Therapists aren't always what we call a good fit with certain patients. Like people in general, we don't all get along perfectly or feel totally comfortable with everyone.'

'Sam's right,' added Laura. 'Naturally, I want the best for my patient. In this case, although it feels a bit like failure, I don't think I'm the best person for the job.'

'It doesn't help either,' said Sam, 'that you both have jobs that sometimes place you in jeopardy, which can't be easy, considering that you care so much for each other. You can't help but worry, it's natural.'

'You aren't kidding, Sam! Now pour me some more wine,' said Laura. 'I think I need it tonight. Anyway, I hope you understand why I've been so worried lately.'

Jackman poured them all another drink. 'Yes, I do, and for my part, I'll try to let you do the job you're so good at. This man is a lucky bugger to have you all fighting his corner.'

* * *

That night Jackman lay awake, thinking about what had been said. He wondered what on earth could be so wrong with this patient to bring an expert hurrying to the Fens from the other end of the country at such short notice. He had a terrible feeling that Laura was in danger. Before Sam left tomorrow, he would ask him if he would consider staying with them for a while. If his job was going to take him away at night, Sam could be here. The thought of her seeing a dangerous patient alone in the old mill building filled him with dread, but Sam's presence would give him peace of mind.

Decision made, he tried to sleep. But sleep didn't come. The nights were becoming difficult for him. As soon as darkness fell, he started to imagine those poor women waking up to find that a menacing stranger had been in their homes. Even now the bastard could be slipping through an unsuspecting woman's window or treading silently into the room where she slept. He imagined a hand stretching out to touch her skin.

Jackman held Laura tighter, and heard her murmur something in her sleep. 'Oh, Laura, I have to get him,' he whispered softly.

'And I love you too,' she murmured in her sleep.

Jackman smiled.

* * *

Ratty had mixed feelings about leaving Ma alone at night, but his compulsion to get out of that static had become overwhelming.

It had been a strange day. He'd noticed the Old Bill drive by earlier — they were obviously keeping tabs on him — and he'd made sure they got a good look at him, even going so far as to wave. He hoped they'd clocked his car too, still parked in the same place and now with a film of dust over the windscreen. Ma had been fretful, complaining about her painful ankle and swollen leg, and cursing old age.

When he could stand it no longer, he borrowed his mate's car and returned to the house he'd seen the night before. Earlier in the day, after the rozzers had gone, he'd driven over in daylight and kept a watch on it for almost an hour. The occupant had gone out for a while, in the little Micra he'd seen in the garage, returning with a couple of bags of shopping. All was as he'd hoped.

Now, once again, he parked out of sight some distance from his target property and made his way through the shadows towards it. Ah, the freedom of the night!

It occurred to him that it had been almost three weeks since he'd been inside a house. Now, like an addict desperate for a fix, he craved that powerful feeling of complete control that penetrating someone else's private and personal space conferred.

He was a few doors away when he saw a man approaching from the opposite direction, and he stood in the shadows, his back against a wall. It was a late-night dog walker, probably some insomniac using Fido as an excuse to walk himself tired. Dogs could be a problem with their highly developed sense of smell. They would know he was there, however much he kept out of sight. It was whether they chose to acknowledge his presence that was the problem. Thankfully, this pooch was more interested in other smells.

Ratty took a deep breath and slipped into the garden of Peartree Cottage.

The window above the conservatory roof was open, as it had been the night before. Together with the convenient drainpipe, the window ledges and the tiled roof on the garden room, getting in would be a doddle.

He was about to spring forward and scale the wall when he felt a sudden pressure against his Adam's apple, closing his windpipe, stifling him. He struggled to breathe, clawing at this thing tightening around his throat. The night grew blacker as consciousness faded. The dark hours, Ratty's safe place, were not so safe after all.

# CHAPTER FIFTEEN

As Jackman drove into the police station car park, a marked car flew out past him and headed off down the road. Then the figures of Stacey and Jay came hurrying towards him.

'Glad you're here, sir,' panted Stacey. 'We've just had a call that a body's been discovered in a cottage garden in Welby Road, Saltern. From the description, we believe it could be Ratty Jones. We're attending. Will you come, sir?'

'Of course. I'll see you there.' He got back in the car and called Marie, glancing across at her motorbike parked in its usual spot.

'Morning, boss. Overslept, have we?'

He chuckled. 'No, we have not. I'm downstairs in the car. Someone suspected to be Ratty Jones has been found dead in a garden in Welby Road. Coming?'

In seconds, she was hurrying out through the back door. 'Dead? As in an accident? Did he finally lose his footing clambering up someone's roof?'

'No information as yet. But with everything else that's going on, I'm not even daring to make a guess at what's happened to him.'

They found out soon enough. Dr Mason was already there.

'Garrotted,' he said. 'With something fine and very strong by the looks of it. Probably wire. Not quite what I expected when I was told to attend a sudden death.'

Marie and Jackman, now clad in protective suits, glanced at each other. Wire had been used to bring about the death of Nan Cutler. Was this the work of the same man? And if so, why?

'Garrotting is a rather, er, professional way of killing someone, isn't it?' said Marie.

'Well, it's quiet, that's the thing. A bit of a struggle and they're gone. Used to be the silent assassin's favourite method of dispatch.' Jackman stared at the still form of Ratty Jones. It was him all right. He looked at the nearby uniformed officers. 'Who found him?'

'Dog walker, sir.'

'When was that, Officer?'

'Around forty-five minutes ago, sir.'

'He's been dead for some time,' added Dr Mason. 'Probably since last night, but the forensics people will tell you more.'

Jackman nodded. 'Thanks for turning out, Doc. We've got it now.'

The good doctor wasted no time in hurrying from the scene.

'I think that took our Doc Mason by surprise,' Marie said.

'He's not the only one.' Jackman nodded towards Stacey Smith. 'Our Stacey looks a tad shaken.'

'I'm not surprised,' Marie said. 'She and Jay have been spending a fair amount of time out at the Teasel Woods caravan park recently. And it is a bit of a shock, you must admit. Ratty's been part of policing around here for donkey's years. He was quite famous. I bet there's not a copper for thirty miles that doesn't know of Ratty Jones and his mad mother.'

'Ah, yes. The mother.' Jackman called to Stacey and Jay. 'We need to break the news to Ma Jones, I'm afraid.'

Stacey nodded. 'We've just been talking about that, sir, and if it's all right with you, we'll do it. We aren't exactly on friendly terms, but at least we're familiar faces, and she understands we were trying to help him.' She gave Jackman a weary smile. 'Even if she'd never admit it.'

'Well, if you're okay with it, I suggest you go now. We don't want the grapevine getting to her first. News of this sort spreads like wildfire.'

The two left immediately.

'Okay, let's get the facts, shall we?' Jackman said. 'Marie, go and find the first responder and we'll see what we actually know.'

Marie went to speak to the uniforms. Jackman looked towards the house and saw two women huddled together in the doorway. One would undoubtedly be the householder, the other was probably a concerned neighbour or a friend.

Jackman stood looking down at the body. Poor Ratty was a pathetic sight. Most people would say he deserved his bad ending, considering all the people he'd frightened in his night-time excursions, but Jackman couldn't help feeling sorry for him. Ratty had led a pretty miserable existence. His only solace had been getting inside some stranger's house, a place where a normal, comfortable life was led. Just being there, completely unseen, touching the belongings, sitting in a chair for a moment or two, running a hand down curtains that had no holes in them.

Jackman sighed. Really there was no excuse for what Ratty did, but he was harmless. Unlike their other night stalker. The man now roaming their streets at night had malice on his mind, and an endgame that Jackman daren't even contemplate. And now he had the streets to himself.

'Guess who's the first responder, boss?' Marie had appeared beside him, accompanied by none other than PC Simon Laker.

'Glutton for punishment, aren't you, Simon?' Jackman said.

'Something like that, sir. I admit I did ask to be told if anything involving either of our two midnight cowboys turned up . . .' He stared down at the body. 'I only live a few roads away, so I was here as soon as it was rung in.'

'So, what occurred?'

'A local man, out walking his German shepherd. Suddenly the dog pulls him violently through the gate here and starts growling at something in the shrubbery. The owner investigated and found the body. He alerted us and then told the lady who lives here.' He pointed to the cottage. 'Her name's Miss Louise Armstrong — the woman on the right, sir, in the green half-jacket. She told me she'd heard something in the garden around midnight or so, but she has regular visits from foxes and hedgehogs — who can make one heck of a racket, apparently — so she didn't take any notice.'

'Have Forensics been called?' Jackman asked.

'Yes, sir. Should be here any minute. We've got everything ready for them. We're keeping everyone out of the garden area and temporarily blocking access into this end of the road. There'll be some contamination from the dog and the owner, but hopefully there'll be something for the SOCOs to find.' He looked at Jackman. 'Are we thinking this could be the work of our picture thief?'

Jackman shrugged. 'It's too soon to say, Simon, but we know he's more than capable of it.'

Marie pointed towards the road. 'Look. Spike and Cardiff. Forensics are here.'

Soon the two forensics officers were suited up and hauling their metal cases of equipment towards the tent.

'No Prof this morning?' asked Jackman.

'Up to his neck, sir,' said Spike. 'We had a lot come in last night, so he's sent the troops instead. Cardiff is photographer, and I'm playing Prof Wilkinson — forensically that is, I won't attempt the camp humour!' He looked at the body. 'Oh! A garrotting. I haven't had one of these since training. And this one's textbook: straight line ligature mark, probably far more force applied than necessary — common in garrottings.' He stood up. 'Okay, Cardiff, go for it. Special attention to the ligature mark, and his hands as well. He might have grappled with the killer and got some hair or skin under his nails.'

'You got it,' said Cardiff. 'And there's quite a bit of damage to the foliage around the site. Ah, I think I see a footprint. I'll get that for sure.'

'He's trained you well,' Marie said, impressed.

Beneath his mask, Spike smiled. 'Right, and this is the point where you ask about time of death, and I—'

'Faff around and keep us guessing — yeah, I know the routine,' said Marie. 'So how about you just give us your guesstimate and we can all save time.'

'From the general appearance, I'd say somewhere between midnight and two a.m.'

'Thank you, Spike. That didn't hurt too much, did it?'

'Just don't tell the prof that I caved in so easily. He'll be disappointed in me.'

'My lips are sealed,' Marie said.

While Jackman half-listened to their banter, his thoughts kept straying to Laura's patient. Was he dangerous? In what way? He forced himself to concentrate. 'So, that ties in with when Miss Armstrong heard what she thought was a hedgehog in the garden.' He turned to Spike. 'You'd say he died here, would you? Exactly where he's lying now?'

'No doubt about it, sir,' said Spike. 'No drag marks, nothing. He was waiting in the shrubbery, watching the house, and his killer attacked him from behind. He struggled with the attacker, probably trying desperately to get his fingers under the wire, failed and asphyxiated. You can see the face is congested and there are conjunctival petechial haemorrhages in his eyes. He died very quickly.'

One consolation, Jackman supposed.

'I'm surprised he went out at all, especially after being warned off by Stacey,' said Marie. 'To all appearances, he was terrified that he might get blamed for something the other man did.'

'From what I've heard, it was an obsession with him,' Jackman said. 'He probably couldn't help himself, and being cooped up with his mother got too much for him. I expect he never thought this other creep would go for him.'

'How wrong he was.' Marie glanced over at the cottage. 'Better go and speak to Miss Armstrong. She's probably a bit shaken.'

'Hello?' Cardiff had been busy behind the cordon. 'Nice clear print here, sir! The soil was recently dug over, so it's quite loose.'

'Can you tell what kind of footwear it is?' Jackman asked.

Cardiff checked her camera. 'We'll need to do a proper comparison, of course. But from the smooth sole and the logo, I'd say it's the same as the one we lifted from the house in Leetoft.'

'Curiouser and curiouser,' Jackman said.

'He's got rid of the competition,' Marie said. 'He wants the midnight hours to himself. But how did he know where Ratty would be? He hasn't been out for a while.' She exhaled. 'I'm guessing he's been watching Ratty for some time. He probably knew exactly where he and Ma Jones lived.'

'Well, he certainly followed him last night, didn't he? On his last nocturnal trip.' Jackman was surprised at how much this death had affected him. Ratty was hardly an upright, law-abiding citizen. Where was his usual detachment? *Come on, Jackman — concentrate.* 'Okay, let's talk to Miss Armstrong and then head back to the factory. Spike and Cardiff don't need us looming over them like a pair of vultures.'

'Speak for yourself,' said Marie with a grin. 'I'm nothing like a bloody vulture.'

For the first time that morning, Jackman smiled.

* * *

Stacey was dreading the visit to Ma Jones, and judging by his silence, so was Jay.

As they neared the caravan site, Jay gave a huge sigh. 'Hate this bit.'

'Me too,' said Stacey. 'It never gets any easier.'

'I did wonder. But I suppose you learn how to read people better, how they'll react?' Jay asked hopefully.

'Nope. You can never tell how anyone's going to take it.' She turned into Teasel Woods. 'Hello? What's all this?'

Parked in front of the Joneses' caravan was an ambulance and another vehicle. People stood around in groups, looking sombre.

Stacey pulled up and they hurried to the site manager's office. 'What's occurring, Mr Moore?'

'Old Ma Jones, Officer. She's dead.' The man's face was white. 'I found her.'

Stacey glanced at Jay. 'Why weren't we called, sir?'

Harry Moore looked puzzled. 'Why would I call you? I called an ambulance the minute I saw her, but it was too late. The other vehicle belongs to a first responder from the fire service.'

'How did she die?' asked Jay.

'Heart, I suppose. I wasn't actually in the caravan when they were dealing with her. They're still there, waiting for an undertaker to come and collect her. I've been trying to get hold of Ratty but his phone's switched off. He's gonna be devastated, poor sod. Oh, and his mate wants his car back. Where is the silly bugger? He oughta be here.'

Stacey decided not to say anything to Moore just yet. Ratty's mother dying at the same time as her son was just too much of a coincidence. It needed investigating. Meanwhile, the body was about to be carted off to the undertaker. 'Oh shit,' she murmured to Jay as they hurried across to Ma Jones's van, 'this could be a bloody crime scene, and the world and his wife have been tramping all over it. Jay, tell them not to move her, and get everyone out of there stat. I'm ringing the DI.'

Having made the call, she hurried over to where Jay was talking to the paramedics.

'Sorry, lads,' she said, 'but this may not be as simple as it seems. Can you tell me what you found when you got here?'

'The site manager called it in,' said the tall one. 'He knew the old lady always got up early and he noticed her curtains were still closed. He knocked but received no answer, so he went in using his emergency key. She was still in bed and didn't respond when he spoke to her. Des got here first,' he indicated to the fire service responder. 'When we got here it was clear she'd been dead some hours.'

'Nothing disturbed?' asked Stacey.

'It's a bit of a tip, but no sign of any struggle or anything. I'm sure she died in her bed.'

His crewmate added, 'We pronounced her dead, but just to cover our backs we rang the local doctor that deals with most of the people who live here. He said he'd seen her recently, and she wasn't in the best of health. Considering her age and her medical history, he wasn't surprised in the least that she'd died, so we were quite happy to contact the undertaker.'

'We'd have got you guys out here straightaway if we'd been in any way concerned,' the tall medic said. 'You know us, we call CID at the drop of a hat. We don't get paid enough to take the responsibility.'

'So what's the problem?' asked his crewmate.

Stacey lowered her voice. 'Her son was murdered last night — but keep that to yourselves for the time being.'

'Shit! I see why you're so bothered,' said his crewmate.

'Yeah, of course.' His colleague shook his head. 'That *is* weird, isn't it? He gets murdered, and his mother drops dead on the same night.'

'Even so,' said the tall one. 'I'd swear it was a natural death.'

'Let's hope so. Meanwhile, I'll have to wait for the DI, and then the pathologist if he thinks it's necessary.' She smiled at the two paramedics. 'I don't want to hold you lads up.'

While she waited for Jackman to arrive, Stacey began to wonder if she'd overreacted. Then she considered the way that Ratty had been murdered, in cold blood, and that his killer could also send a harmless ninety-year-old crashing down the stairs to her death. He could easily have suffocated another frail old woman.

DI Jackman and DS Evans arrived in the wake of the undertaker's black-windowed vehicle, looking like part of a funeral procession. Stacey was happy to leave it to them to decide about Ma Jones's end. Jackman assured her that she'd done the right thing and called the pathologist.

Stacey couldn't help thinking that mother and son might have died at exactly the same moment. Which meant, of course, that his killer couldn't have murdered her. But in a way, that made it all the more spooky . . .

She took a deep breath and went to help Jay disperse the people still loitering in hopes of seeing — what, exactly?

'There's nothing to see here, folks. Just go home now and let us do our job.'

Somewhat reluctantly, the people dispersed. 'You look shattered, Stace,' Jay said. 'You okay?'

She nodded.

He didn't pursue it, and she was grateful. What a lucky sod she'd been to get paired up with this remarkable young man. How different he was to the constables she usually encountered.

Half an hour later, Jackman called to them from the static. 'Cardiff's satisfied that it's death by natural causes. She suspects Ma Jones suffered a DVT in her damaged leg and a clot travelled to her heart, causing a heart attack. The old lady's being taken to the morgue.'

'Our two paramedics will be mightily relieved,' said Stacey.

'You might like to contact them, Stacey, and let them know there'll be no comeback,' said Jackman. 'We'll close up the caravan and make sure the site manager knows that no one goes in there until we say so.'

'Shall we tell him what happened, sir?' asked Jay.

The DI nodded. 'Yes, but just give him the bare bones. No details, and definitely no mention of a connection to the other murder.'

Stacey and Jay went to find their car. Stacey glanced at her watch and was surprised to see it was still only eleven in the morning. She'd had enough of today already.

# CHAPTER SIXTEEN

'Blimey, mate, we're a bit thin on the ground!' Kevin Stoner looked around the deserted CID room. Seated at his desk, Charlie Button was the only person left.

'Ratty Jones got taken out by the midnight stalker last night,' Charlie said. 'The boss and the sarge are out at the crime scene, Robbie is chasing up people connected to the women who had their pictures stolen, and Max isn't due in until later.'

Kevin took off his jacket and hung it over the back of his chair. 'I think I've hit on something important. It's about Nan Cutler.'

Charlie looked up, interested. 'Oh?'

'Our sweet old lady has a backstory that needs investigating. As far as I can tell, it involves a woman who's done a disappearing act, and a child, a boy. Other than that, I'm in the dark. I need to tell the boss. We'll have to dig deeper into her past.' He was sure this was the missing link in the chain. He'd seen it many times as a local bobby. You happened to speak to just the right person, the one with a little more inside knowledge than the others, and it sent you off on a trail that led to solving the case. And it was he, Kevin, who had gleaned this nugget from Nan's old church. Kevin badly wanted to prove himself in CID. He wasn't ambitious. He didn't want to outshine the others or anything like that, but he did want to prove himself worthy of the support DI Jackman had given him.

'Gary'll be back in a moment, Kev,' said Charlie. 'He's working the same line as you, isn't he? He'll be very interested.'

'Interested in what?' Gary appeared through the door carrying three coffees. He grinned at Kevin. 'I saw you come in, mate, so I grabbed you a drink too. What's occurred then?'

Kevin told him about his trip to Holy Trinity Church, and about the possible witch-hunt against Nan Cutler.

'Aha! So she's not the nosey parker she was made out to be. That is significant. And who is this Andrea Becker woman?'

'That's my first job for today.' Kevin logged into his computer.

'Want a hand? The lead I was following has turned out to be another dead end.' Gary sat at his desk and stared at the pile of memos in front of him. 'All my other enquiries so far show her to be a thoroughly nice woman, a good friend and very caring. Other than being a bit opinionated and fussy, I can't find anything actually malicious about her.'

'I'm sure my friendly churchwarden would agree with that,' said Kevin. 'What I want to do is find out where this Andrea woman went, and if she remarried. We need her new name — and we really need to talk to her.'

Gary was already looking at his screen. 'You say she lived in Connaught Road?'

'Yeah, which can't have been nice for Nan if she and this woman didn't get on.' He frowned. 'I reckon the place to start is with Nan's neighbours, Lizzie and Eric Coupland.'

'Right. I'll just do a swift check, see if the name Andrea Becker comes up anywhere, and if that fails, you and I could do some legwork.'

Some fifteen minutes later, Gary pushed his chair back. 'All I've come up with is a mention of an Andrea Becker doing the refreshments for a fun run, and that's three years ago. Apart from that, nothing. Not even a speeding ticket.'

Kevin grinned. 'Then we should hit the road. It'll be like old times, won't it? Nothing like a good old house-to-house.'

* * *

Half an hour later they were sitting in Lizzie Coupland's lounge drinking tea and eating home-made lemon drizzle cake. In her Black Sabbath T-shirt and ripped jeans, Lizzie certainly didn't resemble the perfect little housewife, but she made exceedingly good cake.

She sat opposite them, Iron Maiden mug in her hand, frowning. 'Andrea? Andrea Becker, you say?' She sipped the tea thoughtfully. 'Oh, I know who you mean — Andi! I never knew her surname. She was married to a lorry driver who was away a lot. I think his name was Felix. Good-looking man — German, I believe. He had lovely manners and very good English.'

'Can you tell us which house she lived in, Lizzie?' asked Gary.

'I'm not sure of the number but I can show you. It was near the bottom of the road on the right-hand side. More cake?'

'I daren't, thank you!' Kevin said. 'But it was delicious.'

Gary also refused, rather wistfully. 'Did you know her well, Lizzie?' he asked.

'No, not really,' she said. 'She was a funny bundle, as my mum would have said. Not my sort. A touch of kippers and curtains, I reckoned.' She smiled. 'All airs and graces — another of my mother's sayings. It means people who like you to think they're better than they really are. And this is pure gossip, so don't hold me to it, but we were all pretty sure she had another man on the go when hubby was away. I can't be doing with that. We make our choices and it's down to us to make the best of them. Take my Eric. He's certainly no oil painting, but he's got the heart of a blue whale. He has his faults, but don't we all?'

Kevin smiled. 'A "funny bundle." My gran used to say that too. But in what way was Andrea one?'

'Secretive. She was very secretive, and she always seemed to think you had a bad motive for everything you said. Like, I'd ask where Felix had gone off to. I knew he went on long trips, so I was just asking where he'd gone. You know, being polite, neighbourly. Well, Andi would give you a look that said, "Why do you want to know that?" In other words, "Mind your own business." On the surface she seemed like everybody's friend, but I got the feeling that there was a very different woman underneath. I gave up in the end.'

'But she was on the church committee at the Holy Trinity, and had — well, still has, apparently — some close friends there. That doesn't even sound like the same woman, does it?' asked Kevin.

She shrugged. 'I reckon all those good works were a cover for her infidelity. Either that or a guilty conscience. What I *do* know is that our Nan hated her. None of us dared even mention Andi's name in her hearing. She knew her from somewhere else, but I have no idea where. Andi only lived here for around eighteen months, then one day she was gone. Nan was practically dancing in the street!'

'But she never said why she hated her?' asked Kevin.

'Never. All she would say was that Andi was a wicked woman and she prayed that the good Lord would see fit to cast her into the fires of hell.'

'Blimey,' said Gary. 'So much for Christian forgiveness! I wonder what caused it?'

Lizzie shook her head sadly. 'I guess no one will ever know now.'

Kevin wasn't so sure about that. 'Did Nan ever mention a boy she was especially fond of, Lizzie? He would have been around ten.'

'Not directly, but I know there had been a child somewhere in her life. Not a grandchild though. We know all about them.' Lizzie looked pensive. 'It was just little comments she made, and then she got so emotional that I never liked to press her. I once showed her some school photos of our Tommy, and she looked at one and said, "Oh, what an angel. He looks so like my—" Then she flustered on about something else. That happened several times over the years. So yes, I'd say there had been a boy that was special to her.'

'But no one ever visited her with a little lad?' said Gary.

'Never. Most of her visitors were people from the church. Oh, and old Mrs Cooke. Now, if our Nan opened up to anyone, it would have been her. She and Avril Cooke go back years.'

'Where can we find her?' Kevin asked. This Avril sounded promising.

'Cedar Lodge. Warden-controlled flatlets in Doncaster Street. Ask anyone for Avril and they'll point you to her. She's in her nineties and fit as a flea. She has one of those mobility scooters, and every Thursday afternoon she used to hare around here for tea with our Nan. Regular as clockwork, she was. Even in the rain. She had one of those plastic covers, looked dead funny.' Her smile faded. 'Oh dear. She's going to miss our Nan something rotten.'

'Before we go, Lizzie,' Kevin said, 'did you know, or suspect, who Andrea was having an affair with?'

She stared into her tea. 'Look. It was just gossip, so please don't tell anyone what I said.'

Kevin smiled at her. 'This is all off the record, Lizzie. Just a chat. Your name won't come into it.'

'A man named Roger Hereward. I saw them together once or twice, but I never let on, not to anyone. He's married too, with three kiddies. I haven't seen Roger around for ages, and now I come to think of it, I never saw him again after she disappeared from Connaught Road. Rather points in one direction, doesn't it?'

'Very much so,' said Gary. 'Now, if you would just show us her old house, we'll leave you in peace.'

They walked almost the length of the street before Lizzie stopped. 'This was it. I'm afraid I don't know who lives there now, it's changed hands twice since Andi left. I suspect it's a rental these days.'

They thanked her and she trotted off home.

'The old lady with the mobility scooter sounds promising,' Gary said.

Kevin agreed. Before they left, they rang the bell of number thirty-two.

The door was opened by a middle-aged woman with a pronounced Eastern European accent. Kevin's heart sank. Whichever Baltic country this woman came from, one thing they all shared was a profound dislike of the police. The friendly neighbourhood bobby was unheard of in Eastern Europe.

He smiled at her and showed his warrant card. 'I'm sorry to trouble you, madam. We're from Saltern CID. We're trying to trace a woman who lived at this address a while ago, and we wondered if you could help us. Her name is Andrea Becker.'

The woman looked from his card to his face. 'I am sorry. I rent this house from my cousin. I know no one who was here before.'

Kevin knew a lost cause when he saw one. He thanked her and they left. 'One last try next door then it's off to Cedar Lodge. You okay with that, Gary?'

'Yup. You take the left and I'll do the right.'

The houses at this end of the road were pretty standard three-bed semi-detached. All were fairly well kept, with the exception of the old Becker house, which looked shabby by comparison. Kevin opened the gate to a very neat front garden, full of healthy-looking shrubs, along with various bird feeders and water bowls. He saw that the house had a name — Robbin's Nest, with two "b"s.

A grey-haired man opened the door and greeted him with a smile. 'Are you from the council?'

'Sorry, sir, no. The police.' Kevin offered his card.

'Oh, fine. Well, how can I help?'

'We're looking to trace a woman called Andrea Becker, sir. She lived next door a few years back, and we're anxious to find her.'

The man's smile disappeared. 'Oh. Her.'

Kevin saw Gary coming through the gate. No luck at his house, obviously.

'This is my colleague, sir. May we come in?' Kevin asked politely.

The man held the door open and stood aside. The lounge he showed them to was dated but tidy. 'Have a seat, Officers. I was expecting a visit from the local council about the rubbish in next-door's garden. It's going to attract rats before long. It was bad when the Becker woman left, but it's getting worse now.'

'I'm afraid we can't help you with that, sir, but anything you can tell us about Andrea Becker would be most useful.' Kevin flashed a hopeful smile.

'She left ages ago, her and her fancy man. Felix — that was her husband — was out driving that day. He was a long-distance lorry driver, and the poor devil had no idea what had been going on. He was devastated when he got back. I had to give him a brandy for the shock.'

'Did you know the man she left with, sir?' asked Gary.

'Skip the sir, Officer. My name is Don Robbins. They had no idea I knew him, but I've got a good memory for faces, and I recognised him as the owner of a builder's yard down near the station, name of Hereward. I'd see him sneaking in the back way when Felix was off on long haul.' He pulled a face. 'None of my business what folks get up to, but I was really sorry for Felix. He stayed on for around three months, but he couldn't hack it without Andi. The place was getting into a terrible state, so he sold up and moved on.'

'Do you have an address for him, Mr Robbins?' asked Kevin.

Don Robbins stood up. 'As a matter of fact, I do. I said I'd forward his mail for him. Our postie used to drop the letters off with me and I'd send them on.' He went out of the room to look for it.

'That's a stroke of luck,' whispered Kevin. 'The husband might well know about Nan Cutler and what happened to make them hate each other.'

Gary nodded. 'Absolutely, and I get the feeling Mr Robbins wasn't keen on her either.'

'Here it is.' Robbins was back, holding out a slip of paper. 'He lives Fenchester way now.'

'I gather you weren't too friendly with Andrea, Mr Robbins?' Kevin said.

Robbins looked uncomfortable. 'It had nothing to do with her infidelity. As I said, that was her business. But I'll be frank, she was a hypocrite, and that's something I can't tolerate. Say what you mean, say something decent or shut up. Don't say one thing to one and something different to another. She was little short of Mother Teresa to her cronies at the church, but I saw a different side. And it wasn't exactly spiritual.'

'Anything specific that you can remember?' asked Gary.

Robbins looked at them. 'Has this got anything to do with old Nan Cutler?'

'It's part of an ongoing inquiry, sir,' said Gary.

Don Robbins narrowed his eyes. 'Because one thing that does spring to mind is an argument I overheard between Andi and poor Nan.'

Kevin lit up. 'Do you recall what was said, Mr Robbins?'

'I'm not likely to forget. Andi was vitriolic. And they were both shouting at the top of their voices, so I couldn't help but hear.' He made a face. 'Actually, it was horrible. I can hear it now. Nan knocked on the door and asked Andi to stop bad-mouthing her at church. She said that yes, they had their differences, but that was personal, and they shouldn't air their dislike for each other in front of her friends. Andi called her an interfering old witch, and if she chose to meddle in other people's lives, she should expect consequences.' Don Robbins took a deep breath. 'Nan hissed back, "If you'd acted like a human being in the first place instead of a callous, heartless bitch, I'd never have had to interfere!"'

'That's harsh,' said Gary.

'Oh, it went from bad to worse. They got so heated I lost the thread a bit, but it was about a child — a boy, I think. Whatever had happened, Nan was extremely protective of this lad, while Andi got more and more vindictive. She said she'd see Nan drummed out of the church. As I said, it was horrible. In the end, I just had to go around. I could see Nan having a coronary or something if it wasn't stopped.' He sniffed. 'I got no thanks, of course, but it did break it up.'

'Can you recall if the boy's name was mentioned?' asked Kevin hopefully.

'Do you know, I've always wondered what could have been so serious as to cause such distress and anger between those two. I've been over and over that conversation in my head, and I think — only think, mind — I heard the name Teddy mentioned. Just once, that's all.'

'As in Edward?' asked Gary.

'I suppose. I'm not even a hundred per cent sure I heard it at all, but I think I did. Teddy, yes, that's it. Nan said something like that darling Teddy never deserving to be around a woman like Andrea.'

A child called Teddy. Kevin recalled the photo that had been torn from Nan's album. The one with the name ending in "Y". He glanced at Gary, who nodded slightly. He got to his feet. 'You've been a great help, Mr Robbins. We'll leave you our cards, and if you think of anything that might be relevant, or if you hear of anyone who knows the whereabouts of Andrea Becker, please call us.'

'I will.' Robbins showed them to the door. 'This is serious, isn't it? I mean, CID? You can't tell me it's a traffic violation.'

Gary patted his arm. 'We can't talk about an ongoing investigation, Mr Robbins, I'm really sorry. But as my colleague says, anything you think of, just ring us.'

Robbins stood watching them walk back to their car. He looked utterly baffled. Kevin laughed. 'I get the feeling our Don is a bit of an old gossip.'

'Thank heavens,' added Gary with a grin. 'What would we do without them?'

# CHAPTER SEVENTEEN

When Kevin and Gary got back, Jackman and Marie were in the CID room having just added the name Reginald 'Ratty' Jones to a new whiteboard.

'Ah, good,' said Jackman. 'As soon as Stacey and Jay get here, we're going to have a meeting. Charlie tells me you two are on to something?'

'Kevin is,' said Gary generously. 'He's done all the graft, I just rode shotgun.'

'Excellent. Go and grab a drink, the others are on their way back.'

Twenty minutes later the team were gathered in front of the whiteboards. Each reported any new information they had managed to garner, and Jackman gave a summary.

'So, it would appear,' he said, 'that either our killer doesn't want anyone else lurking in the shadows while he goes about his business, or Ratty saw something he shouldn't and had to be terminated. Whatever the motive, we don't think Ratty's death has anything to do with the murderer's main objective. And from what Kevin and Gary have found out, that could hinge on a child called Teddy.'

Kevin raised his hand. 'Sir, we could well find out more after lunch, when we go back to see Nan's old friend, Avril.

We called earlier but she was out at the hairdresser. We left a message to say we'd be back after two. She was close to Nan, saw her every single week, so if anyone knows something it'll be her.'

'I agree. Make that a priority, and well done for finding out what you did about this Andrea Becker. She needs finding and interviewing, as does her ex-husband, Felix.' Jackman looked at Max and Charlie. 'Would you two follow that up, please? I want Becker brought in here and interviewed, and remember, if her old neighbour and the churchwarden are to be believed, she's not the charitable, good-natured Christian her churchmates believed her to be. Read between the lines, and rattle her cage if you need to, okay?'

'Our pleasure, boss.' Max grinned. 'Charlie and I enjoy a spot of cage rattling, don't we, mate?'

Charlie smiled. 'Certainly makes a refreshing change from filing reports.'

'Right then. Robbie, can I leave it to you to chase up Forensics? Ask them if they would do the PM on Ma Jones as soon as possible. Beg if necessary. I have to know for certain that she died from natural causes. I need it officially confirmed. Her son was murdered, and she died on the same night. I must rule out any connection, wildly improbable as it would seem.'

'Leave it with me, boss,' said Robbie. 'I'll even take them a cake if it helps.'

'A bribe always helps, Robbie.' Jackman smiled. 'And a proper coffee might clinch the deal.' He turned to their three uniformed colleagues. 'Perhaps you'd pay a call on our four victims of the night stalker, and ask each one of them if a child called Teddy has any significance for them?'

Stacey, Jay and Simon nodded in unison.

'No problem, sir,' said Stacey. 'We'll do that this afternoon. Oh, and sir, we've located the car that Ratty used to travel to Peartree Cottage. He parked it about quarter of a mile away. Is it okay for the owner to collect it?'

'Yes, it won't be needed for forensics. Ratty just borrowed it to fool you guys.'

'And it worked,' Stacey muttered. 'I really thought we'd frightened him into staying at home. I wish I'd come down on him harder now.'

'Not your fault,' said Jackman. 'It's like an alcoholic needing a drink. He couldn't help himself.'

'Even so, I still feel bad. Not that I dreamed he was in danger. I just didn't want him getting in the way of our investigation or finding himself locked in a cell for something he hadn't done.'

'Apart from nailing his feet to the caravan floor, Stacey,' Jackman said, 'you couldn't have stopped him. He was an adult, albeit one with issues, so let it go. Our priority now is to find Teddy.'

* * *

Annie Carson slept better that night. She put it down to the fact that she was doing something concrete instead of wallowing in fear and self-pity. It was approaching lunchtime and she'd already located the address and phone number of the fourth victim of their night stalker. Natalie Miles lived in Old Fleet, and it just so happened that she was known to one of the other ladies, Sylvia Wilson. Sylvia had rung her earlier that morning. She said that the police had mentioned Natalie, but she hadn't thought about it at the time. Later, she realised that Natalie was a friend of her sister-in-law, Patsy, who also lived in Old Fleet. She had rung Patsy, who confirmed it. So, after lunch, she and Callum were going visiting again.

Just as she was preparing some lunch, her son came into the kitchen.

'Mum! There's been another murder. It's just flashed up on Facebook. One of my friends just sent me a video someone's posted showing all these police cars and CSIs in blue suits in a garden in Saltern. Do you think it's him? Has he killed someone else?'

Annie shivered. Her son was looking at her anxiously. 'I have no idea, but it could be, I guess.' Little point in lying

157

to the boy, he was bright enough to know it was perfectly possible.

'Then why don't you ring this other lady now, rather than drive there? You've got her number from Sylvia. You're always telling me not to put things off. I reckon you should get all those ladies round here this afternoon. This psycho is dangerous!'

She smiled at his enthusiasm. 'Okay, skipper, good idea.' She placed a plate of sandwiches in front of him. 'Eat up, and I'll go and ring her.'

It wasn't an easy call to make and it was pretty strained at first. Then Natalie began to see what she was trying to achieve.

'I'm sorry if I seemed a bit negative at first,' Natalie said. 'I'm still trying to come to terms with the thought of that beast being locked inside the house with me. It just keeps going round and round in my head. If Patsy hadn't come and stayed with me, I'm not sure how I'd have got through the night. I'm a bit of a wreck, I'm afraid. What you're saying does make sense though. I'll happily come over today if the others are going to be there. I think we have a lot to discuss. I just want to be home before nightfall.'

'Oh, naturally. I fully understand that. Let's say two thirty, and I'll let you know if there's any changes, okay?'

Natalie agreed, then asked tentatively, 'Could I bring Patsy with me? I have a back injury, so she'll be driving.'

Annie said that would be fine. She gave Natalie the address and her mobile number and ended the call. She then contacted the others, who all said they would come. She glanced at the clock. She had an hour and a half to tidy the house.

She went back into the kitchen, bolted her sandwich and made them both a drink. She then raced around, hoovering the lounge and tidying away the scattered books and magazines. She worried that she had no cake to offer, then remembered some chocolate biscuits she'd been saving. Those would do.

Sylvia was first to arrive, pleased to hear that her sister-in-law Patsy would be joining them. 'Now, there's a lass with her head screwed on,' she said. 'If we get too bogged down, our Patsy will get us thinking clearly again.'

Sylvia was right. They needed a Patsy. The rest of them were still too raw from their experiences and could well get overemotional. Her only concern was when it came to delving into their pasts, which could bring secrets to light. Would Callum's presence be a constraint? She supposed she'd just have to play it by ear. She really didn't want to send him from the room.

Soon, they were all seated in her lounge. Annie took a deep breath. 'I really appreciate you all taking the time to be here. I think we could be a great help to the police in getting this dreadful man off the streets.'

After a few shy moments, they were all chatting animatedly, sharing their experiences and fears. If nothing else, this meeting would be good therapy, Annie thought.

'Ladies,' she said, 'I expect that, like me, you were all asked by the police whether anyone had come into your house in the last few months — like plumbers or electricians, for example.'

'Who might have had the opportunity to check for photographs,' Fleur Harper said.

'That's right. In case you've forgotten, Callum has made a list of the kind of people you might have let in. Callum?'

Consulting his trusty notebook, Callum began to intone: 'BT or Openreach engineers, plumbers, electricians or central heating operatives . . .' The list was exhaustive.

Although all of them had had one or two from the list in their houses, none had visited them all. Annie went to make tea and left them talking.

After the drinks and biscuits had been handed out, Natalie, who had been very quiet up to now, suddenly said, 'I did have one caller, come to think of it.'

Everyone looked at her.

'A Sky engineer. He said he needed to check the serial number on the Sky box, as they were finding faults on a particular batch.'

'Me too!' Sylvia cried, 'I'd forgotten that. He was only there for a couple of minutes and said mine was fine.'

'And me,' added Fleur. 'Around three weeks ago it was.'

Then Annie remembered the 4x4 with Sky Sports emblazoned across the rear windscreen. A man in a blue-and-black polo shirt with Sky embroidered on the shoulder and an ID card around his neck had told her exactly the same thing. 'That's how he got in! That's our link, ladies. And I remember him clearly.' She described the man, and the others all agreed with her, adding odd details that they recalled, until they had a very good picture of him.

'Did anyone recognise him from anywhere?' Fleur asked.

'He was a complete stranger to me,' said Sylvia.

The others concurred.

'If none of us know him,' mused Annie, 'why did he pick on us?'

'It has to be something to do with those pictures of the boys,' said Natalie. 'But what?'

'Yes, what?' said a small voice.

Annie went to where her son was sitting perched on a footstool and hugged him. 'Sorry, my love. Would you prefer to go and watch TV or listen to your music? Maybe this is all a bit much for you.'

'No way! I'm one of those kids in the pictures you're talking about.' He paused. '*And* I'm the record keeper. You guys need me.'

'He's right,' said Patsy, speaking for the first time. 'Callum might just provide some insight that you're all missing. I think he's very useful. If he hadn't produced that brilliant list of possible callers, no one would have remembered the Sky engineer.'

'Which is a vital clue,' added Fleur. 'Now we'll be able to give the police a clear description of the night stalker.'

As the meeting began to wind down, Patsy helped Annie carry the cups out to the kitchen. 'Patsy,' Annie confided, 'I think we'll have to find a time to talk when my son's not around. I know I can't keep him off school forever, but he's all I've got now his brother's left home, and frankly until the police know what's going on, I'm terrified for his safety. But right now I want to find out if any or all of us has something, um, irregular in our past concerning the children in those photos. You know, like a custody battle or a doubt regarding parentage. Anything that could give rise to ill feeling. You don't kill an old woman of ninety for no reason at all, do you?'

'You're right there. But you're going to have a problem leaving Callum out of it, aren't you? Does he have a close friend whose parents would be willing to invite him out for a day? Or for a sleepover?'

'He's getting too old for those, and he's a bit of a loner now his brother has gone into the RAF.'

'Is his brother stationed locally?' Patsy said.

'RAF Marham in Norfolk. Not far at all. Why?'

'What would be the chance of a flying visit? Excuse the pun.' Patsy raised an eyebrow.

'Ah, right! Good idea! I'll text him tonight. If he can spend some time with Callum, I'll be able to slip out and meet you all alone. We've done really well today, but I think there's a lot more to it than this.'

'I hate to say it,' Patsy said, 'but I think you're right.'

Before they left, Annie addressed the group. 'I've been thinking. I would still rather the police didn't know we're meeting like this, in case they object. So maybe just one of us could ring and say she'd recalled the Sky man's visit?'

'Aha, and then they'd phone each of us and we could say, oh yes, we'd forgotten about him,' said Sylvia. 'So, Annie, would you ring and give them the description?'

'Happy to,' she replied. 'They'll have the information, and our mini-crusade remains a secret. Perfect.'

* * *

Not long after everyone had left, PC Stacey Smith and Jay Acharya knocked at Annie's door.

'Thank heavens for that,' said Stacey. 'At least you're in. We wanted to speak to everyone involved in these night-time visits, but the others are all out. Can we come in, please?'

Annie opened the door and showed them into the lounge, where Callum was just slipping his precious notebook under a cushion.

'How can I help?' she said, pointing to the sofa. 'And would you like some tea?'

'Er, no tea this time, thank you.' Stacey looked at her. 'Annie, does the name Teddy mean anything to you?'

'As in bear?' She frowned, puzzled.

'As in a boy's name,' said Jay.

Her frown deepened. 'No, not that I can think of. It's a bit old-fashioned, isn't it?'

The two police officers turned to Callum. 'Do you know anyone with that name, Callum?' asked Stacey.

He shook his head. ''Fraid not. I've never met anyone called Teddy.'

'Can I ask who this Teddy is, and why he's so important?' Annie said.

Stacey and Jay glanced at each other. Jay said, 'It's just a name that's been mentioned in connection with Nan Cutler. We're following it up, in case there's a link to the photographs.'

'I'm really sorry, Officers, but it means nothing to me.'

Annie watched them go. Teddy. Did one of the others know who he was?

# CHAPTER EIGHTEEN

Kevin and Gary were lost in admiration. With her friendly face and gentle waves of silver hair, Avril Cooke could have passed for a woman in her seventies. They offered their condolences on the death of her friend. She told them how much she had enjoyed Nan's company, saying she would miss their weekly visits.

'We understand that Nan fell out with a woman from her church, someone who lived in the same street as her.'

'Oh, the Becker woman,' Avril said dismissively.

'Can you tell us what it was about?' Kevin asked.

'Has *she* got something to do with Nan's death? Only it wouldn't surprise me. Wicked, wicked woman!' Avril's eyes filled with tears.

Kevin leaned forward and touched her hand. 'Please, don't distress yourself, Avril. She didn't cause Nan's death. We need to know as much as we can about Nan and her life and why she felt so strongly about Andrea Becker, so we can build up a picture of what happened.'

'You were her dear friend,' Gary said. 'She might have confided in you. We need to know the truth in order to catch whoever did this to her. Please, if you know something, tell us. For Nan's sake.'

Avril seemed to rally. 'My dear young men, I wouldn't think of keeping anything to myself if it would help catch the person who ended her life so cruelly. Nan is dead now, nothing I say can hurt her anymore. Ask me anything you like. But I have to say, I don't know as much as you seem to believe. So . . .' She took a deep breath. 'During her long life, Nan did a lot of volunteer and charity work, especially after her husband died. She was a Samaritan, and she helped out as a volunteer counsellor at a women's refuge. There, she provided many women with an impartial listening ear and a shoulder to cry on. That was where she met Andrea Becker.'

Kevin noticed the way she almost spat the name out.

'Now. You need to understand what kind of woman Becker really is. And that isn't straightforward.' She paused for a moment, thinking. 'Andrea Becker had a magnetism that attracted people to her. She appeared to be in control of everything — the ideas person, the organiser. Beneath that capable exterior lay a need to gather vulnerable women around her so she could feed off their praise and adulation. The refuge and the church were ideal places to meet such women.' Avril frowned. 'I'm talking from experience, because she almost bewitched me too, at one point.'

'Go on,' Kevin urged.

'Anyway, you want to know about Nan's experience, not mine. It began at the refuge. Becker was also a volunteer there and appeared at first to be a veritable angel. She seemed to have endless time for the damaged women and their children.' She grunted. 'Of course she did. She was revelling in their adoration. To start with, Nan supported her and admired her apparent selfless dedication to helping others. Then she began to see through it.'

'How?' asked Gary.

'Nan thought Andrea was getting too involved with one or two of the women, and was doing more than listening, which was all they were supposed to do. Becker was suggesting that they deal with their issues in a certain way, and imposing her own, sometimes radical, ideas.'

Kevin knew that counsellors should never interfere or voice their opinions. He could see why Nan Cutler would have become concerned.

'Then a woman that Nan happened to know came into the refuge. Her name was Claire, but I can't recall her surname. They weren't close friends. If that had been the case, Nan would have had to keep well away from her. As it was, she knew something of Claire's situation.' Avril sighed. 'Claire had her little boy with her.'

'Teddy,' Kevin said.

She raised an eyebrow. 'You know about him?'

'No, we've just heard the name mentioned,' said Gary.

'Teddy was the perfect example of a child caught in the middle of a toxic relationship.'

'Is there a reason why you're speaking of him in the past tense, Avril?' asked Kevin.

'It's not what you're thinking,' she said. 'It's just rather a long time ago now. I'm afraid I never did know what happened to Teddy. One day Nan stopped speaking about him, and that was that.'

'Can you tell us what you did know up to that point?' Gary said.

'Well, Nan told me that Andrea Becker became almost obsessed with this Claire, and also with her son. The next part is vague, because Nan became so agitated whenever the name came up. I never did get to hear the whole story, but I believe that somehow Becker managed to convince Claire that she and the boy would be better off living with her instead of in the refuge. I think she told Claire that the child would have his own room. Said they'd have a much better life until somewhere could be found for Claire and him to live safely away from her husband. Nan became quite close to the lad and began to fear for him. I think he told her quite a lot about his father and mother's relationship. He also described all the wonderful things Andrea had said he could have if they went and stayed with her. You know young boys, they're easily impressed, and he hated life in the refuge. Nan did everything she could to convince them to stay. But one day, when Nan arrived, she was told they had gone.' Avril sighed. 'She was utterly devastated, but never really explained why. I believe she knew something about Andrea that had scared her badly. For weeks, she fretted over Teddy. Then something happened. Don't ask me what it was, but after that, no matter how hard I tried to encourage her to talk, she never mentioned Teddy again.'

'Could you give us the name of the refuge, Avril?' Kevin said. 'They'll have records, I'm sure. We need to know Teddy and Claire's surname.'

'I'm sorry, my love, but Nan never said. As you well know, those places don't advertise themselves. No one who has anything to do with them, including the women who stay there, can divulge the address or telephone number, for fear of abusive partners finding them.'

'We have lists at the station,' said Gary. 'What town was it in? We'll check it out.'

'Right here in Saltern-le-Fen,' Avril said.

'Ah, well that simplifies things. We have two listed. Let's hope they have a record of Teddy.' Gary scribbled in his notebook.

'One small point,' added Avril. 'Unfortunately, it won't help you two lovely policemen. Teddy wasn't his real name. It was a pet name that Nan used. I have no idea of his proper name.'

*Great!* thought Kevin. Another stumbling block.

They thanked Avril for her help and made their way back to the station. As he drove, Kevin said, 'I'm not sure our Claire and her boy are going to be as easy to trace as we'd hoped. If they were accepted into a refuge here in Saltern, they wouldn't be locals. They could have come from anywhere.'

'That went through my mind too,' said Gary. 'Refuges only accept women from out of the area, it's safer that way. And there's nothing to say that Claire is her real name either. Women often adopt another name to make it harder for their abusers to find them.'

*Oh boy.* Kevin's excitement was fading fast. So much for pinning all their hopes on Avril Cooke. They had certainly learned something, but was it enough to move the case forward?

\* \* \*

Jackman and Marie listened to Kevin and Gary's story. To their evident surprise, a slow smile spread over Jackman's face. 'Don't look so downcast, lads. There's one thing that stands out to me, and it might answer a simple but very important question.' He paused, watching for their reactions. 'You said Nan became close to the boy she called Teddy, and Teddy told her quite a lot about his mother and father's relationship, did you not?'

Kevin nodded, then groaned. 'Oh, of course! You think that's the reason Nan had to die.'

Jackman nodded. 'I do. We've been wondering all along if Nan knew something, and now we know she did. I think it's Teddy's father who's stealing pictures and killing people. His son told Nan something, and whatever it was got her killed.'

Marie let out a low whistle. 'I've been wondering why I keep remembering that old case — the father at the school gates, desperately hunting for his estranged children. Our killer is looking for his son, isn't he?'

'It would fit,' Jackman said. 'Picture the scenario. Wife can't stand any more of his abuse and checks herself and their son into a refuge out of the area. He spends ages looking for them until, somehow, he discovers where they went. But did he find them? Or did they move on again?'

'I'm betting they got away, or why would he still be hunting for his son?' said Marie.

'What if, in desperation, the mother surrendered the child to social services,' said Kevin, 'and the father's trying to find where the boy has been fostered?'

'Maybe.' Jackman went across to the whiteboard and stared at the photos of the boys. 'They're of a similar age, but there are differences in appearance, even hair colour.'

167

'Maybe the mother coloured the boy's hair,' said Gary. 'But you'd know your own child, surely? I mean like . . . immediately?'

'What if he doesn't actually know him,' said Kevin pensively. 'What if the mother took the son away from him much longer ago?'

'Go on . . .' Jackman said.

'Well, say the father's been in jail, for instance. Mother never takes the kid to visit, never sends photographs, maybe never visits herself. Then he gets out and wants to see his son. Maybe he's aggressive, even dangerous. She's terrified and takes off with the boy. He traces her to this area, and, well—' he held up his hands — 'who knows what happened next?'

Jackman nodded slowly, then looked across to Marie. 'I do believe that our Kevin has come up with a very believable chain of events, don't you, Marie?'

'Startlingly believable, I'd say! Smart thinking, Kev.'

Kevin shrugged. 'I could be way off, but even if the actual circumstances are different, he could still be hunting for a son he either hasn't seen for a long time or has never seen at all.'

'Well, I think we start with trying to discover the identity of the woman known as Claire. There are only two registered women's refuges in this area, one run by Women's Aid and the other by Shelter. So we tackle them first, and we do it by phone. We can't have men in plain clothes turning up unannounced. You know how it works. If anyone needs to go in person, it should be Marie or Stacey.' He looked over to where Robbie, Max and Charlie were still working at their desks. 'Max? Charlie? Any progress with Andrea Becker or her husband yet?'

Max looked up. 'Can't find the woman yet, sir, but we've made contact with Felix Becker. He's now living in Leicester with his sister. He's coming in to see us tomorrow morning, and he's bringing a photograph of his ex-wife.'

'Excellent. That'll be a great help. All we have is a fuzzy image from a newspaper clipping about a church function, which could have been anyone.'

'I'm not sure he'll be too much help, boss,' said Max. 'I reckon she damaged him badly.'

'Even so, it will help build up a clearer picture of her.' He looked at Charlie. 'Do we know if she actually did go off with this Hereward, the owner of the builder's yard?'

'No, sir,' Charlie said. 'She ditched him soon after she did a runner from Felix. I get the feeling Hereward was a means to an end, and once she'd got away, she dropped him too. He crept home to his wife, only to face divorce. Becker's proving very hard to trace.'

'Keep at it, Charlie,' said Jackman.

Robbie was just setting his desk phone back in its cradle. 'That was the prof, boss. He hasn't finished the post-mortem yet, but he wanted you to know that all early indications show natural causes for Ma Jones's death. He said it looks as though Cardiff was right about a blood clot from her leg.'

Well, that was something. It was sad that she'd died alone, but at least she hadn't been murdered, and she hadn't had to suffer the shock of hearing how her only son had died. 'Okay, I think for now we can assume that Ratty Jones was an accidental victim. He simply got in the way.'

The door to the CID room opened and Stacey and Jay entered, looking excited.

'Sir,' said Stacey, 'Annie Carson called. She told us she had a visit from a Sky engineer who came into her house to check for a faulty Sky box. She gave us a pretty good description too. We rang the others, and they'd all had visits from the same engineer. We believe that's how he knew where the photographs were, sir.'

This was a step forward. 'So, what *does* our man look like?' he asked.

'White male, approximately five foot ten or eleven, smartly cut brown hair, rather sharp features, appeared an athletic type, but not muscly — thin, more like a runner than a weightlifter. He was wearing black workmen's trousers with multi-pockets and a black leather belt, and a blue-and-black polo shirt with SKY embroidered on the right shoulder. Annie said he sounded like a southerner, maybe London but not Cockney.' Stacey closed her notebook.

Jackman wondered at this. 'That's very detailed, isn't it, for a man who was only in her home for a short time.'

'Annie is very observant, sir,' said Stacey. 'Plus she's cursing herself for forgetting. She told us he made a point of having her check his ID card before he came into the house. She said he was friendly and polite, and she thought at the time that it made a refreshing change from some of the workmen and engineers who'd come to the house. Sadly, she can't recall the name on the card.'

'Even so, I'm surprised that all but one of the women forgot to mention him,' Jackman said.

'We decided it was because of the trauma they had all suffered, sir,' said Jay. 'They're all still reeling from it, so it's not surprising they forget things. And as Sylvia Wilson said, it was such a fleeting visit, and required no further action. Basically, he just checked the serial numbers.'

'Put like that, Jay, you're probably right.' Jackman turned to the whiteboard and stared at it. He then walked across to the second whiteboard and tapped the image of the man hanging around at the school gates. 'We should show this to Annie Carson, see if it rings bells, although I think this guy is shorter than the one she describes and possibly less wiry.' He looked at Stacey. 'Show her anyway. If our killer is looking for his boy, then it stands to reason he'd be watching the schools.'

Jackman looked at the clock. 'We can't do too much more this afternoon, but we've made good progress today. Let's keep up the momentum. Tomorrow, we have new avenues to follow. Robbie, check out Sky and those serial numbers, please, but Felix Becker is your main priority.'

'Yes, boss.'

'Stacey and Jay, you stick with Annie, and also that guy haunting the school gates.' He paused. 'By the way, where's Simon?'

'He went back out to check on the owner of Peartree Cottage, sir,' said Stacey. 'He was concerned about her, plus he wondered if any of the other houses along there might have home surveillance cameras in their gardens. Our mates have done a house-to-house, but he thought we might get more from their CCTV.'

'Good move. If you see him, ask him to keep me updated.' He turned to Kevin, Gary and Marie. 'Our main objective will now be Claire and Teddy. Marie, you can start with the women's refuges. Gary and Kevin, join in with Charlie and find out where the hell that Becker woman went when she left Hereward. Thank you everyone for all your hard work.'

Jackman felt more positive about the investigation now. If this was a father hunting for a son that he hadn't seen in years, or maybe had never seen, it would answer some of the questions — like why steal photos of different boys? The answer was that he *had* to, because he didn't know what his son looked like now.

As the others worked away, Jackman decided it was time to go and update the super. Ruth would be relieved to hear that their investigations were moving forward, albeit not as fast as she would have liked. He started up the stairs, then stopped halfway and took out his phone. He hadn't had the chance to ask Sam if he could stay for a while. So far, every time he started to broach the subject, Laura appeared.

'Hello, Sam. Jackman here. Are you free to talk?'

Sam said that he was, and Jackman explained how anxious he was about Laura being alone at Mill Corner while she was seeing this rather disturbing patient.

'I don't think for a moment that he's a danger to her, Jackman,' said Sam. 'After all, he's pinned all his hopes on her.'

'And if she decides that she and this man "don't fit" — isn't that how you put it? — might he not be upset? And if he's unstable, we all know how unpredictable these patients can be if their equilibrium is disturbed.'

Sam said, 'For your peace of mind, my friend, of course I'll stay for a while. But, please, try not to worry unduly. I promise I'll give you my impression after I've seen the young man for myself, and if I find him in any way unsettling, I'll make quite sure that she doesn't see him again.' He chuckled. 'Now, what excuse do I make for inviting myself to stay?'

'Let's stick to the truth, Sam. This case I'm on is ramping up, so I'm going to be working some very late nights, and it will give you the opportunity to discuss her patient with her while I'm out of the way.'

'I'll tie things up here and be at Mill Corner by late tomorrow afternoon, okay?'

'Perfect! And thank you, old friend. I owe you one.'

Jackman walked into Ruth's office with a much lighter tread.

## CHAPTER NINETEEN

Annie Carson was just about to prepare supper when her phone rang. It was PC Jay Acharya.

'I'm sorry to bother you, Annie. But I wondered if I could ask you a personal question? I promise it's pertinent to the investigation.'

'Okay . . . go ahead.'

He cleared his throat. 'We need to know if Callum is your natural son or if he's adopted. As I said, it could be important.'

'I gave birth to Callum in Saltern Cottage Hospital, the year before it closed down.'

'I appreciate that, Annie,' said Jay. 'Thank you, and I'm sorry I had to ask.'

'Why did you want to know?' she said.

'It's an avenue we are following, Annie. Nothing for you to worry about. But there is one other thing. We have a photograph of a man. It's not very clear, I'm afraid, but if I emailed it to you, could you tell me if you think it might be your Sky engineer?'

'Of course. You have my email address, send it now and I'll look at it straightaway. Hang on.'

The attachment came through. Jay was right, it wasn't clear at all. 'Sorry, Jay, but even though it's pretty grainy and you can't see his face properly, I'd say no. This man is a different build to the one who came here, and I think he's younger too. I'd put our bogus engineer in his late thirties, early forties. This man looks younger than that.'

After the call, Annie went to the fridge and took out an open bottle of rosé. She poured a glass and sipped slowly, wondering about what he'd said. Why would the police want to know if Callum was adopted? Annie called Sylvia and asked her if she'd had a call from the police. She had. One of her two grandsons was adopted — the old story of trying unsuccessfully for years, adopting a baby and then falling pregnant.

After that, Annie phoned the rest of them. All had been asked the same question. Two of the four boys were adopted.

By the time she'd finished her wine, Annie had worked it out. She rang Patsy and told her.

'You're right. Your unwanted visitor is looking for a particular child, isn't he? Maybe it's his.'

'That's what I thought,' said Annie. 'And I can't help feeling some relief, because it puts my Callum out of the running. No matter how many times they tell me the killer never visits the same house twice, I'm terrified for my boy. Now I'm even thinking about him returning to school after the weekend.'

'I'd feel the same in your place, Annie,' said Patsy. 'And I thought the way you handled the police was very clever. I understand why you want to keep our meetings a secret. They might think you'd formed a vigilante group and intend to take the law into your own hands.' She paused. 'Have you had a chance to contact Andrew yet?'

'Yes. He's got a forty-eight-hour pass. He's coming tomorrow morning and staying the night, so I'll be able to get away without Callum.'

'Would you like me to ring the others and sort out a time and a venue?' Patsy offered. 'I can text you, so that Callum doesn't get suspicious.'

'That would be great. Thanks, Patsy.'

Patsy's text came after dinner. Callum had just declared that he was going to tidy his room, ready for his brother's arrival.

*2.30 at Natalie's in Old Fleet. See you there. P*

Excellent. Annie was certain now that she and the three other women had not been chosen at random. Now they just had to discover the reason.

\* \* \*

It's hard to deceive a psychologist. Jackman was on his way home and wondering what Laura would think about Sam suddenly coming to stay when he'd always refused to do so in the past. Maybe she'd ignore her suspicions in her pleasure at having him around. Sam was the father she'd never had, after losing her real one far too early.

Jackman determined not to act the mother hen this evening. He had to try and hide his anxiety over this patient and what he might do.

\* \* \*

Marie, on the other hand, was perfectly relaxed, and looking forward to dinner with Ralph after a satisfying day. Tomorrow, she had an appointment with the supervisor of the larger of the two women's refuges. She had provided the supervisor with the dates she was interested in, thanks to Avril, and the supervisor could easily check their records for the details of Nan's time with them. An added bonus was that a woman who still worked there remembered Nan, so she'd hit on the right place.

Marie rifled through her wardrobe. How come every single item of clothing she possessed was either motorcycle gear or workwear? Maybe it was time to do a little shopping. Fine, but it didn't solve tonight's problem, did it?

They were going to a new restaurant that had opened in a pub just outside Saltern-le-Fen. According to Ralph, it had a tempting vegetarian menu, and he was delighted to have an opportunity to try it. Marie was delighted too, but it had nothing to do with the menu. When her husband died, her life had gone with him. Only by riding hard on her motor-bike could she recapture some of the joy she had once known. Now she felt as though a breath of spring had stirred her dull existence, like a new leaf unfurling. She thought of Gary. Did he feel the same, now that he was possibly embarking on a new life with this woman? Neither of them had meant to turn into loners, life had just sent them down that path. Now they were both treading new ground.

She opted for a simple white silk T-shirt, black trousers and a smart black leather blazer that she was surprised she could still fit into, considering its age. She completed her hastily assembled outfit with a beautiful silver and jet necklace that her mother had given her for her twenty-first birthday.

Ralph had offered to pick her up, but mindful of their nocturnal rambler, she said she would meet him at the restaurant, so she could use her car if anything occurred.

It was probably for the best. After so long alone, it would be too easy to rush headlong into an affair that she might later regret. She told herself to take it slowly and enjoy the journey.

Ralph was getting out of his car when she drove into the car park. He waved, his pleasure at seeing her hard to miss. He kissed her lightly on the cheek. 'So glad you made it. We'd better go in and eat, in case one of us gets a call.'

'Lead on,' she said happily. 'I'm starving.'

Marie was mildly shocked when she saw the prices on the menu, but Ralph merely said, 'Tonight is on me. Have whatever you want.'

It was a shame they had to settle for a single glass of wine each, but that was how things were in their job. Ralph smiled mischievously. 'We'll make up for it when we get some proper days off. I've got a bottle of red from Fortnum and Mason at home, just waiting to be shared. We'll celebrate.'

'Celebrate what?' she asked.

'Anything you like. Maybe the fact that I have a rich uncle who gives me wine from Fortnum and Mason. We'll find something.'

Marie laughed. 'Who needs an excuse anyway?'

Conscious of the prices, Marie chose a fairly basic main course, but Ralph put on a stern expression. 'I'm not having that. This is a treat. Push the boat out and go for a starter too. I'm having one.'

It was inevitable that the conversation would turn to work. They were both police officers, so what else would they talk about? Time passed far too quickly. There was so much to learn about this man, and Marie wanted to know all of it, right now.

'I could get used to this,' she said as she sipped her coffee. 'Taking time out, I mean, not spending a fortune in restaurants.'

'Me too,' said Ralph. 'Er, I was wondering if I could tempt you to a meal at my place at the weekend? I'm not a bad cook, or so I'm told.'

Briefly, Marie hesitated. Was it too soon?

But she knew all too well that life was short. She smiled at him over her coffee cup. 'I'll be the judge of that, shall I? Nut cutlets, is it?'

'You wait, Marie Evans! You'll be surprised. You learn to become inventive when you remove meat from your diet.'

'Then bring it on. Saturday evening?'

'Come straight from work. Don't change or anything, just come as you are, and we'll have a relaxed evening.'

Marie smiled again. She'd been doing a lot of that this evening. She approved. It was nice to dress up occasionally, but equally nice to just be yourself. 'Well, okay — if you can hack motorcycle leathers.'

'No problem.'

When they were the only two people left in the restaurant, they decided they'd better leave. These few hours had been the most relaxing she had spent in a long, long time.

* * *

While Marie and Ralph sipped their glasses of wine, Gary Pritchard was seated in his favourite armchair, a glass of brandy and a cup of coffee at his side, chatting on the phone. Twenty minutes, he estimated, and not a single mention of crime, murder or persons unknown lurking in the shadows.

Gilly was easy to talk to, and after the lying thieves and thugs he usually interacted with, her open and easy-going conversation was a rare treat. She seemed so straightforward. They had met several times at his friend John's house, and had gone out together twice — once for a drink in her local pub, the second time to a restaurant in Saltern town. He was already looking forward to another meeting but didn't want to seem pushy. He dared not expect too much.

'Look, Gary, I don't know how you're fixed for the weekend, but it's Nancy and John's wedding anniversary. They wondered if you would join us at the Old Talbot Inn for a meal on Saturday evening?'

Gilly had sounded casual, but was that a hint of hopeful expectancy in her voice?

'As long as the investigation doesn't get too intense, I'd love to,' he said.

'Wonderful! I'll ring and tell them later.'

After another ten minutes or so, Gilly said she'd better say goodnight as she had a couple of other calls to make.

Gary felt like a love-struck teenager, reluctant to be the first to hang up. When, after several final goodbyes, they finally ended the call, he sat for a while with his eyes closed. This woman seemed to understand the importance of his work and accept that arrangements might be cancelled at the last minute. Like him, Gilly had never been married before, but he sensed that somewhere in her past there had been heartbreak. So they had that, too, in common. Maybe they could make it work.

\* \* \*

As darkness fell, not everyone was bidding a tender farewell to a new love. Although this was about love, wasn't it? A love more powerful than a sweet boy-girl romance. This love would last for eternity.

Hidden in the shadows of a derelict summerhouse, he watched. Here, there were no open windows enticing him to come inside. Every curtain was tightly pulled. There was a forbidding atmosphere to the old property. He was not welcome here. Something about this building just did not feel right. The house he had so carefully selected for tonight's *sortie* felt more like a baited trap. Well, it didn't have to be tonight, did it? He'd waited so long for this, it would be foolish to spoil it all through mere impatience.

He turned and slipped away.

* * *

It was one thirty in the morning, and a kid called Baz sat in a petrol station kiosk, waiting for the weirdo on the forecourt to bugger off. He wanted to go home. He'd locked all the doors and was praying that someone, preferably a beefy six-foot-tall lorry driver, would pull in for fuel.

The guy must be stoned, Baz decided. He was on something a lot stronger than booze, anyway. Now he was sitting on the kerb by the diesel pumps, muttering to himself.

Baz had thought about calling the Old Bill, but he knew what they'd say. Just a drunk, deal with him yourself. Tell him to sod off home and sleep it off.

Baz stared out of the kiosk window. Lit up in the harsh glare of the strip-lights, he felt like a goldfish in a bowl. Talk about a sitting fucking duck. His dad would sort the nutjob out all right, but at this time of night he'd probably be paralytic himself. Baz had no choice but to wait until the idiot wandered off again.

He idly wondered about the reinforced glass in the kiosk. How strong was it really? What if the guy turned nasty and lobbed a brick or something — would it hold? There was a lot of money in the safe and no one had collected it tonight.

He stared at the wacko on the forecourt. Why the hell didn't someone pull in? A car full of leery lads, a traffic car even. The local Burger King had closed for a refit, so they would sometimes pull in here for crisps or a sandwich. Just not when he needed them. Baz sighed. Tomorrow he was off to Tesco to try and get a job stacking shelves. He wasn't going to have another night like this, no way.

Suddenly, the man jumped up and ran towards him, throwing himself at the glass with his palms against it, and staring. He didn't seem to see Baz in there. Baz cried out, started back. Then he saw the guy's shirt front. It was stained dark red.

This time, Baz didn't hesitate. He grabbed his phone and dialled 999.

# CHAPTER TWENTY

The first thing Jackman did on arriving was to check through the log of overnight calls and incidents. He was still reading it when Marie arrived. Jackman smiled at her cheerful face and decided to leave off worrying about her new boyfriend.

She sat down opposite him. 'Morning, boss. I gather from the absence of nocturnal telephone calls that our man gave us a night off?'

'Morning, Marie. Seems that way. Nothing reported from Uniform. In fact, apart from an RTC on the main road and some drunk terrorising a petrol station attendant, the night passed without incident.' He noticed that she wasn't wearing leathers. 'Left your brute of a Tiger in the garage today?'

She nodded ruefully. 'I saw the weather forecast before I came out. The warm spell is about to break. Heavy rain and high winds coming in later today, so I opted for the car.'

'At least driving rain will make it more difficult for our Spiderman,' Jackman said. 'People close their windows, and drainpipes can be treacherous. If we're lucky, we could have more than one night off.' He recalled that bad weather had deterred even Ratty Jones.

'It would certainly help us. We need every hour we can grab to try and fathom out what happened to send this man off the rails — and to find out who the hell he is,' Marie said.

'The thought of some youngster being hunted down by a man as dangerous as this is scaring the life out of me.' Jackman leaned back in his chair. 'So, what's your first move today, Marie?'

'Well, I've located the refuge where Nan Cutler used to volunteer, and I have an appointment with the supervisor at nine thirty. She's meeting me in a café close to the refuge, so as not to upset the occupants. I've given her all I have on Andrea Becker and this woman called Claire and her son, so we'll have to just cross our fingers that they keep good records.'

'Let's hope so. Teddy, whoever he is, is the key to this case—' There was a sharp knock on his door and a breathless Stacey Smith leaned around it. 'Sir! The guy who haunts the school gates has been seen at a nearby primary school. I'm on my way, and I'll update you as soon as I have him.' And she was gone.

He and Marie looked at each other. Maybe this would be a good day.

Stacey's visit was followed almost immediately by the entrance of PC Simon Laker, looking almost as excited as Stacey.

'Sir, I've got a picture of our killer.' He placed a print-out in front of Jackman. 'He triggered a nocturnal wildlife camera that one of the houses close to Peartree Cottage had set up to look for badgers. It's a high-resolution camera, and the picture quality is remarkable. I extracted this one from a video clip.'

'Good work, Simon,' said Jackman. 'You really are making an effort.'

'I've got a nine-year-old son, sir. I once took him to the County Fair and lost him. Only for about a quarter of an hour, but it was the worst fifteen minutes of my whole life. I can't bear the thought of the children in those photos being in danger.'

Marie glanced at the image. 'This is very good for a night camera.' She turned to Jackman. 'I suggest we get a copy of this to Annie Carson. See if she recognises her Sky man.'

'We'll get one to each of the women whose homes the killer got into. If they all agree it's him, we'll finally have a description of our man. Can I leave that to you, Simon? Stacey and Jay are off after the schoolyard stalker.'

'Straightaway, sir.'

Simon almost ran off.

'Dare I say it?' Marie raised an eyebrow.

'Uh-uh. Don't jinx it.' He looked down at the image. 'This fits Annie's description, doesn't it?'

'It does,' said Marie, glancing at her watch. 'Better get myself over to that café. Hopefully, we'll get some good news there too.'

'Then I'll stick around and see what Stacey turns up with from the school gates. As soon as he gets here, I'm going to watch the interview with Felix Becker. I'll let the lads talk to him and observe through the camera relay. I'm very interested to hear what the ex-husband has to say about his former wife.'

'Poor sod,' muttered Marie, standing up.

'Indeed. Love leads us to make some very poor choices sometimes.'

'Oh, very philosophical for nine in the morning, boss. I'm off before you get too profound. Ta-ta!'

* * *

As soon as Jackman walked into the interview room and saw the white-faced young man, he knew that this was not their killer.

He was a smartly dressed man of around thirty, with good quality clothes and neat hair. He had given his name as David Michaels, and he swore that he was not doing anything untoward, just his job.

'Okay, Mr Michaels, and what exactly do you do for a living? Not many jobs require you to hang around school gates watching little children.'

'This one does!' he said. 'I'm a private detective. Look at the ID you people took off me when you brought me in. I'm fully licensed and I'm working for a client.'

'I'll need your client's name and contact details for verification, Mr Michaels. Now, can I ask what you're looking for exactly?'

'A young woman named Ellie Carpenter and her two children. There's a file on my phone, which you've also taken. Their details are all there, including photographs. She did a runner with another man, and her husband is trying to find her.' David Michaels was starting to relax a little. 'The man she took off with lives in this area. The biological father believes that Ellie has moved in with him and he assumed she'd try to get the kids into one of the schools around here. I'm just trying to locate them. I've tried all the normal routes and I suspect she's using a different name. That's all, honestly. I'm no pervert, I swear.'

Jackman believed him, and when Stacey appeared with confirmation that he did work for a small company called Fen Investigation, he decided that this whole business had been a red herring. But at least they could rule him out of their inquiry and reassure the parents.

Just in case, he asked Stacey to double check that this Carpenter woman really was the focus of the agency's investigation. While he waited for the confirmation, he asked the man if he had managed to track down the missing wife and children.

'I've had a couple of leads but they came to nothing. I've got pictures of the children, but I can't just start hawking them around the other mothers. The husband made it clear that he doesn't want the fact that he's looking for them advertised.' Michaels looked abashed. 'I hope he doesn't hear about this little fiasco or I'll be slung off the job.'

'I'm sorry about that,' Jackman said, 'but I hope you can see things from our point of view. You've not exactly been discreet, have you?'

'I may not have handled this very well, Detective Inspector,' Michaels said.

'Let's say I wouldn't want you working with me, Mr Michaels.'

Stacey came back in. 'All checks out, sir.'

'Thank you, Stacey. Mr Michaels, you may go. Stacey will take you to collect your things. Thank you for your time.'

Jackman went back to the CID room and wiped the words "School Gates Man" off the whiteboard. He then told everyone there to drop that line of investigation. 'He's not the man in Simon's night camera picture, that's for sure. He's a PI, and not a very good one.'

Max called out, 'Boss, Felix Becker has just arrived. We're off to talk to him.'

'Great, you do the meet and greet. I'll be down shortly to look in from the observation room. Get all you can, Max,' Jackman said. 'His ex is very important to us.'

'You got it, boss. Come on, Charlie! Let's go grill the guy.'

'I think the word is interview, Max,' said Jackman dryly.

'Just my loose interpretation, boss. Never fear, we have it all in hand.'

* * *

Marie had often seen Harriet Burns from the women's refuge around but had no idea that she worked there. She also knew the older woman next to her. Dulcie was from the village of Sutterthorpe and a stalwart of the local community.

'I think you already know Dulcie, DS Evans. I asked her to come along because she remembers the young woman you were asking about. She knew Nan and Andrea too. I took over the refuge somewhat later, so she'll probably be of more assistance than me.'

Though somewhat overweight, Harriet had a perfect complexion, long, dark, lustrous hair and a friendly face. She gave the appearance of being effortlessly in control, a person you instinctively trusted. She would have a calm way with traumatised, desperate, sometimes angry women.

Marie greeted Dulcie and told them as much as she dared about their inquiry.

'I heard about Nan's death,' said Dulcie. 'I still feel bad about the way she was treated. Andrea Becker was a force of nature, persuasive and convincing. Looking back on it, she influenced a lot of people into changing their opinion of Nan. She made Nan out to be interfering and unprofessional, whereas it was Andrea herself who was the interfering one, and her conduct was way out of line.' Dulcie stared down at her untouched cup of tea. 'Everyone held Nan responsible for Claire and her boy leaving the refuge so precipitously. I only realised much later that she had nothing to do with it. In fact, she was trying to protect them.' She sighed. 'I went to see Nan, but by then it was far too late. Claire had disappeared, along with her boy.'

Harriet produced an A4 plastic wallet and handed it to Marie. 'This is everything I have from our records of that year. Everyone who comes to us has to sign a licence agreement, which is basically the terms under which you can stay, including the rent to be charged and all our rules of safety. Claire registered as Claire Woodhall, and her son's name was Leon. She only gave us a mobile number, no other contacts at all, but that's not unusual. These women are escaping from abusive relationships and often travel long distances in order to keep their whereabouts a secret.'

Leon? Was it even the right child?

'Claire required no financial advice or assistance and drew no benefits. We never enquire into the personal affairs of our residents,' added Harriet. 'In fact, if they choose, they only have to give a first name. Claire wasn't referred by yourselves or the Samaritans or any other aid organisation. As long as we have the space, any woman who is in need can come into the refuge via Women's Aid. We ask no questions, just offer support, advice and a safe place to stay.'

Which was brilliant, of course, but of little help to Marie. 'You say this Claire just disappeared, Dulcie? Did you have any idea where she went? We were told that she might have gone to stay with Andrea Becker.'

Dulcie shook her head. 'She didn't go there, I do know that. I was concerned at her sudden departure, and I called round to Andrea's place. This was before I became aware that Andrea was not what I'd believed her to be. She was out, but her husband was there, and he said he'd seen the woman and the child just the once, when Andrea brought them back for tea.'

'And Claire never mentioned anything about moving on, or even going back home?' Marie said. 'I know some women do go back, even after they've made the break.'

'Never in my hearing.' Dulcie sipped her tea. 'But I'd be willing to swear that she would never have gone back to her husband. She was scared to death of him.'

'And the boy?'

Dulcie didn't answer for a moment. 'He was a strange child, Marie. Very insular, hated the refuge and its restrictions. He spent most of his time in their room, although I think his mother did make an effort to home-teach him. No matter how hard I tried, he never spoke more than two words to me that I can recall. Though he did talk to Nan. I remember that.'

*That could have saved your life, Dulcie,* thought Marie. *He talked to Nan and look what happened to her.*

After a few more words, Marie realised that there was little more to be got from this woman. She asked her last question without much hope. 'Did Claire have a friend she might have confided in? Someone she seemed close to?'

'Yes,' Dulcie said. 'Ruthie Grey.'

'Ruthie!' echoed Harriet. 'No one talks to Ruthie.'

Dulcie laughed. 'Ruthie cleans the house, has done since it opened, and she's probably the most taciturn person I've ever met. But she and Claire seemed to have an affinity. If Claire talked to anyone, it would have been her.'

'Is she still with you?' asked Marie hopefully.

'Only a few hours a week. She's getting on now, but she still tries to do her bit,' said Harriet. 'She lives in Church Walk, the last house before the churchyard, a tiny two-up two-down cottage. It's called Thimbledown.'

Marie thanked the women for their help. She decided to take a walk and see this woman of few words for herself. You never knew.

* * *

The door was opened by a sharp-featured, almost skeletal woman who stared out at Marie from beneath lowered eyebrows.

'Mrs Ruthie Grey?' Marie said brightly. 'DS Marie Evans, Saltern Police. I wonder if I could have a word?'

'Why?'

She intensified the smile. 'Dulcie and Harriet said you might be able to help me with my inquiry.'

'Did they really. What inquiry?'

'It's about Claire and her son, Leon.'

There was a slight softening in the expression, then, without a word, Ruthie pushed the door wider and turned on her heel.

Marie followed the retreating back into a cottage kitchen that seemed to have come from another era. She gasped. 'Oh, this is beautiful!' Her gaze travelled from the old range to the butler sink and scrubbed wooden table. There was even a glass oil lamp.

There was a flicker of what might have been a smile. Ruthie pulled out a chair. 'Tell me she hasn't gone back to that bastard. He hasn't hurt her, has he? Or the little lad?'

'No, Ruthie, it's not that. But we are desperate to find them, her and the boy. We suspect her husband murdered Nan Cutler, and he's terrorising women in the area.'

Ruthie sighed. 'Why doesn't that surprise me.'

'So you see,' went on Marie, 'she and the lad could be in grave danger. Do you know where Claire went when she left the refuge? Or even where she is now?'

'If I could tell you, I would, but I haven't the faintest idea.' Ruthie looked directly at Marie. 'We lost touch eighteen months ago. Her phone suddenly went dead, and she never rang me again. I'm afraid the worst might have happened.'

Marie groaned to herself.

'But I do know where she went after the refuge,' added Ruthie. 'I swore I wouldn't tell a soul, but now she could be dead for all I know, so I suppose I can say.'

Marie looked at her expectantly.

'She went to Skegness. A friend of hers from the refuge had a holiday flat there. She wasn't letting it out, so she said Claire could stay for free. Claire had begun to understand that Nan Cutler wasn't the problem, but Andrea. So without a word to anyone, she packed their few belongings and disappeared with the boy.'

'Did she give you the address?' asked Marie.

'Yes.'

'Could I have it, please?'

Ruthie hesitated. 'Get your notebook out, girl. I know it by heart. Didn't want to write it down in case. You never know, do you?'

Marie opened her notebook.

'She ain't there though. After her calls stopped, I took myself off on the early bus one morning, but it was all locked up and the blinds were drawn. A neighbour said she hadn't been there for weeks. Right sad, I was.'

But there was still hope. Even though Ruthie had been unlucky, the police had more resources for tracing missing persons. They'd start with the owner of the property. 'If you could let me have the mobile number too, Ruthie, we might be able to do a trace on it.'

The old lady produced a rather battered phone from her cardigan pocket and scrolled through her contacts. 'Addresses are one thing, but who can remember numbers? Ah, here we are. Not that it'll do you any good, lass. It was the cheapest pay-as-you-go phone in the supermarket. I know because I bought it for her.'

'I really appreciate your help,' Marie said, 'and when I find out what happened, I promise I'll come and tell you.'

Ruthie Grey nodded. She had said all she had to say.

# CHAPTER TWENTY-ONE

Felix Becker was a tall, lean man with a shock of unruly, dark-blond hair.

'We really appreciate your coming here today, sir,' began Max. 'Anything you can tell us about your ex-wife will be a great help with a murder case we're investigating.'

'Murder, Detective? You never mentioned murder when we spoke on the phone.' Becker spoke with a pronounced German accent.

'Well, it's a complicated investigation,' Max said.

'And Andrea is involved in some way? My God! Andrea could be accused of a lot of things, but murder?'

'We're not accusing her of anything, sir. We're looking for some people she knew, and we need her help to find them,' Charlie said.

'Well, okay. I'll help as much as I can, but as you probably know, she left me some time ago. After she went, I discovered that there were sides to her that I never knew about.' He looked down at the table. 'And I've since learned a whole lot more, which makes me feel like a fool for being so naive.'

'Mr Becker, if what the people who knew her say is correct, she deceived almost everyone she came into contact with. And she caused a lot of hurt and pain along the way,' Max said.

'I had a breakdown when she took off with that builder, or whatever he was. It took me nearly a year to even think clearly again.' Becker shook himself. 'But how can I help you?'

'We're sorry to rake up painful memories, sir,' said Max, 'but do you recall a young woman your wife once brought home for tea? Her name was Claire. She had a little boy with her called Leon.'

'Officers, my wife collected people like others collect fridge magnets or Pokémon. There were always people coming and going through the house. I don't remember any Claire — hold on. Yes, actually I do recall the boy. Didn't speak. He was either very shy or maybe just unhappy. If he came from that shelter Andrea worked in, I'm guessing it was the latter.'

'He was from the refuge, sir. Apparently, Andrea was very taken with them. She even wanted them to come and stay with you,' Charlie said.

Felix Becker snorted. 'I've heard that before, many times. What a farce that would have been. Andrea wasn't exactly an angel when she was at home.'

'But you still loved her?' asked Max. 'Sorry to be so personal.'

'For my sins, yes,' Becker said. 'I was completely taken in by her. And she was so beautiful when she was younger.' He had brought an A4 envelope, from which he removed two photographs. One showed him and Andrea on their wedding day — a happy, strikingly handsome couple.

Max looked closer. Even if he hadn't known what he did about Andrea, he would have spotted the look on her face — pure triumph. She had landed her catch, the handsome German.

The second picture, Becker told them, was taken not long before she left him and was the most recent he had. It showed her with two other women outside the church she attended. 'I destroyed all but these two pictures, Officers. They represent the beginning and the end of our relationship.'

The image was clear, her features unmistakable. She had shoulder-length, wavy, dark hair, very dark-brown eyes and a full figure. The Andrea in the picture was an attractive, self-confident, mature and overtly sexual woman. Max could see why this man had been besotted with her. 'This is exactly what we need, Mr Becker. Thank you. Now, did you have contact with her during your divorce proceedings?'

'It was conducted entirely through our solicitors, Detective. I never knew where she was. I did hear that she hadn't stayed long with the man she went off with. No matter how hard I tried, I could not discover her whereabouts. No one had seen her — or if they had, they weren't telling me. She still had some very loyal friends.'

'Any names, sir? If one of her friends knows where she is, it would help us enormously.'

'Well, if she's still living around here, you could try a woman called Lexi Freeman. She used to work in a health food shop in town, the one near the market square. She adored Andrea. If anyone knows where she is, it'd be Lexi.'

'We'll check her out,' said Charlie. 'Thank you.'

'Mr Becker, is there anything you can tell us about Andrea that might explain her behaviour?' Max frowned. 'It looks to me — us — that she needed people to like her and think her special. And she would turn on anyone who failed to respond.'

'Nicely put, Detective. Fundamentally, Andrea was a narcissist. I hadn't been aware of her true nature until after we were married. I do know that she had been rejected as a child and had a deep-seated inferiority complex. But it's my belief that her controlling nature was in her genes. She was aware of this dark side and tried to cover it up with "good works."'

'But she couldn't always hide that dark side,' said Max.

'She could not. She could be vicious, and she used people.' Becker shook his head. 'I don't know why I wasn't the one to make the move. I should have done it years ago. But despite what I learned about Andrea, I still loved her. More fool me.'

'And Nan Cutler?' asked Charlie.

'Oh my! That woman saw through her all right! And she wasn't afraid to voice her opinion. But she was no match for Andrea. My ex-wife was a class act at turning the tables on people who threatened to expose her for what she was. She practically made that poor woman a pariah.'

'And now she's dead,' said Charlie softly.

'You think that's connected to Andrea?' Becker asked. 'Is her death what this is all about?'

'It's connected to that woman called Claire and the boy, Leon. Andrea was doing all she could to get them under her spell,' said Max. 'So maybe she wasn't directly responsible, but certainly indirectly. Sir, would you give your permission for us to contact your solicitor and make enquiries as to her whereabouts? We would need a warrant, which might not be granted, as she is not a suspect, but she might agree to talk to us voluntarily if her solicitor suggests that it's in her best interests.'

'Of course. Anything I can do to help. I still use the same firm, even after I moved away. It's Rigby and Pattinson in Queens Lane, Saltern. I deal with Aaron Rigby.'

'We'll see this Lexi Freeman first,' Max said, 'but at least we'll have another avenue to try if she's no longer around. And you can't remember anything that was said about Claire or Leon?'

Becker shook his head. 'Naturally, I'll give it some thought, but I can't think of anything at the moment. I'm sorry.'

Max and Charlie gave him their cards and told him to ring at any time if he thought of something or heard anything about his ex-wife. Becker stood up. 'If you find her, I don't want to know where she is. At one time I might have done anything to see her again. Now she's the last person I want to meet. Good luck, Officers, and if you do talk to her, don't be fooled. She's not to be trusted for a moment.'

Max smiled. 'Thank you, Mr Becker, we'll bear that in mind.'

\* \* \*

At eleven in the morning, Laura Archer received a call. The distressed voice sent shivers through her. *Oh God! What now?* Freddie Shields's voice was shaking. He seemed to be on the verge of tears, if he wasn't crying already.

'Please can I talk to you, Dr Archer? I don't have anyone else. Please?'

Stifling a groan, Laura managed a calm, 'What's happened, Mr Shields?'

'I can't talk on the phone. Can I come and see you? I know it's not correct protocol or whatever you call it, but I'm desperate, and I mean it.'

Laura closed her eyes and thought quickly. 'Give me ten minutes and I'll see if I can rearrange my appointments. No promises, but I'll try.'

After she'd hung up, she rang Sam Page and told him about Shields's call.

'Tell him to get to the mill in an hour's time,' said Sam. 'I've sorted everything here, so I'll lock up and get to you straightaway. It's a good opportunity to see this patient of yours while he's undergoing one of his episodes.'

Thank goodness for Sam. And thanks to Jackman for engineering his visit. As it was, she had no appointments until the afternoon, both booked to take place in her consulting room here, but she wasn't going to tell Shields that.

'Before I ring off,' Sam said. 'Some good news. I've heard from my contact in the prison service who says that Ashcroft's transfer went off like clockwork. He's now safely ensconced in HMP Gartree in Leicestershire.'

'That's a big relief, Sam. But I must say I was hoping it would be HMP Frankland.'

'Gartree is well equipped to deal with high-profile prisoners, believe me. It doesn't have the reputation that Monster

Mansion does, but if they can handle killers like Fred West and Ian Brady, they can certainly manage Ashcroft. The only thing that worries me — and that would be the case in either prison — is if he gets into a PIPE unit. But enough of that for now. I'll get a move on and be with you as soon as.'

Laura gave it another five minutes, then reluctantly rang Shields. 'If you can get here in an hour, Mr Shields, we'll see you then.'

'We?'

'Professor Page will be here. I told you last time we spoke. He's an eminent psychologist and has the highest connections with specialists in your specific disorder. You are in good hands, Mr Shields.'

'I need to be, as long as it's not already too late.' He swallowed loudly. 'I'll be there in an hour.'

'I'd suggest you take a cab. You really don't sound as if you should be driving,' Laura said.

'Maybe. I'll see. Thank you so much. You're a lifesaver.' The line went dead.

Laura stared at the receiver. Why, oh why, did this man disturb her so much? And what did he mean by it being too late? In her time she had been in some pretty frightening situations, but Freddie Shields seemed to upset her on another level completely.

She went and made herself a strong coffee, still trying to analyse her reactions to this perplexing young man. On the surface, he was a rather ordinary person. He cared for his mother and was sufficiently concerned for his partner's safety to send her away for a while. He was clean, well dressed and articulate. He was obviously educated, though not academic, and he was scared of his condition and what it could mean. So, what on earth was it about him that caused such confusion in her mind?

She was still pondering her reaction to Freddie Shields when Sam arrived half an hour later.

'I can't forget that odd look on his face when he left here last time. It looked like, well, triumph.' She shrugged. 'It's

196

hard to describe, Sam, but it didn't seem appropriate to what we had been talking about.'

'Maybe that's what's disturbing you,' said Sam thoughtfully. 'His expression, maybe his body language too, doesn't match what he's saying. That can be very unsettling.'

Laura looked at him. 'Do you know, I think that's it! He's saying one thing and thinking another! It's confusing, especially when you're trying to get to the bottom of what's causing his condition.' She smiled at her friend. 'It's something I'd like you to keep an eye open for when he comes.'

'Oh, I will. In fact, I can hardly wait to make the acquaintance of your Mr Shields.'

\* \* \*

Charlie and Max hurried into the CID room buzzing with excitement.

'The woman in the health food shop turned up trumps!' Max exclaimed.

'After a bit of gentle Cockney persuasion,' added Charlie with a grin.

'We have an address for Andrea Becker.' Max opened his notebook. 'Thirteen Hilary Court, Main Road, Sutton Bridge. And it's recent!'

Jackman, who had been talking to Marie, gave them a smile. 'Nice one. That's good work, lads! And Marie here has come up with a last known address for Claire and Leon, so it looks like we're all going to have to hit the road. I would say ring the local division and get them to call round, but I think we'll just notify them out of courtesy and go ourselves. Are you two up for a quick trip to Sutton Bridge?'

'Like a shot, boss. I think we need to deal with this lady ourselves. After all, it's us knows what she's really like, isn't it?' Max looked as if he was itching to tackle this one.

Sutton Bridge was about an hour's drive from Saltern-le-Fen, so they would be back early afternoon, hopefully with Andrea Becker in the back seat of their car. So Jackman said,

'If you want to get off immediately, I'll ring the local lads and put them in the picture. Meanwhile, Marie and I are off to Skegness.'

'Come on, Charlie,' Max said. 'Sorry it's not the seaside. No candy floss for you, mate.'

Jackman watched them go. 'How about you, Marie? Fancy that stick of candy floss?'

'Well, I wouldn't mind a nice pot of cockles.' She smiled at him. 'You know, boss, this could be a complete waste of time. Why don't I shoot off there, while you get on with the more important business? I can be there in forty minutes, check it out and be back in no time. Of course I'd have been quicker on Tiger, but it's getting pretty cloudy outside. That weather report could well be right.'

It made sense. The reports were piling up and he still hadn't updated the super. 'Maybe you're right, Marie, but ring me as soon as you know something, won't you?'

'Of course. Can I bring you back some jellied eels?'

He grimaced. 'I'll give those a skip today, if it's all the same with you.'

'Oh well, your loss.' Marie pulled on her jacket. 'I'll ring you later, boss.'

Jackman made calls to the local police in both locations and prepared to brief Ruth Crooke. Then, while everyone was out, he would go over what they had so far. Things were starting to happen, and he wanted to be ahead of the game.

\* \* \*

At the same time as Marie threaded her way between the late-season holidaymakers and watched storm clouds gathering overhead, Max and Charlie were parking outside thirteen Hilary Court. It was a small estate of new builds, mainly lower- and middle-priced housing. Number thirteen was a detached property built to a modern design. Being at the end of a little cul-de-sac, it had a larger garden than the others, wrapped around it on three sides.

Max was disappointed to get no response to his knock. He'd been keen to see this diabolical woman for himself.

He stood back and stared up at the house. It had every appearance of being deserted. The curtains were half pulled — something that his mum used to do when she went away. He'd told her a dozen times that it only drew attention to the place, but she wouldn't have it. You developed a feel for places in his job, and this one felt empty and unloved.

'Round the back?' asked Charlie, indicating to a side gate.

Max nodded. 'Yeah, maybe we can get a butcher's inside if there's a French window. I reckon she's away, don't you?'

'Looks like it.'

They strolled into the back garden. It had been recently planted and had a freshly laid lawn bordered by flower beds and a shrubbery. Trees from an older neighbouring property edged the boundary on two sides.

'Nice little suntrap in summer,' commented Charlie. 'But she needs to learn about weeding or it'll be a wilderness by autumn.'

'Thank you, Alan Titchmarsh,' laughed Max. He tried the back door. 'Locked. Let's check those patio doors. They look like they might lead out from the lounge.'

They started across the flagstones, then stopped, mid-stride.

'Is this what I think it is?' asked Charlie in a low voice.

'Yep. That's blood all right.'

The white uPVC doorstep and the edge of the big patio door were smeared with dark, brownish dried blood.

Max noticed smudged tracks along the paving and on to the grass. 'Someone has dragged someone or something out into the garden. Come on, let's see what the hell happened here.'

When they reached the edge of the lawn, they saw that the soil of the flower bed had been disturbed. They made out two deep grooves.

'I could be wrong, but I reckon those are heel marks,' said Max.

They moved more slowly now, careful not to cause too much contamination.

Charlie tentatively parted the shrubbery, and they edged towards the wooded boundary. Max froze and grasped Charlie's arm. 'Look!'

They were looking down on a mound of freshly turned loose soil. A shallow grave?

'Better make a few phone calls, Charlie-boy,' said Max. 'The boss first, and then the local lads. We seem to be slap bang in the middle of a crime scene.'

Carefully, they retraced their steps to the patio. While Max rang Jackman, Charlie pulled on his nitrile gloves and tested the patio door.

'Bloody hell, it's open!'

Slowly, he opened the door.

And gasped. 'Oh shit! Blood everywhere!'

For a long moment, Charlie seemed unable to tear his eyes away from the scene in front of him. Then he closed the door again.

'Clear the scene if you're going to hurl,' insisted Max. 'Nothing worse for the SOCOs than coppers adding their puke to the carnage.'

Charlie heaved in a deep breath. 'I'm okay. It's the stink. I hate it.'

Max finished his call to Jackman then had a look for himself.

There was no doubt about it. This was where the attack had taken place. 'Blimey! Our prof is going to have a field day with that blood spatter. Looks like an arterial bleed to me.'

He shut the door. 'Jackman's contacting Uniform and Forensics. We need to stay and tie up with them. So much for that weeding. Andrea Becker will never get around to it now.'

'But Felix Becker will get his wish. He'll never have to see his ex-wife again,' said Charlie. 'Someone's seen to that for him.'

'Unless he made sure of it himself.'

Charlie raised an eyebrow. 'You reckon?'

'Not really, but stranger things have happened.'

They returned to their car and leaned against it. 'Hope the circus gets here soon,' Charlie said, gazing up at the gathering clouds. 'If we get a deluge, much of the evidence could be washed away. We need some awnings or tents, and fast by the look of it.'

'Jackman has that in hand. He said it's already pissing down back in Saltern.' Max looked back along the little cul-de-sac. 'Let's see if the neighbours are in. I'd like to know when she was last seen.'

'How about starting with him?' Charlie indicated across the road to an elderly man who was making a big show of cleaning his car's windscreen. 'He's been clocking us ever since we got here.'

Max strolled across the road and took out his warrant card. 'Afternoon, sir. Detective Constable Max Cohen. Could you tell me when you last saw the lady who lives in the house opposite?'

'Oh, well, er . . . must be about three or four days ago, I suppose.' He looked at them with inquisitive, slightly piggy eyes. 'Why? What's she done?'

'Nothing, sir,' said Max lightly. *Other than get herself butchered.* 'Just an inquiry. Could you say precisely when?'

'Let me think . . . Ah, yes, it was definitely three days ago, at around seven in the evening. I was watering the hanging basket when she came home.'

'Alone, sir?'

'Yes, alone.' He glared at Max. 'Look. What's happened? Is she all right? Only she's well liked around here. We're all quite new to the area, and she's been a real brick, helping people out and that.'

*So our Andrea was running true to form.* 'Nice to hear, sir.' He smiled. 'Thank you for your assistance. Other officers will no doubt speak to you later.'

He hurried away, conscious of those porcine eyes following him all the way to the car.

\* \* \*

Jackman had just finished arranging matters with Sutton Bridge when his mobile rang.

'Well, boss. No candy floss, no jellied eels and definitely no Claire and Leon. And no bloody sunshine either, it's tipping it down here.'

Jackman had to smile. Poor Marie. So much for her trip to the seaside. 'Well, at least you were proved right. You said it would be a waste of time.'

'I've spoken to a number of people who live in the same block of flatlets, and one or two of them remember having seen Claire and her son, but not for some time. I do have the name and number of the woman who loaned her the flat, but there's no answer at present. I'll keep trying.'

'Get back here, Marie. You've had no luck, but Max and Charlie's luck was even worse. They walked straight into the aftermath of another of our night stalker's murder games. At least, that's what we assume. A team is already on its way to excavate what appears to be a shallow grave, and Forensics will be wading their way through a sea of blood in the lounge, according to a rather queasy-sounding Charlie Button.'

'Oh my!' Marie exclaimed. 'A bit of rain doesn't seem so bad all of a sudden. I'm on my way back now.'

Jackman went out into the CID room, where Robbie, Gary and Kevin were all hard at it. 'If I could stop you guys for a minute. I have an update . . .'

'He really is clearing up, isn't he?' murmured Robbie. 'Seems like he's getting rid of anyone who had anything to do with Claire and Leon.'

'Looks that way, Rob, but it seems Claire and the boy are still one step ahead of him. Anyone got anything on Claire's history yet?' Jackman was becoming frustrated by the lack of information about this woman.

'Well, boss, Claire Woodhall, the name she checked into the refuge under, seems to have been a pseudonym. I rang Women's Aid and asked how far women might travel to get to a safe place, and on their advice, I started with our own county and spread out from here. Many travel hundreds of miles to get away, but not all do. Some women don't want to be too far from family and friends. I've found four women named Claire Woodhall in the county, and none match the description of the person we're looking for. I extended the search to Yorkshire, Nottinghamshire, Cambridgeshire and Norfolk, and also checked whether it could have been her maiden name, but again, no one tallies.'

'Kevin? Gary? Anything?' They shook their heads.

'I checked the PNC and no one of her description shows up under that name, sir,' said Kevin.

'Two things from me, boss,' Robbie said. 'The Sky man is definitely a scammer. He's called on dozens and dozens of addresses in and around Saltern and the surrounding villages. There *are* no faulty boxes, and the vehicle that Annie described isn't one of theirs. The logo on all their vans is done professionally. Plus, I've been checking out the schools around here looking for a temporary student by the name of Leon, or possibly Teddy.'

'But nothing.' It wasn't a question.

'Zilch, I'm afraid,' Robbie said. 'It was an outside chance, I guess.'

'She took that boy somewhere, didn't she?' said Jackman. 'And given that her pursuer is searching different homes, she placed him into care a while ago. She may have even given him up for adoption. Has anyone spoken to social services?'

'Without a name or an address, sir, it's useless,' said Gary. 'They have too many cases as it is. We need a whole lot more information before we can ask for their help.'

Gary was right. But this boy appeared to be the root cause of a series of murders. They had to find him.

He sat down heavily on a spare chair. 'Okay, let's try something else. We can only assume our killer knows a lot more than us about where Teddy — Leon — actually is. If he's targeting houses with a connection to ten-year-old boys, he's narrowed his search down to this specific area. I think we can assume that's correct so far? One thing we don't know is how he learned about Nan's involvement in the boy's life.

He can't have been following Claire and Leon, or he'd have simply grabbed the child and taken off. No, he discovered it some other way.'

There was a silence, then Kevin said, 'Andrea Becker? What if she was in league with him? What if the real reason behind her attempt to get Claire and Leon to stay with her was to hand them over to the man who was hunting for them?'

'She was certainly devious enough,' said Gary. 'That's a damned good suggestion, Kevin!'

Jackman thought about it. It was a good idea, but he saw a flaw. 'Then why did the killer not just take the boy from the refuge? Or grab him when Claire took him out for a walk?'

'Because he didn't know they were there,' added Robbie thoughtfully. 'We know what an evil witch Andrea Becker was, maybe she was stringing him along, feeding him small bits of information. She might have calculated that she could squeeze a considerable sum of money out of a desperate father.'

'But on this occasion,' said Gary, 'it looks as though she bit off more than she could chew. If the contents of that garden grave turn out to be her, Andrea Becker made a serious mistake by underestimating her "desperate father."'

It was possible. Andrea believed she could control people. Why would a man hunting for his son be any different? If he was indeed desperate, he might even be a total pushover. 'Yes, that kind of situation would suit her, wouldn't it?' Jackman said. 'And she would really shine when she finally presented him with Leon. Once again, she'd be the centre of attention.' He frowned. 'Do we know why she left the man she ran off with? This Hereward fella?'

No one answered.

'We assumed it was because he was a means to an end, but supposing she was seeing another man?' said Jackman.

'As in the killer?' asked Gary.

'Why not? We know she was able to seduce men at will, and if Felix Becker was anything to go by, she knew how to keep them too.' He looked at Gary. 'Speak to Roger Hereward and ask him.'

'Okay, I'm on it.' Gary turned to his computer. 'We've got his last known address, let's hope he's still there.'

His head spinning, Jackman returned to his office and sat down. Until they had confirmation about Andrea Becker, he was stuck. He looked at the wall clock. Marie should be back soon, and with luck Forensics would already be digging in the back garden of thirteen Hilary Court. Even if it wasn't her, someone had certainly met with a sticky end in her lounge.

He took a deep breath and closed his eyes. How many more people were going to pay for having associated with the killer's son?

# CHAPTER TWENTY-TWO

Laura and Sam were with Freddie Shields in her consulting room at the mill. After she'd made the introductions, Sam spent a few minutes trying to put the visitor at ease. But Freddie Shields was clearly in a state of extreme agitation, barely taking in Sam's soothing words. Laura noted that he had ignored her advice to get a taxi and had driven here himself.

'So, what happened to make you so upset, Mr Shields?' asked Laura.

'It was horrible. I went out again last night, Dr Archer. And I almost got arrested.'

'I see,' Laura said, her voice even. 'Well, can you tell us what happened — what time this was, where you went and what you did?'

'It was after midnight. I don't know how I got there, but I went back to the filling station where I'd been before. It seems I was acting like a mad person — shouting and hammering on the kiosk window.' He looked down. 'I must have scared the wits out of the poor kid who worked there. He dialled 999.'

'You drove there?' asked Sam.

'Yes, but I left the car in a lay-by on the other side of the main road. I must have walked right across the A52, but

I don't remember doing so.' He looked at them anxiously. 'I don't remember anything until the police got hold of me.'

For the first time Laura noticed the dressing on Shields's arm. 'You injured yourself?'

'Somehow, although I didn't feel it. The police saw I had blood all over my coat and they found the wound on my arm. One of the officers put an emergency dressing on it, then I dressed it properly when I got home.'

'But you have no idea how you came by the injury?' asked Sam.

'None at all, and as I say, it didn't hurt until much later.'

'And Julia?' asked Laura. 'Is she back with you yet?'

He shook his head. 'I wouldn't let her, and now I'm glad that I made her stay away. What on earth is the matter with me?' He looked from one to the other of them helplessly. 'What am I capable of?'

Sam answered, 'I'd say that something buried very deeply inside you is struggling to manifest itself, Mr Shields, something from your past. It comes to the surface when you sleep and your defences are down. It's a little like a recurring nightmare, but instead of remaining asleep in your bed, a part of your brain — the part that controls movement — is still awake, so you get up. The part that controls cognition is still asleep, so you have no awareness of what you are doing.' He gave Shields a kindly look. 'It's frightening, Mr Shields, but not too uncommon. We need to find out what's troubling you, and when you confront that, I believe the sleepwalking will stop.'

Laura leaned forward. 'You told me that once you went to your father's grave while you were asleep and begged him for forgiveness. Do you think that what's disturbing you might be something to do with your father? Something that happened when you were a child maybe, that's now rising to the surface again?'

'No,' Shields said brusquely. 'He was a good father and I tried to be a good son. It's nothing to do with him, I assure you.'

*He's lying again*, thought Laura.

'You said you'd see if there was somewhere that could take me in, Dr Archer. Because I think the time has come, for everyone's safety, including my own.' He pointed to the dressing. 'To make sure I'm somewhere secure at night.'

Laura nodded. 'Yes, Mr Shields. I've spoken to a sleep clinic, but I'm afraid it's private. To get you seen under the NHS will take much longer. It's a purpose-built facility for monitoring sleep in a controlled lab. It's not intended for long-term stays. Most people only sleep there once, to be tested, but as your case is extreme, they have agreed to do a series of tests on you over several consecutive nights. My hope is that they will pinpoint something medical, rather than a mental health issue.'

'I'll pay. I can't go on like this. I'll find the money. Where is this place?' He looked at her eagerly. 'Can I go tonight?'

'Fenchester, and, yes, if you want, I can ring them and tell them you'll be with them this evening.' Laura didn't like the strange fervour in his eyes, but she was relieved to be free of his sudden desperate visits for a couple of days.

'I was rather hoping that I'd be going to a secure hospital of some kind.' Shields gave a short cheerless laugh. 'Listen to me — normal people never ask to be locked away, do they? But I'm afraid for my sanity, doctors, I really am.'

'The clinic is the place to start, Mr Shields,' said Sam. 'As Dr Archer says, let's rule out a medical cause, but I do urge you to look at your childhood, and try to think of some trauma that you might have suppressed. I'm certain it's some-thing from your past that's at the root of your distress.'

Laura noticed the look of irritation that flitted across Shields's face. If he kept blocking it out like this, she'd never be able to help him. 'Have you managed to talk to your mother yet?' she said. 'Speaking to her might help identify whatever it is you're repressing. She could be the very person to throw some light on it.'

'She's an old lady. I can't lay this on her. Sorry, Dr Archer, but I won't do it.'

'Will she worry about you being away for several nights?' she said.

'I'll tell her I'm spending a few nights at Julia's place. I'll see her during the day, so it won't be a problem.' He crossed his arms and stared at her defiantly.

And that's that, thought Laura. If only she could meet the mother. She was sure that old or not, she would want to help her son.

Sam told Shields about Professor Hugh Mackenzie, who was making a special trip from Scotland to discuss his case. 'We are making every effort to help you, you know. So please, don't despair. We'll get to the bottom of this, and you'll be back to normal again.'

Laura wrote down the address and telephone number of the clinic for him. 'I'll ring them now, before you leave, then you'll know what time to be there.' She made the call, wishing she could hand this man over to them permanently. Then she felt guilty for wishing it. 'Be there at eight this evening, Mr Shields. They'll be expecting you.'

Shields finally drove away. After he'd gone, she and Sam sat in silence for a few moments.

'I see what you mean, Laura,' said Sam. 'What on earth is going on in that head of his?'

When she didn't answer, Sam squeezed her arm. 'You were right to call me in. I think your Mr Shields has another agenda altogether here — my alarm bells are ringing very loudly.'

*Oh, thank goodness*, Laura thought, *so I wasn't imagining things!*

Laura looked at her watch. 'I have a couple of sessions with PCs who have suffered recent traumas, then I have to brief Superintendent Ruth Crooke on how they're doing. As soon as I'm through with that, I thought I might have a word with the crew that went out to the filling station last night. I'd like to hear their take on Mr Shields's behaviour. Is that being unethical?'

'Not in the slightest,' said Sam. 'You're concerned for his safety, that's all. You aren't divulging anything to them, just asking what they witnessed. There's no problem in that.'

'Good.' Laura didn't mention it, but she thought she might drive past Shields's house on her way back. After Sam had expressed his own doubts about her client, she felt more confident. She needed to find out what Frederick Shields was really like, not what he chose to tell her.

While Sam unpacked, Laura switched on her computer. It would be useful to know what type of woman Shields's partner Julia was. He had told her that she was a teacher at Saltern Academy, so she found the website, which had a page called 'Meet Our Staff'. She scrolled down the list of names and photographs, looking for a Julia.

None appeared. Maybe the site was no longer current. No, it had been updated very recently. Maybe Julia was a middle name, and the school had her listed under her proper name. It was possible. She had friends who didn't like their first names.

Laura got up and went to her filing cabinet. She took out the file for Freddie Shields and checked his patient information sheet. His next of kin was listed as his mother, Catherine Shields. The contact number for emergencies was a local one . . . ah, and in brackets, Partner, Julia Emma Taylor, of the same address.

She returned to the computer and once again scrolled down the list of teachers, teaching assistants, supervisors and even trainees, but there was definitely no Julia, and no one with the surname Taylor. For a minute she was tempted to start trawling through social media sites, but stopped herself. This really wasn't something she should be doing. She was a psychologist, not a detective.

Laura frowned. Yet another mystery. Was or wasn't there a Julia in Freddie Shields's life?

* * *

Marie shook the rain from her jacket and went upstairs to find Jackman. As she approached his door, it opened and he hurried out.

'Ah, Marie! Excellent timing. Come with me. Ruth wants to see us, but I'm not sure why. She said she'd like us to meet someone.'

Inside Ruth's office, they found two unsmiling men seated side by side. One, a heavily built young man, looked vaguely familiar.

Ruth smiled her tight-lipped smile when they entered. 'Shut the door, Marie, and please take a seat, both of you.' She turned to the two men. 'This is DI Rowan Jackman and DS Marie Evans, my most trusted detectives. Jackman, Marie, please meet Mr Mark Bannon and his son, Giles.'

So that was it. Giles Bannon! No wonder he looked familiar — she'd seen his photograph.

She glanced at Jackman, who looked as surprised as she was.

'Mr Bannon has asked to speak to me, and I wanted both of you to be present. Mr Bannon?'

Mark Bannon was a tallish man in spectacles with a grey moustache and short, receding grey hair. Years of anxiety and pain were etched into his face. He spoke in a deep, sombre voice. 'Thank you, Superintendent Crooke. In light of recent events here in Saltern-le-Fen, and because you will obviously be aware of what happened to my son's family, I decided to come and speak to you in person.' He drew in a breath. 'I still cannot believe my bad luck in spending months searching for a suitable property for my son only to finish up choosing a town where a murder had just been committed.'

'Unfortunate, indeed, Mr Bannon,' murmured Ruth.

'We're aware of what you must be thinking, and in a way, we can't blame you.' Bannon looked from Jackman to Marie. 'But you should know that my son has been exonerated of all blame. Far from being able to grieve for his terrible loss, instead he was dragged through the courts and wrongfully convicted of murdering the people he loved most. Then he spent years incarcerated in an institution that no decent man or woman should ever have to set foot in. It devastated our whole family.'

As the father continued speaking, Marie observed the son. Giles Bannon could never have slipped through any top window. Which at least cancelled out any suspicions regarding their recent murders. She had imagined him almost emaciated, with the pallor of someone who'd been a long time imprisoned, but he was much fatter than his photos showed him to be, almost obese. Somewhat cruelly, she thought prison food must have suited him.

'But now you're free, and rightly so,' Ruth said to Giles.

'Ha! You think so? I've been hounded out of my home and reduced to spending my days alone with the blinds closed in a lonely place that I barely know. It doesn't seem too much like freedom to me.'

Marie had seen those closed blinds. If Giles Bannon was innocent, then life had indeed been cruel to him. She regretted her thought about the prison food.

'This ordeal,' Giles continued, 'has not only destroyed my family and my home, it's taken its toll on my physical and mental health as well.' He looked almost beseechingly at Marie. 'I don't think I could cope with another inquiry about something I had no part in.'

'And that's why we're here,' his father said. 'To ask for reassurance that you will leave Giles alone. I — we — assure you that he has nothing to do with whatever is going on here. We also wanted to tell you that as of this weekend, his mother and I are taking him away for a few weeks. This has been so unfair on him. We considered moving on again, but that feels like admitting we have something to hide. Plus, the property we've found is perfect for his needs. Giles will be staying and, hopefully, one day he'll become a member of the community, with no shadow hanging over him.' He looked at Ruth. 'I'll furnish you with our travel plans and the contact details of where we're going. I'm sure the media will be covering this dreadful murder, so we'll return when it's all over.'

'If it helps at all, sir,' said Jackman, glancing from father to son, 'we have no reason to look in Giles's direction regarding the case we're currently investigating. It's the work of a very particular kind of person.' He smiled at Giles. 'And he's nothing whatsoever like you, sir. We won't be knocking on your door.'

Mark Bannon looked relieved, but Giles still appeared sceptical. *And why shouldn't he be?* Marie thought. His dealings with the police and the judicial system must have been the stuff of nightmares.

Ruth said that indeed it was a good idea for Giles to absent himself for a while. She promised to do her utmost to ensure that his presence in the area remained unknown.

'No one knows he's here, Superintendent,' said his father, 'and I want to keep it that way. Some people out there have the habit of jumping to ill-informed conclusions. They aren't interested in the truth and would happily incite a lynch mob if the fancy took them.'

'Enough, Dad. Enough. We've said our piece. Now let's just go.' Giles stood up. Marie saw that he was shaking.

Mark stood too. 'I'm sorry. My son is right. If I could just have an email address we can send our details to?'

Jackman took two cards from his pocket and gave one to each of them. 'Use my own personal email address. And, Giles, if anyone does bother you, ring me direct.'

After they had gone, Ruth directed them to sit again. 'Have either of you read the trial transcripts?'

Marie nodded. 'Yes, plus I've been through the media reports.'

'Opinion?'

'The first trial was flawed, full of omissions and with not nearly enough hard evidence. I was surprised they handed down a guilty verdict. But the jury must have seen something I didn't, since they were there day after day, watching him.'

'And what did you think of him today, Rowan?' Ruth asked.

'He's a mess, Ruth. That was no act. He's screwed up, poor man.'

Marie recalled the uncontrollable shaking of his hands, and the twisted, angry look when Ruth had mentioned being free. 'I agree, Super. He's clearly seriously affected by what's happened, but who knows? It could be a guilt thing.'

'Mmm.' Ruth sat back in her chair. 'He's not what I expected. His father certainly seems to have a close eye on him. He and the mother upped sticks too, you know, so that he wouldn't be completely alone in a strange county. Mrs Bannon's family were born here. Now they live in East Saltern, about fifteen minutes from their son.'

'Well, whatever we think,' said Jackman, 'in the eyes of the law he's an innocent man, and we'll treat him as such.' He gave Marie a grin. 'I guessed what you were thinking when you realised who he was, Marie Evans. "Hey up! He'll not get through any top opener that I've ever seen." Am I right?'

'Except for the "hey up." That's hardly Welsh! But at least he's one less name to add to the list of suspects.'

Jackman pulled a face. 'We don't have *any* names on the suspect list yet.'

'And that's worrying,' said Ruth. 'You two better get out of my office and do something about it. I just wanted you to hear all that for yourselves and give you a chance to get to see our new neighbour in person.'

They stood up to go. 'Thanks, Ruth,' said Jackman. 'We appreciate it.' He paused in the doorway. 'By the way, off the record, what did you think? Guilty or innocent?'

She gave him one of her shrewd looks. 'Personally? I'm reserving judgement.'

# CHAPTER TWENTY-THREE

Having apprised her son Andrew of the need to keep his younger brother occupied and why, Annie Carson set off for Old Fleet.

She found Natalie's bungalow, Crosswinds. Patsy opened the door to her, smiling.

'Ah, the great escape. Work out okay, did it?'

'Like a dream. I hate to cut Callum out, but people may want to say things he shouldn't hear.'

When they were all settled in Natalie's lounge, and tea and coffee had been served, Annie took the lead. 'I hate to say this, ladies, but I don't think we were selected at random, as I first believed.'

A rattle filled the silence as the women set down their cups.

'But we knew that,' said Fleur. 'He picked us out because of the photographs we had.'

'Yes, of course, that's partly right,' said Annie. 'But it's more than that. He's looking for a specific child. From the questions the police have been asking, it can be inferred that this man's child was taken from him and either fostered or adopted, and he wants him back.' Annie looked at them. 'The police have asked us all if the children in those photos were ours by birth. They also wanted to know if we had ever known a child called Teddy, isn't that right?'

They all nodded.

'Well, that's the child he's searching for.'

'I agree,' said Patsy. 'It makes sense. But you'll have to go back a few years. This didn't happen recently.'

'Exactly. We need to search our memories for a young boy we may have known in the past, even slightly.' She took a mouthful of tea. 'In my own case, I recall a boy of around seven I was once asked to mentor. My Callum used to go to an after-school club. The kids could do anything they liked — arts and crafts, reading, gymnastics or just play. The club was intended to develop their interests and encourage independence and social skills. I was part of a team of volunteers who helped out.'

'My Jason went to one of those,' said Fleur.

'Well,' Annie said, 'one of the teachers asked me to mentor a boy who'd been abused and was socially isolated. They thought he needed one-to-one contact with someone who could help boost his self-confidence. I tried my best with him, but for two months he hardly said a word. Then his mother took him away.' The memory brought a lump to her throat. 'I'd become quite attached to the little tyke, even though he rarely spoke to me, but then he was gone, and I never saw him again.'

'What was his name?' asked Sylvia.

'Ben.' Even the name made her feel sad. 'Just when I thought I was getting somewhere . . .' She spread her hands. 'Gone.'

She looked at the others. 'Have any of you had any experiences like that, or maybe something more personal? This is no time for holding back, even if the memory is painful or embarrassing. It could be up to us to provide the police with some sort of viable lead. A child could be in terrible danger.'

'Well, I've never spoken about this . . .'

Everyone looked at Sylvia.

'I once actively helped a young mother and her child to run away from her husband.'

'Oh my,' said Annie. 'Can you tell us about it?'

'I'll try. You see, I haven't always worked in that crappy nursery. I was a nurse in the A & E department of Greenborough Hospital. I was particularly good with frightened youngsters and was often called on to calm a terrified child. But this particular boy showed no sign of that. He was just uncommunicative, and although he had a nasty cut on his hand, he didn't even flinch as it was being attended to.' Sylvia had a faraway look in her eyes. 'Actually, the mother worried me a good deal more.'

'When was this?' asked Annie.

'Around four years ago, just before I retired,' she said. 'Anyway, it was clear that what brought them to A & E was just an accident, no hint of abuse, but it was manic that day and there were hold-ups with the attending doctors, so I spent quite a bit of time with the mother. She told me her name was Susie and she was terrified of her husband.' She paused. 'To cut a long story short, I had her to stay with me for a couple of nights, rather than return to her abusive spouse.' Sylvia sighed. 'She went back to him, as victims of abuse so often do, but three days later she was back, with terrible facial bruises and a badly cut lip. This time I urged her to take her child and run, and then go to the authorities and report him. Which she did.' Sylvia fell silent.

'Go on, Sylvia,' Annie urged gently.

'I heard from her a month later. Things hadn't gone well. She'd finished up moving from refuge to refuge, afraid he would catch up with her, but she never went to the authorities. I urged her to let me help her, put her in touch with people who would protect her and the boy, but I never heard from her again.' She gave them a wan smile. 'Not a very happy ending.'

'Sadly, I can't confess to being so caring and helpful,' said Fleur Harper miserably. 'In fact, I'm bitterly ashamed of myself. But as we're baring our souls — or in my case washing our dirty linen in public — here goes.' She cleared her throat. 'I was aware that a woman I knew was being threatened with domestic violence, but I kept quiet and did nothing to help.' She closed her eyes for a moment. 'In my own defence, I was in a very bad place mentally and physically at the time. My own marriage was breaking up, and I've never been strong emotionally. I was a wreck, not coping at all, and I was starting to realise that this would probably cause me to lose my precious son, Jason. Sounds weak and pathetic, I know, but I just didn't have room in my head for someone else's problems.'

Sylvia smiled understandingly at her. 'I think we can all understand that, Fleur. It's a survival mechanism, not weakness.'

'I absolutely agree,' said Natalie. 'Maybe it's time for you to let that guilt go, Fleur. You clearly needed all of your energy to come through it.'

Annie said that sharing her experience might allow Fleur to forget. 'Do you recall the family's name? Or where they lived?'

Fleur frowned. 'I know where they lived, just three doors away from me in Glebe Close, Cartoft, at number nine, but I can't recall their name. I think they had two children, Cassie and Christopher. That's how I knew what went on in their house. Christopher used to sneak out and come to our kitchen via the back gardens. He was a poor little thing, not ill-treated that I ever saw, but he was so quiet and nervous.' She laughed. 'He reminded me of myself when I was a kid. The things he told me about his mother and father used to make my blood run cold. He spoke of it as if it was perfectly normal. Then, as my Bob was on the verge of leaving, I cut the boy off. I will always bitterly regret that.'

'Are they still living there?' asked Patsy.

'Long gone. They did a moonlight flit about the same time as my husband left. Packed up and moved out in the dead of night, apparently.'

Annie was beginning to wonder if, therapeutic as it might be, any of this was relevant.

Natalie said, 'I hate to disappoint, but I can't think of anything involving children, or battered wives. Even my nephew Davy is very much a loner. He'd play in the garden here all day sometimes and never brought a friend along to see the frogs or the newts in the wildlife pond.' She went suddenly quiet.

'What are you thinking?' asked Patsy.

Natalie looked at her friend. 'Do you remember Dylan, Patsy?'

Patsy thought for a moment, then smiled. 'Oh yes. Goodness, I'd forgotten all about him.'

'Me too,' said Natalie thoughtfully. She looked at Annie. 'I'm sure this is absolutely nothing to do with anything, but for a while, when Davy was about eight or nine, he had an imaginary friend. He called him Dylan.'

'We thought he'd taken it from the rabbit in *The Magic Roundabout*,' added Patsy.

'But the odd thing was that he only ever saw Dylan here in the garden. Nowhere else at all. I didn't think much about it at first. After all, lots of children have imaginary friends. My brother had one when we were children.'

'Agatha Christie confessed to having imaginary friends as an adult,' added Patsy. 'They're nothing to worry about.'

'Absolutely. But I was fascinated by the fact that Dylan never came indoors. Davy met him outside and never invited him in.' She frowned. 'I remember once doing some work in the greenhouse and hearing Davy chatting away to himself and laughing softly. It sounded really creepy.'

'Didn't he start taking food out into the garden?' asked Patsy.

'Yes. He'd gather up all sorts of scraps from his lunch and take them outside in a napkin. It sounds innocuous, but the thing is, I never found the napkins afterwards. At that point I started to wonder if there might really be another child.' Natalie shook her head. 'It came to a head when Davy helped me clean out one of the ponds. We took the fish out, put them in big containers and drained the pond. I scrubbed it out and we refilled it and put it back together again. When it was done, as you can imagine, it was pretty muddy around the edges. I went inside to get us some drinks and when I went back out, Davy told me that Dylan liked what we'd done. I said that was nice, he should have helped us. Davy looked really upset and said, "He's not allowed."' Natalie raised her eyebrows. 'There was something in his voice that really worried me . . . but not half as much as when I went out later that evening and found two sets of children's wellington boot prints in the mud by the pond. I knew Davy's, and the others were slightly smaller with a different tread altogether.'

'So there really was another child in your garden?' asked Fleur in amazement. 'Did you find out where he came from?'

'I never did. Davy seemed a bit subdued after that and told me Dylan had gone away. I questioned him about his friend, but he just said that he'd known he would go one day, he never stayed long anywhere. As far as I recall, he never mentioned him again.'

Annie thought about Natalie's story. Of all of them, this one resonated the most. A child that never stayed long in one place. A child that remained unseen. So, despite what Natalie thought, this one was important. Each of them, in different ways, had been in contact with a transient boy. Was it the same one? Their rather vague descriptions did kind of tally. But how on earth would the intruder have known about these occurrences?

They discussed these questions, until Fleur said she ought to get home, as she was still nervous of being out late. That brought the meeting to a close, and Annie made her way home.

Her mind was still spinning when she got in, and she was glad of Andrew's presence. After Callum had gone to bed, she would tell him about her 'investigation', and ask his opinion before she contacted PC Stacey Smith. Annie was afraid she'd been making too much of what could well be irrelevant and petty anecdotes. Andrew would help her put her enquiries into perspective.

# CHAPTER TWENTY-FOUR

Jackman put down the phone. 'It's definitely a woman's body in that shallow grave, and from the description, it's very likely to be Andrea Becker.'

Marie exhaled. 'Hardly a surprise, but nevertheless . . .'

'Forensics will probably check fingerprints from inside the house and compare them with those of the dead woman. The neighbours have confirmed that she lived alone, although she had a lot of regular callers, both male and female, which isn't exactly a surprise either.' Jackman sat back. 'But, as there's no new partner or husband living with her, we might have to ask Felix, the ex-husband, to identify her.'

'Jackman, I could be completely off base here, but I'm getting dead twitchy about the women whose photographs were stolen,' said Marie slowly. 'The suspect seems to like to permanently eradicate anyone who gets in his way, and as we have no idea why he took those particular boys' pictures, what if those women are in danger?'

Jackman groaned. 'We don't have the resources to watch them all, Marie, Uniform are stretched enough providing officers to cover the boys' schools and advise those schools on extra security. And apart from that, we've nowhere near enough proof that they're at risk to get those women into safe houses. It won't happen, I'm afraid.'

'Until one of them finishes up in another shallow grave,' she muttered. 'Then the others will have to be protected.' She looked at him. 'I don't want to scare the shit out of them, they've been through enough, but I think we need to find a way to encourage them to be extra vigilant. They're all far too vulnerable, considering we have a highly motivated killer out there.'

She was right, but how could it be done without adding to their anxiety? 'I'll speak to Stacey and Jay, and Simon too. Maybe they could have a word with their skipper and watch for any night-time activity in or near their addresses.'

Marie smiled at him. 'Thanks, boss. It's better than nothing.' She lost her smile. 'If only we knew who this damned killer was! Then we could throw every man and woman we have out there to look for the bastard. As it is, we're in the bloody dark.'

'Steady on, Marie,' Jackman said. 'It's frustrating, I know, but we'll get him. We're making headway every day, you know that.'

'And people are dying every day. A child is in danger, and we don't even know who that child is. Our headway isn't good enough, is it?'

Jackman was surprised at Marie's sudden burst of negativity. Up to now, she had been amazingly upbeat and positive about the investigation. It was as if someone had thrown a switch. He closed the door. 'Talk to me,' he said softly. 'This isn't like you.'

Marie sank back in her chair and let out a long sigh. 'I'm sorry, Jackman. That was out of order.'

'So, what's troubling you? The real reason.'

'It's silly. It's stupid. And it's not even professional.'

He looked at her in puzzlement, then grinned. 'Call me thick, but some clarification would be helpful.'

Slowly, an apologetic smile replaced the scowl. 'Okay, if you must know, it was seeing Giles Bannon that set it all off. I got to thinking that if he really did three years in HMP Full Sutton for a dreadful crime that, not only did he not commit, but was never given the opportunity to grieve for his wife and child, and there was no one to help him come to terms with what happened. Add to that, the poor sod also knew that their killer was still out there, probably laughing his head off, and most likely would never be caught. It's a wonder he's still able to function at all.'

Jackman nodded. 'It is a worst-case scenario and, as you well know, it's very, very rare.'

'I know, but it got me thinking how important it is for us police officers to get everything right. If we cock up, people suffer.'

'And they'd suffer a lot more if we weren't here and doing our job to the best of our ability. We're only human, Marie, and far from perfect, but we do our level best.' But she knew all this. 'And the rest?' he asked. 'The bit that's really eating you?'

Marie gave him a wry smile. 'You really do know me, don't you, Jackman? Sure, Bannon kick-started it, but what's behind it all is that I suddenly realised I'd found someone I really care about, and it scared me. I married a policeman, and he died too soon. I'm terrified it's going to happen again.' Her voice dropped to almost a whisper. 'Life is so unfair sometimes — look at what happened to Bannon, and to my Bill. I don't want to lose someone else.'

Jackman went and put his arm around her. 'Time for that hug you were talking about yesterday, I think. And before you object, it's *wholly* appropriate.'

'I'm not objecting. But I told you it was stupid,' she said tearfully.

'Far from it. Life deals us some pretty poor hands sometimes. But just think: you, Marie Evans, have just emerged, blinking in the sunlight, from a very long, dark social hibernation. It's an emotional awakening. I know that from meeting and falling in love with Laura. It's a shock to the system.' Jackman sank down on his haunches beside her. 'It will pass, I promise, and you'll be stronger than ever.'

'Now I feel like a real idiot. I can't believe I just offloaded all that onto you.'

'Anytime. I'm your friend, and you were there for me when Laura and I had our big wobble a little while back. We've chosen a career that rarely supports stable relationships, but it's down to us to stick two fingers up and make a go of it.'

Marie finally laughed. 'Thank you, Auntie Jackman. You can stand down now. I feel my sanity returning.'

'About bloody time,' he said, smiling. 'Now, will you please blow your nose, get back on your steed — sorry, bike — and help me catch this killer.'

\* \* \*

Annie had decided to tell Callum about the meeting. She played the whole thing down, describing it as a spur-of-the-moment thing instigated by Natalie. Knowing how little time he had with his brother these days, she had decided to spare him from having to choose between them. Andrew added that it was his fault really, having thought Callum would much rather keep his big brother company than drink tea with a bunch of old women. So, after a few grumbles, Callum had come round, and of course had agreed with Andrew.

Now, Callum was up in his room, talking to one of his friends on WhatsApp, while she and Andrew prepared supper.

She soon came out with the whole story, glad to have someone to share it with.

Andrew took it all in, then laid down the paring knife he was using. 'Mum, you can't sit on this!' He gave her a long look, sighed and smiled. 'It was a great idea, and let's face it, it's worked. But you need to pass it straight to the police. Believe me, they need every single bit of intelligence they can get. For all you know, somewhere in those stories there's some tiny detail that will link to something they know and you don't. It could be vital, so stop what you're doing and ring that number you've stuck on the fridge door. Though to be fair to them, you'd better tell your friends what you've done.'

'When exactly did you get so damned sensible?' she asked, shaking her head.

He grinned. 'I've always been sensible, it's just that nobody noticed. Now, off you go.'

Annie rang Natalie's number, and to her relief, Patsy answered. 'Can you do me a favour . . . ?'

'I'll ring round the others right now, Annie. You phone the police. I was going to ring you myself, because the more I've thought about it, the more I think your son is right. We must tell the police. Keep in touch.'

That done, Annie phoned PC Stacey Smith.

'Let me stop you right there, Annie,' said Stacey almost immediately. 'I'm in the CID room now, and they're finishing up for the day. You need to tell the DI. I'll get him. Hold on.'

And then she was speaking to DI Jackman. She explained that the stories were of a rather personal nature, and he seemed to appreciate what she meant.

'Can I come and speak to you, Mrs Carson? I think I need to hear this from you directly — if I may?'

Annie agreed.

She ended the call, by now somewhat drained, and there was Andrew, a glass of wine in his hand.

'Here you are, Mum. Dutch courage. And open bottles of wine don't last for ever, you know, even in the fridge.'

'Maybe I should save it until after I've spoken to the detective inspector. I reckon I'll be needing it then.'

Andrew grinned. 'You've done the right thing, Mum.'

'Patsy agrees, and she's sensible. She was going to suggest it herself.' She sat down on the nearest kitchen stool. Her face clouded over. 'What are we going to tell Callum?'

'He thinks you two are a team, so bring him in on it. He's no fool, Mum. For his age, he's pretty canny. You've come this far together, and you can't shut him out now.' He gave her shoulder a nudge. 'If anything comes up that you think is unsuitable, give me a nod and I'll suggest we leave you with the inspector for a while and join you again later.'

'My hero,' she said, dangerously close to tears. 'I'm so glad you're here.'

'So am I! Without me around to keep you on the straight and narrow, who knows what would have happened. Secret societies, indeed.' He shuddered dramatically.

Annie suddenly felt a rush of affection for her lovely son, and a massive relief at handing it all over to someone who actually knew what to do with it. 'It's all right, Andrew. I'll hang up the mask and tight pants. My work here is done. Let the professionals take over.'

\* \* \*

The heavy clouds and driving rain made it feel like late evening when Jackman and Marie arrived back at the station. As they raced, heads down, across the car park and into the building, Marie gasped, 'I just hope this keeps our killer out of action tonight.'

Jackman stamped his feet to shake off the drops. 'I guess it depends entirely on his endgame, and whether he's following a strict schedule.'

They hurried upstairs and Marie went off to get some hot drinks. They were staying late to go through all the information Annie Carson and her son had provided.

Spread out on the desk lay a ream of papers and a spiral-bound notebook with a Tardis on the front. Jackman smiled. He'd leafed through it while he waited for Marie to return with coffee and had been most impressed. In fact, he wished that some police officers were as meticulous as this twelve-year-old boy. Dates, times and observations had been listed, followed by references to details he had followed up later on the computer. When Marie arrived with the drinks, he pushed it across the desk to her. 'Take a look. I'm thinking of writing to his careers master suggesting he go into CID.'

Marie looked at it and laughed. 'Puts a few coppers I know to shame, that's for sure.'

Jackman skimmed through his notes. 'I'm not sure what Annie Carson intended with this group. Victim support maybe, or therapy. She's certainly managed to compile an awful lot for us to work on.'

'Interesting too,' said Marie. 'I reckon there might be something in here that will lead us to our man's identity. We have his image, courtesy of Simon. All we need now is a name and we can start the hunt.'

They read in silence. Then Jackman stopped, read again. 'Look! Why didn't I pick up on that when Annie mentioned it?'

Marie looked at him, her mouth slightly open.

'God, I'm an idiot! It was something Fleur said about a boy who used to climb over the fence into her back garden and talk to her about what was going on in his neighbours' house.'

'Yes, I got that.'

'It was a family that did a moonlight flit. What if it was Claire and Leon? And her husband. Of course! The man we're looking for. And I happen to know someone who will tell us exactly who they are.' Jackman reached for his mobile. 'These people lived in my village. And who knows everything that's ever happened there?'

'Hetty Maynard! Your housekeeper.'

Jackman beamed at her. 'Good old Hetty.' He found her number and, tapping his foot, waited for her to answer. 'Len? Evening, Len. Sorry it's late. It's Jackman here. Is Hetty around, please?' He put the phone on loudspeaker.

'Yes, Mr J? Everything all right?'

'Yes, Hetty, just fine. I need your local knowledge. Do you have a few minutes?'

'Oh yes, Mr J, certainly. How can I help?'

'A family — husband and wife and a boy and a girl — who used to live at number nine, Glebe Close. Do you remember them? Or know their surname?'

Hetty said, 'Oh them. Bit of a bad lot, I believe. They were nothing but trouble, or so people said. And the girl wasn't theirs. Cassie was a niece who stayed with them for a while after her parents split up, and the mother took her back when she'd got herself sorted.'

That would be why Claire left with only the boy. 'And their surname?'

'Spiller. Yes, that's it. Jordan and Claire Spiller. The boy was called Christopher, but the neighbours called him Teddy. When he was little, he always carried around this moth-eaten old teddy bear.'

'Thank you, Hetty Maynard. You're a diamond.' At last. A real lead to Teddy. 'Hetty, we were told they did a runner one night. Was that true?'

'Yes, they did. Although not exactly a runner. They owned the house, so it wasn't a case of taking off without paying the rent. But a friend of mine who lived in Glebe Close at the time said they went in different cars. He was on his own, and Claire took Teddy. Next thing we knew, the house had a "for sale" board outside, and we never heard from them again.'

Jackman took down the approximate month and year of this departure. 'What did he do for a living? I presume he did work?'

'Oh yes,' Hetty said. 'That was one of the odd things about him. Never out of work, and good at it too. Just dead jealous over his wife and a bit free with his fists, or so it seemed. He was a roofer. Did special jobs, like stately homes and old churches. He was no labourer, certainly. I saw him once up on the spire of St Mary's, fixing some tiles. Fair turned my stomach to see him swinging around so high up.'

Better and better, thought Jackman. 'One last thing. If I bring you a photograph on my way home, do you think you might tell me if it's a likeness of Jordan Spiller?'

'Of course, Mr J, we ain't going anywhere! See you later.'

He thanked her and ended the call. 'Jordan Spiller, and he's not afraid of heights.'

'So climbing up to a first-floor window would be a doddle.' Marie's smile spread from ear to ear. 'We have a name! And if your dear Hetty fingers him, we're out of the starting gate at last.'

Jackman was certain this was the right man, and Hetty would confirm it. 'Come on, let's call it a day. I'm going directly to Hetty's place, and I'll ring and let you know what she says. We'll start early tomorrow and throw everything at finding this man.' He gathered up the papers. 'I'll get one of the lads to type all this up tomorrow. You never know, the rest of these seemingly disparate incidents could easily be tied to Spiller as well and tell us why he chose those particular women. Thank you, Annie and Callum!'

'And Hetty Maynard. Off you go, Jackman. And don't forget to ring me.'

'Don't worry, I will. How nice to see a smile on my best friend's face again.'

'I'm back on track now,' she said. 'And thank you, Jackman, for getting me through that wobble — and for that illicit hug.'

'You're welcome. Any time it's appropriate.' He grabbed his damp coat. 'Speak later.'

* * *

Jackman was soon standing, dripping, on Hetty and Len's doorstep.

'Oh my goodness, come on in!' cried Hetty. 'You'll catch your death out there.'

Their cottage was a homely place, full of mementos from their long lives together. Anniversaries, souvenirs of different places their relatives had holidayed in, and various other bits and pieces. Being Hetty's house, the place was of course sparkling clean and as dust-free as an open fire and an ancient dog would allow. It wasn't to his taste, but it always felt so welcoming. Jackman loved it.

'Get that down you, lad.'

Len Maynard was handing him a steaming glass in an intricate latticework silver holder. Jackman knew it was one of the precious Moroccan tea glasses their son, John, had brought back from North Africa, but he had no idea as to its contents. Len was a keen maker of hot toddies, served up at every season of the year. Jackman tasted honey and lemon, the rest seemed to consist of ninety-proof rum. Jackman downed it gratefully — he lived three hundred yards away and was the only policeman in the village.

'I always felt so sorry for that little lad, Mr J,' said Hetty. 'You asking about them made me wonder what happened to him. It wasn't the best start in life for a young 'un.'

Jackman pulled his copy of the image from his pocket and unfolded it. Miraculously, it was dry. 'Is this Spiller, Hetty?'

She took her reading glasses from her cardigan pocket and put them on. 'Oh yes, that's him. I'd know him anywhere — right beanpole he was. Thin as a reed.'

Jackman smiled. 'Thank you so much, Hetty.' He lifted his glass in a toast.

'Did he turn really bad, Mr J?' she asked.

'About as bad as they come, Hetty. Can't tell you any more, you know how it is, but I really need to catch him.'

'Well, I must say, I always believed he wasn't quite right in the head. But I thought he had a good side too, which didn't match up with what you heard about him. Like, he could be really gentle, especially with dogs — though he didn't like cats at all.' She glanced at the old dog sprawled contentedly across Jackman's feet. 'He loved our Albert to bits. He saw a Traveller try to steal him from our back garden once, and he really let him have it. I do have to thank him for that. And Teddy never showed signs of any injury. Jordan seemed to really care about the boy. I suppose he took his anger out on Claire. I reckon he's one of those Jekyll and Hyde people.'

'You could well be right, Hetty,' said Jackman. 'Now all I have to do is find him, but if he went off without leaving a forwarding address, that might not be too easy.' He took a sip of the powerful toddy and felt it warm him as it went down.

'Oh, he's still in the area, Mr J,' said Hetty. 'I haven't seen him myself, but you know old John who looks after the churchyard? Well, he has. He mentioned it to me a week or so ago. He saw him walking around the gravestones early one morning and recognised him at once. The Spiller family are all buried there, and John thinks he was looking at their graves. Not the first time he'd been there either — the postie saw him too.'

Jackman began to wonder about this man. Maybe Spiller wasn't quite the devious psychopath he'd supposed him to be. He was pretty sure Jordan was their night stalker, but his motives were suddenly less clear. 'Hetty, do you have any idea of where in the churchyard the Spillers were buried?' he asked.

'Oh yes, lad,' Len said. 'They lies at the back of the church itself, next to them two yew trees. Don't walk widdershins around the church, mind. It's ungodly.'

Hetty smiled. 'He means unlucky. You must always walk clockwise around the church.'

Jackman was aware of the old superstition that if you walked three times anticlockwise around a church you invoked the Devil, and though he didn't believe it, he always made sure he kept the church on his right when he went round it. 'My mum taught me that when I was a small boy, Hetty, so don't worry.' He downed the last of his drink. 'Phew! That was powerful, our Len.'

'Wouldn't do you no good if it weren't now, would it?' the old man chuckled.

Jackman stood up. 'Thank you for your help — and the toddy. I suppose I'd better get home while I can still see straight.'

But Jackman didn't go directly to Mill Corner. He drove to the church. Getting out his Maglite, he locked the car and hurried towards the ancient village church, which in the gathering dark was nothing but a dark shape looming above him. There were three graves belonging to the family Spiller, and on one of them Jackman found a single artificial red rose with a plastic wallet attached to it, a card inside. In the beam of his torch, he read: *My heart has never stopped crying for you.*

Jackman stood and stared at it, oblivious to the rain now trickling beneath his collar and seeping into his shoes. Had Jordan Spiller left this?

Vowing to return it if he was proved wrong, he took a spare evidence bag from his pocket and slipped the flower into it.

He hurried back to the car and drove the short distance to Mill Corner. They had a name at last, but what kind of man was this?

## CHAPTER TWENTY-FIVE

While Jackman wandered through the graveyard, two other men were abroad that rainy night. They paid no attention to the weather, and neither were in their right mind. Both were dangerous. One doggedly pursued his aim, while the other never operated without a contingency plan. This latter man consigned tonight's expedition to one of simple reconnaissance, smiled coldly and went home.

\* \* \*

Marie had just poured herself a glass of wine and was contemplating supper, when her phone rang. Jackman.

'Boss! What news?'

'It's him, it's Jordan Spiller. Hetty and Len have identified him. We start in earnest tomorrow.'

There was something not quite right in the way Jackman said this. 'You sound a bit down, Jackman. You've got the result you wanted, so what's up?'

Jackman gave a little laugh. 'It's nothing, I'm sure, but the picture Hetty painted of him doesn't quite match up to the image I had in my head. I'm afraid we might find that his motives are deeper and more convoluted than we first believed.'

'As if our cases are ever straightforward!' she said. 'So, do you want to expand on that or hit me with it tomorrow?'

'It'll wait, Marie. I'll let you switch off for the evening. We'll tackle it after a night's sleep. And I need a hot shower. I've been standing in the local churchyard reading tombstones in the pouring rain.'

'Er, right, Jackman. New hobby of yours, is it? See you in the morning.'

As soon as Marie ended the call, her phone rang again. What had Jackman forgotten now? But it wasn't Jackman. 'Have you eaten yet?'

'Ralph! Well, not exactly, I'm just weighing up my options — bother to cook or microwave?'

'Do neither. I've had to collect some statements from an address close to your place. Suppose I grab two fish and chip suppers and bring them over?'

'Perfect! Make mine a large haddock, and don't forget the mushy peas and scraps. Oh. But you're a vegetarian. What are you going to eat?'

She heard him laugh. 'I'm what's known as a pescatarian. I do eat fish, although not often. I should be with you in around twenty minutes, give or take.'

Marie found herself smiling from ear to ear. Three meals together in one week! Then she realised what she must look like.

'Hellfire! Twenty minutes! I need at least an hour.' Marie took a quick shower and racked her brains for something to wear. After a few moments of panic, she settled for a pale blue-and-white-striped shirt. She brushed her hair, telling herself that she was acting like a teenager.

She'd just got herself ready when Ralph arrived. They ate at the kitchen table. Ralph had a knack for making her feel totally at ease, and she began to enjoy herself.

'I thought vegetarians didn't eat any animal products, including eggs and dairy,' said Marie.

Ralph sat back. 'Not quite. People who have a totally plant-based diet are vegan. My sister is a vegan. It depends

234

on your reasons. I chose to give up eating meat because of the way animals are factory farmed, but my mother gave me fish once a week for health reasons. I've kind of remained that way. My sister and I fight like cat and dog over it.'

Listening to him speak, Marie realised that she knew almost nothing about Ralph Enderby. So far, they'd had little chance to spend much time together. She hoped that would change very soon. 'What's your sister's name? Is she younger or older than you?'

'Diana. She's two years older than me and lives in the Peak District, near Matlock. She's an equine veterinary surgeon.'

'She'd get on a treat with my boss,' Marie said. 'Jackman is horse mad, and his mother owns a livery stable.'

'Diana's the brains out of the two of us. Even as a kid she was really bright. Me, I'm just a plod — no degrees and no letters after my name.'

'You haven't done too badly, Ralph. We all have different skills.'

'I guess if we were all geniuses it would be a weird world to live in. Diana's amazing with animals, but she's not exactly well-endowed with good old common sense, and she's certainly not worldly-wise. So, yes, I suppose we all have our strengths and weaknesses. And speaking of strength, how's Rhiannon?'

Ralph had met her mother, and Rhiannon had taken an immediate liking to him. 'She's just as wonderful as ever. It was so good to spend that week with her. If there's one place that recharges my batteries, it's in those glorious Welsh mountains with Mum.' She then surprised herself by saying, 'Come with me next time I go, and you'll see what I mean.'

'I'd love to. I'm ashamed to say I've never been to Wales. It was always Ireland for our holidays, as Dad had a brother out there. I think that's where Di got her love of horses — he worked at a thoroughbred breeding stable.'

They managed to talk for a full half-hour without mentioning work, until Marie broached the subject. 'What made you join the force, Ralph?'

'I think it was a need to find independence, something I could be good at in my own right.'

'Because of your sister?' she asked.

'Because of a whole family of high achievers.' He gave a wry laugh. 'Academic success seemed to come easy to them, whereas I struggled. My dad was a senior engineer in a company that built advanced-technology combine harvesters. My mother, Janice, was and still is one of those amazingly capable and confident women that small villages and rural communities rely on. She runs the food bank, organises charity functions, is an active member of every women's group in the area and once a year heads up a committee that puts together an amazing ten-day-long flower and arts festival.'

'She sounds like Superwoman,' Marie said.

'In a rural, villagey kind of way, she is. If I had the power to dish out an OBE, she would get it. But you can see why I needed something to be good at, can't you? The first time I took a drug dealer off the streets, I knew I was on the right path.' He sighed happily. 'And when I was part of a team that solved a really tricky serious crime, that clinched it. I was one of the family at last.'

Marie doubted that he would have meant any less to his parents or his sibling even if he had failed at everything.

'How's your case going?' he asked.

She told him that they finally had a name for their killer and that he used to live in the same village as Jackman.

'Oh, that's a massive step forward, isn't it?' he said. 'Get a face and a name and everything feels like it's shifted in your favour at last. Want me to flag it up as a priority in our area?'

'An attention drawn will go out in the morning to all forces — we reckon he travels about a lot — but please do make your guys aware of just how badly we need to get him.'

They went into the lounge with their coffee. As they sat down, Marie was suddenly reminded of how depressed and angry she'd felt earlier in the day. She resolved to take each day as it came, which included this new relationship. Her phone rang.

She swore. Ralph laughed. Then she laughed with him and answered the call.

'Sorry to disturb you, DS Evans.'

It was the night duty sergeant. 'Yes, Sarge, what's the problem?'

'We believe it's your man again, Marie. Someone has tried to gain access to a property in Skeldyke Lane in Saltern. Scared the occupant half to death. Woman living alone again. He took off on his toes, but I've got several units and a dog handler out there trying to find him. Will you attend?'

'Has DI Jackman been alerted, Sarge?'

'No answer from his mobile and the landline is busy, but I'll keep trying.'

'Tell him I'll see him there. On my way.'

She ended the call and spread her hands.

'Just don't apologise.' He moved closer and looked at her intently. 'I know what this is going to be like, Marie. But I'm still up for it, if you are?'

His kiss seemed to stop time. Then he held her at arm's length, smiling at her, his eyes shining. 'All right, DS Evans. Go and answer your shout. Our time will come.'

'And I'm going to damn well make sure it does, DS Enderby!'

* * *

Marie drove into Saltern-le-Fen, thinking that she'd finally crossed the line and entered new territory. It was daunting, but she was full of hope.

Skeldyke Lane consisted of a scattering of properties along a winding lane leading from the edge of town into the marshes. The house was old, as were almost all of the ones out here. Twilight was now fast turning into darkness, and the blue lights up ahead flashed vividly against the indigo sky.

*This is my world*, thought Marie. *And it's Ralph's too. We both understand the importance of what we do, so we might be able to make it work.* She thought about the rocky road that Jackman had trodden with Laura, and knew it wouldn't be easy, but it was certainly worth trying.

She got out and locked the car. Now it was time for work.

She found the homeowner, a Mrs Owen, sitting at her kitchen table with PC Simon Laker. He really had drawn the short straw, hadn't he? She wondered briefly if he'd known what he was letting himself in for when he requested to be notified of anything connected to their investigation.

He introduced Marie to the white-faced householder. 'Are you up to telling the detective sergeant here what you told me?'

Mrs Owen nodded. 'I go to bed very early, Detective Sergeant. Not much to stay up for these days, not since my husband died. Now I know old houses do creak and groan a bit, but tonight I'd barely settled and put the telly on when I was disturbed by another noise, one I didn't recognise. I knew it was coming from downstairs, and I was terrified, but I thought I'd rather go and face whatever it was than have it come upstairs and find me.'

'That was very brave of you,' said Marie.

'That's what I said,' added Simon. 'I'm a big lad, but even I would have thought twice.'

'You can't roll over and give up just because you're a woman on your own. My Eric would have been down those stairs like a shot, and I try to follow his example when something scares me. "Head on, my girl," he would say. "Problems? Face 'em head on!"'

'And what did you find?' asked Marie.

'A face at the window.' She swallowed. 'It was distorted, horrible. Pressed right up against the glass like some gargoyle. I can't tell you how shocked I was.'

'You don't have to, Mrs Owen,' Marie said softly. 'It's written all over your face.'

'Do you think he meant to scare you, Mrs Owen?' asked Simon. 'Or something else?'

Hazel Owen seemed to think about that for a moment. 'At first, I believed he was trying to scare me, but later I wondered if he had heard me and pressed his face against the window to see where I was. I'm not really certain, but I think it was most likely the latter.'

'We found a workman's tool outside the window, Sarge, one that window fitters use. It's a lever used to remove the trim and panel. Looks like he was about to pop the glass out.' Simon grimaced. 'But Mrs Owen disturbed him and he ran off.'

'Anything from the crews who were checking the area?' she asked.

'Nothing so far,' said Simon.

Marie turned back to Hazel Owen. 'Could you describe him?'

She shook her head. 'No, not at all. I'm sorry. I just saw that nightmarish face, and then he was gone. The shock of seeing him blanked out everything else. I screamed, then when I came to my senses, I rang the police.'

Marie beckoned to Simon and he followed her outside. 'Is it me, or does this not quite make sense, Simon?' she said.

He gave a faint smile. 'I was just going to say the same to you. It's not following his usual pattern, is it?'

'Far too early in the evening for starters,' said Marie thoughtfully. 'Our man goes out late at night. And he's never tried to remove windowpanes before.'

'Plus, I talked to the lady before you got here, Sarge, and she and her husband had no children, so no grandchildren either.' He paused. 'Oh, and she doesn't have Sky.'

Marie went back inside and asked Mrs Owens about any children she might have come in contact with, even if they weren't related.

'My dear, when we realised that we couldn't have a family, we were both devastated, but we decided that if God had intended us to have children, he would have given us some of our own. So we put it out of our minds.' She looked sadly at Marie. 'There have never been any children here, and because it was so painful, I never associated closely with people who had young families. We had dogs and cats instead, and were never without company, until I lost my lovely old Lady the month before last.' She glanced up at a photo of a golden Labrador and sighed. 'But I'm going to a rescue shelter next week to try and find another old girl, hopefully as old as I am, to love and cherish for the years she has left.'

'I'm sorry if I upset you, Hazel,' said Marie gently. 'But it's an important part of a bigger investigation.'

'You didn't upset me, my duck! You've got a job to do, I know. Actually, now I'm wondering what on earth he did want. There's nothing of any value here.'

'Can I take a quick look around?' asked Marie.

'You go ahead, no problem. There's no secrets here.'

The only photos were of Hazel's late husband and a variety of pets going back over the years. So, why try to break in? It felt all wrong.

She went back outside and found Simon. 'It's not him, I'm certain of it.'

'I agree, Sarge. Maybe an opportunist thief? He'd seen she went to bed early and took a chance,' he suggested.

'Something like that. But if that's the case, he's chosen a particularly bad time to start wandering around people's houses at night.'

'You can say that again!' Simon laughed grimly. 'There's something much nastier than him out here at present.'

'And a whole load of vigilant coppers on the beat,' she added. 'Which reminds me, maybe you should ring your skipper and tell him we think it's a red herring. The budget won't cover all this overtime for a failed burglary. If it's not our killer, then it's time to call off the troops.' Marie heard her ringtone and groped in her pocket for her phone.

'Jackman! Where are you?'

'I'm so sorry, Marie. I've only just got the shout. I don't know what I was thinking, but I left my phone in the bathroom, and Laura's been using the landline. What's occurring?'

'It's all right, you can relax. Attempted break-in, but we're pretty certain it's not Spiller. Nothing matches up, and both Simon and I agree that it was a wild goose chase.'

'Then you get away too, Marie. And I'm sorry you got lumbered. Hope it didn't spoil your evening?'

Marie stifled a giggle. 'I'll get over it. See you tomorrow.'

After Marie had spoken again to Mrs Owen and reassured her that her burglar wouldn't be back, she said goodnight to Simon and drove back home.

The kitchen still smelled of fish and chips. Marie caught herself smiling. Besides the remains of the meal, something of Ralph still lingered there too. It was nice.

She made a hot drink and took it up to bed with her, undressed and snuggled under the duvet. It had been a strange day, full of ups and downs. Despite being in the middle of a murder inquiry, she felt oddly at peace.

Marie lay in the darkness and thought about her beloved husband, Bill. She spoke softly to him in the quiet of the room. 'My darling. I've held you here with me for far too long, haven't I?'

There was no answer, but she hadn't expected one.

'It's time to let you go and for me to move on. I won't ever love you less, and we'll meet again one day, I know.'

As Marie closed her eyes, she felt her husband gradually slip away from her, while the room remained warm and full of love. As sleep began to overtake her, she felt the lightest brush of a kiss on her cheek, and a whispered, 'Goodbye, my love.'

# CHAPTER TWENTY-SIX

The morning was still damp and breezy, but the torrential rain had stopped and a weak sun was struggling to emerge from behind the clouds.

Laura decided to drive past Freddie Shields's home on her way in to the police station rather than waiting till later. Her car was a nondescript grey colour, so should Freddie chance to be out and about, he wouldn't notice her. She drew near the terrace of houses where he lived. The road was fairly busy, and she couldn't slow down enough to get a good look at the place, so she turned and made her way back, parking a few houses along, from where she could see the house clearly.

The house was exactly as he had described it, with a slightly uncared-for appearance, as if he'd lost interest in keeping it up. Laura looked closer. The annexe he had spoken of with such pride was obviously costly, but that too looked rundown.

Laura glanced at the clock on her dashboard and saw that there was still plenty of time, so she drove a little further and pulled into the car park at the recreation ground next door. She might be able to get a better look from there. She locked the car and strolled over to the trees lining the boundary and found a spot that would give a fairly clear view of his mother's annexe. The luxury, purpose-built granny flatlet was in worse condition than the house.

'He's neglecting her,' she whispered out loud. Clearly, his condition was occupying his every waking moment, giving him no time to care for his mother and her home.

Laura abandoned her inspection, more anxious than ever.

\* \* \*

By nine o'clock, Jackman and Marie were working flat out. The whole team was now engaged in either hunting down Jordan Spiller or trying to establish a link between him and the women whose houses he'd entered. They were contacting estate agents regarding his rushed sale of the house in Glebe Close, contractors who specialised in church repairs and specialist firms that maintained the roofs of listed buildings. They had asked other forces to send them any information they might have on him and were trawling through the PNC and any other platform they could think of, even Facebook, to try and find a mention of his name.

Max and Charlie had the task of going through the notes provided by Annie, her son and the women's group. They had summarised the women's stories and were now trying to correlate these with actual evidence, which they would then collate and cross-check with the intelligence they already had.

The whole room resounded with the clamour of animated conversation, phones ringing and printers whirring, and with every new development, Jackman would update the whiteboards. He had already reorganised one of them, putting everything under the name JORDAN SPILLER in large capital letters. This was intended to focus the team on their goal and indicated that they were moving ahead.

Just as he was adding another piece of information, he saw Laura walk past the entrance on her way up to see Ruth Crooke. He was disturbed by the look of anxiety on her face.

'Boss? Got a mo?'

Max had raised his hand. Jackman crossed to his work-station and looked over his shoulder. 'Very impressive. You guys have turned what looked like an article from a chat magazine into a proper investigative report.'

'Thanks, boss, but you should see what we're uncovering. Charlie and I reckon that all these women had dealings with Claire and her son, even if they didn't realise it. I very much doubt that they were randomly selected by Spiller in his guise as the Sky man. He was sourcing specific women who had close ties, blood or otherwise, to young boys who were approximately ten years of age at the time he and his wife split up, and who were connected to his son in some way. What we don't know is why.'

'And how he seems to know about all these people,' added Charlie. 'That's the real puzzle. Where did he get all their names and addresses from?'

'It's like someone else was keeping a close eye on them, and then feeding it all back to Spiller,' said Max. 'But if that was the case, then why the hell didn't he act at the time? Why wait until now?' He shook his head. 'Beats me, that's for sure.'

Before Jackman could answer, PC Jay Acharya burst in and hurried across to him. 'Sir! We've just had a call from Saltern St Matthew's School. One of their pupils is missing.'

Jackman stiffened. 'Do we have a name, Jay?'

'Yes, sir. Davy Frances. One of the boys from the photos he stole. It's Natalie Miles's nephew.'

A silence fell over the whole room. It had started.

Jackman closed his eyes briefly. 'This is what we dreaded might happen. Okay, everyone. Listen. Marie and I will attend. And while we're out, I want you all to work your arses off looking for everything you can find on Spiller and where the hell he might be. Robbie, go tell the super. Say I'll ring her the moment I know what's occurring.'

'On my way, boss.'

'Jay, I want you and Stacey with us.'

Marie was already pulling her jacket on.

* * *

They drove across Saltern on blaring two-tones.

'Ah, shit! Our worst nightmare,' murmured Marie. 'He's finally stepped up his game.'

'At least we now know what his endgame is,' said Jackman. 'We always thought something like this might be on the cards, but damn it, we're one step behind him as usual.'

The school was smallish and modern: single storey, open plan with lots of glass. The various teaching spaces were divided from one another with brightly coloured panels — science labs, art rooms and the gymnasium. Marie seemed to recall that it had won an award for educational design.

As soon as they arrived, they were hurried to the head-master's office.

Without preamble, Jackman asked for a concise statement of exactly what had happened.

The head, a Mr Jonathan Lewis, asked them to sit and, his face still showing the shock of what had happened, gave them the story.

'We were made aware by yourselves and the parents that there was a small possibility that young Davy might have attracted the attention of someone who intended doing him harm, so we increased our security — without drawing attention to it, as we had no wish to frighten the pupils.' He looked from Marie to Jackman. 'All our staff had been instructed to keep an eye on Davy, and we raised the alarm at once when he failed to attend his second class of the morning.'

'He was present for the first one?' asked Jackman.

'Yes, he's never late and always commits fully to the subjects that interest him. He's a studious boy, Detective Inspector, not a particularly gregarious one, but generally liked and respected for his love of nature.' The head began to pace his office. 'He left the first class, which was English with Miss Dawson, but failed to report to Mr Cooke for science.'

'And none of his classmates saw him go?' asked Marie, slightly incredulously.

'The science block is some way away, in a different area. Plus, after each class, there is a small amount of time allowed for pupils to speak to their teacher if necessary or use the toilet facilities. We are an academy, Officers, and as such are able to set our curriculum according to the needs of the students. Davy wasn't part of a group and didn't have any particular friends. As I said, he was not a gregarious child. He would have gone on his own. It doesn't surprise me that he wasn't noticed.'

'And the entire school has been searched?' Jackman asked.

'Immediately. We have a protocol for security issues. The pupils were asked to remain in their classrooms and not to move out of them. We've spent a small fortune on CCTV equipment and have recently employed a registered security guard. He and the caretaker, plus myself and my deputy, did a thorough search, and your people are now checking the school and the grounds again.'

'We need to see that CCTV footage,' said Jackman. 'Immediately.'

Marie knew that the footage was their best chance of discovering what had happened, but even so, she didn't hold out much hope.

'Come with me.' Jonathan Lewis went to the door. 'My secretary is already checking through it with one of your officers.'

In the general office, they found PC Simon Laker with the school secretary, their eyes fixed on a screen.

'We've located him twice, sir,' said Simon. 'On both occasions he was walking alone along a busy corridor, then — nothing. There are a lot of areas covered by the surveillance cameras — the exits and entrances, most of the corridors and all the classrooms and halls. It'll take a while, but we'll keep at it.'

Marie could sense impatience rolling off Jackman in waves.

'Okay, do that,' he said to Simon, and turned back to Lewis. 'Have you had anyone unauthorised come into the school today? Deliveries? Maintenance men? Anyone unexpected?'

'No, no.' He shook his head. 'And there are no supply teachers here at present, it's just my regular teachers and admin and catering staff, and our permanent caretaker and groundsman.'

'No extra ancillaries or helpers at all?' said Marie.

Lewis frowned. 'Certainly no one new, although we do have two student teachers from the local university observing the classes, and our PE teacher, Mr Fawcett, has a scout for one of the county football teams in this week. But they're all carefully vetted and checked, I assure you, as is Mr Edwards. He's been with us, two days a week, for almost a month now, from the Wildlife Conservation Society. He's been giving talks on conservation science and wildlife management. A lot of the youngsters are very interested in helping to save wildlife.'

'I'd like to talk to all of these people, Mr Lewis, and can I just ask—'

'Mr Lewis, sir? Sorry to interrupt, but it's important.'

They all looked round to see a plump woman in a pleated skirt and floral print blouse standing in the doorway. 'One of my class recalls seeing Davy, sir.'

'Which child was that, Miss Lloyd?' the head asked.

'Lindy Hopson, sir. She's a very reliable girl. She saw him about five minutes after the English class finished. He was talking to Mr Edwards outside the biology lab. She thinks they went inside, because when she looked back, they were gone.'

Marie glanced at Jackman, who took the image of Spiller from his pocket. He thrust it out towards the headmaster.

'It's a still from a night-vision camera, but would you say this was your Mr Edwards?'

The head took it and then handed it to Miss Lloyd. 'I'd say it is. What do you think, Emily?'

'Oh yes, Mr Lewis, that's Mr Edwards, I'm sure of it. He's so *thin*, isn't he?' She handed it back to Jackman. 'He's such a caring man too. Always got time for the children's questions. I'm sure he's inspired a lot of them to do their bit for the planet and our endangered species.'

Marie gritted her teeth. So, for the past month, a murderer had been teaching conservation to a school of impressionable children. Great. Just great.

'We need to speak to him immediately, Mr Lewis. Can you page him over your loudspeaker system?' Jackman said.

Looking somewhat confused, Lewis turned to his secretary. 'Could you ask Mr Edwards to come immediately to the general office, please?'

A few moments later, the request was heard echoing around the school corridors. Marie already knew there would be no response.

'This biology lab, where is it?' Jackman was on his way through the door.

'I'll take you.' Jonathan Lewis caught him up. 'It's this way, but we did search it and there was nothing there at all.'

Marie hurried along beside them. 'We are rather more interested in where this part of the building is situated. If that's the last time Davy was seen, then there's a good chance that's where he disappeared from.'

The lab was situated in a spur off a main corridor. It was a large room flanked by plate glass along one wall and boards that resembled their own whiteboards along the other. The equipment was all up-to-the-minute. Posters and diagrams and notices occupied the facing wall, and in the far corner, a fire door.

'CCTV on that?' snapped Jackman.

'Er, I think so, although it is probably an external camera,' said Lewis.

Marie looked outside. There was a camera high up on top of a pole close to the perimeter fence. A narrow walkway led through to what appeared to be another car park. 'What's that?' she asked, pointing to the end of the walkway.

'Staff parking, I'm afraid,' said Lewis, in a grave voice. He was beginning to realise what had happened.

'Okay, back to the office. We need to get Simon looking at this area in particular, including the car park. And you, Mr Lewis, are going to tell us everything you know about Edwards, and how the hell he came to be here in the first place.'

They strode back along the corridors in silence. Marie had rarely heard Jackman so abrupt. She suspected he was thinking about his own young nephews, and the danger they had been in during the reign of Alistair Ashcroft. He was probably also wondering, as was she, if enough had been done to safeguard these boys.

After instructing Simon which area he should concentrate on, Jackman turned to Marie. 'Take Stacey and Miss Lloyd and talk to the lass who saw him with Edwards. I want to know exactly what she noticed about the boy's appearance and demeanour.'

'You mean, was he scared and so on?'

'Yes, exactly,' Jackman said.

Marie found Stacey talking to Miss Lloyd outside the teacher's classroom.

'Lucky it was young Lindy saw him, Officers,' said Emily Lloyd. 'She's sensible, not given to overdramatising like some of the pupils.'

Lindy was obviously somewhat overawed at being interviewed by two police officers, but she turned out to be a veritable star witness, even able to tell them a little about Davy's background.

'Davy likes Mr Edwards, and Mr Edwards likes him too. He gives prizes to students who are interested in conservation and come to all his talks. Davy's won three, which is pretty good. Davy's really into conservation, you know, saving butterflies and polar bears and all that.'

'So, when you saw them what did they look like, Lindy? Were they laughing, or did they look cross?' asked Marie.

The girl screwed up her face in concentration. 'Cross? Oh no, Sergeant, but they did look quite serious. They definitely weren't laughing.'

'And the next time you looked they'd gone. Is that right?' asked Marie.

'They asked me that before — the teachers and them. I reckon they *had* to have gone into the biology lab. It's the last room in the corridor. There was definitely no one in the corridor when I went into my science class.'

'Did you think that was odd, Lindy?' asked Stacey.

Lindy looked puzzled at the question. 'No, not at all. Davy was Mr Edwards's wildlife conservation monitor. He tells Davy about any new projects he has planned, and Davy and some others sometimes stay late helping him.'

How sweet, thought Marie bitterly. Grooming the child who liked nature. Must have been easy. She thanked Lindy for her help, and stood for a moment, watching the child walk away.

'I want to be a policewoman when I grow up,' Lindy called back over her shoulder.

'You'll make a very good one, Lindy. You notice things, and you have a good memory.' She smiled at the little girl.

Jackman was sifting through various letters and emails the school had exchanged with Edwards prior to his two-month stint at the school, while Lewis gave an account of the accompanying phone conversations with him.

'It was a purely voluntary arrangement,' explained the head. 'We've had a number of such volunteers before with no problem at all. Experts in all sorts of different subjects often offer to share their expertise.' Lewis was now grey with worry. 'Although Edwards stayed longer than any of the others.'

Jackman gathered up the paperwork. 'I'll need to take all this, Mr Lewis. And I'll need a statement from you detailing every phone call that passed between you and Edwards and his agency.' He smiled a little more amicably at the headmaster. 'In truth, it appears that all the proper checks were done. I'm beginning to see why you believed him to be just who he said he was. He engineered this placement extremely carefully, and these letters and credentials are impressive, considering that they're probably faked. Our people will be able to clarify my suspicions, but there's little doubt that this man you call Edwards is actually a Jordan Spiller, whom we believe to be searching for his son, taken from him by his wife when she absconded.'

Lewis turned even greyer. 'But why Davy Frances?'

Jackman hesitated. 'We aren't sure. The fact that he's adopted may be a factor, though we know Davy couldn't be his because the boy was adopted at the age of five.' He shook his head. 'As I said, we don't know what his agenda is.'

'If he's a father, he won't hurt the boy, will he?' asked Lewis desperately. 'He was so kind with the children, full of all the right values. Or so it seemed.' He looked anxiously at Jackman. 'Is he dangerous?'

Seeing the anguish on his face, Marie lost all her anger. Poor man. He obviously really cared about the children in his charge.

Jackman was choosing his words carefully. 'He is a danger to some, Mr Lewis. As to that particular boy, well, we just have to hope not. He's spent a lot of time and effort getting hold of him — he'd been planning for months, possibly longer — so I don't think he intends to harm him.'

Lewis didn't look too convinced. Nor was Jackman, as Marie knew. But he had to say something to alleviate this man's distress.

Simon Laker called from the adjoining office, where he'd been going through the CCTV footage. 'Sir! We've located him.'

They all sprinted through. Simon ran through the footage again. 'Look. They're leaving by the fire door at the back of the biology lab. And the boy's not being taken against his will, far from it in fact.'

Simon was right. Young Davy Frances was walking alongside Spiller, glancing furtively about him. At one point he was actually ahead of Spiller. And it was Jordan Spiller. His thin frame was unmistakable. He and Davy appeared to be chatting animatedly.

'They pause at the corner, check there's no one there, and then make a run for Spiller's car.' Simon pointed at the screen. 'Then we lose them until they go out of the school gates.' He switched to another camera. 'Here. His car is the red Ford Fiesta, and the number plate is perfectly visible. He's turned right out of the gates, away from Saltern town. Shall I ring it in, or will you, sir?'

'Do it now, Simon,' said Jackman. 'He's had far too much of a head start, but we'll put out an attention drawn, all units.'

Simon made the call.

'Stand the search team down, Stacey,' Jackman said, 'but they're to remain on the premises — discreetly. I can't imagine why Spiller would come back, but just in case, they should stay until the school closes for the day.'

Jackman turned back to the headmaster. 'Mr Lewis, you are free to do whatever your board advises in a case like this. There's no danger to the other students, and Spiller is long gone, so in my opinion it would probably be best to make an announcement just to allay any fears or rumours, and resume normal classes.'

'What? Tell them it was a false alarm and that everything is all right?' Lewis looked dubious.

'The alternative is to call all the parents and get them to collect their children, which would worry the parents, half of whom will be at work anyway. It's important that we keep this from the media until my commanding officers have had time to decide how much to divulge and when.'

'Well, yes, you're probably right,' Lewis conceded. 'If you can assure me that the children are in no further danger.'

'I'll be leaving officers here, sir, and I wouldn't suggest it if I didn't believe that there's no danger to anyone else.' Jackman looked grim. 'Spiller has the child he was after and he won't be back. Now I have to find that youngster and return him to his parents.' Jackman gathered up the paperwork and asked for the access code to the CCTV, so that the IT section could retrieve what they needed remotely.

On their way out, Marie said, 'You might want to have a quiet word with that lass, Lindy Hopson, Mr Lewis. She's a canny girl and could well put two and two together, so be careful what you tell her.'

She and Jackman returned to their car. Marie drove, while Jackman rang Ruth Crooke. Then they sat in silence. Both had similar thoughts. A twelve-year-old boy had willingly climbed into a car with a man he respected and admired. That man was also a ruthless murderer.

# CHAPTER TWENTY-SEVEN

By early afternoon, Saltern-le-Fen police station seemed to have stepped up a gear. People moved about with more purpose. Phones rang and were quickly answered, and messages were relayed with more urgency.

Jackman ticked boxes in his mind. To start with, the follow-up had not gone smoothly. Davy's parents had been difficult to locate — the father worked on a building site up county and the mother was a hospital theatre nurse. Both were now on their way to the station. Box ticked.

He was upset at having missed Laura. He couldn't stop thinking of the haunted, anxious look she had worn. His calls went to voicemail and his texts went unanswered. Finally, during a short coffee break, he managed to get hold of Sam.

'She's just got in, Jackman. She rang and told me she'd had an emergency call to Greenborough, but it turned out to be a false alarm. I'll call her for you.'

'Hold on, Sam.' Jackman quickly explained what was worrying him. 'I don't want to hassle her. Could you talk to her, and if it's anything to worry about, ring me?'

'Of course. Leave it with me.'

Jackman ended the call a little easier in his mind. Sam would keep him updated.

'Boss?' Marie stood in his doorway. 'Max and Charlie are wondering if they could go and have a word with Natalie Miles. They're working on what's connecting the women to Spiller, and since it's her nephew who was taken, they'd like to talk with her in person. Plus, she's been very close to Davy over the years, he still rings her every week. He might have shared something with her that would be of help to us.'

'Good idea. Tell them to go immediately,' Jackman said. 'Then would you ask Gary to go downstairs and get an update on the hunt for Spiller's vehicle?'

After Marie left, he looked again at Spiller's application to do voluntary work at the school. He rang one of the numbers on an official-looking letterhead. He found himself listening to an answerphone message telling him that all their operatives were busy, but if he'd like to leave his number someone would get back to him as soon as they were free. It sounded genuine enough, as did the letters of introduction. Then something began to nag at him. All this had taken time, it had been meticulously planned and set up. Which meant that Spiller knew all along that it was Davy he wanted, and if that were the case, why break into those other houses and steal photos of boys he wasn't looking for? Why steal the picture from Natalie Miles if he was in the middle of planning that very boy's abduction? It didn't make sense.

Jackman thought about those other boys. Then, cursing himself for his stupidity, he rang Annie Carson.

'Annie? DI Jackman here. Can I have a word with Callum, please?'

Annie gave a little chuckle. 'There's going to be no living with him when he knows a DI is asking for him.'

An excited whispering followed. 'Callum here, Detective Inspector Jackman.'

'I need your help, young man. Did anyone ever come to your school to talk about nature and wildlife conservation? I'm thinking especially of a man named Mr Edwards.' He held his breath.

'Oh, yes, Mr Edwards. He usually comes in on a Wednesday afternoon and takes us after school. He's a nice bloke, knows a lot about endangered species and all that. It's dead interesting and . . .'

'You still there?' Jackman asked.

'Well, you mentioning him made me think . . . I remember you asked me if I knew someone called Teddy, and I said no, but some of the seniors don't call him Mr Edwards like we do, they call him Ted or Teddy. I'm sorry but I forgot that.'

'No problem, Callum. What you said about the after-school class is really important. Thank you.' So he was right. 'Can I have another word with your mum, please?'

'Annie, you must make sure your boy never leaves the house. Understand? I'm arranging for someone to come and be with you for a while.'

'What's happened? Is he in danger?'

'I suspect that, in the guise of a wildlife conservationist, our man has been grooming all the boys whose pictures were stolen.' Jackman heard voices in the background. 'Is someone else there?'

'My son, Andrew. He's playing a computer game with Callum. He's on a forty-eight-hour pass from his RAF base and goes back early tomorrow.'

'Could he ask for an extension? I'd be a lot happier if I knew he was with you.'

'I'll ask him and ring you back. But oh, the others . . . Oh, my god, what about them? Natalie has Patsy, but they're alone.'

'I'm arranging protection for them right now. Speak later.' He hung up and called to Marie.

Jackman told her what he suspected. 'Quick, get Robbie to chase up Fleur Harper's boy, Jason, who lives with her ex. Then he and the team should find out if the others have had a Mr Edwards coming to their schools. Tell them not to waste a moment. I need to know that all the boys are safe.'

Jackman arranged for a crew to go directly to Annie's house while Marie briefed the others.

'They're on it, boss. And Gary says Spiller's car has been found ditched — literally. It's lying in a deep ditch along one of the lanes outside Cartoft.'

'His old home, huh?' Jackman wondered if that was significant.

His phone rang. Jackman recognised the speaker at once. Len Maynard never rang him at work. In fact, Len never rang him.

'I've got Hetty here, Mr J. We been chatting, like, you see. She didn't want to bother you, but I thinks it's important.'

'Put her on, Len, and tell her not to worry about bothering me.'

Then Hetty was on the line, full of apologies. 'Well, I had a visitor today. You might remember her — my oldest friend, Elspeth Berridge. She's the one who left the village and went to live with her daughter in Cleethorpes, only to find herself being an unpaid childminder, so she came back and got a nice little flatlet in a warden-controlled block in Saltern and—'

Jackman was very fond of Hetty, but he really didn't have time for Elspeth Berridge's unabridged biography. 'Yes, I remember her, Hetty, but what did she tell you that was so important?'

'Ah, well, she used to live next door to the Spillers, at number seven Glebe Close.'

Jackman's ears pricked up.

'Well, I asked her if she recalled Jordan Spiller and the family and all the trouble they caused, and she got a bit uncomfortable, like.' She lowered her voice. 'Then Len gave her one of his toddies, and she started to talk about them. I reckon she heard a lot through the wall — all the shouting and hollering and the fights — but she never spoke up at the time. She said she thought it weren't quite like people said — you know, him hitting her and all that.'

Jackman glanced at Marie, who was listening on speaker. 'How do you mean, Hetty?'

'Elspeth thinks he was defending himself, and it was her, Claire Spiller, what was doing the hitting.'

Jackman was stunned. Claire the abuser? Was that possible? 'But the neighbours said the little lad had told them some real horror stories about what went on in that house.'

'I think they just assumed it was the father. And who can say what the poor little mite made of what he saw, Mr J?'

'You could be right, Hetty.'

'Elspeth is certain Jordan Spiller loved that little lad to bits. She thinks the mother used threats against little Teddy to make her husband do as she said.'

'Was Elspeth there the night they left, Hetty?' Jackman asked.

'Yes, Mr J, she was.'

'I need to talk to her. Can you let me have her address in Saltern?' Luckily, it was only five minutes' drive from the station. 'Will she be at home now, do you think, Hetty?'

'Yes, she will. One of her neighbours who still drives dropped her off here this morning and collected her over an hour ago. They'll be back at the flats by now.'

He thanked her and hung up. 'Well, what do you make of that, Marie?'

'I'm totally confused, boss. I don't know what to make of it.'

'Me neither,' he said. 'Come on, let's pay a call on old Elspeth Berridge. I want to know exactly what happened the night the Spillers took off.'

* * *

Laura told Sam what she'd seen at Freddie Shields's house. 'I've been itching to get back here and tell you, but it's been hold-up after hold-up today.' She flopped down on the sofa.

'Well, the kettle's just boiled, so I'll make tea, shall I?'

'Oh, please. I'll come with you. We can talk in the kitchen.'

Laura sat down at the kitchen table. 'I've never had a patient cause me so much agitation, and I have no idea why.'

'He's disturbed on a lot of different levels, Laura. He's not a textbook case of one specific kind of psychological illness. What's more . . .' He stopped talking.

'And?' asked Laura.

'And we both suspect him of playing us in some way. I'm beginning to think that the reason you're so baffled by Shields is because something isn't adding up. Maybe his malady doesn't correspond with anything we've seen before because it's not real.'

'You think he's a fraud?'

He poured the water on the teabags and stirred them. 'I don't know what I think. But I shall be very interested to know what the sleep clinic makes of him.' He looked up. 'By the way, what did the police tell you about his escapade at the all-night garage?'

Laura pulled a face. 'They're still on night shift, so I never got to speak to them. But I do have a mobile number that the sergeant gave me. He said to phone after three o'clock.' She glanced at her watch, then pulled her phone from her pocket. 'One of them should be up and around by now.'

Sam listened while she talked to one of the police constables. It seemed from what the man was saying that Shields's account had been pretty accurate.

'And when he'd calmed down, you or your crewmate dressed his wound for him?' Laura asked.

'Oh no, Dr Archer. He already had a dressing on it. I did wonder why, if he'd dressed the wound, he hadn't changed his clothes — they were well bloody. Still, if this sleepwalking thing he told us about is right, then maybe he was still asleep when he put the dressing on. Dead weird, if you ask me.'

Laura threw Sam a puzzled look. 'Did the blood on his clothes look fresh, Officer?'

'Not particularly. As far as I remember, it was sort of brown.' He sniffed. 'Have we messed up with that guy, Dr Archer?'

'I honestly have no idea,' said Laura. 'But if you ever see him out at night again, ring me immediately.'

The constable said he would. 'Glad to, Dr Archer. Good old drunks I can handle, but I'm quite happy to leave the nutcases to you.'

Laura ended the call and sat staring at her phone.

'Why did you ask about the blood on his clothes?' asked Sam, taking milk from the fridge.

She didn't look up. 'Because that officer never actually saw a wound. What if there was no injury? Suppose he didn't cut himself that night.'

'So where did the blood come from?'

'Exactly.'

They fell silent. Sam was having seriously bad thoughts about Freddie Shields. Thank goodness Laura had come to him rather than try to shoulder the responsibility alone.

'Let's take this step by step,' he said at last. 'Laura, ring the sleep clinic. We need some expert help. Hughie won't be here till tomorrow, so let's see what they've come up with.' He wasn't expecting much, however. It was quite common for nothing to occur when the sufferer was in different surroundings.

It was a brief call. 'He never attended,' she said. 'He rang saying he was unwell and asked to rebook for tonight. They agreed, but the person I spoke to said they doubted he'd turn up.'

'Hmm. So, what did he get up to last night?' Sam said.

'I dread to think, but—' Her phone rang.

'Sorry to call back, Dr Archer. It's PC Burton here, we spoke a moment ago. I've just thought of something one of the other night shift crews mentioned when we came off shift. Someone frightened the hell out of a woman who lives alone. I'm wondering if it could be your bloke.'

'Really? What did he do?'

'Pressed his face against the window and scared her badly, but he seemed to have also tried to get into the property by removing a windowpane.'

'Breaking and entering seems a little extreme for our man, but cases like this can escalate. Who should I ask for if I want to know more, PC Barton?'

'Either PC Simon Laker or someone from DI Jackman's team. They attended as it was suspected to be connected to the serious crimes they're investigating. The murders, that is.'

'But it wasn't?' Laura asked.

'No. Didn't fit the suspect's usual MO, apparently. So, if it was someone else, I thought it might be our fruitcake from the garage.'

Laura thanked him and ended the call. 'So, we may now know what Mr Shields was doing when he should have been at the sleep clinic.'

Sam kept thinking about the blood on Shields's clothes. And what of his elderly mother?

'Sam? Are you up for a house call?'

'You read my thoughts. The clinic told us he's unwell—'

'And because we know how anxious he was to attend, we're very concerned about him, are we not?'

'Very concerned.' Sam smiled. 'Drink your tea, and we'll pay a visit.'

\* \* \*

Elspeth Berridge didn't like gossip and was loath to discuss her neighbours, not wanting to 'get folk into trouble'. Jackman and Marie said that by telling them, she'd possibly be helping to find a missing child.

'It's the night they finally left Glebe Close that we're most interested in, Elspeth,' Jackman said. 'Hetty tells me you have a really good memory. Can you cast your mind back and tell us everything you remember about it?'

'It's hard to forget, unfortunately. My Fred was alive then, and he made me promise to let well alone and say nothing to anyone. He said they were going, and that was an end to it. Good riddance to bad rubbish.' She swallowed. 'The thing is, the house was in his name. He told me that himself. He had the decency to come and tell me they were splitting up and would be moving out. He even apologised for all the arguments and said he hoped they hadn't upset me too much. He said that sometimes things didn't work out as you hoped.' She looked from one to the other of them. 'He was very sad when he said that, Officers, I could tell. I just had to ask about the boy, our little Teddy.' She looked down. 'He said Christopher was going with him. They would be staying with a relative for a short while until the sale of the house was finalised, then he'd get somewhere within easy reach of Christopher's school.'

'But that didn't happen, did it, Elspeth?' said Jackman.

'Oh, DI Jackman, you have no idea! That day was just dreadful! Most of their stuff had already been moved out. It was the final clear-up, and they argued the whole day, right through till the evening, when they were due to leave. My husband was away all that day, helping an old friend with his allotment, so I was alone, and, well . . .' She sniffed. 'I just cried. Then, at the eleventh hour, as they say, Claire pushed the boy outside and locked him in her car. She went back inside and screamed at Jordan that he wasn't having Christopher. There was a crash and a shout, then silence. I don't know what I believed at that point. Then Jordan started saying terrible things to her — that he'd find her, that he'd hunt her down and that he'd have his child back, no matter what. I'd never heard him speak like that to her. Never. It was as if he'd suddenly turned into someone else. Then she ran out and got in the car and drove away. Moments later, he emerged. He was staggering and he had blood pouring down his face.' She shivered. 'I'll never forget the look on that face of his. It was anguish, Officers, and hurt, and hatred too. And then he was gone. I never saw any of them again, and I never spoke about it either.'

'Perhaps it might have helped to share it, Elspeth,' said Marie kindly. 'That was a lot for you to bear alone.'

'Thing was,' Elspeth continued, 'Claire was such a pretty thing, and so sweet to everyone except her husband that no one would have believed me. She certainly had a temper on her. Uncontrollable sometimes, it was. Our houses were attached, they shared a wall, so I heard more than others, but they all heard the rows. Everyone thought it was Jordan who was the violent one. Naturally, Claire said nothing to change their minds, so they all felt sorry for her. I often wonder where she took the poor little lad.'

'Seems that she and her son trailed from refuge to refuge, telling people she was escaping her "violent and abusive" husband,' said Jackman.

'But, it wasn't like that at all. Unless . . . I said he changed when she hurt him, then took the boy. Maybe it turned his brain. Maybe he carried out his threat to find her.'

*Maybe you're right*, thought Marie grimly.

'It would serve her right, to be honest, but little Teddy deserved better.' Elspeth gave them a sad smile. 'And that's all I can tell you.'

'You've been amazing, and we do thank you.' Jackman stood up. 'Now we'll leave you in peace. You can forget this sad episode now, it's all in the past.'

'Well, I do feel better for having told someone. But I'll never forget that boy. If you find out what happened to him, will you let me know?'

'Of course,' Jackman said. 'You take care now.'

Outside, they both stopped and looked at each other.

'Claire Spiller went one step too far, didn't she?' whispered Marie.

'I'd say so,' Jackman said. 'Taking his boy like that pushed him over the edge.'

They climbed back into the car. 'So, how do you feel about it, Marie?' Jackman asked.

'I've got mixed feelings,' she said. 'Part of me is relieved, because if he did love his boy that much, he probably won't hurt Davy. But another part is very worried indeed because he's deranged, and that's a scary thought. How about you?'

'Ditto, although I'm leaning towards the scary. Let's get back and see what's come in while we were out. I want this guy caught, but we'll have to be extremely careful how we go about it.'

# CHAPTER TWENTY-EIGHT

This time she wasn't on some furtive reconnaissance operation. Laura parked immediately outside the Shields's house. She and Sam strode up to the front door, rang the bell and waited.

'I swear he's in there,' murmured Laura. There was no movement, nothing to bear this out, but she sensed a presence inside. She rang again. Oh well, maybe she'd been wrong. The place remained silent.

Sam took out his phone and rang Freddie's home number. They could hear it ringing, but it went unanswered.

'I'll try his mobile,' said Sam.

They listened again, but try as they might, they couldn't hear a ringtone.

'He really must be out,' said Sam. 'So, what next?'

'Well, as we are so worried about him, I suggest we ask his mother if he's okay. Maybe we should just say we're friends of his. Announcing that we're his shrinks might give her a heart attack.'

'Indeed,' said Sam. 'What's her name, by the way?'

'Catherine. I think he told me at some point that she prefers to be called Cathy.' She led the way around the side of the house to the annexe.

The moment they saw it close up, all Laura's fears returned. The windows were grimy, the door and window frames covered with dirt and cobwebs. 'This is worse than I thought!' She rang the bell in some trepidation.

They heard it ring inside, but no one came to the door.

Sam rapped hard on the door but to no avail. They looked at each other in consternation.

'When did Freddie say he spoke to her last?' Sam asked.

'He said he talks to her every day. He said he was going to tell her yesterday that he'd be staying with Julia, rather than say he was going to a sleep clinic. He always gives the impression that he spends a lot of time with her.' Laura rubbed at a corner of one of the windows and tried to peer inside. 'Curtains are pulled. It's hard to see in, the windows are so dirty. How can he leave her in such a state? Poor woman! And he boasts about how much he cares for her and how he built her this specially designed granny annexe. From the way he spoke, I thought she'd be living in a little palace. And look at it!'

Sam was making his way along the side of the building. 'It must have been quite something a few years back,' he said. 'These modular buildings cost a pretty penny all right. There's a patio door further round. Let's take a look. Maybe she's fallen asleep in front of the telly.'

Laura followed him, more concerned with every step. What if the flat wasn't the only thing he was neglecting? 'Maybe this wasn't the best idea after all, Sam.'

Sam was standing on a small suntrap patio outside what was undoubtedly her lounge, shielding his eyes to peer in through the glass doors. They had vertical blinds, and Sam was trying to look between them. After a few moments, he turned and stared at her. 'I pray I'm wrong, but I think I can see a foot sticking out from behind a sofa. I think she's had a fall!'

'I'll call an ambulance,' she said, pulling out her phone.

'Hold up for a moment.' Sam looked undecided. 'I really couldn't see much through those blinds. It could just be a discarded shoe, and then we'll have called them out for nothing. We need to get inside and see if this is a real emergency or not. She could be out with Freddie, shopping, or at a doctor's appointment or something.'

They searched for a way in, finally discovering that the door to the kitchen was not as secure as the main doors. Sam gripped the handle hard and shook it. 'There's a lot of play there. A few years ago I would have put my shoulder to it, but I daren't after my arm injury. We need something to prise it open with.'

Laura saw a small wooden shed on the edge of the lawn and ran across to it. It was unlocked, and inside was a jumble of junk and garden tools. She grabbed a small spade and ran back to Sam.

'Perfect.' He wedged the blade edge between door and frame and wrenched it back. The lock popped at his first attempt, and the door flew open.

Before they could even step inside, the appalling stench hit them. They both retched.

Neither had to ask what had caused it. It was unmistakable. Rotting, stinking decomposition.

It was certainly far too late for an ambulance.

'Stay here,' gasped Sam, holding her back. 'I'll go in and look. This isn't for you.'

'It isn't for you either.' She gagged. 'Nor for anyone with a heart, or a sense of smell. I'm coming with you.' She gripped his arm. 'Come on.'

The woman was lying on her side, behind a leather couch in the open-plan lounge area. Blood had pooled, caked and dried around her. It was impossible to see what had happened, but Laura suspected that multiple stab wounds would be found in her upper body. There was no need to go further inside. She had been dead a long, long time. So long that she was unrecognisable, even if they had known her. They had to assume this was Catherine Shields. Who else could it be?

'Okay, we've seen enough. Let's go,' said Sam, his hand over his mouth and nose. 'I'd rather make our calls out in the fresh air.'

She was about to agree when she heard a noise behind her. She froze. She knew exactly who it would be.

'I suppose you're looking for me?'

She turned slowly. Just seeing him was bad enough, but the knife gripped in his right hand almost stopped her heart.

* * *

Natalie Miles was angry. She demanded to know why more had not been done to protect her nephew knowing there was a madman loose in the area.

It took both Max and Charlie, as well as her friend Patsy, some time to calm her before she cooled off and admitted that little more could have been done given the circumstances. Police crews had kept up discreet surveillance on the schools, and the school itself had upped security. Somebody always went to and from there with him — much to his annoyance — and everywhere he went, he was always accompanied by a responsible adult. His home, and that of the other boys, had also been under surveillance by the police.

'To be honest, my darling,' said Patsy gently, 'that man would have found a way, even if your nephew had been shut up in a locked room in a high tower. It's like any criminal — if you have something they want, they'll find a way to get it.'

Max looked at Patsy with interest. 'That sounds like a copper speaking.'

'Fifteen years with Derbyshire Constabulary,' she admitted with a grin.

'That's why I feel so safe with her around,' said Natalie.

Now she had calmed down enough, Max and Charlie lost no time in asking their questions.

'Is he a boy that's easily influenced, would you say?' asked Charlie.

'Oh no. Davy knows his own mind,' she assured them.

'And he's passionate about the subjects he enjoys, Detective,' added Patsy. 'Almost to the point of single-mindedness, wouldn't you say, Nat?'

'Especially wildlife. That's his big love, always has been. As a little one he had me building hedgehog houses and providing woodpiles for beetles and insects and such. I put up bat boxes and more bird boxes than you could count. He was on a one-child mission to save the natural world.'

'Still is, it would appear,' Max said.

'Other hobbies have crept in over the years, Detective,' said Natalie, 'but recently it's been conservation again, in a big way. Someone at his school was advising the children on how they could make a difference to help the natural world and save the planet, and his old passion was rekindled.'

I bet it was, thought Max grimly. 'Did he ever mention the person by name?'

'Oh yes.' She chuckled. 'Mr Edwards said this, Mr Edwards thinks that. Mr Edwards suggests I follow a career in conservation.' She shook her head. 'I said he wasn't impressionable, but his Mr Edwards made a very big impression indeed.'

Patsy looked at Max and raised an eyebrow.

He gave a slight nod. Then he changed the subject before Natalie noticed. 'I know this will be of little consolation, but we're pretty sure that whoever has your nephew doesn't intend to hurt him. We have no proof as yet, but it could be a case of a father looking for his missing son, a boy who may have been given up for adoption. As I say, it's still a supposition, but it's something to hold on to.'

'Time alone will tell,' she said. 'All we can do is pray and wait.'

Charlie looked up from his notebook. 'I'm very interested in your nephew's imaginary friend, the one who turned out to possibly be real. I think you told Annie Carson that his name was Dylan, is that right?'

The two women glanced at each other. 'We've talked about that a lot since Natalie first mentioned it,' Patsy said, 'and we're now almost certain there was a boy. We think we know the reason why he didn't want to be seen.'

'Until last year, there was a big house down the road,' Natalie said, 'close to the level crossing. It was used as a shelter for homeless people. An old couple owned it who'd lost a daughter to an overdose and were trying to do whatever they could to help others who'd fallen on hard times. We suspect Dylan came from there and had been told by whoever was in charge of him not to speak to strangers or tell them his name.'

Charlie wrote that down. 'That's quite feasible. And this place isn't being used as a shelter anymore?'

'The old man died,' said Natalie, 'and his wife went into a home. The house was sold to pay for their expenses. A developer bought it and there's about six houses there now.'

'Did Davy ever say anything particular about his friend Dylan?' asked Max.

Natalie shook her head. 'Not really. He rarely talked about him at all, just the occasional passing mention — I might ask him what he'd been doing, and he'd say "playing with Dylan." I think the most he ever said was that Dylan liked what we'd done with the pond. He did say Dylan loved wildlife, which is all I can recall about him really.'

Max wondered if that was why Davy had been taken. Davy had spent time with this lad, and Jordan might have been hoping that Davy would lead him to his lost boy. He glanced at Charlie and closed his notebook. They should get back to the station.

They stood up to leave and thanked the two women for their help.

'Please find him,' said Natalie. She had a catch in her voice. 'He's such a special boy. I couldn't bear it if anything happened to him.'

They assured her they would do all they could, though both wondered. Davy was in the hands of a man who had been driven insane by the hurt and pain of not knowing where his son was. He could be capable of anything.

\* \* \*

269

'Boss!'

Jackman looked up to see Marie hurrying towards his office. 'I've located an old friend of Jordan Spiller's. He's coming in to talk to us now.'

She sounded excited.

'He worked with Spiller for years, up on the roofs. He knows about his disaster of a marriage, and he says he may have information that no one but him can give us.'

'Is he a local?' Jackman asked. 'How long will it take him to get here?'

'He's local, yes. At present, he's working on the old church at Carrion Fen. He said he'd be here in less than half an hour. His name is Andy Forman. Will you interview him with me?'

'Try and stop me! If he knows him well, then he might have some idea where he would go.'

'I hope so too,' she said. 'Oh, and from the little he said on the phone, I got the impression he'll corroborate everything old Elspeth told us. He said he was going to put us right about Jordan's "wicked bitch of a wife." His words, by the way.'

'I never doubted Elspeth, but it'll be good to hear it from someone else.' This was what they'd been hoping for, someone who knew the real Spiller. Someone who could give them an idea as to what he intended when he took young Davy Frances from his school.

It was a long thirty minutes. Other pieces of information were trickling in, but nothing truly useful. They now knew that the dumped Fiesta hadn't even belonged to Spiller. It was an old courtesy car from a garage on the outskirts of Saltern. It was only used when the better vehicles were all booked out, and the staff there hadn't even noticed it was missing. Jackman looked at his watch.

At last, Marie was calling to him. 'He's here, boss. Interview room two.'

When they entered the room, they found another slim, tall man. Andy Forman bore a considerable resemblance to the picture they had of Jordan Spiller. He was around forty, Jackman guessed, with short, dark hair and a tanned, weathered face, no doubt the result of working outdoors. Andy Forman told them he was originally from Hampshire but had been living in Saltern for the past ten years. He was a specialist in ecclesiastical architectural repairs. 'I love old churches,' he said with a friendly smile, 'and my firm are the best. They're passionate about restoring and conserving them.'

'And Jordan Spiller worked for the same company?' asked Jackman.

'Yes, sir, that's how this lady here got hold of me. Jordan and I worked some tough assignments together. He's a top roofer. Brilliant balance, no fear of heights whatsoever. He's got strength and stamina, and you need both working roofs.'

'We're most interested in his private life, Andy. We've been given a whole lot of contradictory stories about Jordan. Most have labelled him as an abusive husband.'

Andy's face darkened. 'Yeah, all spread around by *Claire*, that slut of a wife of his.' He almost spat out the name. 'She was the abusive one, Detective Inspector, as God is my witness. Jordan's a good man. He didn't deserve any of what happened to him.'

It was hard not to contradict him. After all, Jordan had murdered an old woman in cold blood, stabbed another and buried her in a shallow grave, and strangled a man who simply got in his way. He'd terrorised other women and threatened children, and now he'd abducted a boy. These were not the actions of a good man. 'Well, something happened to cause this "good man" to do some horrific things, Mr Forman. We believe him to be responsible for three deaths — three murders to be precise — and apart from terrifying several women by getting into their homes at night, he has abducted a twelve-year-old boy.'

Andy Forman gaped at him. 'What! I cannot believe that. Not Jordan. Oh my God! It must have turned his mind — everything that happened with that bitch. It's the only explanation. He's a *good* man,' he muttered, and gave a long, shaky sigh. 'All her fault. This is all her fault.'

'Years of mental and physical abuse, and then her taking his boy,' said Marie. 'I know it's terrible, and totally unforgivable, but sadly it does happen. I cannot begin to think what it must be like, but Andy, good people don't commit murder.'

'But it wasn't just that, was it? It was what came afterwards.'

Marie glanced at Jackman. 'You mean, something else happened, after she'd gone off with the boy?' he asked.

'You don't know?' Forman looked at them, shocked. 'His son is dead. Claire killed him.'

Jackman had never been so astounded by a statement. 'Christopher — Teddy — is *dead*?'

'She wrote off her car, and the boy was killed. Worst of all — if anything could be — she ran off and left him in the wreck. He died alone.'

'And Jordan Spiller knows this?'

'Of course he does. He told me about it.'

Jackman stood up. 'Please excuse us for a moment, Andy. I need to talk to my sergeant.'

They hurried out of the room and leaned against the wall.

'He's not looking for his son at all, is he?' whispered Marie.

'Then what *is* he looking for? A substitute?' Jackman said.

'I dread to think.' Marie rubbed her eyes. 'I suggest I get us all a strong coffee and we find out what he can tell us. He's not lying, is he?'

Jackman shook his head. They had been so certain that Spiller was looking for his boy. And now?

\* \* \*

Sam edged closer to Laura. He had to give her the best chance to get out to safety. Shields smiled vaguely, his eyes unfocused, unblinking.

'What happened, Freddie?' Sam asked softly. 'Do you know?'

'I've been trying to tell you. It's been months now, but you wouldn't understand.' His voice was flat. 'And you should call me Mr Shields. We agreed, didn't we, Dr Archer? We agreed.'

'I'm sorry, Mr Shields, you're quite right,' Sam said. 'But look, why don't you put that knife down. It looks really dirty, you could get a nasty infection if you cut yourself with it.'

Shields looked down at the knife as if seeing it for the first time. He frowned.

'Where did you get it, Mr Shields?' Sam asked, keeping his tone even.

'I . . . er . . . I don't know. I think I found it.' He tilted his head. 'Ah, yes. I found it, outside.'

'Then all the more reason to put it down.' Sam smiled. 'How about we all go back into the kitchen, Mr Shields?'

Shields dropped the knife with a clatter, stared at it for a moment and walked into the kitchen.

Pushing Laura round behind him, Sam moved slowly after Shields. 'Sit down, Mr Shields, and we'll have a talk.' Shields obediently sat down. Then, to Sam's surprise, he closed his eyes and his head fell forward.

Laura gripped his arm and whispered, 'Sam. What's going on?'

'Okay, Laura. Very slowly, go outside and call this in — both police and a psych team. Meanwhile, I'll try to keep him stable.' She made to protest, but he shook his head vehemently and hissed, 'Just go!'

Laura took herself outside. As soon as she had gone, Sam sat at the table, opposite Shields.

They sat in silence for a few minutes. Shields lifted his head, stared at Sam and blinked, as if waking from a deep sleep. 'Professor Page? What are you doing here? I didn't know you knew my mother. Has she made you tea?' He sniffed. 'Oh dear, I think she's let the milk go off.'

Another long silence.

Suddenly Shields looked around. 'Why are we in Mother's home?' He frowned. 'And what is that terrible smell?'

He started to get up, but Sam held up his hand. 'Relax for a moment, Mr Shields. You've been asleep. We'll sort all this out in a moment.' He reached across the table and gently patted Shields's arm. 'Sit down again.'

Shields perched on the edge of his chair. He looked at Sam, his eyes wild. 'I need to check on my mother. She might be ill, she might need me.'

'It's all right. Your mother doesn't need you right now. Just relax.'

'I've had another episode, haven't I?'

There was a frantic, scared look in his eyes, and something else that Sam couldn't quite equate. Any moment now, the volcano would erupt. He just hoped that Laura had been able to make that call.

Shields leaped up, his chair crashing to the floor. He ran into the lounge. After a moment of silence, Sam heard a terrible, ear-splitting wail.

'Mother!'

* * *

Having called the police and the psych team and unable to bear the thought of Sam alone in there with Shields, Laura was about to go back in when a terrible cry rent the air and stopped her in her tracks. The door burst open and she was pushed roughly to the ground, her head hitting the concrete path. She groaned and lay still for a moment before she eased herself up.

'Sam!' she murmured, and pulled herself to her feet. 'Sam!'

'I'm okay, it's all right.' Sam staggered out of the door, holding his arm to his side. 'He pushed me into the work surface. I've hit my damaged arm, that's all.' He stared at her anxiously. 'You're bleeding! Laura, there's a lump the size of a duck egg. You need to get checked out, my girl!'

274

She tried to argue but was swept by a wave of nausea.

Sam led her to a garden bench, and they sat down. 'I'm calling an ambulance,' he said, pulling out his mobile.

'And you need that arm looked at, Sam. Oh dear, what have I got us into?'

'I wasn't exactly an unwilling party, was I?' Sam attempted a laugh. 'And thank God we came. That poor woman could have lain there for ever.' He looked around. 'I wonder where the hell he went?'

'I heard a car start. I suppose he's driven off somewhere,' Laura said.

'The police will soon get him,' said Sam.

Laura wasn't so confident but didn't have the energy to say so. She was fighting off an overwhelming desire to sleep. She leaned against Sam, hoping she wasn't hurting his arm. 'Rowan isn't going to be too pleased with me, is he?'

'Or me,' said Sam bitterly. 'I'm supposed to be looking out for you.'

'What do you mean?'

Sam looked guilty. 'Okay, I'm going to throw up my hands. Jackman had bad vibes about your patient, that's why I'm here. And before you object, he was absolutely right, so no having a go at him. He loves you. He was worried about you.'

But Laura was beginning to drift.

'Laura! No sleeping. You've got a concussion, so you must stay awake.'

Then she heard the two-tones, and all at once the house was surrounded by police cars, their blue lights flashing. 'So much for the quiet approach I requested,' she muttered. Not that it mattered any more. Shields was long gone. But where?

Laura succumbed to sleep.

# CHAPTER TWENTY-NINE

Jackman and Marie returned to the interview room and sat down. Jackman apologised for their abrupt departure. Though he didn't say so, he hoped it had given Andy Forman time to assimilate what they'd told him about his friend.

'I thought about it while you were out,' he said. 'And to be honest, the last time I spoke to him — which was months ago now — Jordan sounded different. I'd never heard him speak like that before. He sounded cold, businesslike, as though he hardly knew me. Maybe the Jordan I knew died along with his boy.'

'Do you have his address?' asked Marie.

'Only his old one, but he's not there. I rang him several times and then I went round. No one answered the door. I looked through the windows. Some of his stuff was still there, but a lot was gone, and there was a load of boxes stacked up. I spoke to the bloke in the flat above, and he said he hadn't seen him in weeks.'

'Where was this?' asked Jackman.

'Cartoft village. It's a small ground-floor flat, part of Cartoft Manor. In what used to be the stable block.'

'That's his old home village,' said Jackman thoughtfully. 'Of course! The red rose on the gravestone. The child isn't buried there, but it's his family grave, and that's where he goes to grieve. "My heart has never stopped crying for you." That's what the card said. He'd written it for his boy.'

'Yeah, that sounds like something Jordan would say,' said Andy. 'He said something similar to me, about his heart never healing. He also said that he should have died with his son. I guess I never realised just how badly it damaged him.'

'I'm shocked that he's been living in Cartoft yet no one recognised him. It's a small village — I should know, I live there too — and everyone knows everything that goes on,' Jackman said.

'He did move away to start with, but something brought him back. He became a bit of a recluse after Claire left. And there's a back entrance to the manor that leads on to a little Fen lane that connects with the main A road. He didn't need to even go into the village.'

'I know where you mean. It's called Beales Lane,' Jackman said. 'And I see your point about the manor. I never even knew those stables had been converted. It lies well back off the road down a private drive and behind a whole lot of trees. As soon as we're finished here, we'll get a car round there and see if he's left any clue as to where he went.'

'Can you tell us anything about the car crash, Andy?' Marie asked. 'Like where it happened, and when.'

'I'm not sure how long ago it was. He never said exactly when. He just phoned me one night, months ago, beside himself. I gathered it happened somewhere remote, but he never said where.' He sat back, thinking. 'I asked him how he found out and was shocked as hell when he said Claire had told him. Apparently, she rang him and said he'd never have his son back now.'

There was something odd about this. 'Andy,' Marie said, 'if a body is found in a wrecked car, there's always a major inquiry. There's no mention on the Police National Computer of any RTC involving either her, her son or a car registered in her name. Besides, an unknown child's mysterious death would be headline news. Did you see anything in the papers?'

He shook his head. 'Nothing, and I did look. I googled it. But he was so sure about it that I never thought to question him.'

'So, you only have his word for it. No proof.' Jackman suspected that there had never been any car accident at all. 'Two things spring to mind here: one, that she told him the boy was dead to stop him looking for them. And, two, she wanted to hurt him even more.'

Andy shrugged. 'Maybe. But you didn't hear him. True or not, he certainly believed it. Oh, and she told him she'd changed her name, so maybe your enquiries didn't show anything up because she was using a different name.'

'But he did hunt for her, didn't he, Andy? He did follow her around, desperately searching for his son.' Marie looked at him earnestly. 'People have told us that he swore he'd find them. And you said yourself that he'd changed.'

Andy nodded slowly. 'Yes, he did. And he swore he'd have his revenge. Several times he came close to finding her, once in a hostel and another time when they were staying with someone. But she always managed to get away. Then he went quiet, and I've never seen or heard from him since. Like I said, his phone no longer even registers.' He looked down at the table. 'I did try. I did all I could to reason with him. I begged him to let the authorities deal with it, go the legal route. I warned him that if he hurt her, he'd never get his son back. But he insisted on doing it his way.'

'There's something that's bothered us from the start,' said Jackman. 'Jordan's revenge has extended to people who either helped Claire to get away from him or who were closely involved with his son in some way. How on earth did Jordan know who these people were? Was someone helping him? Maybe someone she knew and trusted was surreptitiously feeding back information to him.'

Andy looked up. 'It's a lot simpler than that, DI Jackman. Christopher told him. Before the mother stole him, Jordan had given the boy a second mobile phone. It was their secret, and it only had his number in it. He'd told Christopher to use it only if he were in trouble or frightened by something. Jordan never rang him, it would have been too risky, but he'd asked Christopher to contact him sometimes.'

Marie groaned. 'I never considered that. I thought the boy believed that his mother was trying to protect him from an abusive father.'

'You have to realise that Christopher was very disturbed, very introverted,' Andy said. 'I swear he didn't understand half of what was going on, but despite the lies his mother told him, the boy still loved his father.' He smiled sadly. 'Jordan had hidden the phone in the boy's teddy bear, and even at the age of ten, he carried the teddy bear everywhere.'

'Teddy.' Marie sighed. 'What a dreadful life for a child.'

'And now we have no idea if he's dead or alive,' added Jackman.

There was a knock on the door and a uniformed constable handed Jackman a note. Jackman read it and immediately stiffened. 'I have to go, Mr Forman. Marie will continue your talk. And thank you so much for coming forward.' He turned to her and in a low voice said, 'It's Laura. She's been attacked by a patient. She's on her way to A & E.'

'I've got all this, just go. And let me know how she is.' This had to be the patient that had been causing him such anxiety, the one she couldn't talk to him about. She turned back to Andy Forman.

'Sorry, Andy. It's an emergency, or DI Jackman wouldn't have left like that. Now, this could be vital. Do you have any idea where Jordan might be right now? We know he has a twelve-year-old boy with him. His name is Davy and he trusts Jordan, who he knows as Mr Edwards. Jordan seems to know a lot about ecology and conservation, and he's been in several local schools recently, talking to the children about wildlife. Does this sound like him to you?'

Andy drew in a long breath, then blew it out slowly. 'As to where he is, I really can't say. But the conservation thing is bang on. It was his hobby, it got him out of the house and away from Claire. He joined all sorts of wildlife charity groups and organisations, and his lad was the same. Loved animals, birds and butterflies and all kinds of insects.'

'We believe the house they lived in was in his name. Is that true?' she asked.

'Oh yes. Jordan earned good money, as do I, we're highly skilled and do a dangerous job. The house was his and he kept it that way. When they first married, Claire was all sweetness and light, but I think he came to see quite quickly that there was another side to her. Her name was never added to the deeds.'

'Is there any chance he has a second property, a bolthole somewhere?' Marie asked.

'He talked of getting something. He said he fancied a chalet or a cabin, preferably close to water, so he could watch the migrant waterfowl, but to my knowledge he never bought anything.' His face took on a thoughtful expression. 'Although, he did have a friend who had what he called a hideaway. Jordan went there sometimes when things got bad. He took Christopher once. I remember him telling me it was his dream to live somewhere like that, really simply, just him and his son.'

Marie felt a sudden flash of hope. If it meant that much to him, had he gone back there again, this time with Davy? 'Do you have any idea of this friend's name? Or where his hideaway is located?'

Andy Forman frowned in concentration. 'What the hell was the guy called? I never met him, and he didn't mix with us roofers. Jordan met him up on the sea bank watching avocets, and they got talking.' He looked at her, still frowning. 'It's gone, I'm afraid, but I'll remember it when I get home, I'm sure.'

Marie gave him her card. 'It's important, Andy. Ring me the moment you remember. But the location?'

'Somewhere out on the river. He told me how he would walk the river path for miles and not see a soul. He reckoned his friend had family problems too, that's how they became mates, and this hideaway was where the guy went when things got really tough at home.' Andy thought hard. 'He never mentioned an actual location, but I got the feeling it was somewhere out Stone Quay way. Do you know where that is?'

Marie went cold. That place held bad memories. 'I know it.'

'I can't swear to it, but that was the impression I got.' Andy Forman looked at his watch. 'I really do need to get back, DS Evans, and I can't think of anything else that might help you.'

She dragged her mind away from Stone Quay and smiled at him. 'You've been an amazing help. Honestly, what you've told us is invaluable. If you do think of that man's name, you will ring me, won't you?'

He stood up. 'Of course. It'll bug me until I remember.'

She thanked him again and escorted him back to the foyer. As she watched him walk away, she finally allowed herself to think about Laura. It would crucify Jackman if she were badly injured. Oh God, what a day!

\* \* \*

'I'm fine, honestly. Don't fuss.' Laura rolled her eyes. 'You're like an old mother hen.'

'Look at your poor head! No wonder I'm worried!' Laura's scan showed no visible damage and no internal bleed. Even so, they would be keeping her in for observation for a while. Sam too had escaped serious injury, just bruising and pain from the site of his old gunshot wound.

'At least you can now talk to me about that patient of yours,' he said. 'As a murder suspect, he's fair and square within our jurisdiction.' Freddie Shields's case was being handled by a different team, as Jackman was embroiled in the hunt for Jordan Spiller, but Laura could at least tell him about her patient.

'I can't tell you what a relief that is,' she whispered, gripping his hand. 'I'm so sorry, darling, you have every right to be angry. We should never have gone to that house, but I really believed he was just neglecting her. We had no idea that . . .' The tears began to flow.

'I'm not angry. How could I be, considering the things I do in my job? You were concerned for someone's safety, I understand that.' He smiled. 'Although I might need to give that Sam a bit of stick!'

'And he would fully deserve it,' said a voice from behind him. 'I'm really sorry, Jackman. I should have had more forethought.'

'Forget it, Sam.' He pointed to a chair next to Laura's bed. 'I'd have done the same myself. The main thing is that Laura didn't go alone.'

Laura gave his hand a squeeze. 'You get back to work now, sweetheart. I'm fine, and Sam's with me. We know how busy you are, and we're expecting one of your detectives along any minute to take a statement.'

He sighed. 'I'm going to have to take you up on that. It's manic, we're at a crucial stage. I'll get you picked up as soon as you can come home.'

Sam shook his head. 'You forget about us. I'll keep you abreast of what's going on, and I'll get us a taxi home. Just go back to where you're really needed right now.'

* * *

Jordan Spiller stared at his boy, standing at the water's edge watching a group of lapwings. He didn't want to take his eyes off him for one moment, he was far too precious. The boy had been fed a false idea of who and what he was, but he would explain it all, and then they could be happy together, in the time they had left.

# CHAPTER THIRTY

Marie was staring at a map of the Fens when Jackman arrived back in the CID room, tracing with a finger the course of the tidal river around Stone Quay. As soon as she saw him, she asked about Laura.

He smiled. 'It wasn't exactly an attack. He pushed her and she cracked her head on the path.'

'Ouch! Poor Laura.'

'They've given her a scan. She has a concussion, but all her signs are good and thank God there's no bleed.' He looked at the map behind her. 'Why the interest in that area?'

'Andy Forman said Jordan used to spend time at a friend's "hideaway." He believed it was located somewhere around Stone Quay. It's by no means certain, and that stretch of the river winds for miles before it reaches the estuary. Try as I might, I can't recall any "hideaway" there.' Marie had avoided the area after her friend died there, and she really didn't want to go back. But . . . 'The weather has calmed down, so I thought I might take Tiger along the river path and the sea bank to see if there's any place out there that fits the bill.'

'Isn't it dangerous?' asked Jackman anxiously. 'Going off the road like that?'

'Tiger likes going off-road. She's built for both the tar-mac and the rougher tracks. She's tackled far tougher terrain than the sea bank, and it would take for ever to send a crew out there on foot. I'll go after work. It might well be a fool's errand, so if I'm off duty, no time will have been lost.' She went back to her workstation. 'Meanwhile, everyone is hard at it chasing up the new info that Andy gave us. Robbie is trying to find anything he can on an RTC involving a child, and Gary and Kevin are trying to trace where Claire might have gone after Skegness. Max and Charlie have been quizzing the boys who knew "Mr Edwards" in case he might have mentioned anything that could lead us to where he's taken Davy.'

'Have we heard from the crew who went to Cartoft Manor?' asked Jackman.

'Stacey and Jay just rang in, and it's exactly as Andy said — deserted, with a bit of his furniture left and a load of packing boxes. The neighbour from the flat above told them he hadn't seen Mr Edwards for ages, although he admits he works shifts. They got a key from the owners of the manor, and they're doing a fingertip search right now.' She looked at the clock. 'I was going to give them a hand, but as I'm going biking, I'd better get away, if that's all right?'

Jackman nodded. 'Just take care. If you come off, it's either head first into the marsh, or the river, or straight down the bank, and you can't get an ambulance out there.'

'All right, Dad.' She rolled her eyes. 'I'll be careful — Guides' honour!'

'You were *never* a Girl Guide!'

She smiled smugly. 'So what? I might have been. I'd have been a brilliant one too.'

Jackman shook his head at her and smiled. 'I think I'll go and join Stacey and Jay for a while. I'd like to take a look through Jordan Spiller's belongings. And I need to know how the lads here might feel about a spot of overtime tonight.'

'Offer them a takeaway, boss. In fact, I'll do my recce and come back and join you. Save me some.'

'Marie,' he said, his smile gone, 'ring me if you see anything that looks remotely like Jordan's hideout, okay? Do not approach any habitation or person alone. I mean it. No heroics.'

'Of course I'll ring. There's that little lad to think of. I wouldn't do anything to jeopardise his safety, you know that.'

'I do, but just be careful, Marie Evans.'

She laughed, gathered up her things and prayed the rain would not return before nightfall.

* * *

'Sure, boss, I'm here for the duration,' said Robbie rather morosely. 'There's nothing at home for me right now anyway.'

'Me too,' said Max. 'We've got my mum and dad staying for a few days, so Rosie will have plenty of help with the twins, and I've already warned her I might be late.'

The others all agreed as well, so Jackman left them working and headed out to Cartoft Manor.

He found Stacey and Jay still searching through the packing boxes. 'Anything of interest so far?' he asked.

'Oh, hello, sir,' said Stacey. 'We were about to ring you. Yes, we've barely started, but Jay just found some personal papers in a folder with a load of stuff from the bird protection people. It's Claire and Christopher's birth certificates, so we now know her maiden name.'

'Brilliant! Well done, you two! Let's have a look.' At last, something tangible.

He wondered why the son had been registered in the mother's name and not Jordan's but concluded from the dates that he must have been born before their marriage. He rang CID and passed on the information to Kevin. 'Her maiden name was Bourne, no middle name, and she was born in Surfleet.' He gave them the relevant dates. 'The boy was named Christopher Edward Bourne. So the nickname

Teddy isn't just due to his old teddy bear.' He told them he'd let them know of anything else that came to light and ended the call.

They found nothing of any interest among Spiller's possessions, everything he owned was functional and utilitarian. The flat itself had no home comforts. It could have made a very nice home for a single person, being quite big, with a spacious kitchen area and a decent bathroom. But Jordan had obviously used it as somewhere to have a shower, nuke a ready meal and sleep. It depressed Jackman to think of the life he led there. 'Is that the bedroom, Stacey?' He pointed to a closed door.

'Mr Courtney, the owner, is looking for a spare key, sir. It's locked, and we didn't want to damage his property unnecessarily. Shall I go over to the house and see if he's found it yet?'

That door bothered Jackman. He stared at it, frowning. Why lock a bedroom door when you aren't living there, unless there's something you don't want people to see? 'Yes, please. Otherwise, I'm afraid we'll have to force it. I want to know what's behind that door.'

He went outside and looked for a window. There was one, but a heavy curtain hung across it, making it impossible to see inside.

Back indoors, Jay held out a small packing box. 'Sir? This one mainly had leaflets about conservation and the World Wildlife Fund in it, but I found this right at the bottom.'

He took out a small, framed photograph of a boy. If Jackman had had any doubts as to who it was, the teddy bear under the boy's arm would have told him immediately.

He was looking at Christopher. Teddy.

'Are you dead, or alive, little man?' he whispered. He looked closer. The boy must have been around six or seven when the picture was taken. He was thin, with a shock of almost shoulder-length blond hair and, sticking out from a pair of grubby shorts, the skinny legs with knotty knees that so many little boys have. There was a strange other-worldly look on his face, as if he wanted to smile but didn't really know how.

'And there's this too.' Jay held up a well-thumbed notebook. 'Looks like names, dates, places and scribbled notes.'

Jackman took the book, flipped through it and saw the name Nan Cutler, heavily circled in black felt pen. He swallowed. 'Bag this, Jay. It's important. I need the whole thing worked into a timeline of events. I think we're looking at a blueprint for murder.'

Stacey appeared in the doorway. 'Mr Courtney can't find a spare key, sir. He thinks he must have given them both to Spiller, but he said to go ahead and force it.'

Jackman gave the door a shake. It wasn't particularly strong. He stepped back and kicked, somewhere below the lock. The door flew back and crashed against the wall.

The room was dark, thanks to the heavy curtain. He looked for a light switch and flipped it on.

It was a good-sized bedroom, the bed a pallet with a mattress on it, pushed up against the wall. A wardrobe stood next to it, the doors open. Most of the clothes were gone. On the wardrobe floor lay a pair of black spandex cycling pants and a matching black jacket. Two large, modern, white-topped folding tables pushed together took up most of the room.

Jackman could see the photographs from the doorway. He went to the tables and looked down on dozens and dozens of them. There were possibly over a hundred pictures there, all of boys between the ages of ten and twelve.

The photographs were laid out in a kind of circular design like the petals of a giant flower, or a mandala. In the centre, circled heavily in thick red marker pen, was a photograph of Davy Frances, edited and cropped to bring it into close-up.

'The chosen one,' he murmured. He felt sick. 'We need Forensics in here. Stacey, ring it in, please.'

Stacey stood slightly behind him. 'Did he take these himself?' Her voice was low.

'Looks like it, though some have been cut from papers or lifted from social media. You can see the stolen photos in the centre.' Which meant that Spiller had been back, without the neighbour noticing. It also explained the heavy curtains.

Jackman stared at the pictures and wondered if he was perhaps starting to understand Spiller's rather idiosyncratic selection process. Until this point, he had never quite been able to make sense of Spiller's actions. The breaking in, the entering of the sleeping occupant's bedroom, the taking of only one picture had never quite made sense. Now it became a little clearer — he wasn't looking for his real son but a child to take Teddy's place. Yes, he wanted a child who would fit the bill, but the break-ins were more likely to be about revenge. Revenge on women who had either befriended or had a connection to the wife he hated. Women who interfered or had failed to do the right thing by his beloved son. When he had stood in their bedrooms at night, he had held their lives in his hands, however briefly. One he had decided to kill. The others . . . he allowed them to live but in constant fear — of the night and for their children's lives.

Stacey had gone to contact her skipper and put in a request for SOCOs. When she came back into the room, Jackman said, 'The one thing that united all the women you've been talking with, Stacey, was the theft of a photograph, wasn't it?'

She nodded. 'That really did put the frighteners on them, the thought of someone stalking the children they loved.'

Jackman nodded slowly. 'It did, didn't it? It looks like he'd already selected his new "son."' He pointed to the central picture. 'Davy ticked all the boxes. Spiller didn't need these photos. He'd already met the children at their schools and had all these clandestine photos that he took himself. He stole those photos simply to make the women suffer — after all, what would frighten a woman more than a threat to a child she loves?'

Stacey heaved a sigh. 'Makes sense, sir. And it worked — they were terrified for the kids.'

Jackman was sorry Marie wasn't with him to see this. He would have liked her opinion, though he daren't ring her.

The thought of her on that bike of hers, roaring along the high sea bank and bucking across the deep grooves dug by tractor wheels, frightened the life out of him. The last thing he wanted was to distract her. He took a couple of photos with his phone to show her later and left the room.

'Can you guys stay on here, or shall I call in another crew to take over from you?' he asked.

'I'm fine,' said Stacey. 'How about you, partner?'

'Me too. I'd like to see it through.'

Jackman thanked them and hurried back to his car. Mill Corner was still in darkness, so he drove on by. He'd had a text saying that Laura wouldn't be discharged until much later that evening, if then, and Sam had chosen to stay with her.

So, a pizza at the station, and the search for the boy in the middle. Davy Frances, the chosen one.

* * *

DS Vic Blackwell sat by Laura's bed. He'd only just returned to Saltern-le-Fen after a year working with a special tactical unit. He had mixed feelings about Saltern, having disgraced himself there through his own stupid actions. Now, however, he was beginning to recover his old reputation as a good copper. Reconciled with Marie, his old crewmate from way back, he had returned to CID. His first case was a homicide, involving a client of the force psychologist, Dr Archer, along with a professor of psychology who had an almost legendary reputation. It was a bit daunting.

He listened carefully to their account of the event that had brought them to the hospital. When he asked for their professional opinion of their assailant, Freddie Shields, he couldn't fail to notice the look that passed between them. Laura admitted that Shields was an enigma, often saying one thing while his body language suggested something entirely different.

'We have our suspicions about what is driving this man, Detective,' said Sam, 'but these are unsubstantiated, and we're

289

loath to share them at this point. We're not being obstructive, we just don't want to give you misleading information.'

'We have an expert in the field of somnambulism arriving tomorrow,' said Laura. 'He will either confirm or refute our conclusions.'

Vic nodded. 'Well, at this point, my job is to find and question him. Then I'll need to rely on forensic evidence to confirm that it was indeed Shields that committed the murder or whether we have to look for a person or persons unknown. But as soon as you can give me your conclusions as to this man's mental state, the clearer I will be about what I'm dealing with.'

'Of course,' said Sam. 'We'll come straight to you when we've discussed it with our expert.' His face darkened. 'What we can say now, Detective, is do not underestimate this man. I'm certain he has some twisted agenda in that head of his, and he'll not take kindly to being deflected from his goal.'

'Did either of you notice what he was wearing?' asked Vic.

'Grey sports pants and a dark hooded jacket with a white logo, though I forget what it was. It was a popular brand, I know that.' Laura closed her eyes and lay back. 'Sorry, but I have the headache from hell.'

'Then I'll let you rest,' said Vic. 'Thank you both. I'll speak to you again soon, probably tomorrow, for a formal statement, and hopefully get your expert opinion of our man.' He stood up. 'You've got my card. Ring me, day or night, if anything occurs to you or — heaven forbid — you see him again.'

The look on Laura Archer's face said it all: heaven forbid indeed.

Outside in the car park, Vic Blackwell rang the station to check on progress. He was told that Shields's car had been picked up on cameras in the town, but then lost after he headed out into the Fens. There were a few cameras scattered around the bigger villages, but most of the area was invisible, a vast unseen blank. All they knew was that he had been heading in the direction of the river. Two of Vic's colleagues had searched the house and removed his personal papers, bank and credit card details, along with other relevant items such as his diary and laptop. So far, his credit card had not been used, and a mobile phone registered to him was switched off, so they'd been unable to locate him that way. As things stood, he was their prime suspect for the murder of Catherine Shields. He was their only suspect.

The concern on Sam and Laura's faces had been warning enough, without professional opinions and psychological appraisals. Freddie Shields needed to be apprehended and locked up as soon as possible. Vic drove away, fast.

\* \* \*

Marie arrived back shortly after Jackman. 'That area is massive,' she said. 'If Spiller is there, I saw no sign of him. All I succeeded in doing was getting Tiger covered in mud. She looks like a trials bike now.' She thought for a moment. 'There were a couple of places that I couldn't actually get to because of the ditches and drains, and I thought I'd try looking at a satellite map. If I spot anything of interest, we could contact our "eye in the sky."' Marie had been dying to find a reason to make use of the newly formed drone unit, and this could be her opportunity. She flopped down in front of her computer. 'I haven't missed the food, have I?'

Jackman smiled. 'No, it's all ordered. Should be here soon.'

'So, while we wait, tell me what happened at the Spiller home.'

He handed her his phone. 'I found this, in the bedroom.'

She stared at the image and let out a low whistle. They'd seen pictures arranged in similar fashion once before.

'We also have a photo of Teddy and some actual details about him and his mother, which is something. Plus, I've got a good idea why he broke in and stole the pictures—'

'DI Jackman!' Kevin called out from across the room. 'I think I've found Claire Spiller.'

A silence descended over the room.

Jackman hurried across to Kevin's desk.

'I've traced her father, sir. He still lives in Surfleet, he's a GP there. I contacted him and he's emailed me back asking for the officer in charge of the case to ring him. He refuses to speak to anyone else. I have his number here.'

Marie looked eagerly at Jackman. Things were moving, but not a moment too soon. Somewhere out on the Fen, a little lad was spending the night alone with a killer.

Jackman beckoned to her and she followed him into his office. 'Have a listen, Marie. It could be important.'

She closed the door and sat down opposite him. He rang the number and the answering voice reverberated around the office, strong and assured.

'Dr Julian Bourne. Can I help you?'

'Good evening, sir. I am Detective Inspector Jackman of Saltern-le-Fen CID. I understand you were contacted by one of my detectives. We're very anxious to speak to your daughter, Claire Spiller.'

There was a silence. Then: 'Might I ask why?'

'Her husband, Jordan Spiller, is wanted for questioning in connection with three deaths, sir, and he has now abducted a child, a boy of twelve. We need to speak with Claire as a matter of urgency. Do you know where we might find her?'

His sigh filled the room. 'Yes, I know where she is, DI Jackman, but as to speaking with her, that's not possible.' Another pause — and was that faint knock a glass being set down? 'This isn't something that can easily be discussed over the phone. Could you come here? I am free tonight.'

'We'll come immediately, sir, if I can have your address?'

'There goes my pizza,' Marie muttered. 'Was it just me, boss, or did he sound sad when you mentioned his daughter?'

'*Not possible* to talk to her? That had a kind of terminal sound to it, didn't it?' Jackman said.

Just as they were hurrying through the CID room, the pizza arrived. 'Eat it all and you lot are for the high jump! Got it?' called out Marie.

'Cold pizza. Ugh.' Jackman pulled a face.

'Cold pizza is better than no pizza when you're as hungry as I am,' said Marie.

* * *

The roads were clear of traffic. Friday night was no different to any other out in the countryside, and they were there in half an hour.

The house looked imposing. Judging by the brass plaque outside, Ferndale, as it was called, obviously doubled as the doctor's surgery. It was an old, well-maintained property. Under the porch light, even the letterbox and doorknocker gleamed.

Julian Bourne was tall, somewhat overweight and dressed casually in a soft cream sweater and dark-brown trousers. He was in his mid-sixties but his wavy hair still carried a hint of brown. He led them through to a comfortable lounge lined with so many bookcases that the room resembled a bookshop or a library.

Bourne indicated to a long leather couch and offered drinks, which they refused. Jackman was eager to get this over as quickly as possible.

'You understand the urgency of our need to find your daughter, sir?' he began.

Bourne picked up a tumbler of what appeared to be whisky from the mantelpiece and took a swallow. 'I hope to answer whatever questions you have. It's my misfortune to know more than anyone about my daughter's life.'

'Is there a reason why we cannot talk to her personally, sir?' Jackman kept his voice soft, believing that he already knew what the reply would be.

'My daughter died last year, from an overdose. I had been trying to help her, first through a psychiatric clinic, then by keeping her here at home. I administered the drugs that the clinic prescribed, and for a while she improved, but her mental condition never properly stabilised. It was inevitable. It often is with cases like hers.'

Jackman wasn't surprised. 'My condolences, Dr Bourne. I'm very sorry for your loss.'

Bourne sank down into a leather recliner. 'To say it's all for the best sounds horribly callous, but as a matter of fact she was desperately damaged, Detectives.'

'I know this must be painful for you, sir,' Jackman said urgently, 'but we have a boy in terrible danger, and we need some facts about Claire, Jordan and their son Christopher, to give us some idea of what Jordan is planning.'

Bourne gave a short, humourless laugh. 'You'll be lucky to understand anything that goes on in that man's head.'

Marie leaned forward. 'Dr Bourne, we have been given a number of conflicting accounts of Claire and Jordan's life together. All of them cite domestic abuse and violence, but some blame him, while others say she was the instigator. Can you tell us anything that might lead us to the truth?'

Bourne put down his glass and folded his arms. 'We were against the marriage from the start. But we would have been against Claire marrying anyone. When she was seven, she was diagnosed with a condition called IED — Intermittent Explosive Disorder. People suffering from this disorder are subject to sudden episodes of aggressive, impulsive, sometimes violent behaviour. The anger they manifest is always grossly out of proportion to the situation. It's believed to be caused by an imbalance in the structure, function and chemistry of the brain.'

Jackman wrote this down, wondering what on earth was coming next.

'When Claire found she was pregnant, she insisted on getting married to Jordan. At the time, she was taking her medication and regularly attending therapy sessions, and for a time, with Jordan's support, she seemed to be getting on top of it. Even so, we asked her to wait until after the baby was born before they committed to marriage. We didn't know how the pregnancy and the experience of childbirth might affect her condition.'

So that was why the child had her name and not Jordan's.

'To our surprise,' Bourne continued, 'she improved, if anything, and we finally acquiesced to the marriage.' He paused, a rueful expression on his face. 'Sadly, we were so involved with Claire's condition that we never thought to ask ourselves about Jordan and why he was so determined to marry Claire.' He drained his glass.

'He had problems too?' asked Marie.

'He had a very jealous, controlling nature.' He exhaled loudly. 'Theirs was a marriage that was truly made in hell. I should think the reports about their relationship were all correct. Sometimes it would be her, if a rage came over her, other times it was him, eaten up by jealousy. Oh, and Jordan was the most convincing liar I've ever met. If he wanted you to believe something, you believed it.'

The charming Mr Edwards, whom all the kids loved. The neighbour, who called him thoughtful and polite. His roofer friend, who swore that Jordan was a terribly abused husband. They were finding more answers tonight than at any time in the investigation.

'But,' Bourne continued, 'and I must emphasise this, Jordan loved that boy. He adored Christopher. Claire found this impossible to swallow. In her mind, Christopher was hers, and I think she resented the fact that the lad loved his father so much. So she started using him to get at Jordan. Things went from bad to worse. I wanted to step in, but they were adults, and I was told exactly where to take my concerns.' He hung his head. 'I was helpless, and my wife was very ill by that time. I couldn't cope with Claire and her situation as well as worrying about my wife and keeping my practice afloat, so I decided I had to let her go. I was there if she needed me, but there was nothing else I could do.'

What a situation to be in. Jackman truly felt for the man. 'I'm sorry to have to make you relive all this, sir, really I am, but the burning question right now is what happened to Christopher? Jordan told a friend that Claire had had a car crash in which the boy died.'

'My daughter said some terrible things to hurt Jordan. In a rage, she could have said anything. By then, she'd stopped taking her meds.' He shook his head. 'She stopped hauling her boy from refuge to refuge and came home.'

'And Christopher?'

'He's with some wonderful long-term foster parents, in a small village not far from here. I couldn't take him in. I needed to keep him away from Claire, and my wife was dying by then. Fostering seemed the best thing for our grandson until I was better placed to . . .' His voice tailed off.

Jackman heard Marie's sigh of relief. The boy was alive! Christopher would know where the hideaway was. He'd been there with his father when he was younger. 'We're very relieved to hear that, Dr Bourne, believe me. I know this has been traumatic for you, and soon we'll leave you in peace, but I have one last question.'

Bourne looked at him. 'You want to talk to Christopher.'

'We do, for the other boy's sake. His life could depend on it.'

'And it could undo years of painstaking work with a damaged child,' Bourne countered.

'We have only one question. It doesn't have to be me asking it — Marie could, or you, the foster parents, a health-care professional, whoever you think would do the least harm. Please, Dr Bourne?'

'And what is that question?'

'His father once took him to a friend's place, close to the river, possibly in the area around Stone Quay. He called it the Hideaway. We believe it's where he's taken Davy, but it's a huge remote area. It would take days to search and time is not on our side. We need to ask Christopher if he knows where it is.'

After a few minutes of what seemed like endless pondering, Bourne gave a sigh. 'All right, as long as you allow the foster father to ask. He and Christopher are close.'

Jackman nodded. 'I know it's getting late, but please ring him now, so I can confirm our position with the foster parents if necessary.'

Bourne took his phone from his pocket and explained the situation to Christopher's new father.

'He'll do it, Detectives, but not at this hour. The boy is already in bed. Jim Gardner, the foster father, is taking him fishing early tomorrow morning. He'll do it then, and call immediately, at around six or seven.' Bourne stared at them. 'This might sound callous to you, but you have to understand how damaged Christopher was. Jim has brought that lad back from the abyss, but he has to be handled with extreme care if you are to get your answers.'

Jackman nodded. He was bitterly disappointed. It certainly wasn't what he would have hoped for, but it wasn't down to him to jeopardise another child. 'Okay, please, thank him for us. Oh, and the more he can tell us about the actual location of this place, the better.'

Jackman just had to hope that Jordan Spiller wouldn't play out his endgame before sunrise.

# CHAPTER THIRTY-ONE

DS Vic Blackwell was also working late. The strange life of Freddie Shields had begun to fascinate him. By nine o'clock, he had confirmed two things about Freddie — two lies he had told Dr Archer. Freddie Shields was not divorced, because he had never been married. And the lovely Julia, the teacher at Saltern Academy, did not exist.

Now, at nearly ten in the evening, Vic rang Dr Peter Mason, Freddie's GP. He apologised for the lateness of his call and told him what had occurred.

'I hardly know what to say,' said Mason. 'I've been dealing with Freddie for years. I liked the man. I suspected that he was suffering from serious stress issues, which is why I referred him to Dr Archer, but this goes way beyond anything I would have imagined.'

'How about Mrs Shields?' Vic asked.

'Not my patient, Detective. Freddie told me that when she moved in with him, she decided to stay with her old GP. He's Dr Lane-Sykes from the Carvery Road practice, I believe.'

'Did you ever suspect that Mr Shields was being untruthful at all?' Vic asked.

Dr Mason was silent for a while. 'I have to say there were times when I believed him to be hiding certain details from his past. He clammed up when I mentioned his early family life and refused to talk about the possible causes of his adult sleepwalking. I did consider some kind of neglect, or even abuse.' He paused. 'I had hoped that Dr Archer would be able to help, now I feel terrible about referring him to her. Please give her my best wishes for a speedy recovery.'

Vic stared at his notes. He could hear Jackman's team at the other end of the big office, still working, and wondered how often two murderers struck in such a small place simultaneously. Pretty rarely, he hoped. Earlier, Charlie Button had presented him with a grin and a slice of pizza. He had accepted both gratefully. It had felt like coming home.

His desk phone rang.

'Sarge! We've picked him up. We've got Shields. We're bringing him in now, ETA ten minutes. Mind, he's raving like a bloody lunatic!'

'Okay, I'll inform the custody suite so they can clear the area. Get him processed, if you can, and straight into the soft cell. The custody sergeant will organise a medic to assess him.'

'They're going to really love us. And on a Friday night too.' Vic heard shouting in the background and smiled.

'You might well have landed a killer, mate, so I love you even if no one else does.'

He decided it was time to get a caffeine hit and strolled along the corridor to the machine.

'Are we all on overtime tonight?' said a familiar voice.

He smiled at Marie. 'Looks that way. Though my bad boy is on his way to the custody suite. How about you?'

'Jammy git!' she said. 'Ours is still who knows bloody where.' She lost her smile. 'And he's got a kid with him.'

'I heard. Listen, if my guy's the raving lunatic they say he is, I won't be allowed to interview him until he's assessed. I'm sure my DI would let me chip in and help you while I wait for the all-clear, and you know how long that could take.'

'I'll tell Jackman. He'll be chuffed as little apples that you've got that screwball off the streets and away from Laura. Thanks for the offer of help, Vic. It's good to have you back.'

'I never thought I'd miss the place until I left it. It was heady stuff, working with the special tactical lads, but I couldn't wait to get back.'

\* \* \*

Marie returned to her desk. How odd to have Vic back and working in the same CID room. To say that the two of them had a chequered past came nowhere near it. Years ago, he had almost ended her career. Then, more recently, he had saved her life. So she reckoned they were quits. Yes, it was good to have him back and on her side again.

'Listen up, folks! There's little more we can do until first light. The night shift detectives and Uniform will continue to try to locate this hideaway, although our main hope is with Christopher tomorrow morning. So, you can get away now and rest up. Home, everyone!' Jackman called out. 'You've done wonders, now get some sleep. Tomorrow, with luck, we'll know exactly where Jordan's hiding, and we'll go after him. I want you all sharp as tacks for when that happens.' He went across to Marie. 'Can I ask you to get in early, maybe around six? I'm thinking that if we hear from the foster father, it would be best to get out there before Jordan is up and ready.'

'Of course, no problem. Have you heard from Laura?'

'I'm going to the hospital now. Sam was going to get a taxi, but I'll collect them myself.' He smiled at her. 'I can't wait to get her home. I was so scared when I got that message.'

'I know,' she said. 'It showed. Now off you go. Take your lady home and pamper her like never before.'

When Marie got home, she was surprised to see a car parked outside.

Ralph stepped out. He was holding a bunch of flowers. 'I know I shouldn't be here.' He looked like a naughty teenager.

'Why on earth would you think that?' she said, taking his hand. Just inside the door, she pulled him to her. 'Now, Ralph Enderby, where were we?'

* * *

When they got home, Jackman urged Laura to go straight to bed, saying he'd take her supper up to her.

She flatly refused. 'Jackman, my head is spinning — not from concussion but with questions about Shields. You said they caught him. How? And where? And what is he saying?'

'Okay, okay, both of you, sit at the table and I'll make us all omelettes.' While he busied himself at the stove, he relayed what Vic Blackwell had told him before he left. 'They had no idea where he was heading, and he refused to tell them — if he even knew himself. He was in a rage, apparently — wild-eyed and seemingly unable to understand simple commands. On his second attempt to get away, the crew that finally pulled his car over had to taser him.'

'And where was this?' asked Sam.

'Way out on one of the droves that leads towards the river.' The sound of sizzling butter rose into the air. 'He was only caught because a woman out walking her dog rang in to say a drunk was veering all over the road and had nearly hit her precious pet. It was pure luck that a crew was out there looking for a stolen vehicle and was within easy reach.'

'I suppose they didn't tell you what he was ranting about, did they?' Laura wondered.

'Uh, yes . . .' Jackman tried to recall what Vic had said. It was only a passing comment, and Vic hadn't taken too much notice. 'He was furious with someone for taking advantage of him.'

Sam and Laura frowned at each other.

'Who was he talking about?' Laura asked.

'He didn't say, just went on about a so-called friend taking advantage of his generosity.' He shrugged. 'That's all Vic could tell me, I'm afraid.'

'He can't have been referring to either of us,' mused Sam. 'And certainly not Julia, she doesn't actually exist.'

'I suspected as much,' Laura said. 'I googled Saltern Academy, and there was no mention of her on their website.' She shook her head and winced. 'My goodness, he really went to a lot of trouble to make us believe his "Mister Average" act, didn't he? Sadly divorced, wonderful partner, loving mother he doted on and looked after like a loyal, dependable son. Jesus! What a crock of shit. And I fell for it — well, to start with.'

Sam laughed. 'Come on, Laura, you never fell for it! You always knew there was something about that man that didn't add up. That's why you've been so anxious about him.'

'I can second that,' said Jackman. 'I've never seen you so worried over a client.'

He served up the supper. It was plain, but a vast improvement on cold pizza.

'I wonder who they got to assess him,' said Laura. 'I'll be very interested to see their report.'

They all knew that unless Shields calmed down considerably, he would most likely be taken to a psychiatric ward or a suitable mental health unit. It wouldn't be an easy placement because of his status as a prime suspect in a murder investigation. Wherever he went he would have to be closely guarded. 'Your expert gets here tomorrow, doesn't he?' Jackman said.

'Hughie. Yes, mid-morning probably,' Sam said. 'Hopefully, we'll be able to arrange for him to see Shields for himself now he's been apprehended. I can't wait to hear what he'll have to say.'

'Where's he staying, Sam?' Jackman asked.

'I haven't arranged anything yet. I was waiting to see how long he'll be with us, then I'll ring up the inn on the main road. He might even need to get back tomorrow evening. He has a very full schedule.'

'If it helps, I'll get Hetty to make up the bed in the third bedroom. He's welcome to join the rest of us here.'

Sam looked relieved. 'That'd be perfect, Jackman. If it's no trouble?'

'None at all.' Jackman smiled at Laura. 'You'll be here tomorrow, sweetheart. Ask Mrs M to sort that out, will you? I've got to go in at the crack. Tomorrow could be the day we bring in our other deranged killer.' He would have liked to talk to her about Jordan Spiller, but she was flagging, and to be honest, so was he. 'Time we all turned in, I reckon. It's been one hell of a day for us all.'

He set his alarm for five, and finally drifted off to sleep, excited at the prospect of capturing Spiller and recovering the boy, but fearful of what the day might hold if things went wrong.

\* \* \*

Dotted in their various homes around Saltern-le-Fen, the other members of the team were also wondering about the day to come.

Surrounded by his family, Max felt unusually apprehensive. Maybe it was having the people he loved around him that made him so anxious. Maybe it was the fact that a child was involved. He drew closer to Rosie, breathed in the faint scent of her perfume and prayed for a good outcome.

\* \* \*

Gary lay in bed wishing he could tell Gilly of his fears. They talked every evening now, especially when he was working late, but he was reluctant to offload his work problems on her. She kept telling him he could share his worries with her, she had broad shoulders. He found that wonderfully reassuring. It had been many years since anyone apart from Marie had spoken kind and caring words to him. Now he'd found that person, all he had to do was stay safe.

\* \* \*

Robbie tossed and turned. He had mixed feelings about the day to come, most of them negative. He knew they were dealing with someone in the grip of insanity, and that he had a twelve-year-old in tow. The possible consequences were almost too grim to contemplate. He got up and went to the kitchen. It felt empty and cold without Ella. Too late to phone her now. He sat on a stool at the breakfast counter and put his head in his hands. Why, oh why had he let her go? He stood up, padded back to the bedroom and picked up his phone. So what if it was after midnight? There would never be a right time to tell her how he felt, so why not now? He found her number and listened to her phone ring.

\* \* \*

Charlie Button slept soundly, thanks to a hefty shot of his father's Rémy Martin. Before sleep overtook him, he shivered with excitement. Tomorrow would be a bloody good day. Like the Mounties, they'd get their man.

\* \* \*

Further away, in less comfortable surroundings, a man and a boy lay in sleeping bags on two camp beds placed side by side. While the boy slept, the man lay awake listening to the water lapping and the boy's regular breathing, and was at peace. He stared into the darkness, holding the moment as long as he could, because it would soon be over.

# CHAPTER THIRTY-TWO

It was still dark when Marie rode into the police station. It was difficult to recall a time when she had felt more alive. This was an important day, a crucial one for Davy Frances. But in the chill morning air of the open stretch of Fen road, uppermost in her mind was not the coming rescue operation but the image of Ralph eating toast at her kitchen table. It looked so right.

As she slowed, closer to the station, she set that image aside, and by the time she walked into the silent office, she was one hundred per cent focused on Jordan Spiller.

Jackman strode in just moments later. He too had a determined look on his face, his expression free of the previous weeks' anxiety about Laura.

'He'll remember. He has to,' he said. She smiled. He'd spoken without preamble but she understood. The same thought had been on her mind too.

'He will,' she said. 'If he loved his father, then it would have been a special time, one he wouldn't forget.'

'I just hope that this foster father has as strong a rapport with the lad as his grandfather believes.' Jackman went into his office and checked his computer for reports of any incidents that had occurred overnight. 'Thankfully, nothing of any concern to us.'

Marie smiled at him. 'Then it's time your sergeant brought you a coffee before we start biting our nails.'

They drank their coffee and mulled over possible locations for the hideaway. 'There were three places I couldn't get to from the sea bank,' Marie said, sipping her drink. 'None looked particularly promising when I checked the satellite pictures, certainly none worth getting the drone up for.'

'Andy only thought it was in the direction of Stone Quay. Maybe he was wrong. It could be anywhere.' Jackman stared up at the wall map of the Fens. 'The place is a maze of waterways. I've often had fantasies of owning a little cabin somewhere among the tiny creeks and lagoons, where I could watch wildfowl from dawn to dusk.'

Marie was slightly surprised at that. He lived in a sleepy village as it was, pretty well out in the countryside. But on reflection she understood what he meant. There were times when you needed to leave the police force parked up and be somewhere you weren't liable to be called out at any time of day or night. A cabin out in that water-world would be ideal.

She jumped. Jackman's mobile phone was ringing.

Dr Bourne's measured tones filled the office on loud-speaker. 'Christopher has told Jim everything he remembers. I hope it helps you. Do you have a pen handy?'

'Yes, yes, ready,' snapped Jackman.

'They did call it the Hideaway. To reach it, they drove past the marina, then turned off and took the long, straight road towards the sea bank and the old bird reserve at Stone Quay. At the T-junction they took the lane to the right and veered away from the river. He wasn't sure about the exact directions at that point but mentioned passing a sluice where he had seen a grey heron in the water. Just after that, another lane heads down to the marsh. The Hideaway was on a creek that led back into the tidal river and was quite close to the estuary.' Bourne took a breath. 'And that's all he remembers.'

'How did he cope with being questioned?' asked Jackman tentatively.

'Apparently, it was quite strange,' said Bourne. 'For days, Christopher has been going on about wanting to see his father. Jim said that if he'd been a fanciful man, he would have said the boy sensed something was wrong. He's been kept away from the media reports, so it couldn't have been that. Anyway, talking about a happy time he'd shared with his father didn't stress the boy out at all.'

Jackman thanked the doctor and went immediately to the wall map. 'Do you know this spot, Marie? I don't.'

She tried to visualise the lanes but failed. From the map, it wasn't an area you would particularly want to visit. The lane went nowhere, ending at the river. It wasn't a beauty spot, had no car park, nothing. This was further out than she'd been on her bike. She hurried out into the office and searched her computer for the satellite image.

'Come on, come on,' she urged as it slowly downloaded. 'Okay, so here's the bird reserve.' She followed the route they'd been given and found the sluice, the lane, and then the river. She zoomed in closer. Yes! 'There's something here, boss!' she called out. 'It's not very clear, but there's a small building right up by the creek.'

'Now we have a dilemma.' Jackman stood behind her, staring at her screen. 'Do we just get out there, mob-handed, and try to rescue Davy Frances, or should I get the drone unit to do a recce first? That would be my first choice, except that Spiller might spot it. They aren't terribly noisy, certainly nothing like the helicopter, but out there, you could well hear it.'

'And then he could run, taking the boy with him,' said Marie. 'Or worse.'

'Exactly.' He stood for a while, pondering. 'I hate to do this, but I think I'm going to leave the decision to Ruth. After all, if we cock up, she carries the can. Plus, she needs to authorise the manpower and backup for the operation. Maybe it should be down to her.'

Marie grunted, her eyes still on the satellite map.

'I know that look, Evans,' said Jackman warily. 'What's worrying you?'

'I think I might have been there before.' She looked closer. 'Well, not there exactly, but over here.' She pointed to a place on the map marked End Point, about a quarter of a mile from where they believed Spiller to be. It was right on the edge of the estuary and had a flat pier where small craft could anchor up. 'I went there on obbo once when we were looking for smugglers. The thing is, there's a farm track and then a lane that leads down to End Point. It's pretty rough, but we made it easily in a 4x4. I think the track connects up with the river lane.' She moved the map and pointed again. 'Look, there! That means there are two ways in and two ways out. And the track I was telling you about is flat as a witch's tit — he'd see us coming a mile away.'

'So, we'd need to approach using the route that Christopher's given us?'

'Absolutely. That way has the high sea banks and steep drains and culverts to shield you from view. Plus, that's the way Spiller used to go, so he probably still does. But does he know about the rough track to End Point?'

'We have to assume that he does,' said Jackman. 'If he's been going that way for years, he'll know the area.' He placed his hand on her shoulder. 'Ring the others, get them in ASAP. I'm going to contact Ruth and get her decision. I want to be out there as early as possible. If that kid's still alive, he's on borrowed time. There's only so long Spiller'll be able to maintain whatever pretence he's concocted.'

He hurried away. He was right. Even the trusting Davy was going to smell a rat at some point, unless he was very gullible, which wasn't the impression Natalie Miles had given them. Yes, Jackman was right, the boy was on borrowed time.

* * *

Vic Blackwell woke up with a start. Wound up after the capture of Freddie Shields, he hadn't gone to bed until the early

308

hours of the morning, and even then he'd slept badly, wondering if he'd get a call with a report on Freddie's mental state. Still not knowing, he rang the station custody sergeant, and was told that Shields should be fit enough for questioning after a good night's sleep and then a further check that morning.

He ended the call, dragged himself out of bed and into the shower, already worrying about Shields. Apparently, as soon as he got to the station, Freddie had become compliant. He apologised for his behaviour and ceased to struggle. He kept asking for Dr Archer or Professor Page, appearing to have no recall of his earlier encounter with them. He claimed to have fallen into a deep sleep and only came to when he was tasered. Vic believed that story about as much as the one about Father Christmas coming down the chimney. He'd seen plenty of game players in his time in the force, and he was pretty sure that Shields was one of them. How likely was it for a man to go from ranting lunatic to reasonable citizen in the space of an hour? Come on! Vic stood rinsing off the soapsuds, thinking about what the crew who brought him in had said. Apparently, Shields had raved about some person who had "taken advantage of him." The uniformed officers had believed Shields was referring to a recent event, which was odd, because at the time he was supposedly fleeing a crime scene.

Vic stepped out of the shower, towelled himself dry and padded over to his jacket, slung over the back of a chair. He took out his notebook and thumbed through it. Something didn't add up.

He read it, reread it and cursed. He pulled on his clothes and, skipping breakfast, locked up and ran out to his car. He needed to look at the log and see what the crew had actually said.

When he entered the police station, everyone was busy preparing for an operation. He needed to move fast. He got to his desk and switched on his computer. Soon he was reading exactly what the crew had reported. Vic jumped up and ran to DI Jackman's office.

'Sir! Before you go, please listen to this.'

Jackman looked at him, mildly surprised. 'Sorry, Vic, but we don't have much time. We have the drone unit already on their way.'

'I think I can help.' Vic looked at him, begging him to listen. 'Shields! The man who hurt Dr Archer. He was apprehended on the Fen lane towards Stone Quay. I've only just realised that he wasn't heading *out* that way, he was coming back!'

Jackman stared. 'Okay, tell me everything. But hurry.'

'The crew who nabbed him were looking for a stolen car taken by joyriders, and Stone Quay is a favourite spot for setting them on fire. The thing is, they met him coming towards them as they went down to the river. He was ranting about someone taking advantage of his generosity, someone who had gone somewhere without his permission. He mentioned the words "his hideaway."'

'So Shields knows Spiller!' Jackman's eyes flashed. 'And he's still downstairs in the custody suite?'

Vic nodded.

'Come on! If you're right, he can tell us what we'll be up against when we get there.'

It seemed to take hours to get the custody sergeant to sanction an unscheduled interview prior to a second psych assessment, but finally Shields was brought to the interview room.

He seemed puzzled by their questions, claiming to know nothing about his arrest. He had no memory of driving at all.

'Then please tell us about the Hideaway, Mr Shields.'

'The Hideaway? Why?'

Vic could sense Jackman almost quivering with tension.

'Please. Just tell us about it, I'll explain why in a minute,' Vic said urgently.

'It's little more than a hut down on Lapwing Creek. It belonged to my grandfather. He collected samphire and caught eels and sold them in the local market. He used to have a little rowing boat moored there. When he died, he left it to me, and I'd go there whenever I needed some space. That's all there is to it.' He still looked puzzled.

'But you allowed a friend of yours to use it too,' said Jackman impatiently. 'Jordan Spiller?'

Shields nodded. 'So what? He was screwed up over his wife and needed somewhere even more than I did. And he loved the water and the birds. That's how we met.'

'And he's there now?'

Shields gave them a blank look. 'How would I know?'

'You were screaming that someone had taken advantage of your generosity, Mr Shields, and you were driving away from the area.' Vic leaned forward. 'Think! You went there last night. You saw that someone else was already there and you were angry. Am I right?'

Shields looked as if he were about to cry. 'A car. I vaguely remember something about a car. And yes, I was scared and upset. I needed peace, solitude. I suppose it must have been Jordan, but I haven't seen him in ages.'

'Tell us about the building itself,' Jackman demanded.

'Well, it's nothing but a wooden shack — one room with a sink, a Calor gas camping stove, an old sofa, a camp bed and a table and two chairs. It has a small petrol generator out back, along with a privy — well, an earth closet. And that's it. It's just my grandfather's hut.'

'Is there anything about the area that we should know, Mr Shields? Anything dangerous?' Jackman glanced at his watch.

Shields shrugged. 'Not really. Only the marsh at high tide, when the water can run deep and fast. Further up, at End Point, there's a wicked eddy that forms in the water every so often, and you don't want to get into that.'

'Finally, there are two ways of approaching the hut, is that right?' Jackman was already on his feet.

'Yes, one by a farm lane from End Point and other via Stone Quay and past the sluice. That's the road we usually use.' He stared at Vic. 'What's going on?'

Jackman was already at the door.

Vic looked at the man opposite him. He certainly didn't seem like someone who would murder his own mother. 'We think a kidnapped boy is being held in your hideaway, Mr Shields. DI Jackman is on his way there now.' He ended the interview and stood up. 'I'll let you get some breakfast and I'll be back for your formal interview as soon as the custody sergeant allows after your final assessment. Thank you for your assistance.'

\* \* \*

'Our RV point is Stone Quay.' Jackman watched Marie pulling on her crash helmet. 'Are you sure about this?'

'Oh yes. Tiger can get to places that a car isn't able to. It could be useful. I'll meet you there,' Marie called back.

'The drone unit is already en route. Ruth insisted on it.'

She nodded, revved her bike and roared off towards the gates.

He wasn't happy, but then he never was when Marie headed off on that machine. He beckoned to Gary and Kevin. 'Robbie? You take Max and Charlie. Stone Quay, twenty minutes. RV there.'

Robbie gave him a thumbs up and headed for a waiting vehicle.

As they drove, Jackman wondered what would have happened if Freddie Shields had turned up at the Hideaway last night. Both men were probable murderers, and old mates or not, neither would have been happy to see the other there. His money would have been on Spiller doing away with Freddie. Spiller was determined to carry out his plan and would allow no one to get in his way.

While the others chatted, Jackman remained silent. Ignoring his worries about alerting Spiller and putting Davy's life in danger, Ruth had called out the drone unit. She had been adamant that they were not going to proceed with such a difficult operation without first seeing what the terrain was like. The new drone was their own property, paid for from the Proceeds of Crime Act, which — ironically — meant that it and the officer training to pilot it had been funded from cash donated by convicted criminals. It was available for their exclusive use twenty-four-seven, and as it could scan a large area in very little time, it would be invaluable in many different situations. It was a top-of-the-range model with the ability to supply them with photographs, live-link and recorded video, and thermal images, so they would know immediately how many heat sources there were in or around the hut. It was a great piece of kit, but he still had reservations about what Spiller might do if he, or even Davy, happened to notice it.

When they arrived, he found Marie talking to the drone pilot, explaining what they knew already and what they needed to know before they approached.

'Just how loud is that thing?' asked Jackman, staring at the six rotor blades on the drone.

'Not too bad. Like a large fan or a garden strimmer, I guess, but out here on the Fen, you know how sound carries.' The officer shrugged. 'There's a bit of a breeze today. I'll try to approach into the wind, which should carry some of the sound away, but he could hear it, I can't deny that.'

'How long will it be up there for?' asked Marie.

'For the shortest time possible,' he said. 'I'll grab your images, check the surrounding area and lanes, and get back to base.' He addressed Jackman. 'I have to operate this within my sight range and I'm not allowed to exceed 500 metres. I'll ferry her to the closest point, then she's all charged up and ready to go.'

Jackman nodded. 'We'll be moving to an area owned by the waterways people. It's close to the creek but can't be seen because of the sea bank. Send her up from there and I'll make sure we're ready to go the moment we've seen the images. I want my officers all over that place as fast as possible.'

As far as they knew, Spiller had no gun, and although he was deemed highly dangerous, a threat assessment had found the deployment of a firearms unit to be unnecessary.

Jackman knew that Ruth had thought long and hard about this, but knowing a child to be involved, she had declined the use of firearms. So, it was down to the element of surprise and a volume of officers going in fast and hitting Spiller hard. He was pretty sure Ruth would have alerted the tactical support team, who would be standing by in case things went pear-shaped, but hopefully they wouldn't be needed.

In ten minutes they were ready — uniformed officers and detectives. Jackman took a deep breath. It was time to make a move and take up position closer to the Hideaway. He nodded to the drone pilot. 'Okay. As soon as we get to within striking range, send her up.'

* * *

Vic Blackwell sent a young detective out to get him something to eat and a proper coffee. By now, his stomach was groaning audibly.

Just as he prepared to take a bite out of his sandwich, his desk phone rang.

'DS Blackwell? Spike here in Forensics. The prof has asked me to give you a prelim update on the death of Mrs Catherine Shields.'

'Thanks, Spike, what have got for me?' He grabbed a pen.

'She died from multiple stab wounds. It wasn't a frenzied attack, and there were no defensive wounds on the hands or arms. From the blood spatter patterns, we are pretty certain that she was killed while she was asleep in her chair, then dragged behind the sofa. From their depth, the wounds were made with considerable force and very deliberately.' He paused. 'Oh, and the killer was right-handed, by the way. The instrument used was a kitchen knife found at the scene, with traces of her blood still on it. Exactly when she died has been hard to establish, Sergeant, but we believe around a week ago. The central heating was operating on a timer, so there was no average temperature to use as a gauge, and rigor mortis had long since passed, so we're working on insect activity, mainly the blowfly.'

Vic stared at his sandwich and sighed.

'Apart from that, there's nothing much to tell you, Sarge. The full report will be with you in a day or so, hopefully. Cause of death is confirmed but the prof is running a screening test to see if she was sedated prior to her death. There were sleeping pills found in her bedside cabinet.'

Vic thanked him and was about to hang up when Spike continued.

'One last thing,' he said. 'She wasn't actually malnourished, or showing signs of having been mistreated, but it appears that she existed on a rather poor diet, and from the condition of her muscles, seemed to get little exercise. Not sure if that helps you, but as they say, "That's all, folks!"'

There was nothing there that he didn't already know, except for the time of death, and the fact that she hadn't been exactly cosseted. *A week ago, eh?* He would need to get a precise idea of her son's comings and goings around then. He looked at the office clock. Too early to interview Shields. Maybe he'd take another run out to the house and have a quiet look around that annexe now the circus had moved out. He finished his sandwich, left a message for his DI and left.

\* \* \*

Hugh Mackenzie had told Sam that he planned to drive down immediately after breakfast and spend a day with him, maybe two. He was practically buzzing after being told what their patient had done.

Sam ended the call and smiled at Laura. 'He can't wait to see him.'

'Rather him than me.' She pulled a face. 'Although I feel I have to see this through.' She sat down at the table and buttered her toast. 'I hate to mention this at breakfast, but how long do you think that poor woman had been dead?'

'Well, it's not really my field, I'm glad to say, but it wasn't within the last few days, that's for sure. Maybe a week to ten days ago? Something like that.'

'So he sat there feeding me the loving son routine — Mother said this, Mother said that — and all of it was a lie.'

'Not just a lie. He'd actually killed her by then.' Sam shivered at the thought of Laura sitting in her mill house consulting room talking with a man who had recently stabbed his own mother.

'Jackman was right, wasn't he?' she said. 'All along, he knew I was in danger.'

'So did you, Laura.' Sam stared into his mug of tea. 'We can't always interpret the warning signs our mind is giving us. We dismiss them as overreaction or simply think we've misunderstood.' He sighed. 'Ours is not a straightforward profession, my dear. Our cases are never black or white, and our subjects are all either disturbed or damaged.'

There was a knock at the door and Hetty Maynard bustled in.

'I saw your cars still outside. Everything all right, Dr Archer?' She stopped. 'Oh my! Your poor head! That looks so painful!'

Assuring her it looked worse than it was, Laura went on to tell her that they were having another visitor who'd be staying for a day or so.

'Right, then I'll start up there, Dr Archer. I'll get fresh linen on the bed and prepare the room. And I'll try not to get in your way today.'

Laura smiled. 'Don't worry about us, we're going over to the consulting room later. Just do what you normally do, and we'll be there if you need us.'

Hetty stopped in the doorway. 'Forgive me for asking, but have they found that poor Jordan Spiller? I've been worrying all night about that man.'

'Not yet, Hetty,' said Laura, 'but I'm sure Rowan will tell you as soon as he knows anything. He said you'd been a great help to him.'

'Poor lad,' Hetty said. 'I can't help thinking it ain't right what the good Lord dishes out to some folks.'

Did she mean Jordan or Teddy? Sam wondered. Same difference really, they were both messed up through no fault of their own. Though it seemed that Jordan had decided on more deadly means for handling his problems.

# CHAPTER THIRTY-THREE

Just before they left Stone Quay, Marie took Jackman aside. 'Humour me on this one, Jackman. Tell someone to get a Stinger down to End Point. Have it placed across the entrance from the track to the quay's hardstanding area. And keep it well out of sight.'

He looked at her briefly, then hurried over to the officer in charge of the uniformed team.

Hearing him issue the request, Marie felt better, but only a bit. She had part of a conversation going around in her head, something Andy Forman had said in their second talk with him. It had been haunting her since she rode across to the Fen to this place. It would mean nothing if they succeeded in getting into that shack area and securing both Jordan and Davy, but should they escape together it could mean everything.

Jackman raised his arm, and at once a dozen pairs of eyes were fastened on him. 'To your vehicles. We're moving out. And do the last stretch as quietly as possible, no revving engines and no hitting the blues and twos on pain of death!'

* * *

Before long, the team had pulled in, and Marie dismounted and pushed Tiger for the last one hundred metres.

They couldn't yet see the Hideaway or the small area around it. Their view was obstructed by a high man-made grassy berm that flanked one of the tributary water courses that flowed into the river. There was a small parking area, used by the waterways maintenance workers, and from there the lane led directly to the creek and the lonely little hut.

The drone was sent up, and soon they had their images. 'There are a lot of heat sources,' the drone pilot whispered.

Marie threw a puzzled glance at Jackman. 'How come?'

'Animals.' The officer pointed to the screen. Below them was the shack, and around the back, several pens and small shelters.

'He's got animals? Why on earth . . . ?' Jackman said.

Marie suddenly twigged. 'That's how he got the boy there! Wildlife conservation. Look!'

The pictures were incredibly clear. So much so that they could identify a fox in one of the pens.

'Where's the humans? That's what I need to see.' Jackman looked closer.

'Here, sir,' the operator said. 'In that structure with the netting front. Looks like an aviary. That's one of them. The other is in the hut. Both are moving about independently, neither restricted in any way. It's a considerably smaller person in the aviary, so that'll be your boy.'

'Then get your drone out of there, Officer, right now.' Jackman whispered to Marie, 'If Spiller is inside, then he might not have seen it. We have one chance at this, but we must move fast.' He raised his voice just enough to be heard by the waiting officers. 'Ready, everyone. Go! Go! Go!'

Marie's mind emptied of all other thoughts but their goal. She moved forward, a step behind Jackman. Their plan was to leave the shelter of the car park using the lane and rush the shack in a pincer formation, surrounding it. If Jordan and Davy weren't together, so much the better, but they couldn't guarantee it.

As it turned out, their plan came to nothing.

They rounded the bank and ran towards the ancient shack — and heard the roar of an engine. A powerful 4x4 cannoned away on to the farm track that led to End Point. Jordan must have heard the drone! For a moment they were left standing, helpless. Then Marie tugged on Jackman's arm. 'The Stinger! Check it's in place. I'm going after him.' Already running back to where she had left Tiger, she yelled out over her shoulder, 'Remember what Andy said? Jordan wanted to die with his boy! Davy is his substitute son! He's going to drive them both off End Point!'

She leaped into the saddle and roared off, causing a number of startled police officers to jump into the shrubs. Jordan believed his son had died alone, and his mind just couldn't handle it. He was going to try to make it right with Teddy and die along with his boy. Poor little Davy! An innocent who happened to end up at the centre of Jordan's twisted nightmare fantasy. She opened the throttle.

The track was grim to say the least, riddled with potholes and deep, water-filled grooves from numerous massive tractor tyres. It was a challenge, even to a rider as experienced as Marie.

She finally saw the vehicle up ahead and wondered how best to play this. If the Stinger had been deployed properly, it would stop the car, no question. But had they managed to find a traffic car equipped with one at such short notice? Not all cars carried them, and not all officers were allowed to use them. What then? How could she stop him without either getting killed herself or causing an accident that could injure Davy?

But it was impossible to think while negotiating this nightmare terrain. As she had done so many times in the past, Marie Evans would wing it. Right now, she needed to concentrate on staying alive.

\* \* \*

When Vic Blackwell was finally given permission to interview Freddie Shields, he paused for a moment at the observation window. He saw Shields seated beside a snappily dressed, well-groomed man in his fifties, who had lawyer written all over him. He wasn't known to Vic, and he certainly wasn't one of the duty solicitors. He turned to his DC, Denise Gordon, and asked her if she recognised him.

'Oh shit, Sarge, that's Carrington. He's a first-class . . .'

She didn't need to go on. But Vic had met people like Carrington before, and he had his ways too.

He took his seat, prepared to go precisely by the book. Carrington wasn't going to trip him up on interviewing procedure. He pressed 'record', stated his name and introduced those present. He then explained the reasons for Shields's arrest and laid out the charges against him.

The interview went much as he'd expected, with Carrington objecting to practically every question put to Shields.

'Detective Sergeant! This man is suffering from a serious condition. Not only is there written confirmation of this from his own GP, he is being seen as a patient by your very own force psychologist. What further proof do you need that he is clearly in need of medical help, not locking up in a police cell.'

'Mr Shields will be seen later today by an eminent specialist in his specific condition, Mr Carrington. But we also have to consider the fact that Mr Shields's actions led to the hospitalisation of that same force psychologist, namely Dr Laura Archer, as well as Professor Samuel Page, both of whom, as you are aware, were trying to help Mr Shields. *And* he resisted arrest in such a violent manner as to require restraining by the legal use of a Taser, both for his own safety and that of others in the vicinity.'

'My client has already expressed sincere regret at causing injury to Dr Archer, but as it happened during an episode of deep somnambulism, he can hardly be held responsible.'

Carrington's tone now carried less conviction. 'And this also applies to his arrest. So, I really must insist that unless you have irrefutable evidence that this man is responsible for his mother's death, you must let him go.'

'Mr Carrington, his prints are on the knife that has been confirmed as the murder weapon. That is evidence,' stated Vic politely.

'He has already told you that he found it in the garden and picked it up. Of course his prints will be on it! That does not mean it was he who used it.' Carrington glared at him. 'I would like some time to talk to my client.'

Vic suspended the interview.

'Well, Sarge,' Denise began once they were outside, 'you kept your cool there. What will Carrington do next, do you think?'

'I reckon he'll advise Shields to remain and see this expert psychologist. Then he'll weigh up his options.'

'Carrington likes to back winners, Sarge.' Denise gave him an impish smile. 'And I got the impression his heart wasn't in this one.'

'Let's hope so.'

Ten minutes later, they left the interview room for the second time. It was as Vic had predicted — they would await the expert.

* * *

Behind her, Marie heard two-tones and caught the flash of blue lights in her mirrors. Who were they warning to get out of their way on this lonely track — a hare and a couple of pheasants?

Ahead, she could now see the opening to the flat concrete area that was End Point, and heading towards it, the 4x4. It would all come down to the next few moments, and whether her request for a Stinger had been met.

As they drew even closer, she noticed another, smaller entrance to the quay, just metres to the left of the main one.

At one time the lane entrance had been closed to traffic, but the gate was long gone. This smaller passage must have been for pedestrian access.

The big vehicle showed no signs of slowing down. Oh God, she was right! He was not stopping.

Now she was close to his tail. Marie accelerated hard. As he powered through the gateway, she veered off and flew through the narrow gap, then flung the bike into a skid and braked hard.

What happened next unfolded in slow motion. She knew that she was between the car and the water — it was all she'd been able to think of to make him automatically brake and swerve and prevent him killing the boy. Or . . . But she refused to think of the alternative.

The dreaded impact never happened. The Stinger had been deployed. The vehicle's tyres deflated, and it veered off in an impressive skid and came to a halt facing back up the lane, about five yards from Marie.

All around them, police officers erupted as from nowhere and surrounded the car. All Marie could see were the wide eyes and the open mouth of the terrified child.

'Step out of the car. Now!' The command rang out, followed by silence. Only the 4x4 could be heard quietly hissing.

Marie dismounted and went slowly towards the frightened boy, who was struggling to open the door. She smiled. 'It's going to be okay. Just relax.'

Then Jackman was there, with all the team behind him. He stepped through the circle of uniforms and asked for quiet. He moved towards the driver's door, keeping well back.

'Jordan? I'm Detective Inspector Rowan Jackman. It's over now. All over. Will you please unlock the doors and let Davy out? He's frightened, and we need to help him.'

Jordan Spiller looked at Jackman, blinking. 'Who's Davy?'

Marie wondered how they were going to play this. She had a good idea that to Jordan, the boy in the car was his beloved Christopher, his Teddy.

And as she'd also suspected, Jordan was refusing to be parted from his son. The car was locked, and Davy Frances was starting to panic. Marie could hear him begging "Mr Edwards" to let him out. Jordan seemed calm at present, but Marie feared that could all change in an instant, if they made any attempt to force the car open. Spiller now had his arm around Davy.

Jackman had stepped back and was talking urgently with his uniformed counterpart. She suspected they were going to bring in a police negotiator. The Fenland constabulary deployed a brilliant team of highly trained crisis negotiators throughout the area, each one with their particular skill set, on call twenty-four hours a day, every day of the year. Marie looked at the ashen-faced boy and prayed they would send the best they had.

\* \* \*

Hugh Mackenzie studied Laura's notes on Freddie Shields, asking questions as he read. When he came to the end, he gave them a broad smile. 'Fascinating! What an interesting subject he is.'

'Do you believe that these terrifying episodes are real?' asked Laura.

'Not for one moment,' Hugh said, a hint of mischief in his expression.

Laura was speechless.

'But my word, am I looking forward to meeting him.'

Laura and Sam looked at each other. 'Hughie, you are a breath of fresh air!' Sam said. 'We had our doubts about him, but he was so convincing. He completely took in the GP he'd been seeing for years.'

'Well, I'm a suspicious old sod by nature, but what I see here is a calculating mind. To serve his own ends, he's drawn on a common childhood condition that he probably did have, and he's done one hell of a lot of research into adult somnambulism. What those ends were, the police will have to find out. They're going to have a very interesting case to solve. And, if you've no objection, I'd like to be part of it. Unless I'm hopelessly wrong, which I never am, they're going to be in sore need of an expert witness.'

Laura felt a weight lift from her. All her fears had been validated. She smiled gratefully at Hugh Mackenzie. 'I have to admit, I'd started to doubt myself.'

'Relax, Laura. And our Freddie might yet convince me otherwise.' He laughed. 'Although I very much doubt it.'

Sam looked at his watch. 'We can head over to Saltern-le-Fen whenever you're ready. Or we can wait till after lunch — he's not going anywhere right now.'

Hugh stood up. 'Oh, let's go now. And then if you're up to it, Laura, I'll treat you both to lunch.'

Laura gently touched her still swollen head. 'Thanks, but I'd better sit this one out. You and Sam go.'

'We'll ring you when we're through at the station,' Sam said, looking concerned. 'Are you okay?'

'I'm fine, honestly,' she assured him. 'It's probably excitement. I've never been so happy to hand over a patient.' She exhaled. 'I'm going to go and put my feet up. I'm still supposed to be following hospital instructions, so don't fret.'

After they had left, Laura had a sudden urge to ring Jackman, but she knew today was important, so she sent a text telling him she loved him.

# CHAPTER THIRTY-FOUR

Marie felt stiff and her joints had begun to ache. She had spent most of the past hour on her haunches on the concrete quayside, making sure to be in full view of Davy.

The negotiator was good, probably one of the best she'd heard, but even so, he was getting nowhere. She stretched her aching shoulders and stood up, reluctant to move out of Davy's sight, but she had to talk to Jackman. She mouthed, 'I'll be back,' and sprinted over to where Jackman was deep in conversation with Superintendent Ruth Crooke.

'It's a long shot, Super, but please hear me out.' She turned to Jackman. 'This can't go on much longer. Any minute, he's going to blow. Ring Dr Bourne and tell him to get Christopher's foster father to bring him down here. If Jordan sees that his real son is still alive, we might be able to save Davy.'

Ruth dismissed her suggestion as preposterous. Jackman listened to each of them in silence. He said, 'Marie is right, Ruth. Christopher has been going on about seeing his father for a while now. I'm sure that if it's explained to him in the right way, he'll want to help. He's not a baby anymore, and he needs to put that part of his life behind him. I say yes. Will you sanction it?'

Those thin lips of hers almost disappeared. Ruth took a deep breath, then nodded. 'Ring Bourne and get me the address and I'll get a fast car to them. I just hope this doesn't go bloody tits up, that's all. They'll crucify us.'

'I'll let the negotiator know. He'll need to keep Jordan as calm as he can until the car gets here.' This could mean at least another thirty minutes, and they didn't yet know if the foster father and Christopher would agree.

Marie returned to squatting in the boy's sight. The next twenty-five minutes seemed to stretch on for ever. Thank heavens for the negotiator, who heroically managed to keep Jordan together until the car arrived. She saw Jackman race towards it and speak urgently to the man accompanying Christopher.

The lad stood silently beside the police car. So this was Christopher. Teddy.

He looked like a miniature version of his father — stick thin. And pale — his face, his hair and his eyes, especially his eyes. His pallor was accentuated by the white T-shirt and faded stonewashed denim jacket, jeans and white trainers.

Jackman nodded towards the negotiator, who told Jordan that DI Jackman had some very important news for him, something he really needed to hear. He stepped away and Jackman approached the car, speaking slowly and clearly.

'Jordan, I want you to listen carefully. You have been very unfairly treated and lied to, simply to hurt you. But now you need to hear the truth, and I will prove this to you in a moment.'

Jordan moved his head slowly from side to side. Marie heard him say, 'Not listening. Not listening.' Davy flinched as his grip on the boy tightened.

'Jordan Spiller!' Jackman raised his voice. 'Your Christopher is not dead! He never died alone in a car crash! Your wife wanted to hurt you, so she lied to you.'

'Oh no, my son's here with me. You're wrong, you're wrong.' The voice scared Marie. It had the high, sing-song quality of insanity.

'I'm not your son!' wailed Davy. 'I'm Davy Frances! Let me go!'

'Shh, my boy, hush now.'

Then, without warning, Christopher broke free of his foster father's hold and ran towards the car. Jackman went to stop him, then held back.

'Dad?'

Silence fell.

'Dad?' he repeated.

A low keening came from the car. 'Noooo! You're not my Christopher! You can't be Teddy!'

'Dad. It's me.' Then he took something from under his jacket.

It was a battered teddy bear. He held it towards his father like an offering.

Jordan Spiller did not move.

Marie held her breath.

Spiller let go of Davy, unlocked the car and stepped out. 'Son?'

At once, Marie wrenched the passenger door open and pulled Davy towards her. She held him tightly to her for a moment, then ushered him away to safety. When she next looked back, Spiller was in handcuffs and staring at his boy. Then he said, 'I always loved you, son.'

'I know, Dad,' Christopher said.

Then it was all over. A cacophony of voices and engines broke the silence. All Marie wanted now was to get on her bike and ride away. She wanted to phone Ralph.

She was checking Tiger over for any damage after her earlier stunt act when she heard Jackman behind her.

'You really are a Welsh witch, aren't you? If you hadn't guessed what he was planning, we'd be standing here waiting for the underwater retrieval team to bring up a submerged car and two bodies. How did you do that? How did you know?'

'Andy's words had been going round and round in my head,' she said.

'And skidding that monster of yours to a halt in front of a speeding vehicle. You scared the shit out of me! I don't think I'll ever forgive you for that, Marie Evans!'

'On reflection, probably not my best move, but I knew you wouldn't let me down with that Stinger.' She attempted a smile.

'That bloody thing arrived just minutes before you did! Hell, we could have been dredging you and that motorcycle of yours out of the Wash along with the rest.'

'But you didn't, did you? Don't overreact, boss.' She pulled on her helmet, got on the bike and grinned at him. 'We always get there in the end, one way or another.'

As she rode away from the busy scene, she glanced back and saw Jackman standing apart from the others, watching her. He was shaking his head.

# CHAPTER THIRTY-FIVE

Laura finally got her wish, and Marie and Ralph came over to Mill Corner for dinner. It turned out to be a rather different sort of evening to the one she had originally planned. Yes, Marie and her new man would be there, but so would Sam and Hughie, who had been staying with them for the past month, and DC Vic Blackwell.

Autumn had well and truly arrived, bringing cold evenings with a hint of early frost. It had taken them all a while to settle down after Saltern's two recent serious cases, but at last they could all relax and enjoy an evening together, eating and drinking, and dissecting the cases one last time.

Laura liked the colder weather because it meant they could light a fire in the lounge. The warm glow of the embers and the soft lighting made the room look cosy and inviting. They would go there after dinner, and Jackman would open one of his precious bottles of cognac.

Now Laura was polishing glasses and checking that everything was ready for seven. Like a lot of people, they never used the dining room, but always gathered around the big kitchen table. Hetty Maynard had kindly brought her a large home-made blackberry and apple pie. Laura had been tempted to pass it off as her own but knew she'd be rumbled.

'How's it going?' Jackman wandered in and kissed her lightly on the nape of her neck. 'Can I do anything?'

'I think I've got it all in hand,' she said, looking around. 'I hope everyone's hungry, I've definitely over-cooked!'

'Well, you *have* invited four coppers, so I don't think you'll have much trouble getting rid of it all.'

'Ralph's a pescatarian. I hope he likes what I've made for him. We haven't had dinner guests for so long I'm getting all flustered. I used to be able to do this sort of thing with one hand tied behind my back.'

'Well, you look pretty organised to me, which is lucky because I hear a car drawing up. Here goes, sweetheart. Let's have a lovely evening.'

The meal was a great success, and it seemed no time at all before they were ensconced in the lounge in front of the fire, each holding a glass of brandy.

'I hate to talk about work,' said Jackman, 'but we've been so busy with the Jordan Spiller case I've missed out on what's been going on with the creepy Mr Shields.'

'And in my case,' added Vic, 'Shields has occupied my every moment, and it looks like he will for some time to come. Isn't that right, Hugh?'

Hugh Mackenzie nodded vigorously. 'Oh, very true! The media will have a field day when that case goes to court.'

'Why will it get such a high profile?' said Ralph. 'Surely he confessed in the end?'

'Oh yes, he did that all right,' said Vic with a grin. 'I almost needed a bucket just listening to his "confession." Yes, he *believes* that he must have killed his mother, after a lifetime of mental abuse, but he still blames his somnambulism for it. Hugh's right, it's going to make a blinding court case.'

'Was he really mentally abused by his mother?' asked Ralph.

'Who knows?' said Vic. 'So far, we only have his word for it, and he's told so many lies it's hard to separate truth from fiction.'

'Like about his lovely partner, Julia,' added Laura. 'And the marriage and divorce that never happened.'

'He's a killer, bottom line. The whole thing was planned, I'd swear to it. It's just going to be a bastard to prove,' Vic said.

'We'll do it, my boy, never fear.' Hugh beamed at him. 'Shields has clearly been studying the case of Liam Reece, who got an acquittal on the basis of being a somnambulist. I'm certain that somewhere in that house of his, or hidden deep in his computer files, you'll find a mention of it.'

'Even down to the comment about injuring himself and feeling no pain — all lifted straight from the Reece case,' added Sam.

'But he never injured himself at all, it was just a dressing. The blood was probably his mother's,' said Laura.

'And when we challenged him on that a few days later, he said it was only a superficial wound and he healed quickly.' Vic shook his head. 'I'm just glad I've got you three as expert witnesses. And thankfully none of you think he's telling the truth.'

Jackman had been staring into the fire. 'Even so, it all comes down to admissible evidence, absolute proof, and we all know what a smart defence lawyer is capable of. I don't wish to put a dampener on your hopes, but this could run for years.'

'Oh joy!' moaned Vic, and everyone laughed. He looked at Marie, then across to Jackman. 'Anyway, enough about Shields. You guys had a bloody tough one too. *And* another head case.'

'I'm so glad it's over,' Marie said. 'Though I don't think it'll ever be over for some of the people involved.'

'Marie's right,' said Jackman. 'A night stalker, no matter what his motives, leaves damage in his wake. There are women in and around Saltern who will now struggle to sleep, leave their lights on at night and wake sweating and terrified at the slightest noise.'

'But they're doing their best to overcome it,' said Marie. 'In fact, Annie Carson's little team of investigators has morphed into a kind of victim self-help group, and they're finding both friendship and ways to work through it.'

'Hats off to them,' said Laura. 'That takes determination and courage.'

Jackman laughed, 'And Callum Carson, Annie's son, is definitely looking towards a career as a detective, so something good might come of it.'

'Talking about youngsters, Davy Frances is none the worse for his ordeal,' Marie said. 'Apparently he had the best time with "Mr Edwards." They spent hours keeping watch on an abandoned seal pup on the bank of the creek, waiting for the mother to return. That's how he got Davy to go with him. He asked for the boy's help and told him they were assisting Greenpeace to keep it safe from dogs or people who might kill it. Jordan had been trying to save injured birds and animals for months apparently. The back of the hut was like a mini wildlife sanctuary. The boy was told that his parents had given their consent to him staying with Jordan for a few days to watch the seal and help with the other animals.'

'He had a mobile phone, didn't he? All kids do. Surely they'd have rung him,' said Ralph.

Marie laughed. 'You haven't met Davy. He hates technology. He left it at school in his bag. Oh yes, and he likes proper books too, not Kindles.' She looked across at Jackman. 'He's another one that's found a vocation amid this mess of a case. He says he's going to work with a wildlife rescue organisation. He's already had all the injured animals and birds removed from Lapwing Creek, and with the help of his school, has ferried them to a "hospital" he's set up in an old disused outbuilding in the school grounds.'

'No lasting trauma from his abduction and that time in the car?' asked Laura. 'That's surprising.'

Marie looked thoughtful. 'He's a very unusual boy, Laura. He's mature beyond his years. He said he was sure being separated from his beloved son had messed up Mr Edwards's mind, but he was a good kind man at heart who loved wildlife and cared deeply for his animals. He said that the short time he'd spent in that hut with his "friend" and the animals was the most peaceful and rewarding of his life.'

'Of course he had no idea what Jordan had planned when he put him in the car,' Jackman said. 'It will come out in the media, but I hope Davy doesn't get to hear about it for many years.'

'What will happen to Jordan Spiller?' asked Hugh. 'He's a man with two sides all right, an angel to some and a devil to others.'

Jackman swirled his brandy, causing the reflections of the flames to catch the glass and flash like golden shooting stars. 'There's a lot of evidence that's been gathered from each crime scene, starting with his blood on the wardrobe door in Nan Cutler's house, and frankly, I can't see him denying any of it. As long as he's fit to stand trial, he'll get life, no doubt about it. He deliberately murdered three people and intended to kill Fleur Harper as well, for rejecting Teddy when he needed her, but he sensed something damaged in her too and changed his mind. He'll go down for sure, but personally I think he will serve his time in a secure psychiatric hospital like Broadmoor.'

Laura thought he looked rather sad at this, and maybe he was. Spiller could have had a very different life if his wife had not taken his son and told him the most terrible lie of all, that his boy had died alone. Young Davy was quite right. It had messed with his mind, and he'd set about either obliterating or terrifying anyone who expressed the slightest sympathy with his treacherous, lying wife. And he kept seeking out his son in another child. Not all killers were born evil. Some were simply the product of another's dark heart.

Laura sat up in her chair. 'Okay, guys. Let's talk about positive things, shall we? I hear that Robbie and Ella are back together, which is great news. But now for the million-dollar question — well, Marie?' She grinned wickedly at her friend. 'I've been absolutely *dying* to ask . . .'

**THE END**

# ALSO BY JOY ELLIS

## THE BESTSELLING NIKKI GALENA SERIES

## JACKMAN & EVANS

## DETECTIVE MATT BALLARD

## STANDALONES

**Thank you for reading this book.**

If you enjoyed it please leave feedback on Amazon or Goodreads, and if there is anything we missed or you have a question about, then please get in touch. We appreciate you choosing our book.

Founded in 2014 in Shoreditch, London, we at Joffe Books pride ourselves on our history of innovative publishing. We were thrilled to be shortlisted for Independent Publisher of the Year at the British Book Awards.

www.joffebooks.com

We're very grateful to eagle-eyed readers who take the time to contact us. Please send any errors you find to corrections@joffebooks.com. We'll get them fixed ASAP.

Lightning Source UK Ltd.
Milton Keynes UK
UKHW012023111221
395493UK00001B/127

9 781804 050309